Flocks of Praise for Donna Andrews and her Meg Langslow Mysteries

Duck the Halls

"Andrews leavens the action with her trademark humor, including dueling Christmas dinners and an extravagant—and extravagantly funny—live nativity scene."

—*Publishers Weekly*

"Meg, as well as her quirky extended family, makes this humorous cozy a holiday treat."

—*Booklist*

Six Geese A-Slaying

"Produces at least one chuckle—and sometimes a guffaw—per page. Joy to the world, indeed."

—*Richmond Times-Dispatch*

"Andrews . . . scores points for her witty writing and abundance of Yuletide tinsel and tradition." —*The Columbia*

"Firmly in the grand tradition of Agatha Christie's Christmas books." —*The Globe and Mail* (Toronto)

The Good, the Bad, and the Emus

"Andrews's readers, who have come to expect a little silliness, fun-loving characters, and endings that are tough to predict, won't be disappointed." —*Publishers Weekly*

"Andrews has a gift for working a mystery into the antics of an oddball circus, writing with a kind and smiling attitude toward weirdness. . . . This volume, like its predecessors, can be read for sheer joy of the prose.

—*New York Journal of Books*

Cockatiels at Seven

"Suspense, laughter, and a whole passel of good clean fun."

—*Publishers Weekly*

"More fun than seven cocktails—and a lot safer, too."

—*Richmond Times-Dispatch*

"The plot, in true *You Can't Take It With You* fashion, involves plenty of snakes, as well as the titular cockatiels and assorted exotic birds. The author has a fine sense of pacing and a droll . . . sense of humor. This is character-driven fiction, and Andrews maintains the action within the confines and sensibilities of her town-and-gown setting."

—*The State*

The Penguin Who Knew Too Much

"Deliciously daffy." —*Publishers Weekly* (starred review)

"Andrews always leavens the mayhem with laughs. So march yourself down to the bookstore or library and check out *The Penguin Who Knew Too Much*."

—*Richmond Times-Dispatch*

"Andrews's eighth Meg-centric mystery moves along like the best beach reads." —*Entertainment Weekly*

"The levelheaded, unflappable Meg takes it all in stride. . . . This eighth cozy in the series makes the most of humorous situations, zany relatives, and lovable characters." —*Booklist*

"A classic whodunit . . . wraps suspense, humor, and a screwball cast of characters into a mystery novel with stand-up quality." —*about.com*

"Always a treat." —*RT Book Reviews*

"Andrews has mastered the art of writing farce with style and wit." —*Mystery Scene*

No Nest for the Wicket

"Fun, lively, charming." —*Publishers Weekly*

"Andrews strikes just the right balance between comedy and suspense to keep the reader laughing and on the edge of one's seat. . . . Fans of this series will no doubt enjoy this installment, while new readers . . . will be headed to the bookstore for the earlier books."
—*RT Book Reviews* (4 stars)

"Any day when I start reading about Meg is cause for delight." —*Deadly Pleasures*

"As usual, Andrews is a reliable source for those who like their murder with plenty of mayhem."
—*Kirkus Reviews*

"Andrews's talent for the lovably loony makes this series a winner; to miss it would be a cardinal sin."
—*Richmond Times-Dispatch*

"I can't say enough good things about this series, and this entry in it." —*Deadly Pleasures*

"Hilarious . . . another winner . . . keeps you turning pages." —*Mystery Lovers Bookshop*

Crouching Buzzard, Leaping Loon

"If you long for more 'fun' mysteries, à la Janet Evanovich, you'll love Donna Andrews's Meg Langslow series." —*The Charlotte Observer*

"There's a smile on every page and at least one chuckle per chapter." —*Publishers Weekly*

"This may be the funniest installment of Andrews's wonderfully wacky series yet. It takes a deft hand to make slapstick or physical comedy appealing, yet Andrews masterfully manages it (the climax will have you in stitches)." —*RT Book Reviews*

Revenge of the Wrought-Iron Flamingos

"At the top of the list . . . a fearless protagonist, remarkable supporting characters, lively action, and a keen wit." —*Library Journal*

"What a lighthearted gem of a juggling act . . . with her trademark witty dialogue and fine sense of the ridiculous, Andrews keeps all her balls in the air with skill and verve." —*Publishers Weekly*

"Genuinely fascinating. A better-than-average entry in a consistently entertaining . . . series." —*Booklist*

ALSO BY DONNA ANDREWS

Lord of the Wings

The Nightingale Before Christmas

The Good, the Bad, and the Emus

The Hen of the Baskervilles

Some Like It Hawk

The Real Macaw

Stork Raving Mad

Swan for the Money

Cockatiels at Seven

The Penguin Who Knew Too Much

No Nest for the Wicket

Owls Well That Ends Well

We'll Always Have Parrots

Crouching Buzzard, Leaping Loon

Revenge of the Wrought-Iron Flamingos

Murder with Puffins

Murder with Peacocks

Two Deadly Doves

Six Geese A-Slaying and Duck the Halls

Donna Andrews

Minotaur Books

A Thomas Dunne Book
New York

A THOMAS DUNNE BOOK FOR MINOTAUR BOOKS.
An imprint of St. Martin's Publishing Group.

www.thomasdunnebooks.com
www.minotaurbooks.com

ISBN 978-1-250-07438-6 (trade paperback)

Our books may be purchased in bulk for promotional, educational, or business use. Please contact your local bookseller or the Macmillan Corporate and Premium Sales Department at (800) 221-7945, extension 5442, or by e-mail at MacmillanSpecialMarkets@macmillan.com.

First Edition: October 2015

10 9 8 7 6 5 4 3 2 1

Six Geese A-Slaying

To Caroline Willner,
Mother of Mayhem

Acknowledgments

To the folks who made this possible:

At St. Martin's Press, many thanks to Ruth Cavin, Hector DeJean, Andrew Martin, Toni Plummer, and Pete Wolverton. More thanks to Ellen Geiger, my agent, the crew at the Frances Goldin Literary Agency, and to Dave Barbor and others at Curtis Brown.

My writing groups provided moral support and manuscript reading—the Rector Lane Irregulars (Carla Coupe, Ellen Crosby, Laura Durham, Peggy Hanson, Val Patterson, Noreen Wald, and Sandi Wilson) and the Hellebore Writers (Erin Bush, Meriah Crawford, M. Sindy Felin, Barb Goffman, and C. Ellett Logan). And thanks once more to the friends and family who kept me relatively sane while meeting a tight deadline: Stuart and Elke Schlager Andrews, Aidan and Liam Andrews, Kathy Deligianis, Suzanne Frisbee, David Niemi, and all the Teabuds.

Special thanks to Dina Willner for allowing me to borrow the Mother of Mayhem, and to the late Caroline Willner for a decade of friendship.

Chapter 1

December 23, 8:30 A.M.

"We wish you a merry Christmas
We wish you a merry Christmas
We wish you a merry Christmas
And a happy New—"

"Bah, humbug," I said.

Under my breath, of course. As Caerphilly County's reigning Mistress of the Revels, I didn't dare let anyone hear me badmouthing Christmas or showing less than the brightest of holiday spirits. I took a deep breath and straightened my holly wreath headdress before saying anything aloud.

"Could you please tell the drummers and pipers to stop drumming and piping immediately?" I finally said. Shouted, actually, to be heard above the din.

"They won't like it, Meg," my brother, Rob, shouted back. "They're having a competition to see who can make the most noise."

"I never would have guessed," I muttered. But I kept smiling as I said it. And I reminded myself that muttering wasn't particularly inconspicuous in weather so cold your breath smoked.

If only someone had warned me beforehand that "Mistress of the Revels" wasn't an honorary title. It meant

I was in charge of organizing Caerphilly's annual holiday parade.

This year's theme was "The Twelve Days of Christmas." The twelve drummers drumming were represented by twelve members of the Caerphilly College fife and drum corps, while the pipers piping were eleven assorted bagpipers—currently playing in at least eleven different keys.

The drummers outnumbered the pipers, especially since they'd also brought along twelve matching fifers. But the bagpipers seemed quite capable of holding their own in the noise department. They were definitely going to win if this turned into an endurance test. The drummers were already showing signs of fatigue, and the bagpipers hadn't even hit their stride yet. And while "Silent Night" and "The Little Drummer Boy" are both lovely Christmas carols when played separately, they didn't work well when played simultaneously by dueling groups of musicians.

None of which would have bothered me if they'd been doing it farther off—say, down in the cow pasture where they'd been asked to muster. Why did they insist on hovering right across the street from our house, all too near the spot in our front yard where I'd stationed myself, clipboard in hand, to check in the arriving parade participants?

"Go and tell them—" I began, and then stopped. Rob looked at me expectantly. He was quite dashing in one of the medieval costumes we'd borrowed from the Caerphilly College drama department. The blue brocade tunic matched his eyes, and unlike some of the volunteers, he was skinny enough to get away with wearing tights. As one of the ten lords a-leaping he was going to be a smashing success.

But as an enforcer, Rob would be a disaster. I knew what would happen if I sent him over to quell the riotous music. He'd ask them politely. They'd ignore him—if they even heard him. A little later, I'd go over to see why they hadn't shut up and find Rob taking bagpiping lessons or practicing his leaping in time with the fife and drums.

Some things you have to do yourself.

"Never mind," I said, as I turned to head in the direction of the musical duel. "Go make sure none of the other leaping lords have hopped off anywhere. And can you check the Weather Channel and get the latest prediction on when the snow will start? I'm going to—damn!"

I'd stepped in something squishy. I remembered that the eight maids a-milking had recently strolled by, leading their eight purebred Holstein milk cows.

"Please tell me I didn't just step in cow dung."

"Okay, you didn't just step in cow dung," Rob said. "I'm pretty sure the cleanup crew has been by at least once since the cows came through here."

"That's a relief," I said. Though I was energetically scraping my foot on the gravel anyway.

"So that's almost certainly camel dung."

As if that made a difference. I lost it, briefly.

"Can't those stupid wise men keep their beastly camels out of the road?" I snapped. Rob had turned to go and either didn't hear me or pretended not to. It occurred to me that perhaps I shouldn't be so harsh on the wise men, since Michael Waterston, my husband of six months, was one of them.

"Don't blame the stupid wise men," came a voice from behind me. "It was my fault."

I turned around to see an enormous, bushy-bearded figure clad in a peculiar feathered garment. One of the six

geese a-laying, I realized—I'd have recognized that immediately if he'd been wearing the goose head and had been
waving wings instead of a pair of brawny arms covered with
thick hair and a colorful collection of biker- and wildlife-
themed tattoos. But never mind the incomplete costume—I
was just glad to see its wearer.

"Clarence!" I said. "You made it!"

"Wouldn't miss it for the world," he said, giving me a
bear hug.

"So this is one of the six geese a-laying?" said a nasal
voice with a hint of a Southern drawl. I glanced over to see
who was talking and saw a tall, cadaverously thin man in
jeans and a faded brown parka. And he wasn't just tall compared to my five feet ten—he even looked tall standing
beside Clarence, who was six and a half feet tall and almost
as wide.

Brown parka was scribbling in a pocket notebook.
Around his neck he wore a small silver digital camera and
a lanyard with a laminated badge.

"You must be the reporter from *The Washington Star-
Tribune*," I said.

"Are you—" he paused to look into his notebook. "Meg
Lansdowne? The parade organizer?"

"Meg Langslow," I corrected.

"J. Ainsley Werzel," he said. He stuck out a hand and I
shook it, somewhat awkwardly, since he was still holding
the ballpoint pen in it.

"So, one of your geese, I presume?" he repeated. He
stuck his pen behind his ear and grabbed his digital camera, apparently intent on getting a festive holiday shot of
the ferrets inked up and down Clarence's arms.

"And also one of our vets," I said. "This is Dr. Clarence

Rutledge. He'll be helping look after the welfare of the many live animals appearing in today's parade."

I winced inwardly at how stilted I sounded, like something out of a press release from the town council. But better stilted than dimwitted.

Clarence shook the reporter's hand with a great deal less caution than I had. He was so used to enduring the teeth and claws of his more recalcitrant patients that a mere ballpoint pen wound meant nothing to him. Werzel was the one who winced.

"Damn," Werzel said, as he continued to gape at Clarence. "I wish my photographer would get here already. You haven't seen him, have you—short guy with a big Nikon?"

I shook my head.

"Damn," Werzel repeated. "He said ten minutes half an hour ago. Ah, well."

He stood looking around with an odd expression on his face, as if tracking down the source of a bad smell. I checked my foot again. No, it was clean. And when I took a deep breath, the icy air held only the tantalizing odors of the coffee, cocoa, and spiced cider at a nearby refreshment stand. I could hear sleigh bells jingling in the distance, and strains of Christmas carols drifting from various parts of the yard. A brace of cousins hurried by pushing a cart loaded high with poinsettias, and several small children dressed as elves were handing out candy canes, courtesy of the Caerphilly Candy Shop. What could possibly be causing that sour face?

"Quaint," Werzel pronounced.

"Quaint what?"

"Clearly that's going to have to be my angle on this story. Quaint."

He nodded as he said it, and a satisfied expression replaced the frown. He couldn't have been here more than five minutes, the parade itself wouldn't start for hours—and he'd already decided on his angle?

"Pity I can't think of something more sexy," he said, shaking his head.

Not that he'd tried.

"I've never really considered Christmas all that sexy," I said aloud.

"It's all a big conspiracy by the stores," he said.

I hoped that wasn't going to be the theme of his story. But then, I didn't have high hopes about the story anyway. The Caerphilly Town Council members might have been thrilled when they heard that the *Trib* wanted to cover our event, but I was far more pessimistic about how much could go wrong today. Not to mention more cynical about how ridiculous an unsympathetic reporter could make us look if he wanted to.

And why was the *Washington Star-Tribune* sending a reporter to cover our parade, anyway? Caerphilly County and the town of Caerphilly were in rural Virginia, two hours south of Washington, D.C., and the *Trib* rarely mentioned their one claim to fame—the small but prestigious college where my husband taught in the drama department. Our parade drew good attendance each year, but mainly from the county itself and from nearby counties even more rural than we were. Why wasn't Werzel covering more glamorous sights closer to home, like the national Christmas tree and whatever holiday parades and festivals the greater metropolitan Washington area had to offer? He could have written a clichéd story about our quaint country parade without leaving his desk. I was convinced Werzel had an ulterior motive—to make us look not only quaint but ridiculous. Unfortunately, if that was his plan, I couldn't think of any way to stop him.

The ten lords a-leaping danced past, with Rob in the lead. They had all strapped sets of Morris dancing bells onto their shins, and their procession sounded like "Jingle Bells" on steroids. I couldn't help smiling as they passed. Werzel didn't even look their way.

"I mean, what's so special about yet another Christmas parade?" he asked, when he could make himself heard again.

"Holiday parade," I corrected. It was a reflex by now. "We've decided to make this year's parade as diverse and multicultural as possible."

"That's nice," he said. "Of course, in a place like this, I guess multicultural means you've asked both the Baptists *and* the Episcopalians."

He doubled over laughing at his own joke.

"Not exactly," I said.

Just then a large, mud-spattered truck eased to a stop near me and an elderly woman wearing a large, jewel-trimmed turban stuck her head out of the passenger side window.

"So where do the elephants go?" she asked.

"Anywhere they want to," I said. "But see if you can convince them they'd like to wait in the sheep pasture across the street."

"No problem," she said, as the driver eased the truck over in the direction I'd indicated.

"Elephants?" Werzel asked, looking slightly wide-eyed.

"For the Diwali part of the parade."

"Diwali?"

"The Hindu festival of lights," I said. "It's their major winter holiday. Elephants are customary, I understand. Why don't you go watch them unload?"

Werzel nodded and stumbled after the truck. I smiled. Maybe the elephants would save us from the quaint stereotype. And if not—well, we could live with quaint.

"Nothing like elephants for human interest, is there?" Clarence said.

"For some kind of interest," I said. "I wouldn't necessarily call it human, with just the elephants and this Werzel fellow involved. But with any luck, he'll have so much fun photographing the elephants that he'll be in too good a mood to be snide."

"I should go over and check out the pachyderms," he said. He sounded quite matter-of-fact—but in addition to being one of the town veterinarians, Clarence was the official veterinarian for the Caerphilly Zoo, so he had treated elephants before. "That reminds me—sorry about the camel dung, but one of them was limping, and I was taking him for a walk to check it out."

"Please don't tell me we have an injured camel," I said, clutching my clipboard anxiously. "The zoo's only got the three camels. It just won't have the right effect at all if the wise men come riding in on two camels and a ten-speed bike."

"Oh, don't worry—" Clarence began.

"Meg, dear," I heard my mother say.

Chapter 2

I tensed and reminded myself that Mother wasn't necessarily reporting a problem or making a complaint. Still, I took a deep breath as I turned to see what she wanted. She was standing behind me, dressed in an elegant cobalt blue velvet Victorian party dress, complete with a matching parasol.

"You look lovely," I said. Which was true. Rob had inherited his aristocratic blond looks from Mother, whose hair, in her sixties, was still a rich if implausible shade of gold. As usual, I felt dowdy by comparison. Years of practice helped me refrain from patting at my own wayward brunette mane whenever I saw Mother's sleek coif. And was it fair that well short of forty, I already had to fight to keep my figure from turning matronly, while Mother was still as slender as she had been in high school?

I could tell she was eyeing my costume with dismay. I'd dressed for warmth and comfort, and then thrown on one of the county-issue shepherd's robes—cheap, one-size-fits-all garments that some past parade organizer had had made several decades ago so volunteers who didn't have their own costumes could throw on a robe and blend in. Since no one had bothered to launder the robes for years—if ever—the only people who ever wore them were those like me, who didn't remember till the last moment that they needed a costume. I suspected that once the parade was over, Mother would have a few words to say about my appearance.

Of course, I had no idea what her own stunning costume had to do with Christmas, but at this point, I didn't much care.

"I'm glad you like the costume, dear," Mother said, beaming a gracious smile at me and smoothing a bit of the dress's black lace trim.

"By the way," Clarence said, "the house looks lovely."

"Thanks," I said. "But it's all Mother's doing."

Mother beamed widely.

"Really?" Clarence said. "It's fantastic!"

Of course, Clarence already knew Mother had done the decorations. But he'd come to know our family well enough to guess that nothing was more guaranteed to put her in a good mood than a compliment to her decorating skills.

The house really did look fantastic. The exterior of our once-dilapidated three-story white Victorian was now in immaculate condition, thanks to the Shiffley Construction Company and Michael's and my depleted checkbook. Left to my own devices, I'd have stuck electric candles in the front windows and a tasteful wreath on the door and called it quits. In fact, and given how busy I was with the parade, I'm not sure I'd even have managed that. I'd assumed that Mother would expend her holiday decorating energy on their summer cottage—actually a farmhouse that she and Dad had bought, on the next farm down the road from Michael and me. But when she realized that hundreds—perhaps thousands—of holiday tourists would be seeing our house with its minimalist holiday décor, she'd immediately offered to take care of the decorations and had enlisted a small army of helpers from the ranks of the Hollingsworths, her vast extended family.

Every single stretch of roofline, including all the dormers and gables, was trimmed with a three-inch fringe of icicle lights. Every shutter, window-frame, and doorway was outlined with evergreen garlands trimmed with red bows. Every window had been painted to look like stained glass and behind each set of brightly colored panes glowed not only a flickering electric candle but a small constellation of prisms to reflect and scatter the light. Fortunately, Mother's taste didn't run to reindeer on the roof, but she had sent a team up to drape it with a giant banner that read "Peace on Earth." A pair of Christmas doves the size of turkeys hovered over each end of the banner, pretending they were holding it up, though in reality that function was performed by a sturdy cable around the chimneys on either end of the main house. A wreath the size of a truck tire obscured most of the front door, and more evergreen garlands made a festive path down to the mailbox. As we watched, the cousins were arranging the cartload of poinsettias into a bank of red and green on the front porch.

It wasn't exactly my taste, but considering that I hadn't lifted a finger to bring it about, I wasn't going to complain. I just had to remember not to fetch the paper in my bathrobe for the rest of the holiday season—in the three days since Mother's crew had finished it, the house had become a minor local tourist destination.

Even as we spoke, another family group flagged down a passerby to take their picture on our front steps. All in all, the decorations were a smashing success, and boded well for the interior design business Mother had announced she'd be opening in the spring.

"Thank you, dear," she said. "I just stopped by to ask where the Dickens are."

"Where the dickens are what?" I asked.

Mother allowed a small note of exasperation to creep into her sigh.

"The Dickens *characters*, dear," she said. "For the *Christmas Carol* float. You know—Scrooge, Tiny Tim—"

"Oh, right." I checked my clipboard. "Front yard, to the left of the walkway. Who are you, anyway?"

"You can tell she's having a bad day when she can't recognize her own mother," Clarence said, almost managing to keep a straight face.

"I'm playing Mrs. Cratchit," Mother said. She floated off toward the front yard, pausing briefly to straighten the evergreen garland decking one of the trash barrels. As Mother was fond of saying, it's those little details that really make a design.

"I thought the Cratchits were paupers," Clarence said.

"They were. Poor as churchmice. Mrs. Cratchit is described as 'dressed out but poorly in a twice-turned gown, but brave in ribbons, which are cheap and make a goodly show for sixpence.'"

"Have you memorized the whole book?" he asked. "I'm impressed."

"Only parts of it," I said. "The abridged version. Michael's rehearsing for his one-man *Christmas Carol* show, so by the time he's ready, I'll have the whole thing down pat."

"Oh, wonderful! When?"

"Six P.M. tomorrow night at the college auditorium; tickets ten dollars at the door; proceeds to benefit the Caerphilly Children's Fund," I rattled off.

"What a lovely way to spend Christmas Eve," he said. "I'll be there. Meanwhile, don't worry about Larry. He's fine."

"Larry?" I repeated. My glance strayed down to my clipboard. Was I missing a Larry?

"Larry the camel."

"Oh, that's right. Trust Dr. Blake to name his zoo's camels after the Three Stooges."

"A wonderful sense of humor, your grandfather."

I made a noncommittal noise. Less than a year ago we'd learned that Dr. Montgomery Blake, the world-famous conservationist and animal welfare activist, was Dad's long-lost father. I was still working on thinking of him as "Grandfather" instead of "Dr. Blake." I hadn't yet begun learning to appreciate his odd, curmudgeonly sense of humor.

"Anyway," Clarence was saying. "Larry always fakes a limp when he wants attention. I've got them feeding him some camel treats, and he'll be fine by parade time. By the way, you do realize that you sent the elephants to unload in the pasture where the drummers and fifers are rehearsing, right?"

"Yes," I said. "If you're heading there anyway, see if you can convince the drummers and fifers that all that racket they're making could spook the elephants."

"It would if they kept it up," he said, frowning. "Where do you want them to go instead? The musicians, that is."

"In the cow pasture behind the house. It's farther away—and downwind."

"You don't really intend to inflict a dozen bagpipers on a herd of defenseless cows?" Clarence said, with mock fierceness.

"There are no cows in the cow pasture at the moment," I said. "It's too full of Boy Scouts—they had their annual pre-parade campout there. And good luck spooking them—Rob was out last night helping ride herd on them, and he reports that they laughed at all his scariest ghost stories."

"This modern generation," he said, shaking his head. "Well, I'm off to cope with the camels and elephants."

Of course the moment he left, I wondered what he meant by camel treats. Did one of the leading pet food companies manufacture such a thing? And if not, what did you use to bribe a sulking camel back into good humor?

I could ask him later. I looked back at my check-in sheet. I was using a tiny self-inking stamp of a holly leaf to mark everyone present and accounted for. I smiled with satisfaction at the almost unbroken garland of leaves marching down the right-hand side of the page.

I accepted a piece of peanut brittle from a small angel with red pigtails, and a cup of eggnog from a passing cousin. I waved at a local farmer who strolled by herding a small flock of white turkeys with red bows around their necks. Evidently they were marching in the parade—which meant, I hoped, that they wouldn't be anyone's dinner this holiday season. Someone in the front end of a reindeer costume, complete with a battery-powered flashing red nose, wandered by scanning the crowd as if he'd lost something. Probably whoever was playing the hind legs.

"Aunt Meg? We're here."

My twelve-year-old nephew, Eric McReady, appeared at my elbow, at the head of a swarm of brown-clad shepherds around his own age. The Boy Scouts. Eric had recruited the local troop, who would be earning credits toward the next rank by performing public service. They'd be acting as mobile cleanup crews, with groups marching in the parade behind the camels, the elephants, the horses, and all the other large animals. Had the bagpipers evicted the Boy Scouts from their campground already? Or had Eric succeeded in getting his volunteers to show up on time?

Either way it was good news. I smiled as I stamped them as present.

"Are we really going to have a white Christmas?" one of them asked.

I glanced up at the sky again. I'd been doing it so often all morning that I was getting a crick in my neck. The latest forecast I'd heard called for a small storm to dump two to six inches of snow on us sometime today. Normally two to six inches would have constituted a fairly large storm by central Virginia's standards, but the meteorologists were almost ignoring it to focus on the massive storm system currently pummeling the Midwest and scheduled to unload another six to twelve inches on Christmas Eve.

"Yes," I said. "I just hope it waits until the parade is over." Or at least until the tail end of the parade was closer to town than our house. I had no desire to be snowbound with half the population of Caerphilly. Or with the dozens of animals we'd recruited for the parade—for this evening, I'd arranged quarters for the animals in town, in the barns belonging to the Caerphilly College Agricultural Sciences Department. I only hoped the snow would hold off long enough for them to get there.

"Snow! Snow! No school tomorrow! No school tomorrow!" chanted a dozen voices, as the Scouts capered around me in what I assumed was a snow dance.

Yes, two to six inches were more than enough to cancel classes. In their enthusiasm, they seemed to have forgotten that the schools were already closed tomorrow for the Christmas Eve holiday. In my school days, we'd have called this a wasted snow. But that didn't seem to bother the exuberant flock of miniature shepherds.

"Ten-hut!" Eric called.

Behind him the rest of the shepherds fell into formation, saluted in unison and then clanged their shovels against their buckets.

"Cleanup patrol reporting for duty, ma'am," Eric said.

"Thank goodness you're here," I said. And thank goodness they'd stopped calling themselves the Dung Fu Fighters and other worse names. "We just had a camel incident over there," I added, pointing to the offending spot.

Most of the troop scurried over toward the small pile of camel dung and began squabbling to see who got to shovel it up.

"It's okay if Cal helps us, isn't it?" Eric asked.

I glanced down at the small form at his side—much smaller than any of the other shepherds. A round brown face peered out of his hood, and I recognized six-year-old Calvin Ripken Burke, the youngest grandson of our Baltimore-born chief of police.

"As long as it's okay with his grandfather," I said.

Cal grinned, and ran over to join the rest of the crew.

"His brother is home sick with a cold," Eric explained. "So Chief Burke asked me if I'd look after him. Otherwise he'd have to stay with his grandmother and march with the choir. Cal would much rather shovel . . . um . . . dung."

"You're a good egg," I said. "Here—I made a list of the animals that are marching today. It would be great if you could assign a squad to follow each group."

"Roger," he said. "I'm going to do the elephants myself!" With that he ran off to organize his troops.

All by himself? Well, he'd learn. Then again, as the youngest of my sister Pam's six children, Eric was always running as fast as he could to keep up with his siblings, and was doomed to become a teenage overachiever. The parade cleanup was in good hands.

And it sounded as if Clarence, reinforced by the threat of stampeding elephants, had finally resolved the piper and drummer problem. Now I could return to checking in the remaining participants and keeping them from causing too much trouble before the parade started. Which would be in . . . a little over three hours.

I glanced up at the sky. No snow yet, thank goodness. Cold as it was, any snow that fell would undoubtedly stick around.

"What's wrong?"

I turned to see my husband, Michael, tall and resplendent in his wise man's costume.

"Just fretting over the weather again," I said, giving him a quick kiss. "You look very dashing. Have you got your myrrh?"

"Yes, ma'am," he said, giving a deep, elegant salaam that went well with the vaguely Middle Eastern costume. "Not with me, of course; it's on the prop table in the barn with the frankincense and fake gold. Your grandfather's giving a lot of the kids camel rides, so I thought I'd see if you needed any help. So nothing's wrong?"

"Nothing," I said. "Well, except for the fact that they keep changing their minds about when the snow will start, but there's nothing you can do about that. Most of the participants are already here, and it's not even nine."

"Which means we have to put up with them for the next three hours," Michael said, frowning.

"Cheer up," I said. "That gives us plenty of time to send out a posse for anyone who doesn't show."

"Or better yet, plenty of time to round up a replacement," Michael said. He waved at a brace of tuba players in Caerphilly High School band uniforms. "No one is irreplaceable."

"Except possibly the camels," I said, as I pointed dramatically to the left to steer the tuba players toward the rest of their band. "There are just two people left that I'm at all worried about."

"Who?"

"The Virgin Mary," I said. "For the nativity scene float."

"The one who's nine months pregnant."

"Only eight," I said. "Maybe eight and a half. The costume's bulky. No one will notice."

"Tell me again why we cast her as Mary?"

"Her father-in-law owns a flatbed truck," I said. "The only one we could find large enough to hold the nativity scene."

"She's perfect for the role, then."

"It's really the truck I'm worried about," I said. I glanced down the road again, hoping to spot it. "We can replace her, but if the truck doesn't show up, the Holy Family will have to walk all the way to Caerphilly. And then there's Santa. He's only a couple of miles away, and what do you bet he'll be the last to show up. Of course, on the bright side, at least we won't have to put up with him for too long. Frankly, if there's anyone I'll be happy to see the last of when the parade's over, it's him."

Chapter 3

"Oh, Mr. Doleson's not so bad," Michael said.

"Compared to whom?" I asked. "Scrooge? The Grinch? W. C. Fields with a hangover? Attila the Hun?"

"I admit he's a total grouch and can make 'Good morning' sound like a mortal insult," Michael began.

"Not that I've ever heard him say anything as polite as 'Good morning,'" I muttered.

"But at least he's a reclusive grouch, so we don't have to see him more than once or twice a month."

"Wish we could say the same for some of my family," I grumbled. "I can't remember the last time we had dinner for two. But Ralph Doleson's not my idea of a proper Santa."

"I don't think he's anyone's idea of a proper Santa," Michael said. "But he's practically the only guy in town with the requisite white beard and round belly who's also short enough to fit into the existing costume. You know how cheap the town council is—they would never pay to replace a perfectly good costume that's only used once a year."

"Well, at least it's only once a year," I said. "And—speak of the devil."

The short, round, rather toadlike figure of Ralph Doleson was slouching our way. He was lugging a garment bag and a battered canvas duffel that I assumed contained his costume. He'd obviously made an effort for the occasion. He had on a clean pair of overalls. And in an unprecedented fit of vanity, he appeared to have shampooed his beard. Though not his long, stringy hair—a good thing he'd be wearing the Santa hat. His face wore its usual surly expression.

I glanced casually at my watch. Nine o'clock on the dot. He might be lacking in social graces, our Santa, but at least he was punctual. Anyone who arrived from now on was officially late, and would receive the faint frown, the stern scowl, or an actual lecture, depending on how late they were and how penitent they seemed.

"Morning, Mr. Doleson," Michael said.

Doleson looked up, scowling as if Michael had hurled a string of insults at him.

"Do you expect me to get dressed in that barn of yours?" he snapped. "It's full of children and animals."

A Santa who hated children and animals? I was about to snap back that the barn was the only men's dressing room we had and he could change in plain sight if he liked, but fortunately Michael stepped in.

"Of course not," Michael said. "We've cleaned out one of the more private outbuildings for you. Wouldn't do for the kids to spot Santa changing into uniform, now would it? Here, let me help you with your luggage."

Doleson snorted, but surrendered the garment bag and the duffel and shambled off in Michael's wake.

"One of the more private outbuildings?" I repeated. Maybe elegant estates had outbuildings. We had sheds, in various states of disrepair. Though they looked better than usual at the moment. Mother's decorating crew had gift-wrapped the more disreputable-looking ones for the season, with green plaid paper and perky red bows, and decorated the rest with wreaths, evergreen garlands, and fake snow that would soon become superfluous.

I managed not to break out laughing when Michael

bowed and gestured grandly toward the door of the pig shed. Michael must have done a good job of charming the old reprobate. Mr. Doleson peered through the door, nodded brusquely, and stepped in. Trust Michael to save the day and restore my good mood.

The pig shed was the perfect place for Santa. We didn't have any pigs, so the shed was rarely used. We'd stashed Santa's sleigh there overnight in case the snow started slightly earlier than the weatherman predicted. The sleigh was an old horse-drawn wagon with boards nailed along both sides to hide the wheels. The boards were painted to look like runners, and I'd spent several hours the night before scraping off peeling paint, touching up the design, and then literally watching the paint dry—I'd had to run several space heaters to get the air warm enough for it to dry, and I didn't think it was safe to leave them untended.

Most years having a fake sleigh on wheels worked better than a real one, given how rarely we got a white Christmas in central Virginia. But how well would our ersatz sleigh work if the snow got very deep before the end of the parade? I shoved the thought out of my mind. The Shiffley Construction Company was on call for snow removal duty, standing by with snowplow attachments on all their trucks and tractors. If that wasn't enough—well, there was nothing more I could do now.

With the sleigh crammed into it, the shed wasn't exactly palatial quarters but it was extremely clean—I'd made sure of that before we shoved the freshly painted sleigh inside. Mr. Doleson would have enough room to change in privacy, and he could spend the rest of the time until the parade began in the relative comfort of the sleigh's padded back seat. Since Michael reappeared without him, I assumed Mr. Doleson was satisfied, and I stamped a particularly

heavy-handed holly leaf beside his name on the participants' list.

"Mission accomplished," Michael said, reappearing at
my side. If—"

"Professor Waterston?"

Michael turned to see a short, plump, elderly woman
dressed in a Mrs. Claus outfit, holding something wrapped
in red foil and trimmed with green ribbon.

"Merry Christmas, dear," Mrs. Claus said. She handed
him the parcel and tripped away.

"Who's that?" I asked.

"The dean's wife, I think. More to the point, what's in
this?"

"Another fruitcake," I said. "Do you like fruitcake?"

"Not particularly," he said, frowning as he teased open
one end of the foil to verify its contents. "Why?"

"Someone has it in for you, then. There's a rumor going around town that you do."

"Oh, no," he said. "I know how that got started. Professor Braintree's holiday tea."

Dr. Edith Braintree was the chair of the committee that,
in a few months, would decide whether to offer Michael
tenure at Caerphilly College. If they turned him down,
he'd have a choice between settling for a lower-paid ad-
junct position for the rest of his career or looking for
someplace else to start another seven-year tenure quest.
Thus the committee had much the same power over our
future as the jury has over the defendant in a criminal
trial—though at least no one expected accused felons to
have tea with the jurors, lose to them at racquetball, and
buy cases of Girl Scout cookies from their daughters.

"She seemed so pleased when I took a slice," Michael
went on, "I got a little carried away and said it reminded

me of my mother's fruitcake. And before you ask, no, Mom never made fruitcake that I can remember. I don't know what came over me."

I knew perfectly well—tenure fever. I hadn't told Michael, but tenure fever was the real reason I'd gotten stuck with organizing the parade. If the mayor had called up and tried to charm me into the job, I could have managed to keep saying no until he gave up and went looking for another victim. But when Dr. Braintree called, full of flattery and enthusiasm, implying that not only the town but the college would be so grateful if I'd agree to take the post . . .

"I suppose we can manage to eat up a fruitcake eventually," Michael was saying.

"Can we eat up seven of them?" I said. "Apparently there's a large hidden cult of fruitcake bakers in town, all eager for new converts."

"Oh, dear," he murmured. "Probably not. Don't any of your family like fruitcake?"

"Good idea," I said. "We'll regift them to out-of-town relatives."

"What a devious idea," he said. "I like it. I'll leave this one with you, then, and if you don't need me for anything I'll go help your grandfather with the camels."

"Have fun," I said. "And—"

Just then we heard a shout from the pig shed.

Chapter 4

Michael and I both started running toward it, as did several other people nearby, but before any of us reached the door, it slammed open and a small black and white furball sailed out, propelled by the toe of Ralph Doleson's boot.

"Keep that damned rodent away from me or I'll sue!" he bellowed. "I'm bleeding, dammit!"

Yes, he was bleeding ever so slightly. Nothing that wouldn't stop in a few seconds if he held his wounded finger up and wrapped something around it instead of holding it down and waving it around vigorously.

The rodent in question was our family dog, Spike—eight and a half pounds of pure meanness wrapped in a deceptively cute and furry exterior. He'd landed outside with a yelp, and took a few seconds to catch his breath, but then he launched himself toward Mr. Doleson, who swore, and slammed the door so hard the wreath fell off. Spike barked furiously at the door for a few seconds, then retreated so that it wouldn't hit him in the face when it opened, and lay down with his head on his paws to wait for his enemy to emerge.

It would have been cute if I didn't know how serious Spike was about revenge. And if I hadn't been so tempted to help him. I strode over and knelt down to check him for wounds—wondering, as I did, who had been brave or foolish enough to decorate Spike's collar with a red-and-green velvet bow the size of his head.

"What a jerk," Rob said. I was so focused on Spike that I started at his voice.

"Spike might have bitten him first," Eric said.

"You know he hardly ever bites strangers unless they bother him first," I said. "And even if Spike started it, Doleson seriously overreacted."

"I think we should report him for cruelty to animals," Michael said, in what someone who didn't know him might think was a calm and unemotional voice. I could tell he was furious.

"Wait till after the parade," I said. "Then we'll get him."

"I'll talk to the chief about it," Michael said.

I nodded. Spike seemed okay, so I began jotting down the names of the potential witnesses in my notebook-that-tells-me-when-to-breathe, as I called my giant, spiral-bound to-do list. Apart from Rob, Michael, and me, at least half a dozen respectable citizens of Caerphilly had witnessed Mr. Doleson's act. Not to mention Ainsley Werzel, who was staring at the door of the pig shed with an outraged look on his face. Maybe Werzel and I had just gotten off on the wrong foot. I made a resolution to be particularly friendly and helpful next time I talked to him.

"It's my fault," Rob said. "I put Spike in there because I thought it would be safer than the barn, and you know how he hates being confined. I'll put him in his crate."

"Get Clarence to check him out first," I said. "I didn't see any blood or obvious injuries, but it's possible he's broken a bone or two and is so fixated on his prey that he just hasn't noticed yet."

"And don't be silly," Michael said to Rob. "Your failure to crate the small evil one does not give Ralph Doleson the right to drop kick him across the yard. I'll find Clarence and send him over."

I returned to my post to continue checking in stragglers, though I kept walking over to look at Spike until Clarence arrived. He examined the patient, and gave me a thumbs up before leading Spike off to the safety of his crate in the kitchen.

I breathed a sigh of relief. Spike wasn't technically our dog. Michael's mother had dumped him on us several years ago when her doctor advised her to see if a trial separation helped her allergies. We'd become resigned to the fact that he was with us for the long haul. But I knew Mrs. Waterston would have a fit if she heard that anything had happened to Spike.

For that matter, I'd developed a grudging fondness myself for the small evil one, as we'd nicknamed Spike. He had more guts than sense, and was not only capable but fond of biting the hands that fed him. On at least one occasion, though, he'd accidentally saved my life. Ralph Doleson had not heard the last of this.

"Let me know if he tries to file charges," a voice said. I looked up to see the tall form of Jorge Soto, one of the programmers who worked at Mutant Wizards, my brother's computer game development company.

"Thanks—I've already got you on my list of witnesses to the dog-kicking."

"Not the first time he's done something like that," Jorge said. "I live at the Pines, you know."

I nodded. Ralph Doleson owned the Whispering Pines, a former hot sheets motel that was now a grungy garden apartment building. Rob technically lived there, too, although for the last couple of months he'd been spending most of his time in one of the unused bedrooms on the third floor of our house.

"He doesn't like dogs," Jorge went on. "We've had a

couple of cases at the Pines where people who had dogs found out Doleson was teasing and mistreating them till they tried to bite him, and then calling the police on them."

"What a jerk!" I said.

"Yeah. I mean, if he doesn't like dogs, he should just put in a no-dogs rule. He owns the place; no one could argue with him. But I think he likes causing trouble."

"I wish we could fire him as Santa," I said. I tucked my notebook away and headed for the refreshment stand. The adrenaline charge induced by Spike's encounter with Doleson had faded, leaving me feeling suddenly tired and in need of warmth and caffeine.

"Why don't you fire him?" Jorge asked, falling into step beside me.

"Hard to find a replacement on short notice," I said. "Especially one who can fit into the tiny costume."

"Can him anyway," Jorge said.

The lady at the refreshment stand smiled and handed me a black coffee without my even asking for it. Maybe I'd been hitting the coffee a little too often this morning.

"How can we possibly have a Christmas parade without Santa?" I asked.

"Holiday parade," he said, with a grin. Obviously he'd heard my knee-jerk correction to other people.

"Holiday, yes; but still—without Santa?"

"In my country, Santa's optional."

"Santa doesn't bring you presents?" I took a deep gulp of my coffee.

"No, in Costa Rica, Baby Jesus brings the presents."

"So you don't have Santa at all?"

"No, we have him," Jorge said. "Santa—St. Nicholas, that is—brings Baby Jesus. He's like the chauffeur."

"I never knew that."

"When my parents were little, they didn't have Santa at all. But once we kids started seeing a lot of American Christmas movies, they had to have some way to explain to the kids what the fat guy in the snow suit was all about. Not sure if it's just my parents or if it's widespread in Costa Rica, but that's how I was brought up."

"I wish we were having a Costa Rican holiday parade, then, but I think around here the kids would be heartbroken if we didn't have a Santa."

"Yeah," Jorge said. "I guess they don't know that behind that beard is the meanest man in town."

With that he waved and wandered off. I finished my coffee and could already feel my energy level rising. I'd crash later—I'd been running on four or five hours of sleep a night for the past week—but for now, I was okay. I squared my shoulders and turned back just in time to see the long-awaited arrival of the flatbed truck for the nativity scene. Our heavily-pregnant Virgin Mary waved cheerfully at me from its passenger window. Things were looking up.

Clarence had even stopped the piping and drumming, thank goodness. I could see the musicians straggling across the road in small groups, heading for the cow pasture. Followed by several tourists with cameras. Well, the musicians were a picturesque sight—the drummers and fifers in their red, white, and blue Revolutionary War uniforms and nearly every one of the bagpipers wearing a different plaid with his full-dress kilt. Given the temperature, all of them probably had matching blue knees by now—should I have someone check them for signs of frostbite?

"There you are!" My father bounced into view, his round face beaming. His exuberance erased whatever last bits of stress I'd been feeling. Dad adored Christmas—adored holidays generally in fact, and was in seventh heaven at being able to help with the annual holiday parade. No present I could possibly have given him would have made him happier. Well, okay, maybe announcing the prospect of another grandchild would have beat the parade, but Dad was one of the few family members who took it on faith that Michael and I had been working on that project since our Memorial Day elopement, and he had never demanded periodic updates on our progress.

He was carrying his black medical bag. I hoped this meant that he was prepared for any emergency that might need his medical skills, and not that we'd already had one.

"Where do you want the boom lift?" he asked.

"I don't know that I want a boom lift at all," I said. "Who brought it, and why? Does one of the floats need repairing or something?"

"It's going in the parade, of course!" he exclaimed, and from his expression I could see that he was clearly astonished at my lack of enthusiasm for the boom lift. "The Shiffleys brought it. Don't you have it on your list?"

I flipped through the pages of my checklist, baffled. Had I, in a moment of mental derangement, approved the addition of a boom lift to the parade? Perhaps decked in holly, evergreen, and red ribbon, and carrying a banner saying "Merry Christmas from the Shiffley Construction Company"?

"There it is," Dad said, pointing to an item on my list. "The Clayville Congregational Church Choir."

"I thought they were just marching and singing," I grumbled.

"They're calling it 'Angels We Have Heard on High.' They're all wearing angel costumes, and they're going to have the soloists up on the platform, scattering confetti. Biodegradable confetti, of course. Don't you remember?"

"Silly me," I said, although this was the first I'd heard of the Congregationalists' plans. "How about putting the boom lift over there by the side of the road? Just beyond the elephants."

"Elephants? We've got both of them, then? Splendid! That means I get to ride one!"

Dad scurried off, and a few minutes later, I saw the boom lift chug slowly by, with Dad twenty feet in the air on the platform. It appeared to be driving itself, unless the person standing up on the platform with Dad was the driver. I'd been wrong about the holly and red ribbon—they'd covered up as much of the boom lift's industrial orange frame as possible with sky blue crepe paper, and stuck several giant cotton clouds to it at random intervals.

The choir members followed in the boom lift's wake in twos and threes, most of them already wearing white choir robes, white wings made of cotton batting and silver glitter, and glitter-coated halos.

And there went Werzel, the reporter, stumbling along in pursuit of the choir, snapping away with his tiny camera. So much for our image as an erudite, cosmopolitan community. Maybe I should be glad he'd already pegged us as quaint. Quaint was an improvement over barmy.

Since Werzel's camera looked like the same inexpensive model that I used to take family snapshots, we could always hope that his photos didn't turn out good enough for the *Trib* to use. Where was the promised professional photographer, anyway?

I double-checked my participants list to make sure I had the waiver from the choir absolving me, the Caerphilly Town Council, and the immediate world of responsibility for anything that might happen to the high-flying angels during the parade. Reassured, I stamped the choir in as present and accounted for.

"Not bad for a small town."

Ainsley Werzel had returned. I had to smile—the reporter was clearly struggling to maintain his former air of cool superiority. Score one for the elephants.

I waved and just nodded to him—at the moment, I was busy welcoming Miss Caerphilly County. Werzel stood by with surprising patience while I admired the beauty queen's hair, earrings, nails, makeup, dress, and shoes and gave her directions to the women's dressing room—the living room and library in Michael's and my house.

"So how far is Tappahannock from here?" he asked.

"Forty-five minutes to an hour," I said.

"You're an hour away," he shouted into his cell phone. "I said west of Tappahannock, not in it." He snapped the cell phone closed.

"Photographer's still lost," he said. "So how come you guys have this shindig only two days before Christmas? Most towns have their Santa parade at the beginning of the shopping season so the parents can hear their kids' gimme lists. And the stores can make more sales."

"Caerphilly's parade started out as an event to give presents to the town's poor children."

"You mean poor as in economically disadvantaged?" Werzel said.

"A hundred years ago, when the parade started, people mostly just said poor," I answered. "But yes. And then when the Great Depression came, everyone was economically disadvantaged, and they started the tradition of giving every kid in town a present. So that's what has happened for the last eighty years or so."

He nodded and scribbled some more. I considered telling him that while our curmudgeonly Santa was handing out small presents to all the children, regardless of economic status, in the public ceremony, many of the families who were quite genuinely poor would be picking up additional presents, not to mention food and warm clothing, from stations set up by the various churches and community service organizations.

I decided against telling him. If he bothered to use the information, it would make Caerphilly look good, but I doubted he would mention it. And more important, most of those proud, struggling country families were embarrassed enough at having to accept handouts. It would be the last straw to have some reporter from a big city paper taking intrusive pictures of them doing so.

"And there's a big festival," I said instead. "Baked goods, barbecue, craft sales, lots of raffles, judging the quilting and cooking contests, performances from many of the local musical groups and church choirs—sort of like a big church bazaar and a county fair rolled into one."

I could see his eyes glaze over. Good; we were safely back in quaint again. Maybe he'd skedaddle back to Washington after the parade and the county's unemployed and working poor could collect their turkeys and warm coats in privacy.

I turned to greet the delegation from the nearby clown school, which involved receiving multiple joy buzzer handshakes and having innumerable coins pulled out of my ears. I heard Werzel's camera clicking, and cringed.

But when I'd dispatched the clowns to their staging area, I turned and found that Werzel was snapping pictures of the Dickens float. Mother and her fellow Victorians certainly were elegant. I smiled approvingly as Werzel snapped shots of the float from various angles. Another triumph for Mother's decorating skills, not to mention her ability to appear completely impervious to both summer heat and bitter cold like today's weather.

Unfortunately, when Mother saw I was free, she furled her parasol and came over.

"Meg, dear," Mother said, "we have a little problem."

Chapter 5

"What little problem?" I repeated. I braced myself—Mother had once described the presence of a black bear in the living room of our vacation cabin as a little problem.

"Those SPOOR people are at it again."

"At what, Mother?"

"SPOOR people?" Werzel echoed.

"Stop Poisoning Our Owls and Raptors," I said. "They're a local environmental group. They specialize in bird-related issues. What are the SPOOR members up to now, Mother?"

"They've brought those protest signs," Mother said. "The ones with the depressing pictures of dead birds on them. I thought you told them they couldn't bring their placards. If they're going to be marching with those signs . . ."

"I did, and they're not," I said. "Where are they?"

"Over by the barn."

"I'll talk to them," I said. "While I do, why don't you show Mr. Werzel the camels?"

But Mr. Werzel wasn't interested in camels, or assumed he could see them anytime between now and the start of the parade. He trailed behind me as I went to straighten out the SPOOR delegation.

They were already dressed in their costumes—SPOOR members would be playing the six geese a-laying. They'd been trouble from the start. Shortly after dawn, I'd had to lay down the law and forbid the entire SPOOR membership from marching in goose costume.

"It's *six* geese a-laying," I'd said. "Not thirty-seven."

"Thirty-eight counting Mrs. Markland," one of them had put in, and the others had nodded approval, as they always did when anyone mentioned their late founder and first president.

"Mrs. Markland died last year," I'd countered. "You're not planning to bring her along, I hope?"

"She's always with us in spirit," one of the members had said.

"That's fine," I'd said. "You can have as many people with you in spirit as you like, whether they're still on this plane or have gone to that giant protest march in the sky. But I only want to see six of you marching in costume in the parade, or I'll get six of the Boy Scouts to replace you."

They'd sulked at that, but had started drawing lots to see who got to wear their elaborately feathered Canada goose costumes and who would simply march along behind in plain clothes, carrying the SPOOR banner. I'd also had to discourage them from including an offputtingly realistic reenactment of egg-laying in their routine. I'd had a private word with Clarence, whom I considered one of the more sensible of the SPOOR members, and he'd promised to keep them in line.

And yet, in spite of everything, here they were blatantly trying to ignore the ban on carrying political signs in the parade.

When I arrived, the six lucky members who would be portraying the geese were doing a Rockettes-style dance number. I had to admit, it was pretty funny, seeing their giant webbed feet kicking into the air in unison, and even funnier when they bent over and waggled their fake tail feathers. I realized I was grinning at the sight, so I paused a moment to settle my face into the kind of stern look that would tell them I meant business. And to see if I could have a word with Clarence. Even in costume, I should be able to spot him, thanks to his towering height.

No tall geese in sight, unfortunately. But I did notice that a dozen other SPOOR members were scuttling around furtively behind some shrubbery. They seemed to be carrying something.

I strode over, parted the bushes, and frowned at them. They were all hovering over a pile of placards. One of them had taken off his coat and was trying to conceal the contraband. The dancing geese broke ranks and came trailing after me.

"I'm confiscating the signs," I said. I began picking up the placards and tucking them under my arm. Something poked me, and I realized that they'd trimmed the placards for the occasion with little bits of holly and evergreen.

"But it's for such an important cause!" one of the costumed geese said.

"Yes, and that's why I asked SPOOR to represent the geese," I said. "Giving you a key, highly visible role in the parade. But you're not going to win over anyone, marching in the holiday parade waving pictures of dead birds."

"They don't all show dead birds," one SPOOR member said. "We've got some with birds that are victims of an oil spill."

"Oh, and that's so much more cheerful than dead birds," I said. "Look, the dancing's great—it should get SPOOR a lot of attention, and then when you are in a forum where it's appropriate to protest, everyone will remember you favorably."

Some of them seemed content with that idea, but the rest were muttering mutinously.

"And if you insist on carrying the placards—"

"We know—you can always replace us with Boy Scouts," one said. "Of course the Boy Scouts don't have costumes."

"They're always prepared, remember?" I said. "I'm sure they could come up with something on short notice."

They nodded, most of them rather sullenly, and didn't try to stop me from taking the rest of the signs.

Werzel fell in step with me as I headed toward the house with my armload of placards. He even nudged a couple back into place when I began to lose my grip on them. It would have been nice if he'd offered to take a few, but he had his notebook out and he was scribbling madly.

"So, you don't approve of this SPOOR thing?" he said. He'd probably taken a few shots of the SPOOR rebellion. I made a note to see if I could borrow his camera, once the parade was over, and accidentally delete anything really embarrassing.

"I thoroughly approve of SPOOR," I said. "It's a wonderful organization. My father's the current president, and I've joined in some of their protests myself. They're doing good work to protect the bird population. But I told everybody from the start that we weren't allowing any political signs or gestures as part of the parade. Not even for political causes I agree with. It's a holiday parade."

Just then, I noticed that one of the geese had followed us and was hovering nearby, clearly waiting for a chance to talk. A very tall goose—Clarence? I looked around for someone to handle the placards and spotted my brother.

"Rob," I said. "Put these somewhere. In the safe room."

"Sure thing,"

"Safe room?" Werzel repeated.

"Our pantry," I said. "It's got a lock on the door. We have

a lot of strangers wandering around the house and grounds today, so anyone who wants a safe place to leave a purse or a laptop can check it in the safe room."

"Good idea," he said. "There's always a klepto in every crowd."

Especially if the crowd included Mother's side of the family. We had several relatives who suffered from what Mother referred to as "a little problem." Michael liked the phrase "insufficiently developed understanding of the concept of private property," but I suspected in at least half the cases in my family the so-called kleptomaniacs were actually drama queens with an unquenchable thirst to be the center of attention. Not that I was going to mention this to a reporter.

"And while you're in the house, give Spike a bathroom break, okay?" I said to Rob.

"Roger."

Jorge Soto came up to help Rob with the placards and I turned back to the goose.

"Can I help you?" I asked.

The goose took its head off, revealing Clarence's shaggy mane.

"Sorry about that," he said. "I've been telling them repeatedly that signs were completely inappropriate. Not that they've been listening."

"I understand," I said.

"It's just that—"

He glanced at Werzel, who was holding his pen poised over his notebook as if waiting to take dictation.

"Can we have a little privacy here?" I asked.

Werzel cocked his head as if he didn't quite understand what I was saying.

"Beat it," Clarence said, his voice an octave lower than

usual. He scowled at Werzel, and tried to cross his arms to assume a menacing posture. Of course, the goose costume wasn't designed for arm crossing, and it looked more as if he was trying to fold his wings in prayer, but Clarence still looked remarkably menacing. Werzel got the message and hurried off. Clarence turned back to me.

"Look," he said. "I just wanted to give you a heads up about something. Feeling is running rather high among some of the SPOOR members."

"About the protest signs? Don't they understand—"

"No," he said. "About Santa."

"Is there something environmentally unsound about the concept of Santa?" Staying politically correct seemed to get harder every year.

"Not Santa in general, just your Santa."

"You mean the Santa the Town Council foisted on me," I said. "I would never have cast Ralph Doleson as Santa."

"No, you've got more sense," he said. "But remember what happened with him this summer? Oh, wait—it was while you and Michael were on your honeymoon, so I suppose you didn't hear. Well, in late June—oh, look!"

I turned to see what he was pointing at. The wise men were taking their camels for a test ride. The camels alone would have been worth staring at—they were stately and majestic and wore the most elaborate and brightly colored leather saddles, bridles, and other accoutrements I could ever remember seeing. They were even more impressive with the elaborately robed wise men riding them. I looked around, but Ainsley Werzel had wandered off someplace. Ah, well—with luck, none of the photos he took would be used for the article anyway, and the camels would still be around when the photographer eventually showed up.

Michael, at the head of the procession, looked as if he

had been born in a camel saddle—partly because he was fairly good at riding horses, and partly because he was too good an actor to let anyone know that he wasn't quite at ease with Larry's oddly swaying gait. Behind him rode Dr. Montgomery Blake, my grandfather, who had spent so many of his ninety-some years roving various wildernesses for zoological projects and environmental crusades that he was perfectly comfortable riding a camel, horse, donkey, elephant, or any other steed or vehicle you could think of. He had one leg hooked around a protrusion that was the Bedouin equivalent of the saddle horn, and was turned around nearly backwards, shouting instructions at our local police chief, who was portraying the third wise man.

"Chief Burke doesn't look altogether happy," Clarence said, with a frown.

That was an understatement. The chief's normally calm, brown face wore a fierce scowl that would ordinarily have reduced his officers to abject terror lest they be the ones who'd screwed up. Under the circumstances, I suspected the scowl was a deliberate attempt to hide absolute panic. But I had to hand it to him—he hung on gamely as the procession lurched and swayed its way past the house and headed down the road.

"Aren't they going the wrong way?" asked a child's voice at my side. Cal Burke stood, shovel and pail in hand, staring anxiously at the camel procession as it disappeared around a curve in the road.

"They're just taking a practice ride," I said.

"Hmph!" Minerva Burke, the chief's wife, had appeared, wearing the maroon satin choir robe of the New Life Baptist Church. She shook her head as she watched her husband's progress. "At this rate, the old fool will break his neck before the parade even begins. But there's no stopping them when they get a crazy idea in their heads, is there? Cal, go keep an eye on your grandfather."

Cal nodded and scampered off behind the camels. Clarence frowned—was he still worried about Larry's limp?—and followed.

Ainsley Werzel sauntered up. He'd thrown on one of the county-issue brown shepherd's robes and was stuffing his press pass inside it.

"Getting into the spirit of things," he said, when he saw me eyeing the robe.

More like trying to fool people into thinking he was part of the parade and catch them off guard, I suspected.

"So Chief Burke's one of the wise men?" he asked. "Is that okay?"

"More than okay, it's useful," I said. "In the unlikely event of any trouble, we'll already have the police chief and a number of his officers on hand to deal with it."

"Yeah, but isn't that carrying this whole multicultural thing a little too far?" Werzel asked. "I mean, were any of the original wise men African-American?"

Was he making a joke? No, he sounded serious. I was still trying to figure out a tactful way to answer when Minerva Burke spoke up.

"African-*American*?" she said, with a snort. "Not hardly, since it wasn't till fifteen centuries after the Nativity that Columbus discovered what the Indians had already found and a while after that before people started calling it America. Not to mention a couple of centuries till the slave trade brought Africans to this side of the ocean. So, no, there weren't any African-American wise men."

"However," I said, "there's a tradition dating back to the Middle Ages that one of the wise men, Balthazar, was African."

"Just African," Minerva Burke said. "No hyphen required."

"And we've asked Chief Burke to be a wise man to honor that tradition."

"Great, great," Werzel said. He backed off, smiling nervously, until he was about ten feet away—at which point he pretended to become fascinated with one of the musical acts—a barbershop quartet dressed as Christmas trees—and loped off as fast as he could.

"Sorry," Minerva said, shaking her head. "Don't know why, but that man just brings out the mean in me."

"Don't apologize," I said. "You're welcome to chase him away any time you see him hovering near me. I really don't want to have to deal with a reporter on top of everything else."

"I'd have thought you'd be pleased to see he was here," Minerva said. "After all, we've been trying for years to get someone other than the local rag to cover it. And you snagged the *Star-Tribune*—it's a fabulous coup."

"I didn't snag him," I said. "He just showed up. And if that's a coup, it's one that could backfire, big time," I said. "Have you read any of Werzel's articles?"

She shook her head. Not surprising—I hadn't either before the *Trib* called to request directions and a VIP pass. But a quick Google search told me all I needed to know.

"He wants to be Woodward and Bernstein for the new millennium, and they've got him stuck in the Style section, writing human interest stories. So he tries to turn every assignment into a new Watergate."

"But there's no possible scandal he can find connected with our parade," Minerva said. "Is there?"

"No, but that just means he'll drive us crazy trying to

find the smoking gun, and when he fails he'll sulk and try to make us look like lunatics."

"Oh, dear," Minerva said. "Yes, we'd be all too vulnerable on the lunacy angle."

"You should see the article he did on a group of little old ladies up in Loudoun County who make bears for sick children in disasters. He spent most of the article making fun of their accents and their clothes and then toward the end made it sound like he suspected they were using the bears to smuggle drugs or launder money or something. He's trouble with a press pass."

"We can't let him stay!" she exclaimed. "It'll kill Henry if we have more negative publicity. His stomach was in knots for weeks after that nasty business over the summer."

Nasty business? Rather a mild term for a murder and the breakup of a major drug smuggling ring. But perhaps her years in Baltimore, where Chief Burke had been a homicide detective, had made her jaded about the crime level in our more sedate rural community.

"We can't very well chase a reporter away," I said aloud. "The parade's free to the public, as I had to explain several times to that ninny who asked us to give Werzel a VIP pass. And if we tried too obviously to shoo him, he'd get suspicious and really make our lives miserable."

"We'll just have to keep an eye on him, then," she said, and strode away—probably to enlist the rest of the New Life Baptist choir in the surveillance. I wondered if it would make Werzel nervous, being constantly under the stern eyes of at least a dozen dignified black women in majestic burgundy choir robes. I hoped so.

I was, for the moment, blissfully unbothered. Slightly chilled, but unbothered. No one was standing in front of me, demanding private dressing rooms, complaining about their unsatisfactory place in the marching order, or asking where to find the rest of their party. Most of the people with nothing better to do were either lining up to get elephant rides or staring down the road waiting to see how many wise men were still in their saddles when the camels returned. I glanced around to see if Clarence had come back, but either he hadn't or he'd put his goose head back on—I couldn't tell which of the far more than six identical geese was him. His height should have been a clue, but either many of the SPOOR members were unusually tall or the goose heads added a lot of height. I made a mental note to drop over there before too long to find out what SPOOR had against Santa and whether it was likely to cause any problems during the parade. And possibly to confiscate all the surplus goose costumes, just in case.

Maybe I could channel the SPOOR members' energies into fixing up the two bird-themed Christmas trees flanking the front walk. When Mother had given Dad and his SPOOR comrades leave to decorate them, I think she'd envisioned the ten-foot spruces festooned with artificial birds, feather garlands, and perhaps a wee tinsel nest or two. It never occurred to her that the SPOOR thought of the trees as for the birds rather than about them. The garlands of nuts, berries, and popcorn were decorative enough, and the little seed balls were not unattractive, but no amount of red ribbon could possibly make large, droopy net bags of suet look festive. And since the SPOOR members had finished decorating them two days ago, the birds had been demonstrating their appreciation by systematically eating the trees clean. They now had that ratty, picked-over look of store counters on the last day of a really good sale. Yes, I should definitely enlist the SPOOR members to replenish the trees. Maybe I could even donate our surplus fruitcakes to the cause.

But not now. For now, everything was under control. I glanced over at my clipboard and saw that only a few bit players had yet to check in. I stuck my clipboard under my arm, stuffed my chilled hands in my pockets, leaned gratefully against one of our front fence posts, and drank in the fantastical sights and sounds around me.

And they were fantastical—even at my busiest, I realized that. I could have been enjoying it all so much more if I didn't have to feel responsible for it. I felt a brief twinge of resentment at that, and banished it with the thought that by nightfall, my term as Mistress of the Revels would be over. And surely, armed with the memory of this year's experience, I could gather the gumption to refuse if they asked me again. So next year I could take a small part and enjoy the festivities. Maybe I'd learn to juggle or at least get a medieval costume and march with Michael's colleagues who attended every year as jesters. Or help Mother's garden club friends with their traditional flower-themed float. Or maybe just stand at the roadside and be part of the audience.

Yes, everything was going splendidly, and before too long I could return to my own plans for Christmas, which included not only the giant potluck family dinner at Mother and Dad's farm on Christmas Day, but also a quiet Christmas Eve with Michael after his one-man show was over. We'd fended off several dozen invitations from friends and family alike, and were planning to spend the evening in front of the fireplace with a glass of Shiraz and soft carols and—

"Aunt Meg!"

Eric came running up, followed by Cal Burke. They both looked wide-eyed and ashen-faced.

"What's wrong?" I said, nearly dropping the clipboard in my alarm.

Eric swallowed hard.

"I think something's wrong with Santa."

Chapter 6

"Where is Mr. . . . . Santa?" I asked.

"In the pig shed," Eric said.

"Do you know what's wrong with him?"

Eric glanced down at Cal, then shook his head.

"Not really," he said.

But from the look in his eyes, he knew, and it wasn't good news.

"Wait here," I said. "If anyone shows up looking for me, tell them I'll be right back."

Eric nodded.

"And don't either of you say anything to anyone," I added. "Promise?"

Cal nodded.

"We won't," Eric said.

I handed him my clipboard to hold so he'd look more official, and hurried over to the pig shed.

"Meg, would you like some Christmas cookies?" someone called out as I passed.

"Later, thanks," I said over my shoulder. What could be wrong with Mr. Doleson?

Whatever the problem, I was grateful Michael had thought to give Mr. Doleson the pig shed. It was not only private, it was somewhat out of sight of the rest of the yard, so if there was some kind of problem, perhaps we could deal with it quietly.

The shed door was closed. I heard no sounds from inside, so at least he wasn't having another of his cursing fits.

"Mr. Doleson," I called, as I rapped on the door.

No answer. I straightened the wreath on the door and waited another token few seconds before turning the knob.

Yes, there was definitely something wrong with Santa. He was sprawled on the back seat of the sleigh with one boot on and one held in his left hand.

His right hand clutched what appeared to be a stake stuck in the middle of his chest. From his fixed, staring eyes and the amount of blood inside the sleigh and on the dirt floor below, I had no doubt he was dead.

I stood there staring for what seemed like an hour—partly out of shock and partly out of morbid curiosity. I felt guilty about it, but I couldn't help the impulse to drink in every detail while I could. After all, in another couple of seconds, I would call the police and Chief Burke would banish the prying eyes of civilians like me.

I glanced at my watch. Nine thirty-five. Only a little over half an hour since I'd seen him enter the pig shed. I pulled out my notebook-that-tells-me-when-to-breathe and jotted the time down.

Then I stepped out, shut the door, and looked around in all directions for someone I trusted to guard the shed while I went for help. I saw two choir members, assorted shepherds, and a very tall goose, but no one I knew well enough to guard a murder scene.

Then my luck changed. I spotted two figures strolling past. One was a wearing a bulky snowman suit while the other was my cousin, Horace Hollingsworth. At least I assumed it was Horace. All I could see was that the figure was wearing a ratty gorilla suit, but Horace came in his ape costume not only to costume parties but also whenever he could get away with pretending he thought costumes were called for.

"Horace!" I called. The gorilla turned around and stumbled in my direction while the snowman waved and continued on his way.

"Hi, Meg."

Even muffled as it was by the gorilla head, I could tell that Horace's voice was flat and depressed. I made a mental note to ask him later what was wrong. For now, Horace was the perfect person to stand guard. Back in my hometown of Yorktown, where Horace still lived, he was a crime scene technician for the sheriff's department, so he of all people would understand the importance of keeping everyone out of the scene until someone competent could examine it.

In fact, he'd probably be the someone. Since Caerphilly was too small to have its own crime scene technician, York County often lent them Horace when they needed forensic help. Particularly if he was already here, as he so often was these days.

"I thought you were guarding the safe room," I said.

"I locked it up so Sammy and I could have a snack," he said.

"Was that Sammy in the snowman suit?" I asked. Sammy was one of Chief Burke's deputies. "Damn, we could have used him, too."

"What's wrong?"

"Someone killed Santa—Mr. Doleson," I said.

"Have you called 911?" he asked.

"Not yet," I said. I decided not to mention that I hadn't yet pulled myself together enough to even think of it.

"I'll do it, then," Horace said. He pulled a cell phone out of his pocket—well, that was new. The gorilla suit never used to have pockets. Unless Horace had learned to sew, perhaps someone with sewing skills had been helping him improve it. That could be good news—Horace's love life lately had been even worse than usual.

"Great, and don't let anyone in the shed," I said. "I'm going to find Sammy, or Chief Burke, or one of his officers."

Horace nodded.

"Debbie Anne?" I heard him say. Good, he'd reached the police dispatcher. I strode off toward where I'd last seen the camels.

I was in luck. The wise men were returning in stately procession. Ainsley Werzel was busily snapping pictures, and several amateur videographers were following the procession's path with their handheld cameras.

I felt bad about ruining the photo op, but they still had the whole parade to go. I ran out to meet the wise men and fell into step beside the chief's camel.

"I have bad news," I said.

"Something I'm going to have to get down off of this fool camel to deal with?" he asked. He sounded eager.

I nodded.

"Hang on a minute, then. Dr. Blake, how the blazes do you park this thing again?"

"Tell him to s-t-a-n-d," Dr. Blake said.

"Stand!" the chief barked. Curley stopped, and Dr. Blake pulled up beside him.

"Stand, Moe. Now tell him to 'Hoosh!' And lean back while you do."

"Hoosh!" the chief shouted.

The chief's camel stood motionless, while Dr. Blake's beast obediently began the awkward-looking process of folding first his front legs and then his back legs.

"Blast it!" Dr. Blake grumbled. "Moe's rather badly trained, and Curley's a little too eager. Try it again. And lean back, hard."

I began to wonder if I should have told the chief my news while he was still on the camel. Ralph Doleson's rigor mortis would probably have set in by the time the chief finally got back on solid ground.

"Hoosh! Hoosh, dammit!" the chief shouted, and leaned back so far I thought for a moment he'd fall off. But when Moe's front legs abruptly folded, I realized the chief had, accidentally or on purpose, gotten it right. Now that Moe was kneeling, the chief was upright.

"Now lean forward again, quick!" Dr. Blake ordered.

The chief leaned forward, grabbed the front of the saddle, and hung on for dear life as Moe's back end hit the earth with an audible thud.

"Meg, put your foot on his front leg," Dr. Blake said. "Moe's front leg, that is, not the chief's." I complied, a little nervously, because I couldn't remember if Moe was the one who bit.

"Put some pressure on it!" Dr. Blake said, as he reached for Moe's reins. "The idea is to discourage him from trying to get up again while the chief is dismounting."

I leaned on Moe's leg, and the chief slid off.

"I'm good," he said. "You can take your foot away if you like. Now what's the problem?"

I glanced around. Plenty of people were watching us, most of them either videotaping the camel dismounting demonstration or pointing their fingers and laughing. But only Dr. Blake and Michael were within earshot, so I decided this was as good a place as any to talk.

"Someone's murdered Ralph Doleson," I said.

"You're sure?"

"If he's not dead, he's a hell of an actor, and I don't think he could possibly have done it to himself," I said.

The chief closed his eyes for a second as if gathering strength, then sprang into action.

"Right," he said. "Where?"

"In our pig shed."

"You didn't just leave him there?"

"I found Horace and left him to guard the scene," I said. He nodded grudgingly.

"Show me."

"Okay," I said. "You might want to look a little happier. Or at least more nonchalant. I don't see him right now, but odds are that reporter's still lurking around here somewhere, and I bet you don't want him to figure out something's wrong and follow us."

The chief frowned for a moment, as if trying to decide whether I had an ulterior motive or not. And I did, of course, but he quickly deduced it was the same one he had: not letting Ainsley Werzel make Caerphilly look completely ridiculous. His face broke into a slightly forced smile.

"Great idea," he said, rather loudly. "Let's just go and do that while I'm thinking of it." In an undertone, he added, "I'd appreciate it if you could find some way to distract that damned newshound when he turns up."

"Roger," I said.

I strolled over to where Dr. Blake and Michael were standing, holding the camels' reins and posing for the photographers.

"Go away," Dr. Blake said. "You're spoiling the pictures." I ignored him.

"Bad news," I said to Michael. "Santa's dead."

"Who?" Dr. Blake asked.

"Santa," I repeated. "Though I assume Ralph Doleson was the intended target."

"Oh, dear," Michael said. "No bite marks on him, I hope."

"No new ones, anyway. He was stabbed—no way they can blame it on Spike. Look, both of you—keep it under your hat for now. And the chief would really appreciate it if we could keep anyone from finding out for as long as possible. Especially that reporter."

I had spotted Werzel now. If he'd donned the brown shepherd's robe to be unobtrusive, it was a miscalculation. He was so thin that he could almost have wrapped the robe around him twice, but it barely came below his knees, revealing an awkward two-foot expanse of blue denim and a pair of ratty anachronistic brown shoes. And, damn it, he seemed to be watching us.

"We could offer him a camel ride," Michael suggested. "Good publicity for the zoo, you know. He's from *The Washington Star-Tribune*."

"Excellent idea!" Dr. Blake exclaimed. Bashfulness was not one of his failings. He strode over toward Werzel and stuck out a deceptively gnarled hand. He seemed to consider shaking hands a competitive sport—if not a form of hand-to-hand combat—and I'd seen stronger men than Werzel wince after Dr. Blake had greeted them.

"Lovely to see you!" he was saying, as he mauled Werzel's hand. "Meg tells me you might be interested in a camel ride!"

I rejoined Chief Burke and led him over to the pig shed.

"Hey, Chief," Horace said as we strolled up. "We've got a bad one."

"You've been inside?"

"Just far enough to see if he needed medical assistance," Horace said. "And Meg's right—he's definitely dead. No pulse, no respiration, eyes open and fixed."

The chief opened the shed door, peeked inside, and nodded.

"We'll need the medical examiner to pronounce before we can proceed, of course, but I have no doubt you're right. Any chance you can help us out with this one?"

"Be glad to," Horace said, nonchalantly, though I could tell from his expression that he was dying to work the case. Perhaps because he was still relatively new at forensic work, and enjoyed working what he called a "nice, grisly crime scene." After twenty-five years with the Baltimore Police Department, Chief Burke looked as if he'd rather see anything else.

"Meg," the chief said. "Keep an eye open and let me know if anyone's heading this way. Any thoughts on whether he was killed here or just stashed here?"

The last bit, I realized, was directed at Horace.

"Almost certainly here," Horace said. "If he'd been killed elsewhere and brought in here, where's the blood trail?"

The chief nodded.

"Another interesting thing—" Horace began.

"Trouble," I said. "Ainsley Werzel's riding his camel this way."

Chapter 7

"I thought you had someone distracting him," the chief grumbled.

"So did I," I said. "But I guess Michael and Dr. Blake underestimated the power of the press."

"Are there any other doors to this shed?" the chief asked.

"No, but I suppose someone could try to get in or out through the windows," I said. "In's more likely; they're shuttered on the outside."

"Go in and guard the crime scene," the chief said to Horace. "And can you call Debbie Anne and tell her to send Dr. Smoot over?"

Horace nodded and slipped inside.

Ainsley Werzel appeared around the corner of the barn and reined in his camel about ten feet away from us.

"What's going on?" he asked.

"I'll have to ask you to leave," the chief said. "And take the camel with you."

"What right have you—" Werzel began.

"You're about to contaminate a crime scene," the chief snapped. "Now take that thrice-blasted beast someplace else."

Werzel's eyes grew large, and he opened his mouth. Then he shut it again.

"Hut-hut!" he said, kicking the camel. They disappeared around the corner of the barn.

"That was too easy," the chief said.

In the distance, we heard Werzel shouting, "Hoosh! Hoosh!"

"He's not going away," I said. "He's just dumping the camel."

The chief muttered something indistinguishable.

Sammy Wendell, one of the chief's deputies, appeared from the other side.

"Debbie Anne paged me and said to meet you here," Sammy said. "What's up?"

"Homicide," the chief said. "Keep that damned reporter at bay while we work the scene, will you?"

Just then Werzel appeared from around the barn, notebook in hand.

"I'm sorry, sir, ma'am," Sammy said. "You'll have to watch from behind this line."

Sammy held out his hands to define an imaginary line about twenty feet from the shed door. The ma'am, I realized, was directed at me. I went over and stood behind Sammy's line, with an ostentatiously cooperative look on my face. Werzel didn't like it, but he followed suit. For now, at least—if I were the chief, I'd keep my eye on him.

"What happened?" Werzel asked.

"Homicide," the chief said.

"Whoa!" Werzel exclaimed. "Someone offed Santa?"

"The name of the deceased is being withheld, pending notification of next of kin," the chief said. "What makes you think Santa Claus is involved?"

"Stands to reason," Werzel said. "That's the shed where I saw Santa kicking the dog."

"What do you mean by 'kicking the dog'?" the chief asked. From his frown, I realized he thought "kick the dog" might be a hip, new synonym for "kick the bucket."

"Santa had a close encounter with Spike," I said.

The chief closed his eyes and shuddered. He'd met the small evil one before. Then he opened his eyes again.

"We need Smoot, damn it," he said.

"You need what?" Werzel asked.

The chief frowned but didn't answer him.

"It's a who, not a what," I said. "Dr. Smoot is the county's medical examiner."

"Acting medical examiner," the chief said. "Any idea where he is?"

"He's over there on the Dickens float," I said, pointing.

The *Caerphilly Clarion*, our local weekly, was taking its turn at photographing the Dickens float. Not surprising—thanks to Mother's decorating skills, it was one of the highlights of the parade. It featured an enormous Victorian Christmas tree at one end and a London street scene, complete with mountains of fake snow, at the other. Mother and the rest of the improbably well-dressed Cratchits were seated in a pair of velvet sofas at the foot of the Christmas tree, toasting each other with plastic champagne flutes and pretending to open elaborately wrapped presents. At the other end stood Scrooge, surrounded by the Ghosts of Christmases Past, Present, and Yet-to-Come. The Cratchits may have gone upscale, but the ghosts' costumes more or less matched the book—Christmas Past was a tiny blond child in a choir robe; Christmas Present was an enormous robed figure with a crown of holly, and Christmas Yet-to-Come was a specter whose face was hidden in the shadows of his hooded black robe. Okay, the text did say that Yet-to-Come was "shrouded in a deep black garment, which concealed its head, its face, its form, and left nothing of it visible save one outstretched hand." But couldn't Dr. Smoot have found a way to look a little less like the grim reaper? I'd always thought the costume at odds with the holiday spirit of the parade—though strangely appropriate for our present problem.

"I don't see Smoot," the chief said.

"In the hood," I said.

"Oh, good grief," the chief muttered and strode over toward the float.

"What's wrong with him?" Werzel asked,

"We don't get a lot of crime in Caerphilly," I said. "Chief Burke takes it very seriously and very personally when someone breaks the peace in his county."

I didn't see him taking notes.

"Right," he said. "I mean what's wrong between him and this Dr. Smoot?"

I shrugged and tried to look puzzled by the question. I knew exactly what was wrong. The chief was a very by-the-book guy, and Dr. Smoot had recently developed an active interest in the supernatural. There was no way the chief or the town council would offer a permanent appointment to a medical examiner who, in addition to determining the manner and means of death, would occasionally venture an opinion on the likelihood of the deceased's return as a ghost, vampire, or zombie. But since the job paid almost nothing, none of the county's other medical personnel had shown the slightest interest in doing it. The way things were going, the chief could be stuck with Dr. Smoot as acting medical examiner for the rest of his career.

And the chief was still mad about what happened when Dr. Smoot, hearing that one of the New Life Baptist deacons had a severe garlic allergy, took it on himself to determine if the deacon was one of the undead. Apparently Dr. Smoot had seen too many movie vampires cower from a single drop of holy water. Unfortunately, the New Life church wasn't equipped with holy water fonts and the closest equivalent was the pool used for full immersion baptism. The chief might have forgiven Dr. Smoot a little sooner if the *Caerphilly Clarion* hadn't printed a picture of the would-be vampire slayer and his victim being rescued from the watery deep.

Still, the chief was polite enough as he conferred with the sinister, hooded figure at the snowy end of the Dickens float. Then the Ghost of Christmas Yet-to-Come climbed awkwardly down from the float and headed our way at a brisk trot.

"That's just wrong," Werzel said, shaking his head as his gaze followed the running figure. "Phantoms should glide."

Yes, scurrying didn't exactly enhance a sinister ghost's image, but what unsettled me more was the undignified sight of the chief trotting after him. Clearly the chief didn't trust Dr. Smoot not to say something the press shouldn't hear. At any rate, he beat Dr. Smoot to the door of the pig shed. After a brief whispered exchange of words, he held open the door.

"In here," he said.

"Oh, dear," Dr. Smoot said. "Inside?"

The chief closed his eyes, and if I could have read his mind, I bet I'd have heard him counting to ten.

"Yes, in there," the chief said. "That's where the body is."

"It's just that it's a very small shed," Dr. Smoot said. He crept a few inches closer to the shed and peered into the door. Which anyone who knew him would realize was incredible progress. At one time his claustrophobia would have sent him running away at the mere thought of being forced to look into an enclosed space.

"It's bigger than it looks," I said. "And if you like, we could open up the windows. You'd hardly know you were in a building at all."

"I don't see why we can't have more outdoor homicides," Dr. Smoot said. He turned sideways to the door and began inching toward the shed door in crab fashion.

"You might want to leave the robe out there," came a voice from inside the shed. Only Cousin Horace's voice, but at the sound, Dr. Smoot let out a loud shriek, jumped a foot, and then turned and fled.

"Damn the man," Chief Burke muttered.

"I'm sorry," Horace said, emerging from the shed. "I didn't mean to startle him."

"What is he afraid of—ghosts?" Werzel said.

"No, he likes ghosts," I said. "He's afraid of small spaces."

"A claustrophobic medical examiner," Werzel said, with a chuckle.

"Claustrophobic *acting* medical examiner," the chief repeated. "Horace, what—"

Then he looked at Werzel, frowned, and leaned over to whisper in Horace's ear.

They made quite a picturesque tableau—the gorilla and the wise man. Werzel grinned and reached inside his brown shepherd's robe—for his camera, no doubt. He frowned, took his hand out, and began patting his pockets, while leaning over to whisper to me.

"Why is he dressed as a gorilla?" he asked.

"I've forgotten offhand," I said. "But I'm sure it's connected with one of the floats."

I mentally crossed my fingers as I said it. Maybe Werzel would buy the parade excuse and not keep asking other people the same question until he found out that we had cousins who didn't know what Horace looked like as a human.

"Damn," Werzel said. "Where's my camera? I had it right here."

A wave of impatience suddenly seized me.

"I'll go bring Dr. Smoot back," I said, turning to go.

"Good luck," the chief said. "The fool is probably half-way back to town by now. We won't find him for days."

"I'll manage," I said over my shoulder.

I had a sneaking suspicion where I could find Dr. Smoot. I checked my clipboard and wound my way through the crowd of participants to the sheep pasture across the road from our house, where the shepherds keeping watch by night had been assigned to abide with their flocks until parade time.

Clustered near the fence where they could observe what was going on were about thirty prize Lincoln sheep belonging to Seth Early, our neighbor. I also spotted Ernest, the llama I'd given Michael for Christmas. I wondered if Michael was still trying to sneak Ernest into the parade with the sheep. If I had time, I'd have a word with Seth. He could care less that there had been no llamas within five thousand miles of Bethlehem at the time of the Nativity, but if I even hinted that Ernest would take the spotlight off his beloved sheep, that would do the trick.

First things first, though. Finding Dr. Smoot was more important than preserving the historical accuracy of the parade.

The shepherds were all seated on the ground, just as the carol described, except for Seth himself, who was standing in the midst of his flock, wearing a brown homespun shepherd's robe, holding a rough-hewn shepherd's crook, and staring over the fields, seemingly unaware of the dozen tourists snapping his picture. I couldn't blame them—he was attractive in a weathered, forty-something way, and he certainly had his shepherd act down cold, possibly because he was a full-time sheep farmer in real life.

I just wasn't sure it was such a good idea, his planning to march in the parade with a flock of thirty sheep.

"Can't you just bring a couple of sheep?" I'd suggested when I heard about his plans.

"And there were in the same country shepherds abiding in the field, keeping watch over their flock by night," he'd said. I couldn't tell if that was supposed to be a yes or a no.

"Right," I'd said. "But couldn't you just keep watch over two?"

"Two? We're not reenacting Noah's ark. Two sheep are not a flock."

"How about three, then?"

Of course he'd ignored me. He'd learn. Seth's sheep were an adventurous lot. Even when he left them in the pasture, they spent a large portion of their time finding ways of slipping past the fence so they could roam the countryside. And he wanted to take them traipsing halfway across the county? He'd be hunting down stray sheep for days.

But that was his problem, not mine. I glanced in the direction he was frowning and spotted my cousin Rosemary Keenan, or Rose Noire, as she now preferred to be called. She was also dressed in a homespun shepherd's robe—doubtless handwoven out of sustainable organic cotton, since Rose Noire had become a leading light in Caerphilly's environmental and New Age circles. She was patting what at first looked like a heap of black fabric wrapped around her legs.

I'd found Dr. Smoot.

Chapter 8

"Now, now," Rose Noire was saying. "Don't let this undo all the progress you've made!"

I sighed. Rose Noire had been practicing therapy without a license on Dr. Smoot, trying to cure his claustrophobia by encouraging him to act out his related childhood terror of vampires. He was a little less claustrophobic than he had been, but the so-called therapy had sparked his new obsession with the supernatural. Not what I'd call real progress.

"It's just so small and dark," he said.

"Dr. Smoot," I called.

"I'm not going back," he wailed, clinging tighter to Rose Noire.

"You don't have to go in the shed," I said. "We can open all the doors and shine some really bright lights in there, and you can examine the body from outside."

"Oh, dear, there really is a body, then?" Rose Noire asked. "That's terrible. Such negative karma for the whole parade."

"Not to mention a real bummer for the victim," I said. Rose Noire didn't appear to notice my sarcasm.

"I'm going to do a blessing for everyone in the parade," she said, spreading her hands out as if to embrace the immediate world and then waving them around like a conductor.

"Great," I said. I meant it. I wasn't entirely convinced that having my cousin walk around burning sage and trying to beam positive thoughts at everyone would do any good— but if it didn't work, at least it did no harm, and if it did work, I wanted as much of it as possible for today's star-crossed parade. "But please don't tell anyone the reason you're blessing things," I added. "The chief wants to keep it pretty quiet for now, so he doesn't have a crowd control problem at the crime scene."

I was in favor of keeping it quiet, too. If only we could keep the news from spreading until after the parade.

"Of course," she said. "We only want good energy for a holiday parade."

"Any chance you could provide some moral support for Dr. Smoot?" I asked. "The chief would really like it if he could officially declare the victim dead."

"They're not sure he's dead, then? That's a relief."

"I found him, and I'm sure," I said. "But the chief has to follow the law. Dr. Smoot doesn't have to examine the body if he doesn't want to, but they can't really do anything until the body's officially pronounced dead."

Odds were if Dr. Smoot wimped out of examining the body, Chief Burke would enlist my father to perform an expert if unofficial inspection. Dad was both a semi-retired doctor and an avid mystery fan who jumped at any chance to get involved in a real life crime—especially a murder.

"Come on, Dr. Smoot," Rose Noire said, taking him by the arm and gently propelling him along. "Let's talk about this. Think what a wonderful opportunity for personal growth this offers."

I winced at hearing my cousin's new catchphrase. My broken leg this past summer, the loss of Michael's aging but still functional convertible to a falling tree this fall, last week's painful dental work—to her, they were not problems but welcome opportunities for personal growth.

If she used the same line when she heard that Michael's mother was coming for a month-long visit right after the new year . . .

Still, her approach seemed to comfort Dr. Smoot. With me leading the way, she guided him back to the pig shed. A small crowd awaited us, but fortunately it was only police and family. Including Dad, of course. I went over to stand next to Michael.

"How's it going?" I whispered.

"Werzel's going to make us all look like complete fruitcakes in his article," he whispered back.

"Good," I said. "I'm all for truth in journalism."

"On the bright side, he's lost his camera," Michael added. "It's making him quite testy, but the chief's relieved."

Dr. Smoot squared his shoulders and lifted his chin. Rose Noire nodded and patted his arm encouragingly.

"I know you can do it," she crooned.

Dr. Smoot took a step toward the shed. Then he reached inside his jacket pocket and took out something that he was careful to conceal in his hand. He lifted his hand to his mouth and slipped something in.

As if by magic, his spine straightened, his head lifted, his chest puffed out, and he began to walk calmly and confidently toward the shed. He stopped at the door and looked around to smile at us before ducking in.

"Oh, dear Lord, he's wearing the fangs," I muttered.

Michael winced, and we both looked over at Werzel, who was scribbling in his notebook, so perhaps he hadn't noticed. Bad enough that our medical examiner had to be coaxed to the crime scene, but when his grownup equivalent of a security blanket was a custom-fitted set of vampire fangs—

"Of course, the good news is that no one will believe a word Werzel writes if he puts everything in," Michael whispered.

"Thank God for the lost camera," I whispered back.

"Oh, my," we heard Dr. Smoot exclaim from inside the shed.

Rose Noire took an anxious step forward, then glanced at the chief and checked herself. Dr. Smoot popped out of the shed door. His hood was thrown back, his hair looked disheveled, his collar was askew, and if Werzel had missed the fangs before, he couldn't overlook them now, because Dr. Smoot was smiling broadly.

"You didn't tell me about the cauthe of death!" he exclaimed.

"No," the chief said. "Because technically that's what you're supposed to tell me."

"It'th all preliminary, of courthe," Dr. Smoot said, as he adjusted his collar and gathered the shreds of his professional dignity. "We can't tell until we've done the autopthy, but—"

"Can you lose those things?" the chief asked.

Dr. Smoot blinked in confusion for a second. The chief gestured slightly at his mouth.

"Oh, thorry," Dr. Smoot said. He reached into his mouth and extracted the fangs. "As I was saying, we won't know till we've done the autopsy, but my preliminary opinion is that he died from a loss of blood resulting from a wound to the heart inflicted by a sharp wooden object."

"Someone killed him by shoving a stake through his heart?" Werzel asked.

"We won't know for sure until the autopsy," Dr. Smoot said. "But essentially, yes."

Werzel glanced at Horace and then back at Dr. Smoot.

"I love this town," he murmured.

"Do you want me to—" Dr. Smoot began.

"Thank you, Dr. Smoot," the chief said, with a glance at Werzel. "And now why don't we leave Horace and Sammy alone to get on with it?"

"With what?" Werzel asked. "An exorcism, maybe?"

"Their forensic analysis of the crime scene. Horace, you carry on. Sammy, you stay with him and make sure the crime scene stays secure. Meg, do you mind if we use your old office in the barn for our incident center? We'll move operations over there."

Werzel watched as Sammy and Horace stepped inside and Sammy pulled the door firmly shut. Then he glanced around.

"You've done so well," Rose Noire said to Dr. Smoot. "I should get back to the sheep. Just come find me if you start feeling stressed again."

"And I should get back to the camels," Michael said. He went over and began untying Moe's and Curley's reins.

"Elephants for me," Dad added, turning as if to go.

Chief Burke was frowning at something in his notebook. I studied my clipboard and turned to leave.

"Where's your barn?" Werzel asked.

I pointed. He made another reflexive grab for his camera, swore under his breath when he came up with empty air, and headed over toward the barn, pulling out his cell phone as he went.

Michael stopped untying the camels. Dad returned to the chief's side. Sammy popped the door open again.

"Coast clear?" he asked.

"Clear," the chief said. "Round up the rest of the officers and maybe a few reliable volunteers and secure the damned perimeter of my crime scene."

"Yes, sir!" Sammy loped off.

The chief turned back to Dr. Smoot.

"So did the stake kill him, or was it done after he died?" Chief Burke asked.

"I can't tell you till I do the post mortem," Dr. Smoot said.

"I assume the time of death—"

"Impossible to say anything until after the post mortem!" Dr. Smoot exclaimed.

"Impossible for you maybe," I said. "But I can pin it down to a half-hour period."

They both looked at me.

"I was checking people in for the parade, remember?" I said. "I happened to notice that Mr. Doleson arrived almost precisely at nine. I remember thinking he was the very last person to arrive on time. And I looked at my watch immediately after I found him, and it said nine-thirty-five. I wrote it down in my notebook, just in case. So allowing a few minutes for Eric and Cal to find me—"

"Admirable precision," the chief said, with a faint smile. "Of course, given the number of people with easy access to the crime scene during the window of opportunity, I doubt if this case will hinge entirely on the time of death, but you never know."

I nodded. No, odds were the time of death wouldn't crack the case. But it might give alibis to some of the people I didn't want to see suspected. And I realized that Spike, bless his evil little heart, had accidentally prevented Michael from being the last person to see the victim alive.

Maybe I was overreacting, but I recalled that in the mystery books Dad read by the bagful, the last person to see the victim alive was always a key suspect. But between the time Mr. Doleson had kicked Spike out of the shed and slammed the door and the time I'd shown up to find the body, Michael was alibied not only by several dozen parade participants but by the chief himself. I made a mental note to give the small evil one a whole handful of treats next time I saw him.

"The time of death's not the important thing anyway," Dr. Smoot was saying. "Clearly someone thought he was a vampire!" He sounded downright happy about it.

"Halloween's over," the chief said, with an involuntary glance at Horace's gorilla suit. "And while I've heard half a dozen people just today call Mr. Doleson a bloodsucker, do you really think anyone takes that literally?"

"You see a whole lot of those college students running around wearing black," Horace said. "Black clothes, black fingernails, black lipstick."

"That just means that they think they're cool, and goth," I said. "Not that they literally think they're vampires."

"Perhaps the stake's intended to be a symbolic gesture," Michael said. "Suggesting that the killer considers Mr. Doleson's business practices no better than commercial vampirism."

"That sounds more likely to me," the chief said.

"I still think you should assign someone to infiltrate the local occult community," Dr. Smoot said. He sounded as if he wanted to be recruited for the job.

"We have a local occult community?" the chief asked.

"Oh, yes," Dr. Smoot said. "You'd be amazed at some of the things that go on in a seemingly quiet town like this."

"No, I wouldn't," the chief muttered.

An idea struck me.

"Dad," I said. "What kind of wood is the stake made of?"

"Now that's an interesting question," Dad said. He turned to the chief. "May I?"

The chief frowned slightly and tightened his lips. I had the feeling that the only reason he was putting up with what he would normally have called interference from civilians was that we'd all been moderately useful, especially in fending off the press. But this was pushing his limits. Finally he nodded.

"But don't touch anything," he snapped. "We haven't fingerprinted that thing yet."

"No, no," Dad said. "Of course not!"

He placed his hands ostentatiously behind his back, stepped into the shed, and peered at the stake, both through and over his glasses. And then he pulled out a magnifying glass to reinspect the wood. He paid particularly close attention to the areas where the bark still clung.

"Probably holly," he said, as he stood up. "Very light color, close-grained. I'd say *Ilex opaca*—the American holly. Is that significant?"

" 'Out upon merry Christmas!,' " I declaimed. " 'What's Christmas time to you but a time for paying bills without money; a time for finding yourself a year older, but not an hour richer.' "

The chief and most of the other bystanders were looking at me as if they thought I'd suddenly lost my mind, but Michael joined in on the rest of the quote.

" 'If I could work my will,' said Scrooge indignantly, 'every idiot who goes about with "Merry Christmas" upon his lips should be boiled with his own pudding, and buried with a stake of holly through his heart.' "

"*A Christmas Carol!*" Dad exclaimed. "Of course!"

"Christmas Carol?" the chief echoed. "Like 'The Holly and the Ivy'?"

"It's a quote from Dickens's book, *A Christmas Carol*," I explained. "Something Scrooge says."

"So you think the murderer was making a statement about Christmas, not about Mr. Doleson's character?" the chief asked. He was scribbling frantically in his pocket notebook.

"No idea," I said. "Maybe it just struck the killer as appropriate. After all, Scrooge was a miser, and Mr. Doleson was no philanthropist."

"I still think you should look at the local occult community," Dr. Smoot muttered.

"Or maybe the murderer just thought he was being clever," Horace said. "Using a weapon that fit in with the theme of the Christmas parade."

"Holiday parade," I said, out of reflex. "You know what it does prove?"

Chief Burke frowned, but paused his scribbling and looked up at me warily.

"This was premeditated," I said. "The killer had to cut that stake from a holly tree and sharpen it. Or at least deliberately bring it here."

"It's not something connected with the parade?" the chief asked.

"Most of these people can't be relied on to march in the right direction," I said. "Do you think I'd trust any of them with sharp sticks? No, sharpened holly stakes are not a part of the parade."

"Didn't think so," the chief said. "But you never know. Dr. Smoot, perhaps you could—"

"Right," Dr. Smoot said. "Get on with it. You need to work the scene."

"If there's anything I can do to help," Dad said. He sounded so wistful.

"The more eyes, the merrier," Dr. Smoot said. He reinserted his fangs and ducked back into the shed.

"Excellent!" Dad said, following him.

Okay, Dr. Smoot was an absolute loon, but he'd just made Dad's day—possibly his whole year—so he was all right in my book.

The chief didn't even protest when I sidled up to stand beside him and peer through the open door of the shed. I almost wished I hadn't. Thanks to the several powerful lights that Horace had rigged up to illuminate the scene, I noticed something I hadn't seen before. A long brown feather sticking out of the pool of blood that had collected on the floor.

I pointed it out to Chief Burke.

"Is that significant?" he asked, frowning over his glasses at the feather.

"We'll collect it, in any case," Horace said. "But you'd expect to see a few feathers in a chicken coop."

"Yes, but this shed isn't a chicken coop—never was," I said. "It's a pig shed. And I cleaned it pretty thoroughly before I dragged the sleigh in here to dry. I didn't want any leaves or feathers or other stuff to land on the fresh paint. I think I'd have noticed an enormous feather like that floating around."

The others looked at the feather with new interest.

"Dr. Langslow, you're the birder," the chief said. "Any thoughts on the feather?"

"Hmm. . . ." Dad said. He whipped out his magnifying glass again and began studying the feather. Horace turned his flashlight so Dad would have more light, and I stuck my head inside the door, so I could watch. I winced when I realized what I was seeing.

"I'm afraid I can't help you too much," Dad said. "It's not a native species, I can tell you that. Some kind of commercial feather, I suspect."

"I know what it is," I said, closing my eyes with exasperation. "It's a goose's tail feather."

Chapter 9

Horace held up the tail feather and peered at it.

"No, no," Dad said. "I don't see how this could come from a goose. It's—"

"Not a real goose," I said. "One of the six geese a-laying. The SPOOR members. They're all dressed up in Canada goose costumes, complete with tail feathers that look a lot like that."

"Oh, dear," Dad said, shaking his head. "You're right—it could be part of their costumes. But I'm sure no one in SPOOR would commit murder."

"I'm not," I said. "Some of them are total loons."

"They're very passionate about birds and the environment," Dad said. "But I can't imagine . . . oh, dear."

As president of SPOOR, he clearly wasn't happy about the fact that his fellow environmental activists had just become prime suspects.

The chief, on the other hand, brightened.

"So this tail feather belongs to one of the six people dressed up as geese?" he asked. Clearly he thought his life had just gotten a lot easier.

"Not exactly. Only six of them are marching in the parade in costume. But a few more than that showed up in costume and had to be dissuaded from joining in."

"How many more?" the chief asked, with something closer to his usual mid-case scowl.

"Thirty-seven in all," I said.

"Thirty-eight, counting Mrs. Markland," Dad put in.

"Yes, but Mrs. Markland was here in spirit only, last time I heard. She wasn't here in costume, shaking her tail feathers all over the yard."

"In other words," the chief said, "there are thirty-odd people running around in costumes that could have shed this feather."

"Odd's definitely the word for them," I said. "And they've been running around, practicing their high kicks and line dancing all morning. And shedding feathers like crazy, I imagine. So if someone wanted to cast suspicion on SPOOR . . ."

"Oh, good point!" Dad exclaimed.

The chief didn't seem as charmed by my analysis.

"So as evidence, it might be pretty darn useless," he said, scowling down as if it was the poor feather's fault.

"I'm sure many people have it in for SPOOR!" Dad proclaimed. "In our quest to preserve the natural habitat we have no doubt angered many vested interests."

The chief made a noise that sounded suspiciously like a growl and stepped back out of the shed.

Horace bagged the offending feather and whisked it out of sight.

"You don't really think one of the SPOOR members could possibly have done it, do you?" Dad asked.

He sounded so forlorn that I hesitated to say what I really thought—that yes, it was not only possible but probable that the killer was a SPOOR member—or if not, SPOOR could easily collect a quorum to elect the killer to honorary membership.

Dad must have read my answer on my face.

"Well, if it was someone from SPOOR who did it, I'm sure they meant well," he said.

"Where's Meg?" I heard someone outside say. I reluctantly pulled my head out of the shed.

"Right here," I said.

Minerva Burke was standing beside her husband, which meant that either the chief's officers hadn't completely secured the perimeter of the crime scene yet or they weren't suicidal enough to try and keep Minerva out.

"People are starting to ask what's wrong. And quite a few of them have questions for you."

I glanced at my watch, and flinched when I saw how close to parade time we were.

"Chief?" I asked.

He looked up with a slight frown of preoccupation.

"I hate to bother you when I know you're swamped but—well, you're swamped. Would I be correct in assuming that I should start looking for another wise man to take your place in the parade?"

For a second, his face lit up with relief and utter joy. Then he quickly rearranged it into an expression of apologetic regret.

"I'm so sorry," he said. "I know it puts you in a bind, and I really was very flattered to be asked, but under the circumstances—"

"Henry!" Minerva Burke exclaimed. "You don't mean you're going to leave her high and dry without a wise man?"

"No, I'm not going to leave her high and dry," the chief snapped back. "I'm going to give her back the costume, and she's going to recruit a new wise man from the hundreds of suspects milling around here trying to mess up my crime scene."

"She can't get just any old person to play a wise man!" Minerva exclaimed. "For one thing, ninety percent of the people here are scared witless of those fool camels. Much too scared to even get up on one," she added, which meant she'd figured out that her husband wasn't deliriously happy about climbing back in the camel saddle.

From the look on the chief's face, I could tell he thought scared witless was a sensible attitude toward dromedaries.

"And it needs to be a person of substance," she went on. "Someone with standing in the community. Someone . . ."

"Preferably someone black," I said. "Sorry if that sounds blunt, but in spite of that medieval tradition I mentioned to the reporter, I did some research and found out that Caerphilly's never had a black wise man in the parade before. And some of the Town Council members put up a surprising number of objections. Of course, they pretended it was because you've only been in town seven years, but . . ."

I shrugged and let the sentence trail off. The chief's eyes narrowed, and he gave me a tight nod, as if to say he wasn't all that surprised and he knew exactly which council members I was talking about.

"Of course, I pointed out that I'd been in town even less time than you had," I added. "And I told them since they'd made me Mistress of the Revels in spite of being such a newcomer, I didn't see the problem in the chief being a wise man."

"I heard you'd threatened to resign if they didn't approve Henry," Minerva said. "We appreciate that."

I shrugged. I'd threatened to resign at least a dozen times, usually over far more trivial matters, and wouldn't have been all that broken up if the council had accepted any of my resignations.

"So, about that replacement wise man," the chief said. "How about Lucas Hawes?"

"No way you're going to take away our only half-decent

baritone who's not down sick with the flu," Minerva countered. "What about your cousin John?"

"He's all involved in the Kwanzaa float," the chief said. "What about Reverend Pratt?"

I left the two of them to argue it out. I had no doubt that Minerva Burke would find an acceptable substitute wise man for me.

I saw a bigger problem headed my way. Eric and Cal Burke were peering around the corner of a nearby shed. I hurried over to head them off.

Chapter 10

"You guys shouldn't be here," I said. "It's a crime scene. And you know how stern Cal's grandfather is about letting anyone near his crime scenes."

"Yeah, I know," Eric said.

"Eric, dear," my mother said. She appeared behind the boys, trailed by one of Chief Burke's officers. The crime scene perimeter was starting to resemble a sieve.

"Sorry, Grandma," Eric said. "I know we were supposed to wait by the float. It's just that Cal was worried. About Santa."

I glanced down to see that Cal was gazing up at me with huge brown eyes that looked perilously close to brimming over with tears. Mother put one hand on Eric's shoulder and one on Cal's. Cal just kept staring up at me.

"I heard on Deputy Shiffley's radio that someone killed Santa," Cal asked. "Is it true?"

"Well," I began. I wished Chief Burke or Minerva were in sight. I didn't know the official Burke family party line on Santa Claus. And I couldn't count on Mother for help. When kids asked the difficult questions, like where babies came from and was there really a Santa, Mother usually managed to have someone else answer.

Cal assumed my hesitation meant the worst.

"It's true, then," he said. His lip was quivering slightly, and a tear started rolling down his left cheek. "Someone killed Santa Claus!"

"No, of course not!" I exclaimed. "Someone killed Mr. Doleson. He was just pretending to be Santa, for the parade."

"Why?" Cal asked.

Was he asking, like his grandfather, why someone had killed Mr. Doleson? Or only why Santa had picked such an unpleasant deputy?

"I don't know," I said. "But I'm sure your grandfather will. You can ask him, later, when he's not so busy working on the case."

"My grandpa's helping, too," Eric put in.

"Yes, isn't it nice that Cal's grandfather is letting your grandfather help with the murder?" Mother said. "I'm sure this will be the most exciting Christmas Grandpa's ever had."

"How remiss of us not to have arranged a Yuletide homicide long before now," I said.

Mother pretended not to hear.

"Now come along, both of you," she said.

Before turning to go, she gave me an approving smile, so I deduced I'd handled the Santa issue to her satisfaction. But that reminded me that I had another Santa problem.

I turned to see Chief Burke striding toward me, still dressed in his wise man's robes and turban, and with one side of his flowing headcovering pulled over his mouth, as if he were fighting his way through a desert sandstorm. All I could see was a small patch of brown skin and a pair of dark eyes.

"Very dashing, Ch—Minerva?"

Minerva Burke pulled the cloth away from her face and chuckled.

"If I fooled you at ten yards, odds are I can carry it off on top of a camel," she said.

"But aren't you needed in the choir?" I asked. "Not that I object to you being a wise man—person—but I don't want to sabotage the music."

"Lord, child, we've got four other altos in the choir as good as me, and we're a little short on menfolk with enough gumption to tackle the camel."

"The camel doesn't bother you, I take it?"

"I've survived Henry for thirty years, and raised those two mule-headed sons of his," she said. "I don't see that the camel will be that much of a problem."

With that, she headed for the camel pasture.

Moe wouldn't know what hit him. For that matter, neither would Dr. Blake.

Before I had time to savor the notion, Ainsley Werzel reappeared.

"Have you seen my camera?" he asked.

"Not recently," I said. "Where did you leave it?"

"If I knew that, I wouldn't be asking you, would I?"

I took a breath, discarded the first half dozen things I wanted to say as being too rude, and tried again.

"Sorry, what I should have said was, where do you last remember having it? Do you recall the last thing you took a picture of?"

"No! If I—"

"Meg, where's the cleanup crew?" someone called. "We need them over by the elephant pen."

"Meg, the bagpipers have been playing 'Away in a Manger' for half an hour. Can you make them play something else?"

"Meg, we need—"

"Sorry," I said to Werzel. "Things are a little chaotic right now. I'm sure your camera will turn up sooner or later. Why don't you tell me what make and model it is and—"

"But I can't cover the rest of the parade without a camera!"

"See that guy over there with the antlers on his head," I said, pointing to Jorge. Why was Jorge wearing antlers and a sweatshirt with "Blitzen" stenciled on it? Had the programmers from Mutant Wizards organized some kind of reindeer-themed float they'd forgotten to tell me about? I pushed the questions out of my mind.

"You think he's got my camera?"

"No, but if anyone can round up a digital camera for you to borrow, he can."

"But I need my own camera!"

"Fine," I said. "If I find it, I'll let you know."

"But—"

I turned away to deal with some of the other problems. Suddenly, rebel bagpipers and elephant manure didn't seem so bad.

But time was moving on, so I tried to deal as efficiently as possible with the several dozen participants who surrounded me, all shouting their questions, problems, requests, and complaints. I'd have been more sympathetic if most of them weren't asking questions I'd already answered, reporting problems someone had already solved, complaining about things I couldn't do anything about, or making requests they should have thought of six weeks ago.

"No, you can't use your loudspeakers to play 'Let It Snow' the whole time you're marching," I told the people from the Ski Club float. "The Caerphilly High School Band is marching right behind you, and you'll drown them out. But I'll ask them to go heavy on the snow-themed songs."

"Meg, can't we be closer to Santa Claus?" one of the Caerphilly Morris Dancers asked. "We've worked out this great routine to 'Santa Claus is Coming to Town.' It's so perfect—the bells make it really sound like a sleigh!"

"It's a great idea, but we really need you toward the front of the parade," I said. "We're a little weak on pizzazz up there and—would you excuse me?"

"But—"

"Bathroom," I said. "Right back!"

I turned and ran toward the house, growling, "Bathroom!" at anyone who tried to waylay me. Once I got to the house, I ran into the bathroom off the kitchen—not to use it, but because even my family don't usually follow people into the bathroom. I took a few deep breaths. Then I took out my notebook and flipped to the section on the parade. Just looking at it made me feel a little better. I crossed off a few items that I'd done or that had taken care of themselves, took a deep breath, and was just writing another item when I heard a knock on the door.

"Meg?" It was Michael. "You okay?"

I stuck the notebook and pen back in my pocket, opened the door, and walked out. He, Rob, and Dad were standing in a circle around the bathroom door, worried looks on their faces.

"I'm fine," I said. "The parade isn't. We don't have a Santa."

"We can find someone," Michael said.

"Someone who fits the costume?" Rob countered. "Not too many people around here who can fit into a costume that short—where did they get it, anyway, the kid's section of the Costume Shack?"

"Irrelevant," I said. "Since the costume has a great bloody hole in the center of the chest—no one would want to wear it even if Horace hadn't already packed it up in an evidence bag."

"Meg," Dad said. "I could do it. I already have my own Santa suit, remember?"

I remembered very well. When we were children, Rob and I had been firm believers in Santa Claus long after most kids our age had become cynical Santagnostics, in part because we had such dramatic proof of Santa's existence. I still cherished the Polaroid Cousin Alice had taken, showing a blurred figure in a red and white suit, standing in the middle of our familiar living room, placing a present beneath the tree I'd helped decorate. Later on, I'd helped to create blurred Polaroids myself, or more recently blurred digital shots, to thrill my nieces and nephews.

Between the Polaroids and Dad's practice of getting up in the middle of the night on Christmas Eve to stomp around on the roof, shaking a string of sleigh bells— wearing the suit, of course, in case any of the grandkids woke up in time to peek—Dad had a lot of practice at Santa.

He was certainly a lot closer to my idea of what the jolly old elf should look like than Mr. Doleson had been.

"Okay, Dad's Santa," I said. "But we don't have a sleigh for him to ride in—the sleigh's part of the crime scene, remember?"

"Can't we just have him ride in a car?" Michael suggested. "We could use my convertible, so he could wave and smile at everyone."

"Yeah, but it lacks that certain something," Rob said. "No offense, Michael—love your new car, but convertibles are pretty humdrum in a parade."

For once I agreed with Rob.

"I have it," Dad said. "I have an inspiration! One that will make this Santa's most dramatic arrival in the history of the parade."

"This doesn't involve the boom lift, does it?" I asked.

"The boom lift? I hadn't thought of that," Dad said.

"Then don't start."

"If we could rig up something that looked like a chimney that would ride along beneath the boom lift," he said. "And I could tie a rope to myself and—"

"Don't even think of it," I said. "We already lost one Santa. We're not going for a double header. Can you imagine how traumatic it would be to the children of Caerphilly, seeing Santa take a forty-foot fall from a boom lift? Go back to whatever idea you were having when I made the mistake of mentioning the boom lift. What was that, anyway?"

"Have you seen Clarence's new motorcycle?" Dad asked.

Maybe I'd been too quick to reject the boom lift.

"It's not a bad idea," Michael said. "If we try to rig up a makeshift sleigh, it's bound to look just that—makeshift. But this—well, once they find out what happened, everyone will understand that we had to do something, and meanwhile, it's bold, it's new, it's in keeping with your goal of not having a boring, old-fashioned Christmas parade. Holiday parade," he corrected himself.

Yes, and was he forgetting how much certain members of the town council hated some of my non-traditional ideas for the parade? If I sent Santa down the road on a motorcycle, they'd freak. They'd never let me hear the end of it. They'd—

They'd never, ever put me in charge of the parade again, not if Michael and I lived here in Caerphilly for the next fifty years.

"You're on," I said. "Biker Santa it is. Rebel with a Claus."

"I'll run over to the farmhouse to get my suit," Dad said.

"I'll find Clarence," Michael said.

"I'm going to find my camera," Rob announced. "This is going to be awesome."

They all scattered. I pulled out my notebook and flipped it open to the page where, a few minutes before, in the bathroom, I had written "Find Santa." I pulled out my pen to cross it off, and instead of relief, I felt a wave of anger.

Someone had deliberately knocked off Santa at my parade. Someone who hadn't cared that the dead body could be—and was—found by two innocent children. Someone who hadn't cared that Ralph Doleson was about to do the one genuinely worthwhile thing he did all year. Someone who couldn't just wait until the parade was over and Mr. Doleson had gone back to his daily routine. Okay, the murderer hadn't done it to inconvenience me, but he—or she—did it on my watch. I had to do something.

Instead of crossing off "Find Santa," I changed it to "Find Santa's killer."

Chapter 11

As I strode outdoors again, I flinched slightly as the cold air hit me, and then forgot about it as I dived back into parade preparations. I felt more like my usual self again. Better than usual. As I stalked through the yard, I dispatched problems, answered questions, settled arguments, and calmed attacks of stage fright, almost without thinking. I was looking for a particular person. I headed toward the barn, where I'd last seen the six geese a-laying and all the surplus geese.

There were at least two dozen SPOOR members still wearing forbidden goose suits, which meant I had to keep my eye on them. It occurred to me that if they organized themselves in groups of six and each group slipped into the parade at a different point, it would take me a while before I could tell for sure that I wasn't seeing the same six geese bumbling into the wrong part of the parade by mistake.

Then I realized that Chief Burke would solve that particular problem for me. He'd undoubtedly confiscate all the goose costumes so he could figure out which one had shed the tail feather found at the crime scene. If he didn't, I'd do it myself, and tell SPOOR I was doing it on his orders.

I smiled slightly as I scanned the geese, who were happily milling around, unaware of how close they were to being plucked. From a distance, they all looked alike, but when you got a little closer, you could see subtle differences in their forms. Some were taller or shorter, fatter or thinner, neatly groomed or covered with haphazard, flyaway tufts of feathers. Slightly apart from the rest I spotted a goose that was taller and more angular than most. Its costume seemed more professional—the feathers all lying neatly and elegantly as they should. Including, I couldn't help noticing, a seemingly complete set of tail feathers.

When I got a couple of steps closer, I could see that this particular goose was reading a paperback book.

"Ms. Ellie?" I called. "Is that you?"

The goose turned, and took its head off. I was right. It was Ms. Ellie Draper, the town librarian.

"Good guess," she said, tucking the headpiece under her arm. I tilted my own head, almost instinctively, to see what she was reading. I was startled to see that the book's cover art was of a skeleton wearing a Santa suit.

"*Rest You Merry*," she said. "Charlotte MacLeod. It's a lot of fun—I must remember to thank your father for recommending it."

I nodded. I hoped the chief wouldn't find out that Dad was recommending Christmas-themed murder mysteries. In the chief's current frame of mind, he'd find it highly suspicious, forgetting that Dad was always recommending seasonally, geographically, or professionally appropriate mysteries to anyone who would listen.

"Anything wrong?" Ms. Ellie asked.

"That depends," I said. "What can you tell me about SPOOR and Ralph Doleson?"

"Oh, dear," she said. "They're not threatening to boycott the parade again, are they?"

Again? I'd heard threats of protests, but this was the first I'd heard of a SPOOR boycott.

"Not that I've heard," I said aloud. "But it's important anyway."

"Or is Ralph Doleson complaining about us again?"

"Not that I've heard," I repeated. "But why would he? Spill. Please."

"Why do I think someone's been making trouble?" she said. "Okay, this happened while you and Michael were in—where was it you went this summer?"

"Nice try," I said. "But Michael and I still aren't telling anyone where we went on our honeymoon. Something happened in June, then."

"We heard that a pair of bald eagles had built a nest in a large oak tree down by Caerphilly Creek. You can imagine how excited we were!"

I didn't have to imagine—when Pam, Rob, and I were children, Dad dragged us to view any number of nests belonging to rare or interesting birds. To us, of course, this usually meant spending an hour or so gazing at lumps of twigs at the top of trees, in the forlorn hope that the nest's elusive maker would put in an appearance.

"Down by Caerphilly Creek," I said. "Let me guess: the oak tree was on Ralph Doleson's property. By the Whispering Pines."

"Near there," she said. "But much closer to the Spare Attic. That off-site storage facility—did you know he owns that, too?"

"Yes," I said. "Michael and I still have a bin there."

"Why in the world would you need off-site storage with this place?" she asked, glancing up at our three-story house.

"We don't," I said. "We needed it before we moved, though, and Doleson wouldn't rent month-to-month. Our final year-long lease doesn't run out till March."

"That man is greed personified," she said, shaking her head.

" 'Oh! But he was a tight-fisted hand at the grindstone,' " I quoted. " 'A squeezing, wrenching, grasping, scraping, clutching, covetous, old sinner!' "

"*A Christmas Carol*?" she said.

I nodded.

"I've been helping Michael rehearse."

"Very apt," she said. "I can't help but think Ralph Dole-son would be better cast as Scrooge than as Santa. Can you suggest that for next year?"

"Get back to the bald eagles," I said. "They were nesting near the Spare Attic and . . ."

"We were going to put up an eagle cam," she said. "You know—a web-based camera so people could watch the parent birds incubate the eggs, and then eventually observe the hatchlings. We had the camera, and some of those nice young men at your brother's company did all the technical work to connect it to our Web site. But when we asked Ralph Doleson for permission to mount the camera on the roof of his building, he refused."

"Did he give any reason?" I asked.

"No. It was just pure meanness," she said. "It's not that it was the only possible place to put it, but it was the only place we could get it installed without special equipment."

"I can see how that would annoy SPOOR," I said. "But isn't all this talk of a boycott a little extreme?"

"If it had been just his refusal, yes," she said. "We tried to explain the importance to him, and he refused again, so we made other arrangements."

"What other arrangements?"

"It was your father's idea," she said.

I winced. I could picture Dad leading a contingent of SPOOR members on a daring midnight raid to install the webcam by stealth.

"He arranged to borrow Mr. Shiffley's boom lift," she said. "So we could put the camera in another nearby tree. But when we went out to do the installation, we found that someone had destroyed the nest."

"Oh, no."

"Including the two eggs."

"Oh, dear," I murmured. "That's a pity."

"It's also a crime," she said.

"I thought bald eagles were off the endangered species list?"

"They went from endangered to threatened in 1995, and were delisted entirely in 2007," she said. "But they're still covered by the Bald and Golden Eagle Protection Act."

"Did you report him?" I asked.

"Unfortunately, we couldn't prove it was Doleson," she said. "We all knew it had to be, but we didn't have any witnesses. So he's going to get off scot free. There's a lot of bad feeling about it among the membership. And then to hear he'd been chosen as Santa!"

"He wasn't chosen, he was a legacy," I said. "If I'd known about the eagles, I'd have vetoed him, but since no one told me anything about this before today . . ."

"I'll tell everyone," she said. "I think it will make a difference. I don't think you have to worry about a boycott—I've pointed out that *you* weren't around when the eagle slaying occurred and might not have known how unsuitable Ralph Doleson was. But next year—"

"I don't think you need to worry about next year," I said. I saw Chief Burke standing nearby, frowning at the large number of costumed geese cavorting in the area. Since Minerva had taken his costume, he was back in his usual suit.

Ms. Ellie followed my eyes.

"Oh, dear," she said. "Something's happened, hasn't it?"

I nodded.

"Was there a reason you were asking about Ralph Doleson? Is he—?"

"Dead."

"Oh, dear," she repeated. "That's terrible."

"I thought you didn't like him," I said. I got the patented librarian stern look.

"I didn't like him, but I didn't wish him dead," she said. "Just elsewhere. Is there some reason the chief's paying particular attention to SPOOR? Apart from the fact that he knows very well how hard we tried to get Doleson arrested and how mad we were that we couldn't?"

"Yes," I said. "And he'd never forgive me if I jumped the gun and told you."

"Oh, dear," she said, shaking her head. "I do hope none of them do anything tasteless when they hear the news. Feelings have been running rather high all summer."

"I'm sure the chief will remember that," I said.

"Yes, and I hope he also remembers that the SPOOR members weren't the only ones at odds with Mr. Doleson. I think the Shiffleys were rather worked up, too."

"The Shiffleys?" I asked. "I didn't realize any of the Shiffleys had become bird-watchers."

"They're not," she said. "But they do—"

"Ladies and gentlemen!" the chief said. He had his battery-powered megaphone. "May I have your attention please!"

The crowd gradually settled down. It consisted by this

time not only of the costumed SPOOR members, but also an ever-increasing number of spectators who'd figured out this was where the best pre-parade entertainment could be found.

"Ladies and gentlemen," the chief began again.

"Geese and ganders!" one goose exclaimed. A wave of laughter rolled through the crowd, and the chief waited it out.

"Ladies and gentlemen," he repeated. "I regret to inform you that we've had a crime here at the parade. And I'd like to ask your help in solving it. Will all the SPOOR members please accompany me to the barn?"

A buzz of conversation erupted, and not all of it sounded happy.

"Oh, dear," Ms. Ellie murmured. "Some of our members don't look as if they feel like cooperating. I'll have to see if I can help."

She strolled over to where the chief was standing and said a few quiet words to him. The chief bowed slightly and gestured toward the barn. Seeing Ms. Ellie and the chief strolling along, chatting amiably, most of the SPOOR members fell into step behind them. The few would-be rebels made a big show of dragging their heels and making it clear with their body language that they were only going to the barn out of curiosity, not because anyone had the right to order them around.

Deputy Sammy came over to talk to me.

"The chief wants to know if you have any trash bags we can borrow," he asked. "We don't have any evidence bags large enough to hold the goose suits."

"There's a whole case of them right inside the barn," I said. "The Boy Scouts were going to use them in their post-parade cleanup."

"Thanks," he said.

And speaking of the Boy Scouts, if Chief Burke was going to confiscate all the goose suits and perhaps detain all the SPOOR members for questioning, perhaps I should find them and see if they really were prepared enough to fill in as the six geese a-laying.

Though why should they have to? An idea occurred to me, and I followed Sammy out to the barn.

"The trash bags are over there," I said, pointing to the corner where they were stored. Rather unnecessarily, since Sammy had already spotted the giant box with TRASH BAGS printed on it in two-inch letters.

"A school bus will be fine," the chief was saying into his cell phone. "How soon can you get it here?"

"A school bus?" I echoed.

"He's taking us to town to be interrogated," Ms. Ellie said.

"Interviewed," the chief said. "Okay, we have thirty-seven SPOOR members here. Is that all of you?"

"Thirty-eight counting Mrs. Markland," several geese chimed in. The chief scowled at his officers.

"And where is this Mrs. Markland?" he asked.

"Since I wasn't her pastor, I couldn't tell you," Ms. Ellie said. "But I can assure you she wasn't here murdering Mr. Doleson."

The chief blinked.

"That's the late Mrs. Markland," I put in.

"She's dead, then?" the chief asked.

"As a doornail," Ms. Ellie said.

" 'I might have been inclined, myself, to regard a coffin-nail as the deadest piece of ironmongery in the trade,' " I quoted.

The chief and Ms. Ellie both turned to frown at me.

"Sorry, total Dickens immersion," I said. "Just ignore it."

"We've found the trash bags, thank you," the chief said. "I'll let you know if we need anything else."

Coming from him, it was a relatively subtle dismissal.

"Great," I said. "But I need something from you."

"What?"

"Six geese," I said.

"The geese are all—"

"Only six," I said. "Look, you can't possibly talk to all thirty-seven at once. Why not take thirty-one of them to town in your school bus, and let the remaining six take themselves there by marching in the parade?"

"The costumes are evidence."

"We've got more costumes," one of the geese said.

"More?" The chief turned to frown at the speaker. "Where?"

"Not here," the goose said, backing off slightly. "But they're over at Dr. Langslow's farm. They don't look the same. They're left over from another event. We could send someone for them."

"You mean the white duck costumes?" a second goose asked.

"They always looked more like geese than ducks anyway," the first goose said. "They're still better than anything the Boy Scouts could whip up on this short notice."

"I've got a key to the farmhouse," I said. "I'll send someone to fetch six of the white goose costumes. If it's okay with you."

The chief frowned. He didn't like the idea, but he also knew how important the parade was to most of the town.

"And you could have some officers march right behind them to make sure they get to town," I suggested.

"My officers are rather busy."

"You could deputize someone. How about asking some of the campus police? I'm sure they'd be happy to help out."

The chief narrowed his eyes. The Camcops were probably already fuming with resentment that the crime had taken place so far off campus that there was no conceivable reason they could use for barging into the chief's investigation. Though that didn't mean they wouldn't try.

"Oh, yes," Ms. Ellie said. "Such a good idea for promoting interdepartmental cooperation. You know how important that is to the town council."

"And the college administration," I added.

The chief had to struggle not to scowl at that. He was all for interdepartmental cooperation as long as it took the form of the Camcops accepting that their role was to give out parking tickets on campus, ride herd on fraternity parties, and stay out of his department's way when any real crime occurred. Unfortunately, the Camcops wanted to claim jurisdiction over any crime committed on campus or in which any of the victims, perpetrators, or witnesses were students, faculty, or employees of the college. Their notion of interdepartmental cooperation was that eventually they'd get around to telling the chief what they were up to.

"Of course, it's a long march," Ms. Ellie said. "Do you think the Camcops are up to it?"

A sudden smile lit the chief's face.

"Yes, that's an excellent idea," he said. Clearly he liked the notion that by asking the Camcops to guard the geese, he was dooming them to a tedious, footsore day. "Sammy, see if you can arrange that."

With that, he disappeared into my office, with Horace and Dad close behind him.

I handed Sammy my key to the farmhouse and he dispatched a deputy to fetch the spare goose suits.

"Now take off the costumes," he ordered. "All of you."

Some of the geese obeyed immediately, but others seemed strangely reluctant to shed their feathered suits. As Sammy and the other officers continued to chivvy them, the reason became clear. The suits were made of heavy polar fleece and covered with a thick layer of feathers. Despite the cold weather, the geese who emerged from their costumes were sweating profusely, and it quickly became evident that the recalcitrant geese were wearing little or nothing under their thick downy suits.

Someone should organize this, I thought. We could borrow a few garments temporarily from the bins where people had been leaving their donations for the clothing drive. Set up separate dressing rooms for the geese and ganders. Guard the exits so none of the geese would attempt to flee. Someone should—

Someone should mind her own business and get back to the parade she's already organizing, I told myself.

But the least I could do was make my suggestions to the chief.

Chapter 12

I popped into the chief's temporary office and found that he, Dad, and Dr. Smoot were studying the murder weapon that Horace had placed on my desk—on a piece of plastic, thank goodness.

Horace was frowning.

"I've seen sticks like that before," he said.

"On *Buffy the Vampire Slayer*, they normally use something shorter and a bit more elegant," Dr. Smoot said. "And in *Dracula*—"

"I mean I've seen sticks like that in real life," Horace said. "Not being used as a stake, either," he added, quickly, as if afraid Dr. Smoot might have real-life observations of vampire-slaying stakes to share.

"Holly's a very common wood around here," Dad said. "There must be hundreds and hundreds of small holly trees in those woods." He waved his hand in a sweeping gesture at the window. The chief contemplated the woods with a frown, as if assessing an entirely new roster of suspects.

"Are you suggesting the killer went out into the woods, whittled himself a stake, and then came back to kill Mr. Doleson?" he asked.

"No, no," Dad said. "The holly stake's not fresh. It's had some time to season. A few months at least."

"So we're back to premeditation," the chief said. "Someone knew Ralph Doleson would be here, prepared a stake several months ago, and smuggled it in here today to kill him with."

"Seems like a lot of trouble when you'd have so many promising weapons already here," Dad said. "Here in the barn alone you have shovels, pitchforks, hoes, crowbars, axes—"

"And a whole bunch of other weapons that the killer turned up his nose at," the chief said. "But I don't think Meg was keeping a bunch of sharpened stakes in her barn, so unless you can show me someone who was—"

"The Boy Scouts!" Horace exclaimed. "They did it!"

We all stared at him.

"You think the Boy Scouts killed Santa Claus?" the chief asked, finally.

"No, but they made the stake! Meg and Michael let the troop camp out here last night, you know. And some of them are doing this whole project where they make their own tents from deerskin, and tent ropes from deer sinew, and so on. They've been whittling tent pegs just like this!"

We all looked down at the two-foot-long stake.

"Well, almost like this," Horace said. "Except a little shorter. But if one of them was sharpening one end of a holly stick to make another tent peg and just hadn't cut it down to the right length yet, it would look a lot like this."

The chief considered this for a few moments, with his head cocked to one side. Then he turned to me.

"You still have these Boy Scouts on the premises?"

"As far as I know," I said. "They were going to spend another night in our field and help with the post-parade cleanup."

"Show me."

I led the way to the campground. It was fairly neat and tidy. Probably a lot tidier than the same boys' rooms were at home. Some of the tents were ordinary modern tents made of faded canvas in various shades of green and khaki. But there were also three teepees made of leather—presumably deerskin. They were painted in reds, blues, and greens in what I gather were supposed to be authentic Native American designs of eagles, deer, buffalo, and other animals. I couldn't help noticing that several of the buffalo looked remarkably like Homer Simpson. The Christmas wreaths over the tent flaps were a nice touch, but I wondered if I should tell their scoutmaster about the accompanying mistletoe.

"I find it hard to believe that the Boy Scouts had anything to do with this," the chief muttered.

"Me, too," I said. "I mean, I know the Boy Scouts have it in for the Easter Bunny, but as far as I know they've always been on good terms with Santa."

The chief just ignored me.

We followed Horace around as he methodically inspected all the tents. The modern ones mostly had mass-produced tent pegs, but the deerskin tents did have hand-made pegs.

"See, they're larger than the commercial tent pegs," Horace said.

"But still a good deal shorter than our murder weapon," the chief said, leaning over to inspect the peg.

"I'll get it," Horace said. He put on his gloves and pulled one up, causing the tent with the Simpson buffalo on it to sag alarmingly.

"Hey, watch it!" came a voice from inside the tent. We all started, and turned to see the round deerskin tent-flap flip open. A scruffy shepherd began to crawl out.

"If I catch one more person messing with my stakes—"

the shepherd began. Then he caught sight of us and stopped not only in mid-sentence but in mid-crawl, with one leg still inside the tent.

"See!" Dr. Smoot exclaimed. "They even call them stakes!"

"Who are you?" the chief said, training his frown on the shepherd.

"Rufus Shiffley, sir," the shepherd said.

"Wilfred's youngest?" the chief asked.

Rufus nodded, and the chief's frown faded.

"Come on out, son," he said.

Caerphilly was still the sort of small town where you carried your family tree around with you, for good or bad. All I knew from their exchange was that Rufus was part of the vast Shiffley clan who lived in the more rural parts of Caerphilly County and neighboring Clay County. Clearly the chief had pegged Rufus, and not unfavorably.

Rufus crawled out, and we could see that he had a cast on one foot. That answered my next question—why Rufus was here sulking in his tent instead of cleaning up after the elephants like the rest of the troop.

"You said 'If I catch one more person messing with my stakes,'" the chief said. "Have other people been around here pulling up these tent stakes, or pegs, or whatever you call them?"

Rufus nodded.

"Yes, sir," he said. "All night long. It was the guys sleeping in the modern tents. They can lose a peg or two and it's not that big a problem, but with this thing, if you don't get all the stakes in the right way, it sags and leaks."

"Has anyone stolen any of your stakes?" the chief said. "Not just pulled them out but taken them away completely?"

"No, sir." Rufus shook his head. "They're all there, see? Well, they were until just now," he added, frowning at Horace.

"Sorry," Horace said.

"You don't have any spares?" the chief asked.

"No, sir," he said. "It's not something you lose that easily, unless someone's playing a joke. I don't know about the guys in the other tents."

"You mind if we borrow the rest of the handmade stakes for a while?" the chief asked. "I realize that will inconvenience you, but we'd be glad to move your gear to one of the other tents."

"Yes, sir," Rufus said.

"Chief?" It was Sammy. "The geese are rebelling."

"Rebelling how?"

"They're all saying that if six of them are allowed to march in the parade, the rest of them are marching, too,"

"Not in costumes, they aren't," I put in.

"How soon will the damned bus get here?" the chief asked, with an annoyed glance at me.

"Well, that's part of the problem, sir," Sammy said. "We're having trouble rounding up a driver, and it's going to be a bear getting it through the crowds until after the parade, so if we just let the geese march themselves to town . . ."

The chief strode off, with Sammy trailing behind him.

"Let's get Rufus moved," Horace said. "And let the chief deal with the geese."

"Right," I said. "Unless—Rufus, would you like to come inside where it's warm? You're welcome to stay in the house."

Rufus looked wistful.

"I'd appreciate that, ma'am," he said. "But I'm sort of supposed to be guarding everyone else's stuff."

Horace and I helped him relocate not only his stuff but

the stuff the other scouts had left behind in the two deer-skin tents. Then we trudged back up to the house. Horace peeled off at the barn. I looked around and realized that I'd left my clipboard, the outward and visible sign of my office, in Eric's hands.

I pushed through the crowd, looking for Eric. Fragments of carols, hymns, and spirituals echoed from every corner of the yard, as the various choirs, bands, and strolling musicians rehearsed.

I walked past one of Mother's brainstorms—what I called Charity Alley. It had been my idea to invite a hand-ful of charity and social service organizations to set up tem-porary stands here at the staging ground, but having them on either side of the path everyone had to take to get to the Port-A-Potties was definitely Mother's idea. From the looks of it, a fairly successful one.

Some people, though, could resist even the most heart-warming of causes. I saw Ainsley Werzel dashing down Charity Alley as if it were lined with piranhas and saber-toothed tigers instead of harmless souls like the uniformed Marine staffing the Toys for Tots booth and the cheerful Salvation Army women with their bells. He spotted me and hurried over as if seeking protection.

"So what's with all this charity stuff?" he asked. "You've got the Salvation Army, Goodwill, Toys for Tots, America's Second Harvest, Kiva, Oxfam—what gives, anyway?"

" 'At this festive season of the year, it is more than usu-ally desirable that we should make some slight provision for the poor and destitute, who suffer greatly at the pres-ent time,' " I quoted.

"The town doesn't look that bad off," he said. "Are you trying to tell me that you've got a lot of poor people here in Caerphilly?"

"No," I said. "I'm trying to quote Dickens. We just thought it would be nice to give people a chance to remember the true meaning of Christmas."

"Nice?" Werzel said. "Every time I turn around, someone's got their hand out. Anyway, I've been looking for someone who can answer a few questions."

"Glad to answer anything I can," I said, though I don't think I managed to feign much enthusiasm.

"So how come it's the town police chief who's doing all this investigating?" he asked. "I thought Virginia counties had sheriffs."

"We do," I said. "But Sheriff Price is getting along—I think he must be ninety by now. He can't do as much as he used to, so when the town hired Chief Burke, the sheriff appointed him assistant sheriff. The police officers and the deputies all report to him. In fact, it's really all one force, so they all get to choose whether they'd rather be called 'deputy' or 'officer.'"

"So this is just a temporary situation, then?" he asked.

"No, it's been going on for five years."

"Five years? Isn't the sheriff an elected official? You haven't had elections in five years?"

"We had them, yes," I said. "And reelected Sheriff Price."

"You reelected a guy who doesn't do anything?"

"A lot of voters do that," I said. "At least we know we're doing it. And he doesn't do anything wrong, which is more than most places can say about their elected officials."

Werzel shook his head.

"I'm guessing he ran unopposed."

"No," I said. "There were two other candidates. But everyone liked Sheriff Price's campaign platform better."

"And just what was his campaign platform?"

"That if elected he'd reappoint Chief Burke as assistant sheriff and stay out of his way," I said. "About the only people who had a problem with that were the felons the chief has put away, and they don't get a say anymore. It was a landslide."

Werzel shook his head and walked away, scribbling in his notebook. I could tell he didn't quite believe me. Clearly he'd been in the big city too long. And he wasn't just avoiding the Salvation Army kettle—he was giving it an ostentatiously wide berth.

A pity we already had someone playing Ebenezer Scrooge on the Dickens float.

Floats. I checked my watch, and realized that the time had flown faster than I realized. I only had thirty minutes until parade time.

I fought back a moment of panic. I'd spent hours rearranging the cards that represented the various floats, bands, and other participants into the optimal order and then negotiating with everyone to keep as much of that structure intact as possible. But with half an hour to go, I suddenly realized that however useful all that planning had been—if for no other reason than to keep my own sanity intact—it was time to let go of my vision of the perfect parade and let the real thing happen. As long as the Twelve Days of Christmas appeared in the proper order at the beginning of the parade and Santa brought up the rear, no one else would know or care if the rest of the participants weren't all neatly arranged in the agreed-upon order.

I headed for what I'd come to think of as the starting line. My nephew, Eric, intercepted me before I'd gone more than a dozen steps.

"There you are," I said, reaching out to take the clipboard he was carrying.

"Aunt Meg," Eric said. "Can you do something about Cousin?"

I was about to say "Cousin who?" and was already looking around for a familiar Hollingsworth face when I remembered that Cousin was the name of the donkey Rose Noire had recently adopted. We'd originally named him after a particular cousin whose obstinate personality resembled a donkey's, but Mother had protested strenuously, and we'd compromised by just calling him Cousin.

I turned to see that Rob was trying to coax Cousin up the ramp onto the truck for the live nativity scene. Mary, Joseph, and assorted shepherds were standing around looking impatient, waiting for their turn to mount the ramp. What in the world . . . ?

I strolled over.

"Why don't you give it up?" I said to Rob. "Clearly Cousin isn't interested in being on the float, and I can't imagine anyone really wants to ride all the way to Caerphilly with an unhappy donkey."

"But we have to have a donkey!" Rob said, continuing to tug at Cousin's lead. "Like all the carols say. 'The friendly beasts around him stood' and 'the ox and ass kept time' and all that."

The elderly ox was already lying down and chewing his cud in a faux rustic pen atop the float, along with two of Seth Early's spare sheep.

"Don't you think you could just let him follow on behind the float?" I asked. "A century ago, Cousin would have had to pull the float, so I'm sure he'd be perfectly happy to walk behind."

"It's just not the same," Rob said.

Just then, Cousin suddenly took a couple of quick steps up the ramp. The abrupt slacking of the rope took Rob by surprise, and he fell backward. Cousin took advantage of Rob's fall to back down almost to the bottom of the ramp. By the time Rob had scrambled up and grabbed the rope again, Cousin once more had all four feet firmly braced, and two of them were back on solid ground.

"They've been at it for half an hour," said a shepherd who was cradling a live chicken in her arms.

Half an hour.

"Rob," I said. "We don't have time to fool around with Cousin. He can walk behind the float."

"But—"

"Rob, move your . . . donkey!" I snapped.

Rob blinked, then slackened the reins and allowed Cousin to back the rest of the way off the ramp. The shepherds and the Holy Family began rapidly filing up.

"Sheesh. You sounded just like Mother for a minute," Rob said. "I just wanted him on the float because I knew there's no way he'd walk all the way to town. What if he stops halfway there?"

He did have a point. Cousin was notoriously lazy—that and his foul disposition had gotten him expelled from the herd of donkeys the zoo kept for giving rides to children. He'd have been on his way to a glue factory if Rose Noire hadn't felt sorry for him.

Inspiration struck.

"Make sure there's someone around to lead him home, then," I said. "He's certainly not going on the float."

I frowned at Cousin, who laid back his ears. Since the rest of the live nativity scene had now taken their places, the ramp was unobstructed. I went to stand in front of it, and crossed my arms.

"In fact, forget it," I said. "Cousin stays behind. Take him back to his stall."

I pointed dramatically to Cousin and then toward the barn.

Cousin, his ears still laid back, walked up to me and butted me with his head. I pretended to lose my balance and stepped aside. Cousin trotted up the ramp and into the pen, where he shoved the sheep aside to attack the hay supply.

"Meg, you're a genius!" Rob said.

"Remind me later to see if Clarence does obedience training for donkeys," I said. "And in the meantime, go find the rest of the leaping lords and bring them to the starting line. And—oh, dear."

The Virgin Mary had just winced and clutched her enormous belly.

Rob followed my eyes and turned pale.

"Should I get Dad?" he said.

"No!" I said. "Dad's Santa, remember? Besides, it's her first. It could take hours."

"But shouldn't she have a doctor? And head for the hospital?"

"She will be heading for the hospital as soon as we get the parade on the road. And Dad's not the only doctor in town. Aunt Penelope's over at the first aid tent, already on alert. She can throw on a shepherd's cloak and ride on the float, and Mary will have an actual obstetrician if she needs one."

I pulled out my cell phone, dispatched Aunt Penelope to the Nativity float, and went looking for Dad, to make sure he was in his Santa costume and not getting ready to preside over a delivery.

I finally spotted him running by with his Santa pants and boots on and the red jacket still thrown over his arm.

"Dad! Where are you going!" I shouted. "And why aren't you in costume yet?"

"Meg, you've got to come see Caroline and her Uzis!" Dad called over his shoulder as he ran past me on his way . . . somewhere.

Uzis?

I ran after him.

Chapter 13

"What do you mean, Uzis?" I asked when I caught up with him. "We don't want any weapons in the parade on top of . . . everything else. Peace on earth and good will to all men, remember?"

"Not Uzis," he said. "O-O-Z-I-Es. It's what you call elephant handlers."

"Silly me," I said. "I thought you called them mahouts,"

"In India, yes," Dad said. "But these handlers are Burmese. Mahouts would have been better—the Burmese don't really celebrate Diwali. But I don't think anyone will notice. Aren't the costumes fabulous?"

We had reached the sheep pasture—now also functioning as an elephant pasture. Yes, the costumes were fabulous—both the oozies' costumes and the elaborate trappings decking the elephants were a riot of bright, contrasting colors and winking jewels. Undoubtedly fake jewels, but still, I hoped Mother didn't catch sight of the elephants and their riders until after the parade, or she'd try to desert Dickens for Diwali.

The fence was solid with tourists snapping photos continuously, like paparazzi on Oscar night, bathing the elephants with the flicker of flashes like heat lightning. Fortunately the elephants seemed oblivious to the tourists. The larger elephant was eating hay, delicately lifting small wisps with his trunk and tucking them neatly into his mouth. The other elephant was having his foot examined by two of the three oozies and an enormous white goose that I assumed was Clarence in one of the substitute costumes. Evidently the geese had won their battle to march into town.

"Caroline!" Dad called out.

The smaller of the two oozies turned, waved to us, and began slowly walking over. I recognized the woman in the jeweled turban who had brought the elephants.

"Meg, this is Caroline Willner," Dad said. "From the Willner Wildlife Sanctuary. Isn't it wonderful that she could bring both of her elephants?"

"Nice to meet you," she said.

I muttered something, but I was almost inarticulate with surprise. From the tales Dad, Clarence, and Dr. Blake had told of Caroline Willner's exploits, I was expecting a strapping Amazon in the prime of life. Caroline was under five feet, plump, and probably in her eighties. She looked like someone's grandmother dressed up to go to a costume party.

"Of course," she went on, "Monty will never forgive me for upstaging his camels. He'll throw a fit when he sees us."

Monty? She meant my grandfather. I didn't recall hearing anyone call him Monty before. And she didn't look the least bit anxious about the impending fit. When Montgomery Blake lost his temper—usually over some environmental or animal welfare issue, but sometimes over people stealing the spotlight from him—most people tried to be in another time zone.

I decided I liked Caroline.

"We should talk later," I said. "Meanwhile—Dad, you need to get your costume on. I'm starting the parade in about five minutes. And tell Clarence to stop playing with the elephants and change into some other costume. We can't have a goose driving Santa into town."

"Relax." I turned and saw Clarence's towering form, now incongruously clad in a bright green Christmas elf costume, complete with green tights and a sporty feathered cap. Evidently it was another larger-than-average SPOOR member ministering to the elephant.

"Don't let Dad get lost," I said. "I know since you guys are bringing up the rear, he'll have plenty of time to get distracted and wander off somewhere—"

"I'll stick to his side and make sure he's ready to roll by the time you're down to the last few floats," Clarence said. "Don't worry."

Reassured, I headed back for the starting line. On the way, I glanced over my shoulder. Dad and Caroline were standing by the larger of the two elephants, patting his trunk and talking away. Dad had apparently put down his red, fur-trimmed hat and coat in his enthusiasm to greet the elephants, and Clarence had picked them up and was hovering nearby like an enormous elfin valet.

As I passed by the shepherds, I stopped to say a quick word to Rose Noire.

"Okay, keep your eye on the Nativity float," I said. "When that takes off—"

"Rise up, shepherds, and follow!" Rose Noire sang, in her light but beautiful soprano voice.

"Right," I said. "And while you're marching behind the float—"

"Leave your sheep and leave your lambs," she sang. "Only we won't be doing that, of course," she added, in a normal tone.

No, more likely the sheep and lambs would be leaving

them, given how badly Seth Early's sheep seemed to be afflicted with wanderlust. A month or so ago we'd found one wedged into the tiny bathroom off our kitchen, drinking from the toilet like a cat. But keeping track of the sheep was Seth's problem, not mine.

"I'm afraid Mary may be starting to have labor pains," I said, getting back to the point.

"Mary?" I could tell by her expression that she was searching our family tree for a pregnant cousin.

"What's-her-name—the girl who's playing Mary on the float."

"Oh, my goodness."

"So if we have to haul her off the float and away to the hospital in the middle of the parade, can you step in as Mary?"

"Of course!" she exclaimed, and immediately threw herself into the role. She closed her eyes, crossed her hands over her heart, raised her chin, and assumed an expression of seraphic bliss.

"Great," I said. "When Rembrandt shows up, I'll tell him you're ready for your closeup. Meanwhile, keep your eye on Mary and Aunt Penelope. And make sure Seth has enough shepherds to fill in for you if needed."

"Right," she said. "And I'll concentrate on beaming her good thoughts for a short labor."

She planted her shepherd's crook in the ground and began staring at Mary with the intensity of a Broadway understudy who has heard the show's star sneeze.

A few snowflakes floated down in front of me as I returned to the starting line.

"You're gorgeous," I muttered to the snowflakes. "But would you please stay up there in the clouds until I get this show on the road?"

As if in answer, they drifted down a little heavier. I shivered slightly, then pushed the cold aside and ceremonially uncovered the partridge.

Mother and the ladies of the Caerphilly Garden Club had done the First Day of Christmas float, building an elaborate and horticulturally improbable pear tree, festooned with both fruits and blossoms along with enough tassels, ribbon, feathers, garlands, and other gewgaws to keep a decorator's shop supplied for a year. It was done in tones of gold and yellow, with a few accent notes of green. Even the car pulling the float was color-coordinated, a butter-yellow Mercedes convertible with an evergreen-and-pear wreath on the front grill.

The partridge—a real partridge, chosen for his phlegmatic temperament from among the partridge flock at the Caerphilly Zoo after Dr. Blake had inspected the cage and pronounced it suitable—was resting under a yellow silk cage cover until his moment in the limelight began. I whisked the cover off, and the partridge blinked and looked around curiously. He looked a little incongruous in his glittering environment—had anyone bothered to warn the ladies of the Garden Club that partridges' feathers were mainly in earth tones? At least they'd had the sense not to suggest dyeing him to match his surroundings.

One of the junior zookeepers, dressed in a jeweled pear costume, was climbing onto the float.

"You've got the stuffed partridge, in case he gets stressed?" I asked.

The zookeeper nodded.

"Okay, let's get this show on the road," I said. "Wagons, ho!"

The president of the Garden Club began waving at the

surrounding crowd while her husband started the convertible and eased the float into motion.

The audience lining the beginning of the parade route set up a hearty cheer.

I directed a small marching band from the middle school into place behind the float, and they launched into the first of who knows how many repetitions of "The Twelve Days of Christmas."

"Turtledoves!" I shouted.

The turtledoves followed—Miss Caerphilly County and her boyfriend, in feathered cloaks, sitting before a large heart made of chicken wire and pink Kleenex. Probably destined to become a large, damp papier mâché heart if the snow didn't hold off, but there wasn't anything I could do about that. I did scribble a quick line in my notebook suggesting that next year's Mistress or Master of the Revels insist on water- and snow-proof floats.

The three French hens rolled by, on their float from the French Cultural Alliance, followed by a fiddler playing "Un Flambeau, Jeannette, Isabelle." Four local auctioneers in blackbird costumes made rather odd calling birds, but the five gold rings were a crowd-pleaser: five local Olympic hopefuls, marching behind a set of interlocking Olympic rings made of hula hoops adorned with Christmas lights. Six Olympians, if you counted the horse one of the humans hoped to ride in the dressage event.

I was admiring the horse, who pranced and tossed his head as if he thought the whole parade had been arranged just to showcase him, when a whining voice piped up at my elbow.

"Are you people ever going to find my camera?"

Ainsley Werzel. Evidently the impending snow had

inspired him to don a quilted down jacket, though I could still see the tail of the brown shepherd's robe hanging down below the jacket's hem. And he was shivering in spite of the jacket, and hunched against the cold. If I'd seen anyone else looking that miserable, I'd have felt sorry for them. In fact, to my surprise, I did feel sorry for him.

I finished shooing the Madrigal Society into place behind the Olympians and took a deep breath before answering.

"No," I said. "We haven't yet found your camera. I'm terribly sorry, but—"

"How can I cover this stupid, miserable parade without my camera?"

Stupid? Miserable? I might be biased, but I thought our parade was pretty damned wonderful. I bit back several satisfyingly withering replies. He was a guest, and what's more, a guest who had the power to make us look like idiots in the *Star-Tribune.* I looked around and spotted my nephew.

"Eric!" I called. "Can you do me a favor?"

He obediently trotted to my side.

"Can you go up to my office and find my digital camera? Mr. Werzel is going to borrow it—"

"I don't want your—" Werzel began.

"Just until we can find his camera," I continued, glowering at Werzel as I spoke, and enunciating every word with icy precision. "We understand that he needs the photos in his own camera, but at the moment we're a little too busy to look for it. I'm sure Mr. Werzel understands that we will do everything we can to find his camera . . . *after* the parade."

"Wow," Eric said. "You're getting really good at that Grandma voice."

He trotted off toward the house. I winced. Had I sounded that much like Mother?

I'd worry about that later.

"Of course, if you're not interested in taking photos of the rest of the parade . . ." I added, turning to Werzel.

"No, no," he said, backing away. "That's great. I could use your camera, sure. Just as long as everyone knows I really need my camera, too."

He backed away for about ten feet, then turned and fled in Eric's wake.

"Six geese a-laying," I called. "You're up!"

The six chosen geese stepped out in formation. I thought they looked more festive as white geese than they had as Canada geese, especially since they'd all hung garlands of holly and red ribbon around their necks.

All the rest of the SPOOR members stood around with drooping shoulders, looking ostentatiously forlorn and bereft. If they were trying to make me feel guilty, they were wasting their time.

"Seven swans a-swimming!" I called.

A tractor lurched into action, pulling the float on which seven budding prima ballerinas from Madame Vorobianinova's École de Ballet were twirling in full *Swan Lake* costume. A chorus of moos behind me announced that the eight maids a-milking were on deck. I could also hear the tambourines of the nine ladies dancing, the morris dancing bells on the shins of the ten lords a-leaping, and any second now the bagpipes would begin droning and the drummers would begin drumming.

"We might actually pull this off," I said, to no one in particular.

Chapter 14

It took an hour and a half to get everyone on the road. Ainsley Werzel borrowed my camera and gave me a wide berth. I had no great confidence that I'd ever see my camera again, but if that was the price of not having Werzel underfoot for the rest of the parade, it was worth it. I could always bill the *Trib*.

About half an hour into the launch, word came back that Mary had definitely gone into labor, and one of the state troopers rushed her and Aunt Penelope to the hospital, but that I was not to worry, because Rose Noire was doing a great job as understudy.

I lost sight of the various floats and marchers immediately after they passed my post in front of the house, but farther along, the road went up a long, gentle slope. If I glanced over my shoulder, I could glimpse the floats and marchers before they disappeared over the crest of the hill toward town.

From those stolen glances, I realized that the SPOOR members, instead of marching in civilian dress, had found their backup costumes and infiltrated the parade in ones and twos, making it look as if we'd inserted white geese into the procession at random intervals as a sort of running gag.

One goose climbed into the convertible carrying the mayor of Caerphilly, who was too polite to kick him out, so the two of them sat side by side, waving to the crowd, all the way to town.

I saw several pairs of goose feet pattering along beneath the sinuous red silk Chinese dragon, and at least one pair beneath a maroon robe in the New Life Baptist choir.

By the time Seth Early's shepherds reached the hill, they were watching a mixed flock of real sheep and faux geese.

Several geese grabbed pails and joined the Boy Scout cleanup squads marching behind the large animals.

There were geese throwing Chanukah gelt from the Jewish Community Center's float, geese dancing along with the Clay County Cloggers, and geese waving and throwing confetti from the platform of the boom lift.

The Dickens float was the last straw. Since Dr. Smoot was still at the crime scene, they'd turned to the surplus SPOOR members to find a replacement. Unfortunately, they picked someone who was much taller than Dr. Smoot, so the phantom's robe didn't come down far enough to conceal the feathered costume he was wearing underneath it.

"Oh, look," Eric said, as the float rolled away. "It's the Goose of Christmas Yet to Come."

"I give up," I said.

Clarence was as good as his word, and showed up just when I needed him, with Dad, in full costume, happily perched behind him, beaming and waving at everyone.

"Wow!" I looked down to see Cal Burke standing nearby. "Santa came after all!"

"That's Eric's grandfather, playing Santa," I said. "But he sure does look a lot more like Santa than poor Mr. Doleson, doesn't he?"

"Yeah," Cal said. And then he ran off happily to join the

crowd of children tagging along in Dad's wake as devotedly as if he were the Pied Piper. I felt a sudden surge of pride—Dad really was a great Santa. For the first time in years, the children of Caerphilly would see a Santa Claus who loved his job and cared about Christmas as much as they did.

" 'He knew how to keep Christmas well, if any man alive possessed the knowledge,' " I quoted to myself. And I felt a sudden sadness that unlike Ebenezer Scrooge, Ralph Doleson never would have the chance of reforming his curmudgeonly ways.

The crowds that had lined the road were dispersing—a few to their cars, while most fell in step behind the children. Were they going to march all the way to Caerphilly?

Part of me wanted to jump in my car and follow the crowd. Or maybe race ahead on foot, hop on one of the last few floats, and enjoy the cheers and laughter of the crowds.

And part of me kept looking over toward the pig shed, where Chief Burke and his men were still doing . . . whatever they were doing. I hadn't barged in for at least an hour and a half now—hadn't even looked that way if I could help it—but I knew they were there. I also knew very well that Chief Burke wouldn't welcome my dropping in to see how the investigation was progressing.

"Nothing I can do about that," I muttered. After all the time I'd spent organizing the parade, I should at least try to enjoy it. Not to mention the fact that every single potential murder suspect I could think of had already gone to town with the parade. I headed for the house to fetch my purse from the safe room.

The kitchen looked as if a hurricane had come through. A hurricane with a bad coffee habit. I couldn't stand to leave it that way, so I made a quick pass through with a trash bag and then loaded and started the dishwasher.

Before the previous owners had added a new, larger pantry much closer to the food preparation area, the safe room had been the pantry. It was a small room opening off the mudroom, four feet wide by six feet deep, with white-painted wooden shelves lining both sides and an old-fashioned Chubb lock on the door.

I was fishing in my pocket for my copy of the key when I realized there was already one in the lock. Not good. I flung the door open.

The inside was a disaster. Had someone ransacked it? Or had whoever took over from Horace simply done a remarkably slipshod job of keeping things organized? I grabbed a few purses at random and searched them, finding plenty of money and credit cards, along with small valuable items like iPods and PDAs. So the chaos wasn't due to a thief hastily rummaging for loot. Just bad oversight. The items neatly arranged on shelves with numbered tags on them doubtless dated from the earlier part of the day, when Horace had been in charge. But the later additions had simply been thrown in. A small pile of numbered tags that should have been attached to items lay on a shelf just inside the door.

I waded through the clutter till I could reach my purse. The SPOOR placards made up quite a large portion of the debris on the floor, so I decided to take them with me and hand them over to whichever geese I could find in town. I began dragging them out of the heap.

I suddenly realized that there was something familiar about the placards. Not the signs themselves, although I'd seen them often enough by now. About two-thirds of them were, as usual, mounted on slats—rough strips of pine one-by-two that I knew would leave horrible splinters in your hands if, like me, you were stupid enough to try carrying one without gloves. They were sharpened to a rough point to make it easier to stick your placard in the ground when you needed to take a break for splinter removal.

The remaining third were nailed to rough wooden sticks, two to two-and-a-half feet long, about an inch in diameter, and sharpened to a rough point.

Just like the stake that had killed Ralph Doleson. And like the murder weapon, they appeared to be made out of holly wood.

I stopped to put on a pair of kitchen gloves before pulling the rest of the placards out into the kitchen and sorting them into two piles. Twenty-four slat placards, all of which looked as if they'd seen quite a bit of use. Eleven somewhat newer placards mounted on holly sticks.

And one placard by itself, with no stick of any kind—though it had a few staples still clinging to the top and bottom center, showing where it had once been attached to something.

I pulled out my cell phone and dialed the chief.

"I'm busy," he said. "Is this important?"

"I think I found out where the killer got the murder weapon," I said.

He didn't say anything immediately.

"Well?" he said, finally. "I'm listening."

Chapter 15

After hearing what I'd found, the chief showed up on the back porch in under five minutes and shook an impressive amount of snow off his coat and boots before stepping inside.

"Did you touch these before you put on those gloves?" the chief asked, nodding at the placard collection.

"Yes," I said. "Not only just now, but earlier, when I confiscated them from the SPOORs. And then I gave them to Rob to lock up in the safe room, so his fingerprints will be on them, too. For that matter, since I found the key in the safe room lock when I got here, anyone could have been in there."

While waiting for the chief, I'd laid the placards out neatly on the kitchen floor. The ones on slats were in two rows where our kitchen table would have been if we hadn't taken it to the barn to serve as a prop table, while the placards on holly sticks were lined up on the other side, in front of the sink and refrigerator. The stickless placard lay in the center of the room in lonely splendor.

The chief pulled out his cell phone and punched a couple of buttons.

"Horace?" he said. "I'm in Meg's kitchen. Can you come over here? Bring your kit."

He flipped his phone closed and continued to stare at the orphaned cardboard.

"We'll need your prints and Rob's for elimination purposes," he said.

"Okay," I said. "And Jorge Soto was helping Rob. And Horace might have touched them when he took them into the safe room. And—"

"We'll follow their history, thank you," he said. "It didn't occur to you to wonder why one of the signs was missing a stick?"

"I didn't notice the missing stick till just now," I said. "I didn't take them away one by one. I picked up the whole pile and carried them off."

"And you put them in here?"

"I gave them to Rob to put in here. Which, wonder of wonders, he actually did. He and Jorge. But you'll have to ask them whether they did it immediately or whether they left them lying around somewhere in plain sight for a while. You know Rob."

The chief nodded.

Horace came in with a blast of frigid air, shook himself like a dog to get rid of the snow, and looked questioningly from me to the chief. Then he took a look at the placards and went pale.

"Oh, my God," he said. "Those look just like—"

"Check that one," the chief said, pointing to the stickless placard.

Horace pulled on a pair of gloves and examined the cardboard.

"You think that thing used to be attached to our murder weapon?" the chief asked.

"I can't tell for sure till I measure these staples against the holes in the stake," Horace said.

"I know that," the chief said. "But if you had to guess?"

"Yeah," Horace said. "The sticks are exactly the same,

and these staples should match the tiny holes on the murder weapon."

The chief took out his notebook and began scribbling in it.

"And look!" Horace said, pointing to something on the cardboard. "A couple of these staples have bits broken off. It's possible that the broken-off bits are still in the stake—which means I might be able to prove that the two were once part of the same staple."

He looked so triumphant and excited that I didn't have the heart to ask what good that would do. Even if he could authoritatively match the two sundered bits of staple, and even if that led us to figure out who had stapled the cardboard on the stake, I didn't see that his forensic staple analysis would get us one inch closer to figuring out who had used the stake to kill Ralph Doleson.

"That's nice," the chief said, in a rather mechanical tone. Clearly he shared my skepticism.

"I know it's a small bit of evidence, and there's no guarantee it will be useful, but you never know," Horace said. "Don't you remember that case in Canada where a few cat hairs proved to be the critical piece of evidence?"

"I do," the chief said, forcing a more cheerful demeanor. "And I completely agree. For all we know, the staple could be the key to the case, and I'm extraordinarily grateful that you're available to analyze it. I'm sorry if I seem a little distracted. It's been a long, hard day."

Horace seemed mollified.

"I should take all of these signs in for possible comparison analysis," Horace said. "Meg, can I borrow some more big trash bags?"

I saw the chief open his mouth to veto the mass sign confiscation—the police station didn't have a very large evidence room, and the overflow usually ended up in the chief's office. Then he closed his mouth again, nodded, and looked back at his notebook. I handed Horace our box of trash bags.

"If you don't need me for anything, I'm going to catch up with the parade and see a little of the festival in town," I said.

"Good idea," the chief said.

Just then the power went out, as it nearly always did when we had heavy rain, high wind, or even a moderate amount of snow. Horace groaned. The chief made an impatient noise.

"We've got flashlights in the pantry," I said. I heard shuffling noises as Horace headed that way. "And there's a spare house key on the key rack. Horace, could you lock up when you leave?"

"Roger," Horace said.

I left them to it.

Outside, the air was bitter and snow was falling down in earnest—little tiny flakes, but so dense that they seriously reduced visibility. Maybe going to town wasn't such a great idea after all.

Of course, if I didn't go to town, Michael would have no way of getting home. And if I was going to be snowbound someplace—which looked increasingly more probable—I wanted it to be with Michael.

I took the truck.

Chapter 16

Luckily the Shiffleys' snowplows and the parade traffic had kept the road to town relatively clear—so far. But I wasn't used to driving on snow, and my heart raced every time I hit the slightest patch of ice. Not seeing more than a few feet beyond the windshield was unnerving. I was relieved to think that Michael would insist on driving home.

I caught up with the parade just as Dad made his triumphant entry into the town square. They'd set up a massive throne on the portico of the town hall, and the crowds cheered hysterically as Dad raced up the two flights of marble steps and then jogged back and forth through the snow along the edge of the portico, fists upraised, looking like a Yuletide Rocky Balboa.

Then several volunteers dressed as elves emerged from the courthouse dragging fake sleds full of real presents, announcing the next part of the festivities. More elves began marshalling the assembled children into orderly lines and marching them up the courthouse steps for their moment with Dad.

I could see volunteers leading the last of the sheep off in the direction of the college barn. Everyone without children or animals in tow headed for the food. I didn't think any of the kids in line were likely suspects or witnesses, so I followed the rest of the crowd.

Every church and civic group in Caerphilly and Clay counties was selling some kind of food or drink. The New

Life Baptists and the Clayville Congregationalists had rival barbecue pits. Caerphilly Presbyterian was roasting turkeys, Trinity Episcopal had baked hams, and St. Byblig's Catholic Church was dishing out its justly famous potato-leek soup. In the interests of ecumenicism, I abandoned my diet for the day.

I ended up in the Garden Club's dessert tent, sampling half a dozen kinds of cakes and cookies, accompanied by a mug of hot chocolate. Everywhere I went I'd been congratulated repeatedly on the success of the parade. The few people willing to talk about the murder were more interested in picking my brain than giving me useful information. Most people seemed to think I was weird, wanting to talk about murder this close to the holidays.

So once I'd filled my dessert plate, I found a place in a back corner of the tent where I could analyze the day's events in relative peace and quiet. And keep an eye on Dad—if I craned my neck just right, I could look past the trash barrels behind the tent to the snow-filled town square beyond. I couldn't quite see him, but from the length of the line leading up to his throne—not to mention the happy faces of the children and parents as they left the square for the refreshment tents—I could tell he was a success.

Just then a figure blocked my view—someone putting something in one of the trash cans. He lifted the lid, dislodging an inch or two of snow. Then he stuffed a pale blue paper bag into the trash. He looked around anxiously to see if anyone had noticed and I recognized him. Jorge Soto. Then he hurried off.

How odd. What was Jorge so eager to get rid of? If he'd just walked up and lobbed the bag into the trash in a matter-of-fact way, I'd never have thought twice about it, but his conspicuously furtive manner caught my attention immediately.

So I'm nosy. I finished my hot chocolate and went out to raid the trash can.

I could ignore the cans whose lids had more than a slight layer of snow, but four of them had been recently opened. The first two I inspected held only plastic bags full of discarded paper plates and cups, but in the third I found the blue bag. Inside was a gray sweatshirt with "Blitzen" stenciled on it. I remembered seeing Jorge wearing it before the parade. It seemed in perfectly good condition—almost brand new. Why had Jorge discarded it?

Could it have anything to do with the dark stains on the front, near the hem? Only a few small spots, but still—

"What's wrong, Meg?"

I jumped, even though I realized it was only Deputy Sammy. On impulse, I showed him the sweatshirt.

"Is that blood?" I asked, pointing to the spots.

He peered at it.

"I'm no expert," he said, finally. "Could be. Or it could just be chocolate. Does this have anything to do with the murder?"

"I don't know," I said. "Here, take it." I stuffed the sweatshirt back into the blue bag and shoved it at him. "Have Horace test those stains, will you?"

He took the bag, holding it as far from his body as possible, as if he thought it might explode.

"If the stains turn out to be blood, the chief will want to know where you got this," he said.

"If the stains turn out to be blood, I'll gladly tell him," I said. "Thanks, Sammy."

I went back to the town square. The snow was still falling, though not as heavily. Most of the kids had gotten through the line by now and the crowds were thinning. I strolled around the perimeter, looking at the Christmas decorations. Here in the heart of town, where the newest buildings dated from the 1920s, the town had gone in for Victorian, heavy on the evergreens with a lot of gold-sprayed pine cones, velvet ribbons, and the occasional cluster of fruit, real or fake. Mother thoroughly approved of the town square. And with the gently falling snow frosting everything, it looked particularly magical. I passed a photographer with a Nikon in his hands and a press ID hanging from his neck—presumably Ainsley Werzel's much-delayed photographer. I was pleased to see him busily photographing one of the more picturesque stores—the toy store, whose window was filled with a model train set running through a magical landscape of cotton snow, cellophane ice, and battery-lit porcelain buildings.

If I'd found Michael, I'd have suggested inspecting the decorations in other parts of town. The street where at least a dozen homeowners were locked in a fierce annual competition to see who could mount the most impressive light display. The dorms, with their funky, non-traditional Christmas displays. And the upscale glamour of the ritzy neighborhood where all the senior faculty lived.

But I was tired and my feet were getting colder by the second, so I decided to climb the courthouse steps. I could watch Dad at close range and scan the thinning crowds for Michael. Or, better yet, I could wait inside the courthouse. I found a bench just inside the door, worn smooth by the derrieres of countless witnesses waiting outside the nearby courtroom. I could sit there to think.

Come to think of it, it might be even easier to think lying down.

I was just closing my eyes when I heard a door open.

"I can't keep covering this up indefinitely," a woman's voice said. "Either you come clean and go to the police or I will."

Whoever she was talking to said something that I didn't catch, though I could tell it was a man's voice.

I lifted my head and peered down the hallway toward the voices. I couldn't see anything, but I heard the door to the back parking lot open and close.

"Idiot," the woman's voice muttered. I recognized it now. Caroline Willner.

I put my head back down and feigned sleep as she strode past me and out the front door, slamming it behind her.

Interesting. Who and what was Caroline threatening to go to the police about? And did it have anything to do with the murder? And if it did, was threatening a very smart thing to do?

Before I could figure out who Caroline was protecting, pretending to be asleep gave way to the real thing.

Chapter 17

I awoke, as I had for weeks, to the sound of Michael declaiming Dickens. Though normally he did it at the other end of our house, not in my ear when I was fast asleep.

"'It was cold, bleak, biting weather,'" he declaimed. "'Foggy withal: and he could hear the people in the court outside go wheezing up and down, beating their hands upon their breasts, and stamping their feet upon the pavement stones to warm them.'"

"That bad, is it?" I sat up and shoved my hair out of my eyes. I had a crick in my neck. However inviting it had seemed when I lay down on it, the courthouse bench wasn't a particularly comfortable mattress.

"'The city clocks had only just gone three, but it was quite dark already,'" he said, more conversationally, as he sat down beside me.

"Actually, it's nearly six," I said, glancing at my watch. "I slept a whole hour."

"You needed it," he said, abandoning Dickens for the time being. "What do you say we go home and start broiling those steaks?"

"The power went out just before I left."

"Okay, grilling the steaks on the back porch."

"Perfect."

We headed back for the truck. The snow had stopped, but the temperature had plummeted into the teens after sunset and the only people left on the square were a couple of church groups packing up their kitchens and striking their tents. Luckily all the Christmas lights and the glowing shop windows made it easy to find our way back to where I'd parked the truck.

"So why did Chief Burke round up the whole SPOOR membership and haul them down to the police station?" Michael asked as we were dusting the accumulated snow off the truck.

I sighed, and as he eased the truck carefully onto the road and drove slowly home, I gave him a rundown on the goosefeather found at the scene and Ralph Doleson's reputation as a despoiler of eagles' nests.

"That explains it," Michael said. "Though if I were the chief, I'd take a close look at Doleson's tenants, too."

"Yes," I said. "I'm sure they have all kinds of motives for killing him. Of course, that only shifts the investigation from Dad's friends to Rob's. Doesn't anyone we don't know or don't like look the least bit suspicious?"

"There were hundreds of parade participants, and thousands of spectators, all milling around today," he said. "I imagine when the police start sifting through his papers and checking his background, they could come up with a few more suspects."

"Like maybe a posse of parents who thought Doleson's surly behavior was ruining their kids' Christmases?" I asked. "Just how did Ralph Doleson get the role of Santa to begin with? He's not my idea of a proper Santa."

"Nor mine," Michael said. "But at least he was an improvement on the last two Santas."

"What was wrong with them?"

"That's right, it was all before you came to town. My first Christmas here, Wilmer Pruitt had the role."

"Wilmer? Isn't he—"

"Serving time down in Richmond for shoplifting, yes," Michael said. "They fired him as Santa a couple of years before. The police department got tired of stationing a burly armed elf on either side to keep him from pilfering the present bag or picking the children's pockets. After they fired Wilmer, the Shiffleys got one of their clan chosen."

"Figures," I said. The Pruitts and the Shiffleys were the two oldest families in town. The Pruitts were rich and treated the town and the college as their personal fiefdom. The Shiffleys had cornered the Caerphilly market in plumbing, carpentry, and every other skilled or unskilled angle of the building trade. The two families weren't exactly Montagues and Capulets, but there was no love lost between them.

"Orville Shiffley was a very popular Santa until the year he showed up completely blotto ten minutes before parade time."

"Shades of *Miracle on 34th Street*."

"Not the first time he'd appeared less than completely sober," Michael said. "That alone wouldn't have disqualified him. A very cheerful drunk, Orville. But they had to find a replacement Santa in a hurry when Orville fell off the 4H Club float and broke his leg."

"Bet Orville wishes he'd stayed in the sleigh," I said. "What was he doing on the 4H Club float?"

"The can-can, apparently. Anyway, Doleson filled in at the last moment, and after that we were stuck with him."

"Doesn't sound as if either previous Santa's a viable suspect, then," I said. "Even knocking Doleson off wouldn't get back their jobs."

"No," Michael said. "After today, I think your father has a lock on the job for next year, if he wants it."

"He'd love it," I said. "I hope someone got a few pictures of him."

"Werzel's photographer did. Which reminds me—I've got your camera in my pocket. Had to find someone to burn Werzel's pictures on a CD before he'd give it up, but I figured if we let him go back to D.C. with it we'd never see it again."

"Has he gone back to D.C.?" In front of Michael, I didn't have to disguise my eagerness.

"No idea," he said. "Let's hope so."

As we pulled in, I saw almost no cars around the house. The few left belonged to relatives who were over at Mother and Dad's farm having an enormous potluck supper. Even the police had gone, though they'd left a padlock on the pig shed door and several miles of yellow crime scene tape wound around it. Given the snow drifts and the arctic cold, I didn't think too many people would drive by to see the crime scene tape, but doubtless it made the chief happy to know it was there.

We went in through the kitchen, to avoid tracking too much snow and mud into the front hall, and I noted with delight that someone—probably Horace—had tidied the kitchen back to normal. Possibly cleaner than normal, if Horace had been involved. Ever since he'd become a crime scene technician, he didn't consider a room clean if he could find any trace evidence in it.

"Nice," Michael said. "Let's see what your mother's minions have accomplished in the rest of the house."

Mother had volunteered to decorate the interior as well as the exterior. She'd had her crew doing the decorations all morning, and we'd both been too busy to check the results. Mother's taste and mine didn't always agree, so I braced myself as we stepped out into the front hall.

"Oh, my," Michael said. "She's done a fabulous job."

I had to agree. Mother had continued the evergreen and red velvet bow motif from outside into the hall. Garlands ran up and down the banisters and around the door and window frames, with sparkly gold bells here and there as accents. Nests of candles surrounded by sprigs of holly decorated every horizontal surface, and an intricately woven ivy globe with a sprig of mistletoe inside hung from the central light fixture.

Evidently she'd rejected our eight-foot artificial tree as highly unsuitable, and substituted a twelve-foot real spruce. She'd probably raided every chic Christmas boutique in the state to find enough glittering baubles to cover it, but I was touched to see a few familiar favorite ornaments that usually graced the family tree tucked in between the sparkly glass balls, gilded cherubs, feathered birds, and other brand-new finery.

The evergreen boughs draping the living room walls were festooned with the holiday cards we'd received from friends and family. I tried not to think how many. I was using the parade as my excuse to send out holiday cards after Christmas. After all, that's why I called them holiday cards. New Year's was also a holiday. So was Valentine's Day. Maybe even St. Patrick's Day.

Michael flipped our stockings up onto the mantel and lit the fire before we checked the dining room. Mother had done it up in a food motif, accessorizing the ubiquitous evergreen boughs with gold-painted carved apples, pineapples, pomegranates, grapes, strawberries, and bananas. More gilded fruit formed a centerpiece on the table, surrounded the candles in the windows, and nested between the dishes and glasses in the built-in china cupboard. King Midas would feel right at home.

She had also dug out all our wedding present silver and arranged the serving pieces in a nest of holly and ivy on the sideboard, giving the impression that if you lifted the covers you'd find an elegant feast.

My stomach growled at the thought.

"It's fabulous," Michael said. "We'll thank her tomorrow. Let's grill."

He went out to the kitchen to find the steaks. I started to set the table—with the good china. Mother's décor deserved it. I was opening the silverware drawer when I heard an odd sound, and went to the living room to look outside.

"Is that what I think it is?" Michael asked, sticking his head out of the kitchen.

"If you think it's sirens, then yes."

A police car raced by with its lights flashing. As they passed our house, they cut the sirens. How odd.

"Where do you suppose it's going?" Michael mused.

A second police car passed, followed by a car that could have been the chief's. It was hard to tell through the tall hedge that separated us from the road, not to mention the fact that they were all going so fast. Dangerously fast, considering the condition of the roads.

"They're going down to the Pines," I said.

"You don't know for sure."

"Where else?" I asked. The road meandered past half a dozen farms, then dead-ended at Caerphilly Creek, where Ralph Doleson had transformed an abandoned textile factory into the Spare Attic and a run-down motel into the Whispering Pines. "And I bet it's something about the murder."

"I suppose we'll find out in the morning," Michael said, looking wistfully at the fire.

"Or we can follow them, and find out now," I said, heading for the hall closet.

"That's crazy," he said. "What if we get stuck in the snow?"

"It would take a lot to stop the truck. And it's only a few miles. We could walk home if worse came to worst. 'Walking in a Winter Wonderland,' like in the carol."

Michael didn't argue that hard for staying in, which meant his curiosity was as bad as mine. We threw on all our warm clothes, climbed into the truck, and set off down the road at a considerably slower pace than the police cars had gone.

Chapter 18

We had to pull over twice on the way to let faster-moving vehicles pass. One was another police car, and the other was a car with D.C. license plates.

"Could that be what's-his-name?" Michael asked. "The reporter?"

"Werzel," I said. "More than likely. I bet he's got a police scanner and overheard whatever's going on."

When we reached the end of the road, we found that the police cars were all clustered in the parking lot of the Spare Attic. All the Pines residents were out in force, watching—some of them with coats thrown hastily over pajamas.

"Maybe you should park the truck by Rob's unit," I said. "We can always say we came to visit him."

"Not that we'll fool anyone," Michael said. "Like, say, the chief, if he asks us what the blazes we're doing here."

But the chief wasn't visible. I assumed that he and most of his officers were inside. The only one I could see was Sammy, who was outside arguing with Ainsley Werzel.

Sammy wasn't really doing much arguing—just standing in front of the entrance with his arms crossed, shaking his head, and saying a few words now and again. Werzel was yelling and gesturing histrionically, like a coach disputing an umpire's bad call in the World Series.

I spotted Jorge Soto in the crowd. Had Horace tested the sweatshirt yet? I wondered. Surely the stains would only turn out to be chocolate. Or maybe barbecue sauce. Or—

Jorge saw me looking his way, left the group he was standing with, and came over. I moved a little closer to Michael.

"What's going on?" I asked.

"Burglary, we think," he said. "We heard sirens, and then all the cops in the county showed up. There's a humongous truck parked on the other side of the Spare Attic—you can't see it from here. We figured someone must have tried to break in. Stupid thing to do. Like there's any doubt that it's related to Doleson's murder."

"Related how?" Michael asked.

"If they catch the burglar, isn't it almost certain they'll have the killer?"

"Maybe someone just tried to take advantage of Doleson's death to burgle the place for some reason unrelated to the murder?"

Jorge shrugged.

"Maybe," he said. "I guess there could be more than one person wanting to break in there. After all, that's obviously where he keeps the dirt."

"Dirt?" I echoed.

"Stuff he was blackmailing people with."

"Doleson was a blackmailer?" I asked. "Are you sure? How do you know?"

"He was a blackmailer, yeah," Jorge said. "And I'm very sure, because he tried to blackmail me."

"About what?" I asked. "Sorry—maybe I shouldn't ask, but—"

"He threatened to turn me over to Immigration if I didn't pay up."

Oh, dear. Was Jorge illegal? Not only did I like him, but he was a key employee at Mutant Wizards. Could the company get in trouble for having him on staff? Even though he'd passed a background check before hiring? Would the police scrutiny surrounding the murder cause a problem for him? Could Rob somehow arrange to sponsor him legally? It would be a small disaster if the company lost him. Then again, if he'd lied about his immigration status . . . and there was that damned sweatshirt.

He must have guessed from my face some of what was going through my mind.

"Oh, don't worry, I'm legal," he said. "Got my green card, working toward naturalization."

"That's a relief," I said.

"But I figure Doleson snooped around in my room—we all know he does it—and found some of the papers I had there. In my spare time, I do volunteer work at the Latino Community Center, helping people cope with the ice."

"The ice?" I repeated, looking down at the snow, slush, and ice at our feet. Surely immigrants had bigger problems to cope with than adjusting to the normally mild Virginia winters.

"Immigration and Customs Enforcement—ICE," he explained. "We don't get many illegals at the center, but even people who are legal need help dealing with the bureaucracy—it's hard enough to do if English is your first language. People who need help getting their working permits renewed. People who are legal but want to apply for citizenship. People in danger of losing their green cards over some minor brush with the law, like a traffic offense. My English is good enough to decipher the forms. And I'm no lawyer, but I know when to call one in."

"That's great," I said. And I meant it; particularly since, given how busy the programmers at Mutant Wizards were, he didn't have all that much spare time to begin with. I hoped I was suspecting him unjustly.

"You pay it forward," he said, with a shrug. "Anyway, I guess when he saw all the immigration information I had, he jumped to the conclusion I was illegal, and thought he'd try to squeeze me."

"Did you report him?"

"I thought of it," he said. "But he was a real vindictive guy. Might try to do something to get back at me."

"What could he possibly do?"

Jorge looked uncomfortable. I saw him glance over to where Werzel was still pacing back and forth like a caged tiger in front of Sammy's guard post. Yeah, smart to make sure the press was out of earshot before talking about blackmailable secrets.

"Before I found out he was spying on his tenants, I sometimes invited the people I was helping over to my apartment," he said. "I don't always know their status when they first come to see me. If they're illegal, I tell them that there's not much I can do and refer them to an immigration lawyer I know. But what if Doleson spotted someone who turned out to be illegal? He could report me and I'd lose my green card like that!"

He snapped his fingers and shook his head sadly.

"It'd be your word against his," I said.

"Yeah, but he'd have his digital photos," Jorge said. "Hard to explain those away."

"Digital photos?"

"He's always taking pictures of people coming and going," Jorge said. "He's been doing it for years—no idea why."

"I can guess," Michael said. "Up until five or six years ago, the Pines was the sort of motel couples went to if they didn't want to be seen together."

"Yeah, it always was a dive," Jorge said, wrinkling his nose as if remembering a bad smell. We all glanced back at the ramshackle building. With several inches of snow softening its contours and hiding some of the shabbiness, it looked almost habitable.

"And it was the only motel like that in Caerphilly County," Michael went on. "So everyone knew where to look for their cheating spouses."

"You mean people were still stupid enough to go there?" Jorge asked.

"You'd be surprised," Michael said. "Not everyone was smart enough to take their infidelities out of the county. But what really did Mr. Doleson's business in was when people found out he used his digital camera to take pictures of everyone who came there. And sold the evidence for a hefty fee."

"You're kidding!" I exclaimed.

Michael shook his head.

"He'd been doing it for years. Of course, until the last few years he used Polaroids. When people learned that he'd supplied evidence in a few bitterly contested divorces, his business disappeared completely. That's why he converted the place to apartments."

"Lucky he did," Jorge said. "Or I'd still be sleeping on someone's couch." Caerphilly's chronic housing shortage was legendary. "Anyway, even if he didn't have anything to blackmail me with, just reporting me would cause a major hassle. I know people who have spent years trying to clear up completely bogus accusations."

"But you think he was blackmailing other people?" I asked.

Jorge nodded.

"Everyone assumed his blackmail business folded when he converted the Pines to an apartment building," Michael said. "I guess everyone underestimated him."

"You know," I said, "this could explain why they kept Doleson on as Santa. Maybe he was blackmailing someone on the town council."

"I wouldn't put it past him," Michael said.

"When they seize his blackmail files, they'll find out," Jorge said. "I'm sure that's what the burglary is all about."

"You think he kept his files at the Spare Attic?" I asked.

"Yeah," Jorge said. "Most of the bins have walls made of chain link."

"I know," I said. "We still have a bin there."

"But Doleson's own storage place is a room with reinforced walls and a huge, fancy padlock on the outside."

"You've seen it?"

"Not myself, but I've talked to guys who have," he said. "And it stands to reason he wouldn't keep anything really valuable in his unit here at the Pines. The walls are like cardboard."

"Like?" I said. "The walls are cardboard, period. One night, when his neighbors were making a racket, Rob tried to pound on the wall and ended up putting his fist through it."

"So the killer is someone Doleson was blackmailing," Jorge went on. "And then the killer came to steal the incriminating evidence before the police have a chance to find it. This could break the case wide open!"

"Or confuse it," Michael said. "After all, if Doleson was blackmailing a lot of people, the killer would be only one of multiple people desperate to remove incriminating evidence."

Maybe Jorge believed his theory that the burglar had to

be the killer, or maybe he wanted us to believe it because it diverted suspicion from anyone who wasn't the burglar. Telling us about Doleson's attempt to blackmail him could be another very clever way to divert suspicion. I was suddenly glad I'd turned over the Blitzen sweatshirt to the police.

Michael and Jorge were so caught up in their discussion that they didn't notice the sudden flurry of activity at the door of the Spare Attic.

The police were leading out their suspects: Clarence Rutledge and Caroline Willner.

Chapter 19

Caroline waved cheerfully at us, as if her midnight arrest for burglary were merely a continuation of the day's festivities. Clarence looked a little more serious, which meant that the grim reality of their situation had begun to sink in with him. Then again, perhaps Caroline, like Dr. Blake, had become accustomed to the occasional brush with the law in her years of rescuing and defending animals. Clarence would get used to being in hot water if he kept hanging around with Caroline and Dr. Blake.

Curiosity got the better of me, and I began to inch a little closer to the action.

Clarence and Caroline were both dressed entirely in black—black coats, pants, hats, shoes, and gloves—though the foot-and-a-half difference in their heights made the effect more comical than threatening. As I moved closer, I could see that Clarence's black garb was largely wool and leather, while Caroline had donned a quilted black velvet coat with faceted jet buttons and a fuzzy black crocheted scarf and hat set. What the well-dressed felon wears to an evening crime. Caroline had also smeared eyeblack under her eyes, the way football players do on sunny days, though presumably it was intended to reduce her visibility rather than to protect against glare. Apparently Clarence had decided that his beard made the black paint unnecessary.

"I'm afraid we'll have to take you down to the station for questioning," the chief was saying.

"Oh, dear," Caroline said. "In this weather?"

The chief scowled at her, but said nothing. I couldn't help myself.

"If you'd wanted better weather for your arrest, you should have picked better weather for your burglary," I said. "Do you need anything? Like the name of a good criminal defense attorney?"

I had pulled out my notebook-that-tells-me-when-to-breathe and flipped to the back, where I keep a list of useful phone numbers—including two local lawyers who had represented wayward friends and family members in the past. I ripped out a clean sheet and began copying the names.

"Thank you, dearie," Caroline said. "But I'm sure we can work this out amicably."

Clarence gave her a startled glance and stuck out his hand. I gave him the numbers. The chief looked annoyed, and Caroline shook her head as if sorrowful over his lack of confidence, but Clarence tucked the paper away in his pocket and seemed a little less stunned.

"Thanks," he said. "Say, could I leave my motorcycle at your house for the time being? I don't think the chief can spare anyone to ride it into town, and there's no place here to lock it up."

"Fine with me," I said. "Maybe Michael would be willing to try riding it back to our house."

"Absolutely," Michael said, stepping forward. "Happy to oblige."

The chief nodded.

"Sammy," he said. "It's getting colder by the minute. Why don't you check out that motorbike so Meg and Michael can be on their way?"

Sammy went over and removed the saddlebags from

Clarence's motorcycle. We watched as he gave the bike it-self a cursory once-over, then nodded. Clarence pulled his keys out of his pocket, held them up so the chief could see them, and then, after the chief nodded his permission, tossed them over to Michael.

"I should get going," Michael said. "In case the snow starts up again earlier than predicted. And while there are still some people coming along behind me to dig me out if this thing gets stuck."

"We'll have someone here for another hour or so," the chief said.

Michael nodded. He climbed aboard the motorcycle, started it, and began riding it slowly across the snow-covered parking lot toward the only slightly less snow-covered road.

I watched while the officers guided Clarence and Caro-line into the back seat of one of the cruisers. The cruiser followed in Michael's wake, with the chief's car bringing up the rear.

There were still two police cars in the parking lot, though, along with an enormous truck that I recognized as Caroline's—the one she'd brought the elephants in.

Had she driven the truck out here in this weather? Or did they have another partner in their scheme, whatever it was?

Where was the animal angle in all this? With both Clar-ence and Caroline involved, there had to be a bird or ani-mal welfare issue behind the burglary. In the several years we'd had a storage unit at the Spare Attic, before moving to our enormous house, I'd never seen any wildlife other than mice in the walls and birds nesting in the rafters. There were probably whole colonies of birds and mice there still—while Doleson might not cherish them and want to protect them, he would never have bothered spending money on extermination. No wonder the Spare Attic was rapidly emptying.

If the place had been a cosmetics testing lab, a fly-by-night puppy mill, or a dog-fighting ring, I could understand their interest in burgling it. In fact, if that had been the case, I'd have been surprised that they'd left Dad and Dr. Blake behind. But the Spare Attic?

Was the burglary related to the murder or just a distraction?

I wasn't going to get any answers here, and I wasn't getting any warmer, either. The inhabitants of the Pines were starting to drift back indoors, and I saw that Ainsley Werzel had taken refuge in his car and was talking to someone on his cell phone.

Make that trying to talk to someone on his cell phone. As I watched, he threw the phone violently onto the floor and I could see him mouthing what I suspected were curses. Cell phone reception in the remoter parts of Caerphilly County was unreliable at the best of times, and tended to shut down entirely in bad weather.

I got back in the truck and headed slowly for home.

Michael was just wheeling the motorcycle into our barn when I pulled into the driveway. I spotted a cluster of vehicles farther toward town, where the road wound through a small stand of trees. I went out to the middle of the road to get a better view.

Michael strolled up beside me.

"Motorcycles are definitely a lot more fun in the summer," he said. "I'm chilled to the bone. What's going on down there?"

"No idea," I said. "Should we go and see?"

"Not me," he said. "My teeth are chattering. I'm going to go in and build up the fire. You should join me."

"In a minute," I said. "There's someone heading this way."

Apparently Michael's curiosity was as strong as mine. Even though his teeth really were audibly chattering, he stayed with me until we recognized Deputy Sammy trudging toward us through the snow.

"Are your phones working?" he called.

"Went out with the power hours ago," Michael said. "And I haven't tried my cell phone recently, but I wouldn't count on it."

"Darn," Sammy said. "Ours aren't working either. And a big old tree fell across the road while we were out at the Spare Attic. No way to get over or around. Do you have a chain saw?"

"Sorry, no," Michael said. "We've got a couple of bow saws."

"Thanks," Sammy said. "But the trunk is two feet in diameter. I don't think a bow saw's going to be much use."

"I'm really sorry," Michael said. "I've been meaning to get a chain saw, but I just haven't gotten around to it."

News to me. I wasn't even sure Michael had ever used a chain saw in his life, and I couldn't think of anything he ever did that seemed to require one. Then again, chain saw cravings were definitely Y-chromosome linked. Michael and Sammy were shaking their heads solemnly, as if Michael were confessing and Sammy graciously absolving him of a serious moral failure. If only I'd known, I'd have given him a chain saw for Christmas instead of the llama.

"Maybe we can borrow one from a neighbor," I said. "Seth Early's only a mile away."

Sammy and Michael looked at each other, then shook their heads, as if admitting that even a chain saw wasn't worth floundering another mile through the snow with temperatures in the teens.

"Meanwhile, invite whoever's trapped on our side of the tree to come in and warm up," I added.

"You're got heat?"

"We've got a fire in the fireplace," I said. "And blankets. And we can make instant coffee on the camping stove. If you're hungry, we could even grill something."

"I'll go tell the chief," he said. He trudged back toward the cluster of vehicles.

While Michael stirred up the fire and started the water for coffee, I readied beds for the overnight guests we'd probably be having. I changed the sheets in Rob's room and the guest room, added extra blankets, and dragged the rest of the available bedding to the living room. Anyone who valued privacy more than heat could drag his bedroll into one of the empty bedrooms, and the rest could have the two sofas or bivouac at the foot of the Christmas tree on our camping mattresses.

"Do you think we've got enough blankets?" Michael asked.

"Probably not, but this is all we have," I said. "And it's not as if we can go out in the middle of the night in a snowstorm and buy more."

"We could borrow some gear from the Boy Scouts—I doubt if they made it back out to their campsite tonight."

"Great idea," I said.

Just then the door opened, and our guests stumbled in. Caroline, Clarence, Chief Burke, Sammy, two other Caerphilly officers, and Cousin Horace. The officers were all carrying plastic garbage bags and powerful flashlights.

"Meg, do you mind if we take the truck and the van into

your barn?" the chief asked. "We can't leave the evidence unguarded, and I can't ask anyone to stay outside with it. The temperature must be in the teens by now."

"Fine with me," I said.

"And I'd like a private room where I can talk to Mrs. Willner," he said.

"How about the dining room?" I suggested.

He thought about it for a moment.

"Fine," he said.

I followed him to the dining room. He flicked the flashlight around, inspecting the room, while I tidied some of the gilded fruit and greenery off the table so he'd have room to work, and lit a few of the oil lamps we kept handy for our frequent power outages. Caroline came in and sat down. Clarence followed her and hovered nearby.

"We don't want to talk to you," Clarence said. "Do we, Caroline?"

"I'm sure we can clear this up," she said. She looked ashen, and I wanted to order her to bed.

"But we don't want to—" Clarence began.

"Fine," the chief said. "You're not talking. You can not talk to me some more later, but right now it's Mrs. Willner's turn not to talk."

"Coffee?" Michael said, appearing with a trio of cups. Clarence grabbed one and fled to the living room after one last pleading look that was wasted, since Caroline was sitting back with her eyes closed. She smiled faintly as Michael handed her the second cup. He handed the third to the chief and left.

"Anything else you need?" I asked.

The chief walked over to open a small door in our dining room wall, pulled the rope until the dumbwaiter was level with the opening, and then ostentatiously propped the door open. Clearly he hadn't forgotten the time last summer when I'd used the dumbwaiter to eavesdrop while he was questioning suspects in another case.

"This will do fine," he said. "Thank you."

I walked out and closed the door.

"I'm going to do some laundry," I called to Michael. Which wouldn't sound implausible to him or anyone who knew me. I clean under stress.

"With no power?" he called back.

Rats. There was that small flaw in my cover story.

"I can still sort the dirty stuff and fold the clean," I called back. And I did go down and throw a load of sheets in the washer, so it was ready to run when the power returned. Then I waited until I heard Michael and Sammy going out the back door.

"We're off to burgle the Boy Scouts!" Michael called downstairs.

As soon as the door closed, I crept up out of the basement and dashed into the powder room off the kitchen. The powder room had originally been a short servants' hallway between the kitchen and the dining room. When indoor bathrooms became popular and servants too expensive, the owners had put a door at the kitchen end of the corridor, installed a sink and toilet, and blocked off the dining room end with built-in china shelves. But since only the back of the shelves separated the powder room from the dining room, sound traveled rather well. And given how much the boards at the back of the shelves had warped over the years, I easily found a chink to peek through.

Chapter 20

Caroline Willner sat at one end of our dining table. The coffee had revived her. She had clasped her hands over her stomach and was smiling benignly at the chief, as if this were a social visit rather than an interrogation.

"So of course, when Dr. Langslow asked me to bring the elephants, I thought it was a wonderful idea," she was saying.

"Yes, I understand that," the chief said. "I mean what were you doing at the Spare Attic this evening?"

"Loading our truck," she said.

"Yes, we noticed that," the chief said. "But according to the records in Mr. Doleson's office, the storage bin where we found you belongs to Mr. Norris Pruitt. You want to tell me why you were burgling Norris's bin?"

"We weren't burgling," Caroline said. "We were helping Norris empty it."

"At 10 P.M. in the middle of a snowstorm?" the chief said. "What's so all-fired important that it couldn't wait till morning? He got snowshoes and a generator stowed away there?"

"We were rather busy earlier," she said. "With the parade and all. And I have to go back to the sanctuary tomorrow with the truck, so this was the only time we could do it."

She sat back, folded her hands in her lap, and smiled innocently at him.

"And Mr. Pruitt will confirm this if I call him?"

"Oh, yes," she said, but her voice sounded a little anxious.

"And you never considered that maybe this wasn't the right time to help Norris with his bin? Right after the building's owner had been murdered?"

Caroline shrugged.

"I'm not from around here," she said. "How could I even have known Mr. Doleson owned the facility without you telling me? I just knew it was Norris's bin."

"And the reason you brought this with you?"

The chief held up a pair of bolt cutters.

"Norris had lost his key," she said. "So careless of him. That was one of the reasons he needed our help."

She sat back and smiled calmly at him. The chief asked her the same questions several times over, in slightly different ways. Caroline remained steadfast and showed no further signs of anxiety. She even smothered the occasional yawn, which meant she was either a consummate actress or not too worried.

Or maybe just exhausted. I was yawning myself.

I heard noises on the back porch—stamping noises, as if several people were shaking the snow off their boots. I tiptoed out of the powder room and set another pan of water over the camping stove to heat as Michael and Horace came in, laden with sleeping bags.

A minute or two later, Caroline Willner strolled into the kitchen.

"Would you like some more coffee?" I asked.

"I don't suppose you have the makings for a martini?" she asked. "I would kill for a martini. That wasn't a confession, by the way, just a cliché."

Michael grinned.

"I could throw one together," he said.

"Make it two," I said.

"Three," he corrected.

"Extra dry, with an olive," Caroline said. "In fact, under the circumstances, I wouldn't say no to an extra olive. Thank you, dear."

Michael went into the pantry to rummage for ingredients. Caroline sat down, leaned back in her chair, and closed her eyes. For a few seconds, she looked every minute of her age, and I wondered if we shouldn't be urging her to go to bed instead of plying her with alcohol. Then her eyes opened and I felt reassured by the slight twinkle in them.

"Your phones really are out?" she asked.

"Afraid so," I said.

"Pity," she said. "I really would like to get word to Norris. He'll be a nervous wreck."

I already suspected that it was Norris she'd been berating back at the courthouse. I deduced from her mentioning Norris that she either thought I knew what she and Clarence had been up to or was too tired to remember that I wasn't supposed to know.

"Just why were you . . . helping Norris Pruitt empty his storage bin in the middle of the night? Why didn't he come himself?"

"Too terrified," she said. "Nerves of butter, that's Norris. Of course, he's wonderful with wounded animals. I've seen him stay up all night nursing an injured falcon or feeding orphaned wolf cubs. But to come out here by himself in the middle of the night? Never happen."

"Why would it have to happen?" I asked. "It's his storage bin. Why couldn't he just come out in broad daylight to clear it out?"

"Your martinis, madams," Michael said, handing us each

an elegant stemmed glass. I took a sip and decided we should have inaugurated this particular wedding present a lot sooner.

"Excellent," Caroline proclaimed. "This one's a keeper, dear. To your first Christmas together."

We all drank to her toast. Technically it wasn't the first time Michael and I had spent Christmas together, but I'd stopped fighting the world's tendency to start the clock on our relationship with the day we'd eloped, forgetting all the interesting times that preceded it.

"Getting back to Norris," I said. "Why couldn't he just clean out his storage bin himself?"

"Didn't have the key," Caroline said.

"He couldn't have just asked Ralph Doleson for another key?"

"Doleson's the reason he doesn't have a key in the first place," she said. So much for not even knowing Doleson had owned the Spare Attic. "Changed the locks on poor Norris, and wouldn't give him a new key."

"Was he behind on the bin rental?" Michael asked.

"No, he was paid up a year in advance, the way Doleson always made people do," Caroline said. I nodded.

"Then what happened?"

Caroline took a long sip of her martini, savored it for a moment with closed eyes, and then swallowed.

"Norris has a little problem," she began. And then she left the sentence hanging, as if she'd said enough for us to deduce her meaning.

"When Mother says someone has a little problem, she usually means the person she's gossiping about is a galloping dipsomaniac," I said. "Is that Norris's problem?"

"Good heavens, no!" she exclaimed. "He's as sober as a judge."

Clearly she hadn't met some of Caerphilly County's justices.

"Then what's his little problem?" I asked.

"He . . . tends to borrow things."

"Oh, that little problem," I said, nodding. "Another kleptomaniac." We had a few of those in the family, too.

Caroline winced.

"Oh, I'm sure that's not it," she said. "He's just curious— always picking things up to look at them. And so easily distracted. He . . . wanders off with things. I suppose the police would call it kleptomania."

"The police would call it larceny," Michael said. "Grand or petit, depending on what kind of things catch his eye."

"Let me guess," I said. "The bin was where Norris stashed the stuff he'd wandered off with while distracted."

"Exactly, dear," she said. "Every few months, we help him empty out the bin and return everything."

"Every few months?" I echoed.

"We have to do it fairly often," she said. "Before he forgets where he's found everything. I suggested labeling everything, but he really isn't very methodical about it. Sometimes, we have a fair number of things we can't identify well enough to return."

"So what do you do with that stuff?" I asked.

"Donate it to Purple Heart," she said. "We used to do the Salvation Army, but Purple Heart picks up—so convenient."

"I should go see if the rest of our guests have everything they need for the night," Michael said.

I suspected what he really wanted to do was find a quiet corner to howl with laughter without hurting Caroline's feelings. I wondered what Purple Heart and the Salvation

Army would think when they learned they'd been oblivi-
ously receiving stolen goods.

"Ralph Doleson found out about Norris's little problem,"
Caroline went on. "And he changed the lock on Norris's
storage bin and has been forcing the poor man to pay him
money not to tell the police."

"He was blackmailing Norris."

"Oh, dear," she said. "That's such a nasty word."

"It's a nasty crime," I said. "So you decided to take advantage of Ralph Doleson's death to steal back the incriminating evidence."

"No, we planned to take advantage of Ralph Doleson's
absence during the parade to steal back the evidence," she
said. "Since I would be down here with the truck, and Doleson would be stuck for several hours in town, giving out
presents. It seemed like the perfect opportunity."

"Until Ralph Doleson was murdered."

"Yes," she said. "That came as a horrible shock to us, and
we almost gave up our plan. But Norris was afraid the
police would start combing through all the bins in the Spare
Attic and become suspicious, so we went ahead, a little later
in the day than we planned. I suppose that wasn't such a
good idea."

I didn't argue with her.

"Does Norris have an alibi for the murder?" I asked.

"He was helping me with the elephants."

"Doing what?"

"Helping put on their trappings," she said. "And fetching
hay and—"

She fell silent.

"Running errands?" I suggested.

She nodded.

"And he was wearing the goose costume?"

Caroline nodded. She probably realized the goose costume was too multicolored to show blood spatter and heavy enough to protect the clothes beneath. She sipped the last bit of her martini and sighed.

"Would you like another?" I asked. "I'm sure Michael would be happy to bartend again."

"No, thanks," she said. "One's my limit after midnight, or should be. Is that offer of a bed still open?"

I showed Caroline to our guest room and made sure she had more than enough blankets. When I came back down, Michael and one of the police officers were unrolling the Boy Scouts' sleeping bags in the living room, as near the fireplace as possible. They'd doused the oil lanterns, but the fire reflected off all the tinsel and lit the room with a flickering golden glow. Someone's battery radio was playing Christmas carols.

It would have been such a peaceful heartwarming scene if our uninvited guests had been relatives instead of cops, and if the back yard wasn't still festooned, under the snow, with crime scene tape. And if we didn't still have an unsolved murder in town.

At least I assumed it was still unsolved. I decided to risk seeing what I could learn from the chief.

Chapter 21

I knocked on the dining room door.

"Yes?"

The chief sounded tired and cranky. I didn't blame him. I peeked in.

"They haven't found a chain saw," I said. "So we're making up beds for everyone."

He nodded.

"I'm putting you in Rob's room," I said. "It's the most comfy, aside from the official guest room, which we thought Caroline should have."

A faint smile.

"Can I talk to you for a minute?" I asked.

He nodded again and leaned back, looking more tired than wary. I came in and closed the door.

"I can tell you what you're going to find when you finish inventorying the contents of Norris Pruitt's storage bin," I said.

"Not another body, I hope." He sat upright again and suddenly looked much more awake.

"No, of course not," I exclaimed. "Only a whole bunch of bright baubles that don't belong to Norris, and would have been returned to their rightful owners if Caroline and Clarence had gotten away with their burglary. Norris is a magpie."

"A chronic shoplifter, you mean?"

"A kleptomaniac, I imagine. And one of Ralph Doleson's

blackmail victims. You did know he was a blackmailer, right?"

"Well, I do now," he said. "I don't suppose you know any more of his victims?"

"Not yet," I said. "I mean, I heard rumors, but—"

I decided to shut up and hope he hadn't noticed the "not yet." He sighed, but didn't give me his usual lecture about not interfering with police business. That alone proved he was exhausted.

I thought of steering him toward Jorge, but decided against it. After all, the chief was investigating all the residents of the Whispering Pines. He'd have talked to Jorge already. And if Jorge turned out to be innocent, he wouldn't appreciate my singling him out. He seemed paranoid—perhaps justifiably so—about coming to the attention of law enforcement. Maybe I'd have a word with Jorge privately, urging him to tell what he knew about Doleson's blackmailing operations.

Then again—Jorge was looking more like a suspect all the time. Maybe I didn't want to have too private a word with him. Not until Horace had had time to test that discarded sweatshirt.

I'd worry about all that later.

"You'll probably find the photos or documents or whatever he uses to blackmail people with when you finish searching the Pines and the Spare Attic," I said aloud.

"Pretty broad area to search," the chief said. "You got any more specific suggestions?"

"They say Doleson has a large and very private bin at the Attic," I said.

"With a big old padlock on it. We'll be looking into that. Of course, we have to deal with Mrs. Willner and

Mr. Rutledge first. At least now I understand why they both tried to confess to the murder."

"They didn't," I said, with a wince.

"Separately."

"I thought Clarence wasn't talking."

"This was in the heat of the moment, when we apprehended them. Now, he's keeping his mouth shut, except to say that as soon as his lawyer is available, he'll confess everything he knows about today's events, and not to listen to a thing Caroline says, because she'll just try to cover for him."

"If you ever arrest me, that won't be my definition of not talking."

"And Caroline keeps saying it was all her idea, and we shouldn't blame poor Clarence. Not that either one of them makes that plausible a suspect. Caroline's too short, and Clarence too well alibied. Thanks to those fool amateur videographers, we can prove he was giving the tourists elephant rides during the whole window of opportunity. But this puts a new light on it."

"It does?" My stomach tightened. I'd thought I was helping get Caroline and Clarence out of trouble. Was my attempt going to backfire?

"They could both be covering for Norris Pruitt," the chief said. "Which could make them accessories after the fact."

"*If* Norris is guilty," I said. "You haven't even talked to him yet—he could have an ironclad alibi."

"We've already talked to him," the chief said. "He was one of your blasted parade geese. One of the ones who's tall enough—I suppose your father told you what he and Horace figured out from the stake's angle of entry."

Dad hadn't, but only because I hadn't talked to him since the parade began.

"Exactly how tall did they decide the killer has to be, anyway?" I asked.

"At least six feet two. That narrows our suspect list down a bit."

"Still a lot of people who qualify."

"Yes, but the list of tall folks with a motive is considerably shorter," the chief said. "And Norris Pruitt has the same blasted lack of an alibi as most of the geese, and what's more, his costume has a noticeable shortage of tailfeathers."

"Oh, dear." Perhaps I shouldn't have repeated what Caroline told me.

Then again, if she and Clarence were helping Norris . . .

"Just one thing," the chief asked. "Were you the ones who reported the burglary?"

"No," I said. "We didn't know about it until we saw the police cars going by. And our phones have been out for hours. Didn't someone out at the Pines report it?"

"No," the chief said. "Their phones probably went out about the same time yours did. And you know what cell phone reception is like out here at the best of times."

"Don't you have some kind of caller ID on your 911 line?" I asked.

"It shows the burglary was reported from Geraldine's Tea Room."

"That's only two blocks from the police station. And Geraldine closes at six."

"Someone jimmied the lock on her back door and used the phone in her office to call in the report."

"Debbie Anne didn't recognize the voice?"

"Debbie Anne said the caller was deliberately disguising his voice," the chief said. "Or her voice. She couldn't rule out a female caller."

"And you thought it was me? No way. Do you really think I'm that shy and self-effacing?"

The chief sighed, took off his glasses, and rubbed his eyes.

"I thought maybe you were snooping around there, saw something suspicious, came into town to report it, and got cold feet at the last minute. Afraid I'd chew you out for interfering. And finagled the lock at Geraldine's so you could report it without being identified."

"Sorry," I said. "But it wasn't me, and I have no idea who it was. Must have been some other bashful good Samaritan."

Someone knocked on the dining room door.

"Chief?" Sammy Wendell opened the door far enough to stick his head in.

"What now?" the chief asked. He sounded more tired than grumpy.

"We've finished inventorying the contents of Mr. Pruitt's bin," Sammy said. He looked as if about to say more, then glanced over at me and fell silent.

"Well?" the chief said. "Read it."

Sammy glanced over at me again, then shook his head and held up a sheaf of papers.

"It's a long list," he said. "Do you want the details or the summary?"

"Start with the summary."

"Okay," Sammy said. "Electronics: seventeen assorted cameras, six iPods, nine cell phones, three portable DVD players . . ."

I closed my eyes in dismay as Sammy droned on. The

list also included jewelry, silverware, purses and wallets—many with the identification still in place—small bits of decorative china and glassware, items of clothing.

Norris Pruitt had been busy. If he'd accumulated this much stuff in just a few months, Caroline and Clarence must have been rather busy, too, after their previous visits to the bin.

Busy covering up for him. Were they still covering up, this time for murder?

I slipped out of the dining room. Sammy was still reading as I closed the door behind me.

"Seven dog collars. Three squeaky toys. Two rawhide bones, partially chewed . . ."

Even without murder charges, Norris Pruitt was in a lot of trouble.

I heard the front door open and turned around to see who it was.

Ainsley Werzel.

"No way back to town tonight," he said. "Haven't you people out here in the sticks heard about snowplows yet?"

"We've heard about them, yes," I said. "But considering how few big snows we get here in Virginia, the county wisely doesn't buy a lot of expensive equipment that would spend most of its time rusting in a garage. And it's not the snow blocking the road; it's a giant tree that—"

"Whatever," he said. "Mind if I sleep in your barn?"

Chapter 22

Better the barn than the house, I supposed, and I was about to give permission when I remembered what else was currently in the barn.

"You'd better bunk here in the living room," I said. "The barn's unheated and—"

"It's okay," he said. "I don't mind. I'm sure you've got a full house. Don't want to be a bother. No room at the inn and all that."

"Yes, but as I was about to say, the police are using the barn right now," I went on. "And I don't think they'd be too happy about civilians being in it."

"Well, if it's no trouble," he said. "I'll take you up on that living room spot."

I had the feeling he could be all kinds of trouble if he tried. His small, restless eyes barely met mine before taking off to examine every detail of the hall, and his fingers twitched slightly, as if he were already mentally composing some kind of sordid exposé. I hoped he knew nothing of Michael's long-ago career as a soap opera heartthrob and his more recent stint as an evil but sexy wizard on a cult hit TV show. Not that there was anything wrong with the fact that, unlike many actors, he'd earned a living during his New York years, but the college was more easily embarrassed. For that matter, any number of my family members had colorful pasts—or presents—that I would rather not see turning up in the *Star-Tribune*. Why couldn't the man have been stranded on the other side of that blasted fallen tree?

I waved him into the living room and was reaching to bolt the door when I heard a timid knock and opened it again.

Horace.

"Hey, Meg," he said. "The chief still up?"

"In the dining room."

Horace nodded and trudged toward the dining room. What was he so glum about?

A few moments later, Sammy came out and went into the living room. I tagged along. Clarence sat staring into the fire.

"Clarence?" Sammy said. "Chief wants to know if he can see you for a moment."

"I'm not talking without my attorney," Clarence said.

"He just wants to show you something."

Clarence thought for a moment, then heaved himself to his feet and followed Sammy. I tagged along again, but hung back just inside the dining room door.

Horace and the chief were staring down at something on the table. I couldn't see what without getting so close that the chief would notice me and kick me out.

"I'm not talking without my attorney," Clarence repeated.

"You don't have to talk," the chief said. "I'm going to talk to you. Do you recognize those?"

He pointed to Horace, who picked up a set of keys in one latex-gloved hand.

Clarence peered, then shook his head, clearly puzzled.

"You don't recognize them? Never seen them before in your life?"

Clarence tilted his head, perhaps sensing that there was a trap behind the words.

"Yeah, I know you're not talking now," the chief said. "But when we can finally get you and your attorney together, we're going to do some talking together. And you can explain to me how Ralph Doleson's keys ended up in your motorcycle saddlebags."

"What?" Clarence jumped to his feet. "That can't be! I've—"

Then he remembered that he wasn't talking and clamped his mouth shut. Clearly he was tempted, though. Points to Clarence, not only for smarts, but for self-control.

"How do you know they're Doleson's keys?" he asked finally.

"We suspected they might be, from this," Horace said. With one gloved finger he singled out and held up a small metal disk with "RAD" engraved on it. "And several of them fit his apartment, his office, and the Spare Attic's front door."

"Someone could have put those in my saddlebags anytime," Clarence pointed out. "The motorcycle was just sitting around parked at Meg and Michael's house for hours before the parade, and then again for hours in town after the parade. And if I'd had his keys, why would we have broken into the Spare Attic? And—sorry. I'm not supposed to be talking."

"You're not forbidden to talk," the chief said. "You're just not required to. Of course, if you want to clear this up tonight . . ."

"I'll wait for my lawyer," Clarence said.

"Tomorrow, then," the chief went on. "Once you've talked to that blasted attorney of yours. In the meantime, I think we could all use some rest."

Clarence, Horace, and Sammy shuffled out. I lingered and watched for a few moments as the chief gathered up his papers.

"Of course, now Clarence has all night to invent an innocent explanation for the keys being in his saddlebags," I said.

He stood up.

"I prefer to think that he has all night to come to his senses and tell the truth," he said. "You still have a room left for me?"

"Room at the inn? Of course."

I led him up to Rob's room, on the third floor. I could see Deputy Shiffley laying out a sleeping bag outside the door of a bedroom at the other end of the hall, so I deduced that Clarence had opted for privacy over warmth and taken refuge there. I wished them all a good night and went down to see what Michael was up to.

I found him sipping the last of his martini and putting the steaks back in the freezer.

"'Scrooge took his melancholy dinner,'" he quoted. "And so forth."

"Does that mean you've already eaten?" I asked. I'd grown used to Michael's habit of speaking in scraps of dialogue when he was directing or acting in plays, but tonight I was too tired to puzzle out his meaning.

He cocked his head for a moment, as if hunting for a bit of Dickens that fit the occasion, and then shrugged.

"Sorry," he said. "I know it's an annoying habit, all this quoting."

"It's interesting," I said. "And this is much nicer than when you were quoting *Who's Afraid of Virginia Woolf?*"

"I'm also too tired to eat now, and I'm even too tired to think of a Dickens quote to say so."

" 'And being much in need of repose,' " I quoted—though not, I suspect, with complete accuracy—" 'Scrooge went straight to bed, without undressing, and fell asleep upon the instant.' "

"Oh, well done!" he said. "Though I think I can manage the undressing part. And since I expect to be in much more congenial company than Scrooge was, maybe we should rethink that falling asleep upon the instant part, too."

"You're on," I said. "We'll see if you're too tired to remember anything from *Romeo and Juliet*."

I peered into the living room on the way upstairs. The fire was dying down. Everyone was asleep, or at least huddled motionless in a sleeping bag, except for Ainsley Werzel. He was standing in a corner, muttering curses as he waved his cell phone around in what I could have told him was a fruitless quest for a signal.

Chapter 23

Ding-dong merrily on high
In heaven the bells are ringing
Ding-dong verily the sky
Is riv'n with angels singing.
Glo-o-o-o-o-o-o-o-o-o-o-o-o-o-o-o-oria
Hosannah in excelsis!
Glo-o-o-o-o—

"Arg," I muttered, from under the covers. "Don't those angels know what time it is?"

"It's almost eight," Michael said, with a yawn. "I expect most angels get up at dawn for choir practice, and think we're pretty lazy, not being already awake to hear them carol."

I stuck my nose out from under the covers and realized that if I kept it out I'd risk frostbite. The odd gray color of the light peeping in through the break in the curtains meant we had not only plenty of snow covering the ground, but also more snow lurking in the clouds overhead, waiting to fall.

"Inconsiderate angels," I said. "You'd think there might be at least one seraph thoughtful enough to say, 'Hey, between the parade and the murder and having a dozen houseguests dumped on them in the middle of the night,

172

they had a hard day yesterday. Let's let them sleep in.' Are there no night owls in heaven?"

"In heaven, certainly." Michael slid out of bed and went over to peer out one of the front windows. "But not, apparently, in the Baptist section. It's Minerva with the New Life choir."

"Someone must have found a chainsaw and cleared the road, then."

"Thank goodness," Michael said. "I was beginning to worry about my show tonight."

I opened my mouth to point out that the predicted second round of snow was a much bigger threat to Michael's one-man Dickens show than even the most enormous fallen tree. But I thought better of it. For all I knew, the meteorologists might have changed their forecasts again. And Michael was already showing subtle signs of pre-performance jitters. Why remind him that he might be getting worked up over a show destined to be snowed out?

I put a pillow over my face. The choir boomed one final, glorious, five-part "Hosannah in excelsis!" into the skies and then, after a brief pause, launched into "We Wish You a Merry Christmas."

"You don't suppose they're really expecting figgy pudding and a cup of good cheer?" I muttered. "I thought your history professor friend said that historically accurate wassail would be mulled beer."

"I'll put on the coffee," Michael said, heading downstairs. "I rather think that would be the suitable Southern Baptist equivalent. Especially before noon."

"Before noon? Try before dawn."

I pulled on my robe and stumbled over to the window. The singers were standing in a circle around our doorstep, their maroon robes brilliant against the snowy yard. Every syllable they sang came out as a separate little white puff, so when the whole choir got going, it looked as if they were sending up smoke signals. It was easy to tell that a couple of the choir members were just mouthing the words.

I could see my own breath, too, which meant that either the power was still off or it hadn't been on long. I flicked a light switch back and forth a few times. Nothing.

The idea of a cold shower in a cold house didn't appeal to me, so I threw on several layers of clothes and followed Michael downstairs.

He had pulled out our camping stove and was heating two enormous pots of water.

"We'll have to give them instant coffee," he said.

"I imagine they won't care as long as it's hot."

Roused by the carolers, our guests were waking up and either gathering at the front windows to appreciate the music or stumbling into the kitchen in search of caffeine. Except, of course, for Clarence, who went outside leading Spike—probably to take his mind off his legal problems with another canine behavioral therapy session.

Just as the water came to a boil, "We Wish You a Merry Christmas" gave way to a solo rendition of "Rise Up, Shepherds, and Follow." I selfishly grabbed one of the first cups of hot water, stirred in the instant coffee, and inhaled the steam as I blew on the top of the cup.

Okay, it was still too early, but the alto voice doing this solo was worth waking up for. I closed my eyes to enjoy both the music and the steam, and jumped when someone spoke at my elbow.

"Is Henry up yet?"

Minerva Burke, resplendent in her maroon robe, billowed into the kitchen.

"Not yet," Michael said, handing her a cup. "I'll start working on breakfast for our guests," he added to me.

"He cooks?" Minerva said. "No wonder you married him. Henry burns toast. Speaking of Henry . . ."

"He's up in Rob's room," I said. "Third floor. Want me to show you the way?"

Minerva nodded, Michael handed her a second mug for the chief and I led the way. But when we reached the second floor landing, she stopped.

"Can I have a word with you?" she asked.

"Sure," I said. I leaned against the banister. "What's wrong?"

"It's this murder investigation."

Had the chief asked her to warn me off?

"Don't worry," I said. "If I think of anything else important, I'll call the chief, and I won't interfere with his investigation by trying to dig up information myself."

"Well, I wish you would." She took a quick sip of her coffee. "I'd like him to spend at least part of the Christmas holiday with his grandchildren, and the way things are going, that's looking less and less likely."

"The investigation's not going well?"

"I have no idea if it's going well or badly," she said. "Not having seen the man since last night. But from the number of messages coming in, clearly it's still going. Someone has to keep working on it, and he's not going to ask anyone to do what he won't do himself. The more he works on it, the higher his blood pressure will rise. As it is, I can't in good conscience give him a piece of my sweet potato pie, and you can't imagine how much Henry loves that pie."

I made a sympathetic noise.

"I picked up tickets to that show of Michael's tonight,"

she continued. "But the way things are going, I'll be by my-self. Again. I was used to doing without him on holidays back in Baltimore. Big city like that, you're bound to have a few people mean enough to shoot each other on Christ-mas or New Year's. But here—well, I expected better."

She shook her head as if sadly disappointed by the in-considerate behavior of the local criminal classes.

"I'm not asking you to interfere," she went on. "But in a small town, people talk to each other more than to the police. Henry should learn to work with that. If you hear something he needs to know, please tell him."

I nodded.

"And if he won't listen, tell *me*. He in the room at the end of the hall?" she asked.

I nodded again and left her to wake the chief. I strolled downstairs and followed the intoxicating smell of cooking bacon into the kitchen.

I heard the chief and Minerva coming back downstairs again. Outside, Horace was handing out steaming cups of coffee, and I could hear cheerful voices chattering and car doors slamming. The New Life choir was moving on in search of new audiences. In the kitchen, I found Rob sit-ting at the table, wolfing down a plate of scrambled eggs and bacon. Michael had both burners of our camping stove going and was frying up more eggs and bacon.

"I made it!" Rob announced, as if reporting a major tri-umph.

"Are the roads bad, then?" I asked.

"Horrible," he said, through a mouthful of egg. "They're pretty full up over at Mother and Dad's. I had to sleep on the couch. By the way—look at this."

He held up his iPhone, which showed a rather nice pic-ture of Michael on the camel.

"That's great," I said.

"Here, look through them," he said, handing me the phone.

I paged through his photos. Rob was getting to be a half-decent iPhone photographer. Quite apart from the good shots of Michael, I wondered if any of his photos might help with the murder investigation. If I could see them full size, that is.

"Can you give me copies of those?" I asked. "Not just the ones of Michael, all of them."

"Sure," he said. "Let me have that for a second." He took the iPhone back and began tapping on the screen. "There. I e-mailed them to you."

"You're getting signal?" Michael said, his hand reaching to the pocket where he kept his own cell phone.

"For now," Rob said. "Out here in the boondocks, it'll vanish again when the new storm gets going."

"That's right—you have Internet access on that thing," I said. "Can I borrow it back for a few minutes? I really want to see what the papers are saying about the murder."

"You just want to see if anyone said anything nasty about your parade," he said, but he handed over the iPhone. "Use it all you like. Snow makes me want to hibernate. I'm going upstairs to take a long nap."

He slouched out of the room.

"So, if the roads are open, will the chief and his troops be leaving soon?" I asked.

"No idea," Michael said. "Sammy thought they'd want to use our barn for a while. At least I assume that's what he meant when he said they were still maintaining their incident command center."

"The chief must have sent him to some kind of training class," I said, as I fumbled my way to the Internet. "Horace always talks that way for a week or two when he's had some new kind of training."

I wasn't as deft at iPhone navigation as Rob—probably because I hadn't spent every waking minute of the last year playing with the thing. But I opened a browser and navigated to the *Trib*'s Web site.

I winced to see that the story about our parade was the third one down on their home page. Did that mean it was on the front page of the print edition? With the headline SANTA SLAIN IN RURAL VIRGINIA PARADE?

"That's awful," I said aloud.

"What's awful?" Michael asked. He slid a plate of bacon and eggs in front of me and leaned over my shoulder.

"What if some kid sees this?" I said, pointing to the headline. "Couldn't they at least say 'Santa Impersonator'?"

"Too long for a headline," he said, peering at the tiny screen. "And I guess they figure anyone old enough to read it doesn't have to be protected."

"That's true," I said. He returned to his cooking and I figured out how to scroll down the article with one hand while eating with the other.

"Just our luck to have a *Trib* reporter here for the murder," I grumbled, through a mouthful of eggs.

"Is it bad?" he asked.

"Could be worse," I said. "And maybe I misjudged Werzel—this is certainly not the slash job I expected from him."

"Probably because it's not his byline."

I scrolled up to the top of the article again.

"You're right," I said. "Good eyes; I didn't even notice that. Who's this Keating person?"

Michael shrugged.

"He must have shown up after Werzel called about

the murder. Or maybe wrote it from the facts Werzel phoned in."

"Good grief," I said. "You should see what it says at the bottom of the article: 'Staff writer Ainsley Werzel contributed to this report.' I feel sorry for him. He hung around all day, had to rough it in our unheated living room overnight, and all he gets is 'contributed to this report.' That's not fair!"

"Maybe that's why he's still hanging around again today," Michael said.

"Werzel? Damn," I said. "Sorry for him doesn't mean I want him around. Maybe he just doesn't know the road is open."

"I think four or five people have already made a point of telling him," Michael said. "He says he's looking for his camera, but I suspect he's on the prowl for dirt."

"Has he reported the camera?" I asked. "Maybe he didn't lose it after all—maybe Norris Pruitt lifted it."

"Not sure he's officially reported it, but I'm sure the chief knows it's missing," Michael said. "Maybe when they catch Norris Pruitt, they'll find the camera."

"True," I said. "It wouldn't be in the stuff they seized from Norris's bin; Doleson was holding that hostage for several months. But unless Norris has undergone a miraculous transformation, he's probably filching things and stashing them somewhere."

Michael nodded. He slid the last of the bacon into a covered dish and turned the camping stove off.

"That should do it," he said. "Werzel just went outside— maybe I should keep an eye on him."

"Or maybe just tell him now that the road's open he should hit it?" I suggested.

"Never wise to antagonize the press," he said. He topped

off his coffee cup, put on his heavy jacket, and went outside.

The idea that Norris might have filched Werzel's camera cheered me no end. Odds were that by the time Werzel got his camera back, the parade, if not the murder, would be old news and whatever embarrassing or unflattering photos the camera contained would never see the light of day, much less the Style section of the *Trib*. Still—perhaps I should ask Clarence and Caroline, if they found it first, to give me a few minutes alone with its delete button.

If Clarence was still outside, maybe I could have a private word with him. I threw on my own wraps and went outside myself. I was still standing on the back porch, adjusting to the cold and looking around for Clarence, when I heard Michael's voice.

"This is Ernest," Michael was saying. "Our first llama."

First llama? I'd been referring to him as "the" llama. And while I had to admit he wasn't much trouble—far less than most human visitors—I wasn't ready for an entire herd of Ernests and Ernestinas grazing in our tiny pasture. Though I feared Michael was.

I started to say so and stopped. Not a discussion I wanted to have in public, and especially not in front of a reporter. But I made a mental note that we needed to have that discussion soon. Meanwhile, I crunched through the snow to the pasture. Michael was leaning against the fence, gazing proudly at Ernest. Werzel looked grumpy, so I assumed he'd seen the "contributed to" credit. And he obviously wasn't enjoying Michael's discourse on the joys of llama ownership.

"Right, right," he said. "So what can you tell me about this Doleson guy?"

Michael and I both immediately put on appropriately

somber, regretful expressions. Michael, of course, was the better actor, but I'd had plenty of experience behaving properly at funerals of relatives I'd hardly met—and a few I'd met and heartily wished I hadn't.

"A terribly sad business," Michael said, shaking his head. I shook mine too, in solidarity.

"Sad?" Werzel said. "Who are you kidding? From what I hear, he was the biggest louse in town. If you liked him, you must be the only two who did."

"I didn't know him very well," I said.

"But any man's death diminishes me," Michael intoned.

"Dickens?" I asked. "Not *A Christmas Carol*, I know that."

"Donne," Michael said.

"Oh, right."

"Done what?" Werzel asked.

"John Donne," Michael said. "Seventeenth-century poet. 'No man is an island'?"

"Oh, I get it," Werzel said, though from his expression I didn't think he did. "Getting back to Doleson—"

"Look, if you're trying to get us to say something snarky about the dead guy, forget it," I said. "We didn't know him very well, but we can still feel sad about someone dying in such a horrible way at a season when people are thinking about holiday celebrations, not funerals."

Michael nodded solemnly. Werzel looked back and forth between us for a few seconds.

"Right," he said. "I'm going to see what the chief is up to."

Chapter 24

Michael and I both breathed a sigh of relief.

"I'm going to rehearse," he said. "I can't do it in the barn with Chief Burke and his men, so I guess I'll stay out here."

"Don't be silly," I said. "The cold air's not good for your voice. Rehearse in the house. I'm used to it, and our house guests will just have to deal."

"I'll probably drive them all out again," he said.

"You make that sound like a bad thing."

Michael did go to the other end of the house, where he could really cut loose and declaim at full volume. Very soon everyone else found it important to be out in the barn or back in town. I never got the chance to ask Clarence or Caroline about the camera.

Our land line wasn't working yet, but I checked in with a few people while my cell phone still had signal. Our Virgin Mary had given birth to a nine-pound baby girl, to be named Noel Grace. Dad got rave reviews on all sides for his performance as Santa. All the parade participants had made it safely home, except for the animals, who were warm and snug at the college barn. But I failed miserably in my subtle attempts to gather information about Dole-son. Did people really know that little about him? Or were they just unwilling to share what they knew? I finally abandoned all subtlety and called several of the worst gossips in town, with no luck. Either no one had any dirt on him or they weren't going to share it within the remaining useful life of my cell phone battery. The signal was getting fuzzy anyway, so I gave up.

Around ten, the snow began again. At first only a few scattered flakes came down at apparently random intervals, like advance scouts. Then, all of a sudden, as if the scouts had sent back particularly good reports, the flakes began coming down more heavily. And not big, damp flakes that promised a wet, sloppy, but short-lived snow. These were tiny, earnest little flakes that meant real accumulation if they kept it up for a while. Which, according to the weather reports I could get on my battery-operated radio, they would.

I didn't tell Michael. He could look out the window for himself, and if he hadn't, no need for me to upset him.

As the snow arrived, the remaining police officers departed, although before they left, they wrapped a few more rounds of crime scene tape around the pig shed, the barn, and several unidentifiable snow-covered lumps in other parts of the back yard.

I wrapped presents, muttering along as Michael rehearsed. Then I packed the borrowed Boy Scout equipment, still muttering.

About noon, I heard the noise of heavy machinery outside—probably the Shiffleys' snow plow going by at close range.

Michael strolled into the kitchen and put the teakettle on the camp stove.

"Maybe we'll make that show after all," he said. So he had been peeking.

A few moments later, I heard the strains of "Good King Wenceslas" out in the yard.

"More carolers?" Michael asked.

"No," I said peering out. "It's the Boy Scouts. Come to

fetch their camping gear, I assume. And looks as if they're starting their cleanup, even though the litter's buried under the snow. They're caroling while they work."

"Excellent," Michael said. "I'd go and help them if I didn't have to rehearse some more."

"Will they bother you?" I asked, suddenly anxious. "I can tell them to keep it down if you need to concentrate."

"What more perfect background music could I have for rehearsing *A Christmas Carol*?" he said. He took his coffee cup and his script and headed back toward his office. I put on my coat, hat, boots, and mittens, picked up my coffee, and went outside.

I had to admire the Boy Scouts' dedication. It was still well below freezing and as in the carol, the snow was deep and crisp and even—three inches of it and counting. It covered everything, including the trash they'd come to pick up. I'd have been tempted to postpone the cleanup until warmer weather. But the Scouts were rummaging all through the yard and up and down the road, excavating even the smallest lump under the snow to fill the huge black plastic trash bags they were dragging behind them.

Randall Shiffley, who owned the construction company and served as one of the scoutmasters, had apparently used his tractor not only to plow snow but also to drag over a Dempster Dumpster, which stood at the end of our yard closest to town. Some of the older Scouts were dusting off the temporary trash barrels we'd scattered throughout the yard, gathering them up, emptying them into the Dumpster, and finally loading the trash barrels onto a big Shiffley Construction Company truck. I was relieved to see that the Scouts gave the various objects festooned with yellow crime scene tape as wide a berth as if they were radioactive.

Randall was sipping coffee from an insulated mug and observing the action with an approving look on his face.

"I had to come out anyhow, to pick up the camping gear, so I thought we might as well make a start," he said. "Get the trash cans out of your way, do what we can. We'll need to come back after the snow melts for the final policing, of course."

"That's great," I said. "You think they'd like some hot chocolate, or maybe some cider?"

"I'm sure they'd appreciate either one," he said. "It's a cold day, and this is thirsty work."

"I'll go make some if you'll help me carry it out," I said. "And I've got a lot of their gear inside—we borrowed it for our unexpected houseguests."

"That's fine," he said. He followed me back to the kitchen and sat at our kitchen table, sipping his coffee, as I heated the milk and cider over the camping stove.

"By the way," I said, "I heard you might be one of the people who isn't entirely broken up by Mr. Doleson's death."

"You heard right," he said. "You probably also heard about when I tried to punch his lights out."

"Over the eagle's nest thing?"

Randall nodded.

"I didn't realize you were that much of a bird lover," I said.

"Well, I guess I like birds as well as the next guy. But this wasn't just any bird. It was a bald eagle. Our national bird."

"Oh, I see," I said, feigning ignorance. "I just heard it was an eagle. Michael and I were out of town then."

"Yes, a bald eagle. Only eagle we usually get in Virginia. And everyone knew Doleson had smashed that eagle's nest, but he was too sneaky to leave any evidence. Not that Chief Burke didn't do his best."

"No wonder all the SPOOR people were so upset," I said. "I'm surprised Dad didn't tell me about it."

"I think your father felt that what happened was his fault," Randall said. "Since he was president of SPOOR when Doleson did it. Which is nonsense—no one blames your father at all. Not much you can do when you've got a sneaky, mean bas—er, scoundrel like Doleson."

Randall still seemed quite worked up about the eagle, even four or five months after the event. Worked up enough to take revenge? I had a hard time believing it. But then, I had a hard time believing Clarence could be involved, either. And I remembered what the chief had said about the killer's height—at least six foot two. Like Clarence, Randall was tall enough to have staked Doleson.

"So yes, I was mad at him," Randall was saying. "And since he was still trying to cause me trouble over punching him, I guess you could say I had a double motive. That what you're asking—whether I could have killed him?"

"Or whether you know anyone who might have?"

"Lot of high words down at the American Legion hall after the bald eagle incident. But not a lot of people mad enough—or stupid enough—to actually do anything."

"Of course, if you're thinking of killing someone, you wouldn't necessarily run around making threats first," I said. "Makes it so much easier for the police."

"True," he said, with a slight nod, as if conceding a point. "Still—there was some talk of boycotting Doleson's businesses, but hardly anyone rents storage units from him anymore, and it's not as if the poor souls living at the Pines have anywhere else to go, so that died down. Most anyone did was get up a petition to get him kicked out of the Santa job, and you can see how much notice the Town Council paid to that."

"It still seems incredible that the Town Council made him Santa," I said. "Do you think he had something on one of them?"

"You mean, was he blackmailing them?" Randall tilted his head as he considered the idea. "It's a thought. If the chief ever finds Doleson's files, maybe we'll find out."

"Ever finds the files—you mean they weren't at the Spare Attic?"

Randall shook his head.

"One of my cousins is a deputy," he said. "He's back out there tonight, searching the Attic and the Pines, top to bottom. And no luck. So either Doleson didn't have files or he kept them someplace they haven't found yet, or someone got out to the Attic before the police did."

"And before Caroline and Clarence did," I added.

He nodded.

"So who do *you* think killed Doleson?" I asked.

Randall tipped his chair back and folded his arms behind his head as he considered the question.

"Plenty of people mad enough," he said. "But it's hard to think of anyone mean enough to do it at Christmas, and risk spoiling the parade like that. Still—the Lord moves in mysterious ways, and if He was moved to call Ralph Doleson home at what might seem to us an odd and inconvenient moment—well, I'm not going to complain."

In other words, good riddance to bad rubbish. I wondered what he meant by Doleson still trying to cause him trouble. Legal trouble, perhaps? I was searching for a tactful way to ask when Randall spoke up again.

"I don't know who killed him," he said. "But I'll tell you who didn't do it."

"Who's that?"

"Norris Pruitt, that's who. There's no love lost between

me and any of the Pruitts, you understand. But Norris? He has the height, yes, and the strength, but he sure as hell doesn't have the gumption. Or the cunning to cover it up even as well as the killer did. And you can tell Chief Burke I said so."

"It's not as if he listens to me," I said. "And after all, the chief knows Ralph Doleson wasn't exactly well liked in Caerphilly."

" 'Oh! But he was a tight-fisted hand at the grindstone!' " Randall and I both started as Michael stepped into the kitchen, declaiming from memory, but carrying the script behind his back.

" 'A squeezing, wrenching, grasping, scraping, clutching, covetous, old sinner!' " Michael went on. " 'Hard and sharp as flint, from which no steel had ever struck out generous fire; secret, and self-contained, and solitary as an oyster.' "

"Yeah, that was Doleson all right," Randall said.

"Actually, that was Scrooge," I said. "Michael's rehearsing. Don't you say his name in there, somewhere?"

Michael consulted his text.

"You're right," he said. " 'Oh! But he was a tight-fisted hand at the grindstone, Scrooge!' " he repeated. "For the show tonight," he added, for Randall's sake.

"A one-man show of Dickens's *Christmas Carol*," I said.

"I heard," Randall said. "I've got tickets. It's still on, then?"

"Far as I know," I said. "Assuming the power's still on at the theater, and anyone can get there."

"Power's fine in town," Randall said. "So far, anyway. And plenty of people can walk to the college theater. But if I were you, I'd head in there now, before the second storm gets going."

I looked at Michael.

"We'd probably get snowed in there rather than here," Michael said. "And that would spoil our plans for a quiet Christmas alone together."

"I could try to bring you back afterwards on the plough," Randall said. "Of course, I can't do anything about the power in the house—odds are that's out till after the second storm. But if I can get through, I'll bring you back."

"But you can't guarantee that even you can get through," Michael said. "How many inches were they predicting? Six to twelve?"

"Ten to fifteen, last I heard," Randall said, looking out the window and nodding. "You don't see many snows like that around these parts."

He sounded as if he approved of the weather's rare burst of industry.

Michael looked wistful.

"You want to do the show," I said. "And I want to see it. Let's get packing."

"You're on," Michael said.

I handed Randall the tray of ciders and hot chocolates and turned to go upstairs.

"Take the truck," Randall said. "No offense, Meg, but that Toyota of yours can't handle what's on the roads now. And as for that little windup convertible of Michael's—"

"No way I'm taking the convertible out in this," Michael said. "The truck it is."

"And if you can be ready in half an hour, you can follow me back to town," Randall said.

Chapter 25

Half an hour later, we were on the road, sandwiched between the tractor Randall Shiffley was using to pull the Dumpster and the truck carrying the Boy Scouts and their gear. We'd packed enough clothes for several days. We didn't know if the rest of the family would come to town to ride out the storm or hole up at Mother and Dad's farmhouse, but just in case, we brought all the Christmas presents and a cooler containing our contribution to tomorrow's potluck dinner. We also brought our camping gear, in case we ended up sleeping on the floor of Michael's office in the drama department building. First Llama Ernest was with us, in an old horse trailer we'd bought in case of just such an emergency, and Spike was in his dog carrier on the seat between us. We didn't even have children yet, and already our days of traveling footloose and fancy free were clearly behind us.

And what were we going to do with Ernest if there wasn't room for him in the barns of the college Agricultural Sciences Department?

I'd worry about that later. First things first: get Michael to the theater, so he could start all his pre-performance rituals. Then I could get Ernest settled—wherever—and look for someplace better than Michael's office for the two of us.

I reached back to pat the pocket where I'd put my notebook.

There was one silver lining to being snowbound in town—at least we wouldn't be completely cut off from hearing any news about the murder investigation. And maybe even helping with it, assuming I could find a way of helping that wouldn't look like interference.

Behind us, in the other truck, I heard the Boy Scouts strike up another chorus of "Jingle Bells."

"This must be how our pioneer ancestors felt, heading west in covered wagons with all their worldly belongings," Michael said.

"Maybe your pioneer ancestors," I said. "Mine stumbled off the ship from England, still seasick, got down and kissed the ground, and refused to stir a step from the Virginia coast. Caerphilly is as far inland as I've ever lived."

He chuckled, and began singing along with the Boy Scouts. I filed away my worries for the time being and joined in.

Caerphilly looked magical, with all the Christmas lights ablaze and the snow frosting the evergreen wreaths and garlands and the red bows trimming them. Even the police station looked welcoming, with candles in all the windows, including the narrow barred windows in the attached jail. Seeing Caroline's truck in the parking lot dimmed my enjoyment a bit, though.

"They'll be fine," Michael said, noticing the direction of my gaze. "As soon as Norris hears they're in trouble, he'll show up and face the music."

I smiled, and nodded, but I wasn't so sure. Norris had been letting Caroline and Clarence clean up after him for years. I wouldn't want to bet that he'd stop now.

Our caravan stopped in front of Dunsany Hall, where Michael's office was, and paused while we dragged our luggage into the lobby. Then I climbed back in the truck.

"You're all right driving in this?" Michael asked, looking around rather dubiously.

"I'll see she gets safe to the college barns," Randall called back.

"And I'll walk back over once I get the llama settled," I said.

The truck peeled off at the courthouse, where I could see a lot of idling cars—presumably the Boy Scouts' parents, come to collect them. I kept following the tractor. The going got rougher as we neared the Ag Sciences barn on the edge of the campus. I slipped and slid into what I hoped was a parking space and not a part of the surrounding organic farmland—it was hard to be sure with all the flat bits uniformly coated in snow. I waved good-bye to Randall and went to lead Ernest inside the barn.

I worried briefly about taking him out in the biting cold and driving snow, but I reminded myself that with his unsheared coat, Ernest was more warmly dressed than I was. After all, llamas routinely braved the cold of the Andes. He could handle a Virginia snowstorm.

He stepped out of the horse trailer, sniffed the frigid air appreciatively, and looked around with interest as I led him to the barn.

Of course, the barn was still occupied by the animals that had been in the parade. Everyone had probably spent the brief interval between storms shoveling out their own houses, and even if anyone had had time to consider taking the animals home, it wouldn't have been safe to try.

So Ernest might not get a stall by himself. I hoped he wouldn't mind.

If Clarence and Caroline were still busy down at the police station and Dr. Blake presumably snowbound somewhere, I should check on the animals.

To my relief, the barn was heated, and I stopped just inside the door to shed my wraps.

The friendly beasts around me stood—Cousin, the donkey, was stretching his neck over the top of a stall, as if begging for rescue. I gave him a wide berth, in case he was feeling crankier than usual. Several sheep were inside the next stall, and the ox and cow beyond them. The various fowl cooed, clucked, or fluttered in a series of coops nearby. The coops all had full food and water compartments, and I could hear the sound of crunching hay from somewhere in the barn, so I relaxed a little. Someone had been looking after the animals.

I led Ernest into the stall with the sheep—since they were Seth Early's sheep, they had probably spent as much time in our yard with Ernest as they had in their own pasture. Ernest seemed happy to see the sheep, and they didn't seem to mind him, so I shut the stall door and breathed a sigh of relief.

I leaned on the door and watched Ernest and the sheep for a few moments. I found it strangely soothing. Maybe a few more llamas wouldn't be such a bad idea. But no more than we could fit in the horse trailer.

I saw a bin of fresh carrots just inside the barn, and I fed a few to Ernest. And then one to Cousin, being careful to pull my fingers back as soon as he reached out for it, since no one had quite convinced Cousin that donkeys were not carnivores.

I could see the camels, Larry, Curley, and Moe, a little farther down, just beyond the cows, and realized that I had never gotten around to asking Clarence what kind of treats camels liked. Well, no time like the present to satisfy my curiosity.

All three camels accepted carrots—Larry and Moe

eagerly, and Curley with an ill-tempered grumble, as though he were only doing it to avoid hurting my feelings.

Strange, but like llamas, camels had a curious calming effect on me. I stood watching their slow, meditative chewing. Almost instinctively, I began doing the breathing exercises Rose Noire was always nagging me to try when I was feeling stressed.

Everything would be fine, I told myself. Sooner or later, the chief would figure out who'd killed Doleson, and if I had the chance, I'd do what I could to make it sooner. The audience might be smaller, but Michael's show would go well; and if we couldn't get home, we had a place to sleep.

Suddenly I spotted a flicker of movement at the other end of the stable, behind some hay bales.

"Who's there?" I called, and reached into my pocket to finger my probably useless cell phone.

Chapter 26

"Don't mind me," a quavery tenor voice said.

A large, disheveled shape swaddled in a voluminous khaki overcoat appeared from behind the hay bales. After a moment, I realized I knew him.

"Norris?" I said. "Is that you?"

He took a step or two closer. Norris Pruitt was tall—taller than Michael's six feet four—and about as pale as a human being could be without actually qualifying as albino. A few tufts of his straw blond hair stuck out from under his tan watch cap. The only spots of color on him were the bright red patches of chapped skin on his cheeks and nose, and the red rims around his pale gray eyes.

"What are you doing here?" I asked, taking an involuntary step back.

"Don't mind me," he said. "I only came to see to the animals. Normally Clarence would be seeing to them, but . . ."

He shrugged.

"But Clarence is down at the police station, answering questions about the burglary he and Caroline committed to help you," I said. I decided mentioning the murder would be a tactical mistake.

"They didn't have to," he said. "I never asked them to."

"You didn't have to. They've been helping you out of jams for years, haven't they? What did you expect them to do when they found out Ralph Doleson was blackmailing you?"

He hunched his shoulders tighter and shook his head. He looked like a wounded bear.

"I'm sorry," he said. He sat down heavily on a hay bale and buried his face in his hands. "I didn't mean to cause trouble." His shoulders heaved as if he were sobbing convulsively.

Was he talking about his thefts or the murder? For some reason I found it hard to think of Norris as a killer. I inched closer, and had to resist the temptation to pat him on the shoulder and say "There, there."

One of the cows stuck her head over her stall door and snuffled at Norris's hair briefly, as if considering whether its resemblance to hay went as far as the taste. Norris reached up and stroked her face absently.

I knew I should call Chief Burke and report that I'd found his missing suspect, but I gave in to curiosity.

"How did you get Ralph Doleson's keys, anyway?" I asked. Norris stiffened.

"Ralph Doleson's keys?" he whispered. "Did I have them? I don't even recall seeing him yesterday. I don't see how I could possibly have . . . borrowed his keys."

"Are you sure?" I said. "Just having the keys doesn't mean you killed him. Since he was blackmailing you, no one would blame you if you went into the shed, found him already dead and—"

"No!" Norris exclaimed. "I could never have done that, even if I had found him. And I didn't. I didn't."

He was rocking back and forth now, and looked so miserable that now I really couldn't help going over to pat his shoulder. I did refrain from saying "There, there."

"You have to tell the chief," I said, as gently as I could. "You can see how bad your hiding from the police looks. Turn yourself in, and tell the chief the truth, and I'm sure

Clarence and Caroline will do everything they can to help you."

He nodded.

"I can call the chief now, if you like," I said.

"No," he said. "I'll call them."

He reached in his pocket, took out a cell phone, and looked at it as if he'd forgotten how to use it.

"I guess I should dial 911," he said, frowning at the cell phone.

"If you like," I said. "Though I'd just use the non-emergency number. Here, let me do it."

He nodded and put the cell phone in my outstretched hand. I punched in the familiar digits—all the more familiar because Norris's cell phone was the same make and model as my own.

"Debbie Anne?" I said, when the dispatcher answered. "Can you tell the chief that Norris Pruitt's over here in the college barn, and he's ready to turn himself in?"

"My gosh," she said.

I said good-bye, cut the connection, and held the phone out to Norris.

"No, you keep it," he said. "It's yours anyway. Sorry."

I did a double take. No wonder the phone had felt so familiar. I took a step away from him as I tucked it back into my pocket.

"Here," he said, handing me something else. "I'm really sorry."

It was my notebook-that-tells-me-when-to-breathe. I stuck it back in my other pocket and put a good ten feet between me and Norris. I could hear sirens in the distance already, so I whiled away the time until the chief and his officers arrived by patting myself down to see if I was missing anything else.

A stray sheep came up and thrust its head at Norris to be scratched. He was still sitting on the hay bale, disconsolately petting the sheep, when Sammy and Horace burst in.

"Hands up!" Sammy shouted. He was aiming his gun at Norris. I backed away and Norris froze with both hands tightly clenched in the sheep's thick fleece.

"Mr. Pruitt?" Horace said.

Norris was staring fixedly at Sammy's gun with his mouth hanging open.

"Mr. Pruitt!" Horace said, more loudly.

Norris flinched, but didn't answer. I suspected he was about to curl up and faint, like a startled possum.

"Norris?" I said gently. He shifted his gaze to me. "Remember we agreed you were going to talk to the police?"

He nodded.

"Sammy and Horace are just here to talk to you," I said. "You don't have any weapons, do you?"

He shook his head.

"Then why don't you hold your hands up so they can see that?" I said.

Norris nodded, and began lifting his hands. Since he hadn't relaxed his death grip on the sheep's wool, the poor animal began struggling and baaing in protest as it felt itself being hoisted up by the fleece.

"Put down the sheep, Norris," I said.

"Put down the what?" I looked over to see that Chief Burke had just arrived.

"The sheep," I said. "That's right," I added, as Norris set the sheep down and patted it apologetically. I breathed a sigh of relief. It was a little unsettling to see how easily Norris could lift a two-hundred-pound sheep. He lifted his hands high over his head and then looked to me for approval.

"That's great, isn't it, Chief?" I said, smiling and nodding at Norris.

"Fine," the chief said. "Sammy, put that fool thing away before you shoot one of the sheep. Mr. Norris isn't going to hurt anyone, is he?"

Norris shook his head vigorously.

"Thank you," the chief said to me. "We'll take it from here."

"Look, Norris was here looking after the animals," I said. "He and Clarence. If—"

I paused. Norris was still very skittish.

"If Norris has to leave," I said, "and Clarence is still down at the station—"

"Don't worry," the chief said. "If we find it necessary to detain both Mr. Rutledge and Mr. Pruitt overnight, I'll have someone look in on the animals."

"You can always call me if you need help," I said. "Or my dad, if you can find him. If Rose Noire's in town, I'm sure she'll be dropping by to check on them, but I don't know for sure she is."

"I'll keep an eye on the animals, Chief," Sammy said. Yes, if there was even a chance Rose Noire might show up, Sammy's crush on her would ensure that he'd take every opportunity to visit the barn.

"I'll help," Horace said.

The chief nodded. His eyes were on Norris, and his body language clearly said that he couldn't wait for me to leave so he could talk to his suspect in privacy.

I fed Ernest another carrot in passing, by way of farewell, and left them to it.

It was slow going outside—not that I minded. I had on enough layers to keep me warm, and I had plenty of time to fill before Michael's show started. Before I had even gone two blocks, the chief and his forces left the barn, bundled themselves and Norris Pruitt into the three police cars they'd come in, and began slipping and sliding slowly in the other direction, toward the station.

As I hiked along, I tried to push Norris and the murder and all the unanswered questions about it out of my mind and occasionally I succeeded for whole minutes at a time.

I exchanged jovial Christmas greetings with various people I passed, all of them so completely bundled up against the biting cold that I had no idea who they were. I wondered if they recognized me or were simply greeting with enthusiasm anyone else brave enough to be out in the storm.

Foot traffic increased as I passed through Caerphilly's small commercial area, and the stores were doing brisk business. Last-minute Christmas shoppers streamed out of the toy and department stores onto snowy sidewalks already crammed with shoppers whose grocery bags overflowed with milk, bread, and toilet paper—Nature's White Sale, Michael called it.

Cars had almost completely disappeared, though, and even trucks and SUVs were getting scarce. Every so often a snowplow would cruise by, with one of the Shiffleys at the wheel, working to keep the roads clear. Of course, they were handicapped by not having the kind of full-sized snowplows you'd find in larger cities farther north, and this particular snow would have challenged the largest snowplow on the planet. The Shiffleys were losing ground. Though knowing the Shiffleys, they'd keep trying until they cleared the snow or until it melted or until they all got themselves stuck in various ditches and snowdrifts. Shiffleys were notoriously mule-headed.

And notoriously good at holding grudges. Was Ralph Doleson's murderer chugging along on one of those snow-plows? If one of the Shiffleys was the killer, Randall might know, or at least suspect. Was that why he was so convinced of Norris's innocence?

Randall had said that Norris didn't have the gumption to kill. I wasn't sure murder necessarily required gump-tion. At least not Ralph Doleson's murder. The killer could just as easily be someone who was scared and angry and cornered and had the strength to kill just by lashing out. If Norris had been carrying the holly stick when he encountered Doleson, and if Doleson had threatened him . . . I could see Norris lashing out. The shock of what he'd done could well account for Norris's dazed state.

Of course, I couldn't imagine Norris managing even the most rudimentary escape and cover-up. But had the killer been clever, or just lucky?

Still . . . I had a hard time seeing Norris as the killer. And if it wasn't Norris, who was it?

Randall Shiffley himself was on the list, unfortunately. I liked Randall, but he could be pretty inexorable when he got an idea into his head. Did he consider slaying a bald eagle a sin punishable by death? I couldn't quite rule it out. And if Randall decided Doleson needed killing, he'd carry out the project efficiently. He had the gumption and the brains. And the anger. Was he really operating the boom lift during the whole window of opportunity?

And Jorge, who claimed not to be blackmailable, but still seemed very worried about Doleson. And who just might own a bloodstained sweatshirt.

Of course, Doleson had other blackmail victims. I knew of two now—surely there were more? And the chief would find them as he continued investigating. Just because he'd found Norris Pruitt didn't mean he was going to ignore other suspects. I should leave the case to him, and stop worrying.

Of course, I've never been very good at leaving anything to other people.

Chapter 27

Back at Dunsany Hall, things were quiet. I passed by the counter that served as the theater's box office, where two people were buying tickets. That was encouraging. I went upstairs to Michael's office. To my relief, he'd left the door unlocked for me.

Spike was there, asleep in his carrier. I let him out and gave him an early supper and a bowl of water. He bolted the food, sniffed dismissively at the water, and began exploring all the exciting new smells that permeated the unfamiliar room.

I sat down at Michael's desk, turned on his computer, and used my illicit knowledge of his user name and password to log into the college's computer system. I wanted Internet access so I could see what else the media were saying about Doleson's murder.

And specifically what line Ainsley Werzel was feeding the *Star-Tribune*. Call me paranoid, but I had the nagging fear that if he didn't get a sexy angle or inside scoop, Werzel would slant the facts or even make stuff up if he thought it would help his story.

This time there were two articles about us listed on the *Trib*'s homepage. Both carried Werzel's byline, so perhaps his persistence had paid off. They were evidently filed this morning after Werzel had found a working phone or computer. The headline read SANTA MURDER SUSPECTS ARRESTED FOR BURGLARY. It made the failed break-in at the

Spare Attic sound like a twenty-first-century Watergate. The accompanying pictures didn't help. No shots from the scene, of course, since Michael had reclaimed my camera from Werzel before the break-in, but they'd found an old shot of Clarence, in his biker's leathers, looking like a thug. Caroline's picture wasn't brand new either—I'd guess it had been taken a good ten to fifteen years earlier, and showed her with what I first thought was a leopard-fur stole around her shoulders. Then I realized that the stole was actually a pair of half-grown leopard cubs, one of which was licking her face while the other appeared to be teething on her hand.

The accompanying text completely left out Clarence's professional identity as a well-respected holistic veterinarian and animal behavior therapist, and merely referred to him as a suspect in "the brutal slaying of Caerphilly County businessman Ralph Doleson." It didn't really explain Caroline at all, but left the impression that she was a rich dilettante who kept exotic animals as pets, rather than a committed animal welfare activist who'd taken in hundreds of abused or abandoned birds and animals, nursed them back to health, and when necessary had given them a comfortable, permanent home at the Willner Wildlife Sanctuary.

Werzel had also written a sidebar on the history of the Caerphilly County Christmas parade. Some indiscreet soul had spilled the beans about Wilmer Pruitt's shoplifting conviction and Orville Shiffley's bacchanalian exploits. In fact, those weren't the only black marks on the parade's history. In the seventies, a group of students from rival Clay County had kidnapped Caerphilly's Santa Claus and paraded him in triumph down the main street of Clayville. They'd returned Santa after a few hours, but not the bag of presents. And one unseasonably warm Christmas in the fifties, Miss Caerphilly County had tried to shed her fur coat and experienced a costume malfunction that was still remembered fondly by the old-timers who'd seen it.

But no previous Master or Mistress of the Revels had had to cope with a murder during the course of the festivities. I sighed. I wasn't sure this was a distinction I wanted.

I jumped as a loud sneeze suddenly resounded through the office. I whirled around to see who had come in, but the door was still closed.

I heard another sneeze, and realized it was coming from near the floor. I peered down and saw Spike standing with all four feet braced against the force of a third enormous sneeze. Then he sniffed slightly and looked up at me as if registering a complaint.

"Sorry," I said. "I'll tell Michael he needs to dust more often."

Spike sighed, trotted over to a chair that stood against the wall, and curled up underneath it.

I turned back to the computer, though I kept glancing over my shoulder. Maybe, along with the dust, I should speak to Michael about having Rose Noire feng shui his office. I recalled her saying that it was very bad to put your desk so you had your back to the door of the room. I could see why. I kept nervously looking over my shoulder to see if someone had snuck in. I'd have locked the door, but it was the old-fashioned kind that could only be locked with a key. If I kept feeling so jumpy, perhaps I'd hunt Michael down and get the key.

The last half of Werzel's sidebar about the parade pretended to give some of the highlights of this year's parade. As I expected, Werzel had gone out of his way to make us seem ridiculous. He didn't feature any of the beautiful or

ingenious floats—only the few really peculiar ones I hadn't
been able to keep out, like the boom lift and the canine
carillon. I was already annoyed by the time I got to the
next-to-last paragraph. Werzel had cornered Caerphilly's
mayor and asked if he or the town council had considered
canceling the parade out of respect for the murder victim.

"Well, no," the mayor was quoted as saying. "I guess that
would have been up to Ms. Langslow."

Gee, thanks, Your Honor. See how fast you can pass that
buck. I could hear him saying it—not that he'd ever said
anything that brief, but I could imagine Werzel plucking
that one quotable sound bite out of ten or fifteen minutes
of blather.

Then I read the last paragraph and exploded.

"Ms. Langslow was not available for comment."

I snarled a few words I didn't normally say aloud. Spike
lifted his head and watched with interest as I pounded the
desk a few times. Not available for comment? The man had
slept by our fire, eaten our bacon and eggs for breakfast,
and been introduced to our llama. I'd answered countless
questions from him throughout the course of the day, and
if he'd asked me that one, I'd have answered it, too. I was
perfectly capable of spinning out a decent answer to
Werzel's question—something suitably sentimental about
knowing that Mr. Doleson wouldn't want to upset and dis-
appoint the children who had loved him in his Santa role
for so many years.

I searched the *Trib*'s Web site until I found a page about
how to make complaints and submit corrections. With a
phone number. I picked up the receiver and then made
myself put it down.

Bad idea. Not complaining to the *Trib*—that was a very
good idea. But a bad idea to call now, when I was still

hopping mad and would come off like a crank or an idiot. I realized I should give myself a few hours to calm down and then decide what to do—write a brilliant and incisive letter of complaint, citing all the facts and all Werzel's omissions and misstatements? Or call to confront his editor in person, once I'd regained my cool and could adopt the icy precision Mother used to such devastating effect in such situations?

Then I smiled. "What would Mother do?" had never exactly been my mantra. But in this case, I realized, I should do exactly what Mother would do.

I consulted the address section of my notebook, picked up the phone, and called one of my cousins.

Cousin Heather had been knocking around the journalistic scene in Washington for a decade or so, and was currently doing her crusading reporter thing at one of the city's alternative papers, writing exposés of political and financial scandals. She claimed that she was blissfully content with her current job and wouldn't even consider a move to the cold, corporate world of the *Trib*. Of course, as far as I knew, the *Trib* hadn't done anything rash, like offering her a job, that would force her to prove her dedication to alternative journalism.

But however scornful she was of corporate journalism, what she didn't know about the *Trib* and every other media organization in Washington, large or small, wasn't worth knowing.

"Mur Cromuf!" she said, on picking up the phone. Maybe I was imagining the sound of crumbs hitting the mouthpiece.

"And a Mur Cromuf to you, too," I said. "Eating a late lunch?"

"Sorry," she said. "Yeah, trying to finish up an article

before I go home to eat my solitary supper. I was going to take your mother up on her invitation to see Michael's show and stay at your house tonight and have Christmas dinner with y'all tomorrow, but it looks as if Mother Nature is going to interfere. The roads are impossible. I meant to call you so you wouldn't worry."

"No problem," I said. I wondered, briefly, how many other people Mother had invited to stay with Michael and me, and whether any of them had four-wheel drive and would turn up on our doorstep in our absence. "Good call, not trying to make the trip. We don't have power, and however bad the roads are there, trust me, they're worse here. Look, while I've got you on the line—what do you know about a *Trib* reporter named Ainsley Werzel?"

"He's a total jerk," she said.

"I already know that."

"And with any luck, he won't be a *Trib* reporter much longer. No idea why they hired him in the first place, or why he's stayed there as long as he has."

"And how long is that?"

"About four months. Of course, you can't just fire people these days, you know. Not in a litigious town like D.C. You have to prove they're completely incompetent. Takes time, even when it's true. Any day now, they'll decide they've got enough ammo and they'll kick him curbside. Meanwhile, they're trying to minimize the damage he can do by assigning him to spin his wheels on nothing stories. How'd you run into him?"

"Apparently one of the nothing stories they assigned him to was the Caerphilly Christmas parade."

"Ouch!" she said. "Sorry. *Trib*'s perception, not mine. So I guess he lucked out, stumbling on your murder."

"It's not my murder," I said. Snapped, really, and then

thought better of it. "Sorry. Touchy subject. And what's the best way to complain to the *Trib* about him?"

"You sure you want to complain?" she said. "Some editors like it when their reporters hit close to home. Makes them feel they're pulling no punches and being a thorn in the side of the establishment and all that. And they'll never hang their reporters out to dry in public. They may read Werzel the riot act back at the newsroom, but they'll defend him to you."

"Even if he's lying?" I explained about Werzel's "unavailable for comment" line with a few acerbic comments about the character assassination he was trying to pull on Clarence and Caroline.

Heather thought for a moment.

"Okay, the no comment thing's not fair," she said. "But technically, it might be accurate. Maybe he was phoning in the story, and his editor asked him if he'd gotten a reaction from you. And he couldn't reach you in the five- or ten-minute window left to get your comment. Me, I wouldn't say someone was unavailable for comment unless I'd tried pretty damned hard over a reasonable period of time and thought they were deliberately unavailable, but Werzel's a sleaze."

"So your advice is to just ignore it?"

"No, my advice is to keep your eye on him. Sounds like he's starting to flail. His editor's probably pushing him. Asking for better quotes, more damning evidence. Werzel's going to try to deliver, whether there's anything to deliver or not."

"Like making things up?"

"Maybe. Or at least making much more glaring omissions and misquotes. If he's already starting to slant things and weasel, there's always the chance that before too long he'll be out without you doing anything. And if you do complain, be very businesslike and make sure you've got at least three real howlers he's pulled. Clear, provable errors. Until then, if you need to vent, don't call the *Trib*—call me."

"Thanks," I said. "I feel better, knowing that the *Trib* already knows he's an idiot. Wish I knew what inspired them to hire him in the first place."

"I heard he started with them as a stringer. They wanted to expand their coverage of Virginia state politics. And they probably remembered his one big story—the Emerson Drood case."

"Emerson Drood?" The name sounded vaguely familiar.

"It was about ten years ago. That politician from some-where near Charlottesville—was it Fluvanna County? Any-way, you remember—the one who pulled out of the House of Delegates race when they found out he'd spent time in a mental institution."

"I remember," I said. "I never could understand what the fuss was. I can think of any number of politicians who be-long in the nuthouse."

"Yeah, but getting committed tends to put off the vot-ers," Heather said. "Especially if you lie about it and some reporter outs you."

"Werzel outed him?"

"Yeah, and then he was the one who tracked Drood down and got that big final interview just before the guy hanged himself in a sleazy motel room. You remember that part, right?"

"Vaguely," I said.

"Anyway, it was good detective work on Werzel's part, tracking Drood down. I'll give him that. And he did get that incredible final interview. But to me there was always something not quite right about it."

"You think he made up the interview?"

Silence for a few moments on the other end of the phone. Then she sighed.

"The guy's such a louse I could almost believe it," she said. "But no, the interview was too solid—had too many new revelations that turned out to be absolutely true. I meant not quite right about the way he got the interview. No way I believe Drood would have talked that much in his right mind. Who knows what kind of tricks or pressure Werzel used? And two hours later, Drood offs himself. Don't tell me the two weren't related."

"Drood committed suicide when he realized how indiscreet he'd been?"

"Maybe. Then again, according to the coroner's report, Drood had a high blood alcohol content—.02 something. Here it is—I've got one of the articles online—.025. Blotto. So maybe Werzel got him drunk and tricked him into giving such a candid interview. Or maybe Drood got drunk after Werzel left, when he realized what he'd done. Either way, don't tell me that remorse and embarrassment over what he'd said didn't contribute to his suicide. Though the more I think about it—maybe Werzel didn't make up the interview, but I wouldn't put it past him to tinker with what Drood said to make it a better story. I mean, the guy wasn't around to contradict anyone, was he? I guess the *Trib* didn't share my skepticism, though."

"But if that was his one big article, and that was ten years ago . . ."

"Yeah, go figure. I guess maybe the *Trib* made allowances for the fact that even the best reporters on a small-town weekly have limited opportunities for big exposés. After his big story, he stayed with the same newspaper—the *Fluvanna Gazette*—until it folded last year. He did a few stories for the *Trib* as a stringer, and somehow he wangled a staff job—maybe he had something on someone in the *Trib*'s HR department. Or maybe someone liked his style—he can be pretty funny, in a mean, snarky way. But the grapevine says he's on thin ice, and the *Trib*'s had him doing way beyond the Beltway stuff, human interest stuff—not hard news. Maybe he figures your murder—sorry, *this* murder—is his last chance to make it big. No wonder he's trying so hard."

"Thanks," I said. "It all makes more sense. I'll keep my eyes open for those provable errors, and hope the *Trib* cans him before he commits any more errors at all."

"Good," she said. "Hey, if the roads get better tomorrow, I could maybe come down for Boxing Day. Will there be turkey left?"

"Probably," I said. "Since right now neither Michael and I nor Mother and Dad have power, I doubt if anyone has even started thawing the turkey. You might get to help us cook it on Boxing Day."

"I'll check with you before I head out, then," she said. "Call me if you need any more scoop on Werzel. Or if you get any scoop I can use."

"Will do," I said, and we hung up.

I sat back and thought about what I'd learned from Heather. I decided finding out Werzel was in the doghouse instead of being the *Trib*'s golden boy didn't make me like him any better. But maybe it would make it easier to put up with him in the short term. He'd get his comeuppance.

"Meg?"

I nearly jumped out of the chair.

Chapter 28

Jorge Soto had opened the door very quietly and was peering in.

"Sorry," he said. "I didn't mean to startle you."

"Not your fault," I said. I glared at Spike, who could at least have barked or something when he heard someone approaching.

What was Jorge doing here?

"Enough to make anyone jumpy," Jorge said, as he stepped into the room. "Knowing that the murderer's still running around loose."

"Is he?" I said. "Chief Burke has arrested Norris Pruitt. So if you think he did it . . ."

"Do you?" he asked.

"Not really," I said.

"You have someone else you think did it?"

"Not really," I repeated.

He nodded.

I was suddenly acutely conscious of how tall Jorge was. Not quite as tall as Michael, but definitely well over six feet. Even across the room, leaning against the wall, he seemed to loom over me. Having people loom over me didn't usually bother me—in fact, at five feet ten, I didn't often get loomed over at all. But right now, anyone tall enough to loom over me was tall enough to be the killer, and that made me nervous. Even worse, this was someone who might have been trying to hide evidence. I eyed the room for possible weapons. I settled on a wrought-iron fireplace set I'd made for Cousin Horace and had yet to wrap. The poker would make a lovely club. I had to fight the temptation to stand up and grab it.

Or was that a good instinct?

"You didn't tell the chief about Doleson trying to blackmail me, did you?" Jorge asked.

Would that question have made me quite as nervous under other circumstances? If we'd been in a public place instead of a small office on a deserted floor of a building that would not begin to fill up with theatergoers for another hour or two?

"No, I didn't," I said. "But I think you should."

He looked relieved.

"Michael and I both think so," I added.

He frowned slightly in annoyance. Was he annoyed because I was nagging him to talk to the chief? Or because I had just reminded him that I wasn't the only person to know about Doleson's blackmail attempt?

"I know you think I'm being paranoid," he said. "But you don't get it. I'm not worried about Chief Burke. He'll find the real killer."

"Even if people don't tell him what could be vital information?"

"If he goes through Doleson's papers, the chief will find whatever stuff Doleson's got that he could use to blackmail people," Jorge said. "And if he's got stuff on me, I'm sure the chief will see it's bogus. Or he'll talk to me and I'll tell him."

"But you're hoping Doleson threw away whatever he'd been collecting on you when he found out you weren't blackmailable," I said. "Okay. Can't you just tell the chief that you suspect Doleson of blackmail?"

"And say what—that there are guys living at the Pines who shouldn't be as broke as they are? Guys who looked nervous every time Doleson came around? And that Doleson lived pretty well, for someone whose sole source of income was a mostly empty storage building and a run-down apartment building? You really think that would help?"

"I don't know," I said. "But as you said yourself, there's a killer out there."

"And the chief would only think I was trying to divert suspicion away from myself."

I stood up, and pretended to stretch my back, as if I'd been hunched over the computer too long. Maybe I could work my way over to the poker.

"Why would he suspect you?" I asked.

"Maybe because they're going to find my fingerprints inside the shed where Doleson was killed."

I couldn't keep my mouth from falling open in shock.

"What are your fingerprints doing there?" I asked.

"From when I was helping clean it up—the night before the parade. Don't tell me you don't remember."

He looked stricken. I shook my head slightly.

"There were a lot of people helping out the night before the parade," I said. "I don't specifically remember seeing you."

"I was helping Rob—remember?"

I remembered that Rob had made a half-hearted effort at cleaning the shed out in the morning, and that when I'd inspected it, I'd immediately rolled up my sleeves and done it right. But if Rob had had anyone helping him, I hadn't noticed.

"Not really," I said.

Jorge groaned, and buried his face in his hands.

"But I was pretty busy, you know," I said. "I'm sure some

of the other people there will remember you. Rob, for example."

"It'd be so much better if you remembered it," he said. Was that a plea to lie for him? Or maybe a threat? Or just an accurate assessment of Rob's potential value as an alibi?

"I'll think about it," I said. "Maybe something will jog my memory. But don't you have something else that's going to need explaining?"

He looked puzzled.

"The sweatshirt you threw away after the parade? The one the police now have?" I decided it would be better not to mention the part I'd played in getting it to the police.

"Oh, damn," he said. He closed his eyes and slumped against the wall.

"Are they going to find bloodstains on it?"

"Maybe," he said. "I don't know. And if those are bloodstains, I don't know whose blood. Could be Doleson's. I helped Rob put Spike in his crate after he bit Doleson, remember? I figured maybe he had some blood on his muzzle and it rubbed off on my shirt. I can't think of any other way I could have gotten blood on it. But do you really think the chief's going to believe that? Especially if—"

"Aunt Meg?"

I jumped, even though I recognized the voice. Jorge jumped too. My nephew, Eric, was standing in the doorway.

"Sorry," Eric said. "I didn't mean to interrupt."

"It's okay," Jorge said. "I was just going. Look," he added, to me, "we need to talk later. Think about it."

About what? Whether I'd seen Jorge helping out with the shed and with Spike? The bloodstained sweatshirt? Or the fact that Jorge had just become a really serious suspect?

"I hear you," I said.

Jorge gave me one more pleading look, then nodded and left.

"Sorry," Eric said again. "I didn't mean to chase him off."

"He really was about to leave," I said. I didn't think Eric needed to hear about my suspicions of Jorge, or how over-joyed I was that my conversation with Jorge was interrupted by a twelve-year-old who, in spite of his recent growth spurt, was still not nearly big enough to be the murderer.

Eric looked anxious. He seemed so young and vulner-able.

Not just vulnerable—upset.

"Did you get through to your parents?" My sister, Pam, her Australian-born husband, and Eric's five siblings were spending the holiday in Melbourne, with the other side of their family. Eric, thanks to severe and persistent airsick-ness, was staying with my parents, as he usually did when the rest of the McReady clan made one of their frequent trips down under.

He nodded.

"They're fine," he said. "They all send their love."

"So what's wrong?"

"Why do grownups always assume there's something wrong?" he said. He tried to assume a look of bored exas-peration that he'd copied from his older siblings during the worst of their teen years, but he hadn't quite mastered it yet, thank goodness.

"Why do teenagers always lump grownups together in that stereotypical us and them way?" I countered. "You're starting it a few months early."

He grinned at that, and looked about six again. But the grin vanished too quickly.

"Besides," I went on. "After everything else that's gone

wrong in the last day or so, I've gotten out of the habit of expecting anything but bad news. If you've got good news, my apologies, and bring it on."

He nodded, but didn't blurt out any glad tidings.

"Kind of a weird Christmas," he said.

Okay, we'd go the indirect route.

"Weird, yeah," I said. "Which makes it normal for our family, right? Remember the Christmas when your grandfather fell off the roof?"

He grinned at that.

"How about the Christmas when Natasha gave everyone live goldfish?" he said.

"The Christmas your Uncle Rob set the house on fire?"

"How about—" he began. Then he took a deep breath. "How about the Christmas when I thought we'd all really blown it? When Santa didn't bring anybody anything?"

"I remember," I said. Eric had been six or seven, and absolutely obsessed with some toy he'd asked Santa for. So obsessed, in fact, that when he woke up at four A.M., he'd crept down to the living room to see if Santa had come through. Our family tradition was to put all the wrapped presents between family members under the tree in the days leading up to Christmas, while Santa deposited his bounty, unwrapped, after we'd gone to bed on Christmas Eve. And we maintained a strict rule that no one was allowed to go into the living room until the whole family was up. Then Dad would fling open the French doors and everyone would exclaim with delight and surprise at all the wonderful things Santa had brought.

"No one could figure out what was wrong that Christmas morning," I said. "Here you were, the youngest—the only one we were absolutely sure still believed in Santa—and no one could find you."

"When I saw that there was nothing under the tree, I knew I must have blown it, big time," he said. "And not just me, but all of us. I figured whatever it was, Mom and Dad hadn't guessed, but Santa knew. And as soon as Mom and Dad saw the empty stockings and all, they'd start asking some pretty tough questions, till they found out whatever it was we did."

"I told everyone it was a bad idea to wait until morning to put the presents out," I said. "I knew, as late as we'd all been up, that we'd be dragging if we had to get up early, and I suggested it was better just to stay up a little longer. But no one listened to me. And even I didn't expect the power to go out and knock out all the alarm clocks so we'd all oversleep."

"And you knew just where to find me," he said.

"The tree house wasn't such a tough guess."

"I always thought it was really nice the way you convinced me that you'd peeked too, just after dawn, and you guessed Yorktown must be toward the end of Santa's run."

"I remember explaining that if we'd all really been wicked, we wouldn't just have empty stockings but lumps of coal," I said, wondering if there was a point to this trip down memory lane. Not that there had to be, but most people looked a little more cheerful when reminiscing about Christmases Past.

"And you never told anyone what I did," he said.

"You told them yourself, a year or two later."

"Yeah, but I was really glad you let me tell them," he said.

I quelled a momentary burst of impatience. Yes, I wanted to get back to my online sleuthing, but something was bothering Eric. He stared down at the floor for a few long seconds, and then looked up to meet my eyes. "I think I might be in trouble."

"How?" I asked.

"You know that reporter?"

"Ainsley Werzel? All too well by now."

"I sort of borrowed his camera."

"Sort of borrowed? You mean you took his camera?"

"Well, when I first picked it up, I thought it was yours," he said. "You have almost the same model. And when I realized whose it was, I remembered that he'd been taking all these nasty pictures of people. Like trying to get them doing something silly or not looking very good. I thought it was really rude."

"I agree," I said. "And I admit, it crossed my mind how much I'd like to steal his camera and erase all his photos."

"But I didn't steal it," Eric protested. "He left it lying around, and I picked it up to give it to him—well, to you, till I realized it wasn't yours—and then I thought if I could just keep it for a few minutes and go someplace where no one would see me, I could look through the pictures and delete any that would embarrass people, and then just put the camera back where I found it. So I stuck it under my coat. And before I got a chance to look at the photos, he started making that big fuss about losing it, and I was embarrassed to give it back."

"I'd just have left it lying around someplace," I said. "Let him think he'd forgotten where he'd left it."

"Yeah, I thought of that," he said. "But Mr. Pruitt was around—Mr. Norris Pruitt. And you know how he is."

"I do now," I said. "Okay, good call not leaving it around for Norris to pilfer. But you could have told the truth. At least the part about finding it lying around. You could have said you picked it up for safekeeping and forgot."

"Yeah, I realize that now," he said. "But Mr. Werzel was

so mad, and it all happened so fast and I didn't think what to do till later. And once he made that report to the chief, I was scared to. Mr. Werzel would have had me arrested."

I shook my head, but he was right—Werzel probably would have tried. Probably still would, if he found out now. And stressed as the chief was by the murder, he might well have been in the mood to teach Eric a lesson.

"What can I do?" Eric asked. "I can't just give it back."

"Maybe you can't, but I can," I said. "Have you got it here?"

He nodded and reached into his pocket to pull out the tiny silver camera. He handed it to me and then sighed as if I'd taken a ton of rocks off his shoulders instead of a few ounces of metal and plastic from his hand.

"You can tell them what happened," he said. "I know I should have brought it back sooner, but I was too scared to do it myself. You can make them understand."

I was going to miss that when he got a little older—that childish confidence that Auntie Meg could fix anything.

Then again, Rob still turned to me regularly to bail him out of scrapes with that same absolute trust that I could and would rescue him.

"You really should have turned it over as soon as Mr. Werzel made that fuss," I said. "You know that."

"Yeah," he said, looking down at the floor. "And if you think I should take it back myself, I will. I just don't want to do it all by myself."

"No, I'll take care of Mr. Werzel," I said. "I'll tell him about you thinking it was mine and giving it to me. Which is the truth—I'll just let him think I was the one who identified it as his camera."

"Thanks," he said. "I promise I won't ever do anything like this again."

"One thing," I said. "Did you mess with his pictures?"

He shook his head.

"I didn't even look at more than the first one or two," he said. "I could tell it wasn't yours."

"Good," I said. "I want to be telling the absolute truth when I say that you had nothing to do with the missing pictures."

"But how do you even know there are any missing?" he asked.

"There may not be now, but before I give this back to him, I plan to look through all of them and delete any that I'd cringe to see published in the *Trib*. For instance, I remember him taking a picture of my rear end when I was bending over to see if Spike was bleeding to death."

Eric grinned.

"So you're going to do the same thing I was going to do."

"You bet. Now run along and sin no more. Leave that to me."

"Thanks, Aunt Meg." He hesitated, then reached over to give me a quick hug before turning to go.

"Oh, Eric—can you do something for me?"

"Sure." He paused in the doorway.

"If you see Michael, could you get him to send someone up with the key to the office?"

Eric grinned.

"So you can keep people like me from bothering you," he said.

"So I can lock it up when I leave," I said. "We've got all the presents here—including yours."

"Oh, in that case—yeah, I'll find him," Eric said. He closed the door behind him.

I stood up to look over the desk at Spike. He was still under the chair, curled up so tightly he looked like a black and white fur hat.

"You're a lot of help," I said. "Next time, bark, will you?"

He ignored me.

I sat back down to examine the camera.

Chapter 29

Luckily, since Werzel's camera was the same make and practically the same model as my own, I didn't have much trouble turning it on. Not exactly a professional photographer's camera. No wonder Werzel had been so desperate for his lost photographer to show up.

Though it was odd that even after the real photographer arrived, Werzel continued looking so insistently for his camera. Especially since he wasn't much better a photographer than I was. His photos didn't have as many of what Michael called "unidentified flying pink sausages"— pictures in which I'd accidentally put part of my thumb or forefinger in front of the lens—but just as many of his shots were ever so slightly out of focus. Or noticeably askew. Or awkwardly framed. The occasional shot good enough to print looked more like an accident than anything else.

I deleted half a dozen embarrassing or unflattering shots of myself and others—shots sufficiently in focus that some editor at the *Trib*, in an evil moment, might have considered using them. Of course, by the time the news about the murder had broken, the photographer had arrived, so odds were the *Trib* wouldn't need any of Werzel's shots at all.

Except, of course, for the shots of Ralph Doleson while he was still alive. Those might have a news value that outweighed their poor quality. My temper flared all over again when I saw the shots of Doleson booting poor Spike out of the pig shed.

Perhaps it was a pity I'd decided to wait until after the parade to report Doleson for animal abuse. If I'd dragged one of the several nearby police officers over to have him arrested on the spot, maybe he'd still be alive.

No use second-guessing things like that, and it wasn't as if it was my fault the killer had found Doleson alone. Like Ebenezer Scrooge, he'd helped seal his own fate by the way he'd lived.

Werzel had snapped a couple of shots of Spike lying in wait outside the pig shed, and then a rather nice shot of Clarence ministering tenderly to the small evil one. And another predictable but amusing shot of Spike sinking his teeth deep into the heavy leather gloves Clarence had taken to wearing when treating his more savage patients, like Spike and the zoo's wolverines.

I reached over and plugged the card reader into Michael's computer. The shots of Spike and Clarence were too good to let go. Before I gave the camera back, I was going to keep copies of them for myself.

I turned back to the camera and clicked ahead. Another couple of photos of Spike, none of them as good as the first few. A distant shot of Michael, Dr. Blake, and the chief on their camels.

Followed by a candid shot of Ralph Doleson, sitting on the seat of the sleigh. He was looking up at the camera as if surprised, and he was holding a boot in his hand.

"What's that?"

I jumped a foot. I'd been staring so intently at the camera's tiny LCD screen that I hadn't even heard Rob open the door and walk in.

"You scared me to death," I said. "I'm definitely going to get Michael to rearrange his office furniture before one of his students sneaks up and gives him a heart attack."

"I bet he doesn't spend much time on the computer with his back to the door like that," he said. "I wouldn't, if I were him. You're the one who gets so wrapped up in the computer that you don't notice what goes on around you."

"Did you at least bring the key?" I asked.

"Key?"

Okay, so Michael hadn't sent him.

"Never mind," I said looking back at the camera.

"What's so interesting?"

"It's a picture of Ralph Doleson," I said, handing him the little camera.

Rob peered at the screen and frowned.

"He's sitting in the sleigh where he was killed," he said. "With one boot on and one off. I only got a quick glimpse through the door, but doesn't this look a lot like . . . ?"

"Like a picture of Santa taken just before the killer staked him," I said. "I got a lot more than a quick glimpse, and that's exactly what it looks like to me, too."

"What's it doing in your camera?" Rob asked.

"This is Werzel's camera," I said. "It only looks like my camera."

"You switched cameras by mistake?"

"That's what it looks like," I said. Which wasn't precisely a lie, but it kept Eric's secret. "Let me see that again."

"No wonder he was so frantic to find this," Rob said.

He handed the camera back. I studied the picture of Ralph Doleson for a few more seconds, and then clicked the button to see what was next.

Yet another of Werzel's badly shot mistakes. A blurry brown shape on the right, a blurry red blob on the left. I squinted, to see if I could figure it out. Rob leaned over my shoulder.

"Closeup of Rudolph's nose?" he suggested.

"No," I said, as my stomach turned over with a wrenching twist. "Blood spatter on the lens."

"Are you serious?"

I turned the camera over and peered at the lens.

"Maybe it's my imagination," I said. "But there is something crusted around the edge of the lens. See?"

I held it out for his inspection. He stared for a few seconds, then turned pale and sat down in one of Michael's guest chairs.

"That's really blood?" he asked, in a slightly choked voice.

"Put your head between your legs and breathe slowly," I said, mentally kicking myself for having forgotten Rob's notorious squeamishness at the very thought of blood.

"Maybe we both just have overactive imaginations," he said.

"I doubt it. No wonder Werzel was so frantic to get it back. He's the killer—and this camera proves it!"

"Wait a minute," Rob said, sounding stronger. "That can't be blood. How could there be blood spatter on the camera, when there wasn't any on his clothes? I think someone would have noticed if he was running around looking like Sweeney Todd."

"I bet there was blood on his clothes," I said. "That's why he suddenly showed up in one of the county-issue shepherd's robes."

"I just thought he was trying to blend in and get into the spirit of things," Rob said. He shook his head, which looked rather odd, since he was still hanging upside down in fainting prevention mode.

"Maybe you thought that," I said. "I knew he had a sneaky reason for doing it, but I just assumed he was trying to make us forget he was a reporter so he could catch people doing embarrassing things."

"We have to tell—"

"I know, I know." I automatically reached into my pocket and took out my cell phone.

And got absolutely no signal, of course.

"You'll never get a signal in this weather," Rob said, peering up at me. "I'm even having trouble on the iPhone. This whole county might as well be back in the twentieth century. Use the land line."

I nodded, and used Michael's phone to dial the police station's non-emergency number.

Debbie Anne, the dispatcher, answered. She'd have answered 911, too, but she'd be less apt to gossip about my calling if I used the non-emergency line.

"Meg!" she exclaimed. "You made it into town! Does this mean Michael's show is on?"

"With or without an audience," I said. "Look, could I talk to the chief for a moment?"

"I'm sorry," she said. "He's not here. He's out at—out of the station."

I had to smile. The chief had probably told her off again for talking too much and telling too much police business to civilians.

"I don't suppose you know where he is," I said.

"I'm sorry," she said. "I can take a message."

"Could you tell him to call me as soon as he can?"

"Can I tell him what it's about?"

Debbie Anne and I fenced back and forth for a few more rounds, with me trying to find out where the chief was and her trying to find out why I was calling, before we settled for a draw. I gave her Michael's office number, told her I'd be there for the time being, and signed off.

"He'll call back," I said.

"Why didn't you just tell her why you called?" Rob said.

"I'm not sure," I said. "Maybe because Werzel showed up at the burglary scene almost as soon as we did. What if he has a police radio? A lot of reporters do. Or what if Debbie Anne says something to the wrong person? I hear a lot of stuff leaks out of the police station, and I suspect Debbie Anne's part of the problem."

"So what do we do now?"

"I don't know," I said. I looked at the phone as I thought it over.

"A watched phone never rings, you know," Rob said. "We should think of something else."

"Such as?"

"If Werzel's the killer, why did he do it?"

"How should I know?" I said. "Unless—hang on."

I turned back to the computer and Googled Emerson Drood.

"What's that?" Rob asked. He came and perched on the desk so he could look over my shoulder. I felt less stupid about not recognizing Drood's name when Heather first mentioned it.

"A state politician," I said. "From somewhere near Charlottesville. He killed himself about ten years ago. If I'm right . . ."

But nothing on the first couple of pages looked promising. Most were pages that mentioned both Ralph Waldo Emerson and Dickens's *The Mystery of Edwin Drood*. A couple of the articles mentioned Emerson Drood's death, but nothing about the circumstances.

"So far this is not keeping me awake," Rob said. "Are you

sure what you're looking for is even available online? Not a lot of newspapers were ten years ago, you know."

"Yeah, and the one I'd really like to see is defunct anyway," I said. "Let me try something else."

This time I typed in "Emerson Drood" and "Whispering Pines" and clicked on the most promising of the resulting links.

"What does the Pines have to do with this Drood guy?" Rob asked.

"Maybe everything," I said, as I scanned down the article. "Aha!"

"Aha what?"

"Fifth paragraph. 'Drood's body was found at 1:14 A.M. on the morning of August 5 by the night desk clerk of the Whispering Pines Motel in nearby Caerphilly County.'"

"Someone was murdered at the Pines?" Rob said, looking pale again. "What room number?"

"It doesn't say," I said. "And the death was ruled a suicide, if that makes you feel any better."

"Not appreciably, but thanks."

"I wonder what the clerk was doing, snooping in the rooms in the middle of the night?"

"Looking for small portable valuables, I imagine," Rob said. "That was one of Doleson's hobbies. So what does Werzel have to do with this?"

"I'm not sure," I said. "But whatever it was, I think Doleson was blackmailing Werzel about it. You heard about the way Doleson was always photographing people who came to the Pines. I bet he had some kind of dirt on Werzel."

"Like maybe that Werzel killed Drood?"

"Maybe," I said. "No idea why he would, though. Werzel supposedly got a dramatic last interview with Drood just before the suicide. Seems more plausible that Doleson knew there was something fishy about that interview."

"What do you mean, fishy?" Rob asked.

"What if Doleson knew that Werzel wasn't there with Drood long enough to get such a long interview? Maybe Doleson eavesdropped and knew Werzel had faked some of the interview."

Rob shook his head as if it all sounded rather weak. I agreed with him. Then I had another idea.

"Doleson was always snooping, right?"

Rob nodded.

"What if Doleson found the body and didn't report it?"

"Why would he do that?"

"Maybe he wanted to loot the dead guy's luggage before calling the police. Or dump the hassle of dealing with the cops on his poor night clerk. Or maybe he was on the way back to his office to report it. Whatever it was, before he could do it, Werzel drives up. What does Doleson do?"

"Grabs his digital camera and starts snapping shots."

"Bingo!" I said, so loudly that Spike woke up and growled at me. "Doleson gets some lovely shots of Werzel entering the room. Then Werzel fleeing the room. And then the dead body Werzel apparently left behind. Werzel's the prime suspect if the police are thinking murder. And Doleson could have made it look even worse—like claiming he'd heard what sounded like a struggle. He's got the perfect ammo for blackmailing Werzel."

Rob whistled.

"Sounds plausible to me," he said. "Why doesn't the chief call back?"

"It's Christmas Eve, he's got a big murder case, and he doesn't know I've got a key piece of evidence."

We both looked at the phone again. It stubbornly refused to ring.

"So are we just going to stay here till it rings?" Rob asked. "No offense to Michael, but it's kind of creepy up here with no one else around."

"Very creepy," I said. "And no, we're leaving. Minerva and the chief are coming to the show—she said so this morning. Let's go downstairs and wait for them, and I can tell the chief in person."

"What if he skips the show to keep working on the case?"

"Then we'll tell Minerva, and she'll help us reach him. Debbie Anne might not put me through to the chief, but she wouldn't stonewall Minerva."

"Great idea," he said.

I shut down the browser and began turning Michael's computer off. Rob went over, opened the door, and stood fidgeting in the doorway.

"The small evil one should go back in the crate," I said, over my shoulder.

"Okay, I'll—damn!"

I glanced up to see Rob clutching his hand, as the tip of Spike's tail disappeared out the door.

"I think we're going to have to start spelling in front of him," I said, as I picked up my coat and purse.

"Won't work," Rob said, over his shoulder. "He's psychic. I'll get him."

He took off down the corridor. I stuck the camera in my pocket and went over to prop the carrier door open. I heard a clatter outside in the corridor.

"Rob?" I called. I stepped out into the corridor and looked in both directions. Only a few scattered bulbs on the night system lit the corridor, but I could easily see that it was empty. No Rob. No Spike. Nothing at all, except for a cleaner's mop and an overturned bucket at the far end of the corridor on the right, where it turned a corner. The noise had probably been Rob tripping over them.

I started down the corridor in that direction. Strange that I didn't hear them, but maybe Spike was traveling even faster than usual. If he'd taken to a stairwell, they could be on another floor by now.

I rounded the corner and almost ran into a cleaner's cart. Then I realized there was a shape lying on the floor beyond it.

"Rob! Are you all right?"

He didn't answer. I knelt down beside him. He was breathing, but his eyes were closed. I reached to check his pulse.

"He's not dead," said a familiar voice.

I looked up to see Ainsley Werzel standing a few feet away. He was pointing a gun at me.

"Now give me the camera," he said.

Chapter 30

"Mr. Werzel? Is that you?" I said. I pretended to be peering through the gloom as I said it, and I talked as loudly as I could, hoping that someone would hear and come to rescue me. Then I realized that no one but Rob and I knew that Werzel was the killer. If anyone else was close enough to hear Werzel's name, they'd make tracks in the opposite direction.

"Shut up," Werzel growled.

"What's wrong?" I asked.

"Don't pretend to be stupid," he said. "I know you're not stupid. Nosy, but not stupid. Give me the camera."

"You don't have to act as if I was stealing it." I pulled the camera out of my pocket and held it out. "I was going to bring it back to you. My nephew thought it was mine and brought it to me—I have one just like it."

I tried to sound matter-of-fact and calm, as if I hadn't quite noticed he was pointing a gun at me. He didn't seem to be buying it. He leaned forward carefully, snatched the camera out of my hand, and then retreated to a safe distance.

He turned the camera on and began pressing buttons. His eyes kept flicking down to the camera's display screen and then back to me. I deduced that he was scanning the photos.

Then he stopped.

"Yeah," he said. "Pretty incriminating shot, this one. But

the great thing about digital cameras is that you can delete anything you like, and no one the wiser."

He pressed more buttons. Deleting his way through the rest of the shots, no doubt. Then he nodded, turned the camera off, and stuck it into his pocket.

"Now pick him up," he said.

"Rob?" I said. "He shouldn't be moved. He could have a concussion."

"Yeah," he said, hefting a long Maglite in his left hand. "I was aiming for a concussion. If you don't want to pick him up, I could whack him on the head another couple of times and we'll just leave him there."

I decided picking Rob up was the better option. I bent down and found Spike there, licking Rob's head.

"Damn," Werzel said. "If the circumstances were different, I could do one of those great tearjerker stories. Faithful hound licking the blood off his fallen master's wound."

Blood? Yes, I could see it now. Just a trickle, that Spike was licking up eagerly. I decided not to explain that it wasn't either devotion or savagery on Spike's part—he just liked the salty taste. He'd have licked the wounds of a mortal enemy—or Rob's face after a sweaty tennis match—with equal fervor. Werzel would find that all too hilarious.

Spike growled a little when I picked Rob up.

"Chill, Spike," I said.

"Put him on the cart," Werzel said.

I draped Rob carefully over the cleaner's cart. He groaned slightly.

"Okay, roll him that way," Werzel said.

I thought of saying something melodramatic like "You'll never get away with this," but I didn't like the twitchy sound of his voice. I concentrated on going as slowly as I could without ticking him off. Slowly was better for Rob's head, and also maximized our chances of running into someone who might help.

But the corridors we rolled through remained disappointingly empty. I realized that we were heading for the service elevator. Spike was trailing behind us.

"Why are you kidnapping us?" I asked. I didn't shout, but I tried to project from the diaphragm, the way Michael was always trying to teach his theater students.

"Shut up and keep pushing," Werzel said. "There's room for two on that damned cart."

I shut up. Not talking to Werzel made it easier for me to concentrate on coming up with an escape plan. Unfortunately, while I could come up with several different ways I could escape, I hadn't yet thought of any way for *us* to escape. And much as I tried to convince myself that if I escaped and ran for help, Werzel wouldn't dare hurt Rob, I didn't believe it. Werzel had already killed at least once— what did he have to lose?

Dunsany Hall was utterly and depressingly empty. The students had long since gone home for the holidays, of course, but you'd think at least one of Michael's colleagues would be dropping by to check on his e-mail or something. We rolled through empty corridors until we reached the freight elevator. No one stumbled on us during the long wait for the ancient machinery to crank its way up to our floor.

"Roll him in," Werzel said, gesturing with the gun. "And kick the mutt out," he added, as Spike tried to follow me.

"And here I thought you were shocked when Ralph Doleson kicked Spike," I said, as I reached down to pick Spike up. "You weren't shocked by what he did—you were shocked to see him. And—ouch!"

Predictably, Spike bit me, and then scampered off the way we'd come.

"Good riddance," Werzel said.

"You're not afraid he'll run downstairs and warn people that there's something wrong?" I said.

Werzel seemed to find that funny. He'd seen Spike in action enough to know that a Lassie-style rescue wasn't too probable. Ah, well. Surely we'd see someone once we got outside.

But when the elevator doors opened and we rolled out onto the loading dock, I realized that between the gathering darkness and the steady snowfall, I could hardly see ten feet. And that no sane person would be lurking in the alley behind the Drama Department on a night like this. And more immediately, that my coat was still lying beside my purse on the floor of the corridor upstairs, where I'd dropped them when I'd found Rob.

"Over there," Werzel said. He gestured with the Maglite. "The blue Subaru." Yeah, I could have guessed that—it was the only vehicle in sight.

I looked from the cleaners' cart to the Subaru. No way I could roll Rob there through a foot of snow, so I carefully picked him up and staggered over to the car.

"In the luggage compartment."

I settled Rob in the back of the Subaru. It already contained several cardboard boxes filled, as far as I could tell, with paper. To fit Rob in, I had to move one box out completely and put it in the back seat. Werzel stood about fifteen feet away, probably to make sure he had time to shoot me if I emerged from his trunk waving some kind of weapon.

Alas, I could see no sign of anything that would make a

good weapon—no wrenches or tire irons. There was a tarp, which I tucked in around Rob to keep him warm. I checked his pulse, which was still steady. As I did, I noticed that there was also a metal can of kerosene at the very back of the trunk.

"My head hurts," Rob said suddenly. Relief flooded my mind—surely it was a good sign if he was well enough to speak. I glanced over my shoulder and found that Werzel didn't seem to have noticed.

"Shh," I whispered. "Don't talk."

"But my head hurts."

"I know," I said. "I'm going to get help as soon as I can. For now, the less you talk, the less your head will hurt."

"Okay," Rob said.

He closed his eyes again. I breathed a sigh of relief. The less Rob talked, the less likely it was that Werzel would decide to whack him again. And if Rob stayed conscious, there was a slim chance he could help me engineer our escape.

Not a chance I could count on, though.

"Hurry up," Werzel said. "Get in and drive."

I got in, hoping it wasn't a mistake. The keys were in the ignition. Werzel slid into the back seat. I started the car and felt immediately and irrationally better. Werzel still had that nasty little gun pointed at me, but I had over a ton of lethal metal under my control. Surely I could find a way to turn the tables on Werzel. Newscasters were always proclaiming that cars were more deadly than guns.

"Where are we going?" I asked aloud.

"Shut up and drive."

Chapter 31

Easier said than done. The Shiffleys had more than enough to do keeping the streets clear. They had no reason to plow the alley behind a building that, except for tonight's performance, would be closed for the rest of the holiday season.

But unfortunately there wasn't quite enough snow to stop the Subaru. Just enough to slow us down. I took as much advantage of the delay as I could, all the while keeping my eyes open for someone—anyone—on the streets.

The Christmas decorations that had seemed so festive when I'd walked past them earlier now seemed to mock me with their cheerfulness. And where had all the hardy pedestrians gone? Clearly the shopping rush was over, and if anyone was planning to brave the snow for Michael's show, they hadn't ventured out yet. We didn't even see any of the snowplows.

"Take the next left."

The next left would be the country road that led out to our house, and eventually to the Spare Attic and Whispering Pines. Not where I wanted us to be going at all. I wanted us to stay in town, where there was at least a fighting chance of encountering someone. And where we were closer to the hospital I'd be rushing Rob to if—no, make that when, dammit!—I turned the tables on Werzel.

"Left?" I said. I tried to sound surprised and maybe even cheerful. "Onto our road? But it's a d . . ."

I let my voice trail off.

"Yeah, it's a dead end," he said. Then he laughed. "A real dead end."

"If I were you," I said, "I'd be heading away from Caer-philly. I mean really away, not just out into the countryside."

"I will be soon," he said. "Need to do a few things first."

I didn't like the sound of it. Not "We will be soon," but "I." I wanted my stint as his unwilling chauffeur to end on my terms, not his.

Relief washed over me when we got to the turnoff. Clearly the Shiffleys were rethinking their attempts to keep every road in the county plowed. Where the turnoff should have been was only a solid bank of snow they'd ploughed off the highway.

"Don't shoot the messenger," I said, as I slowed to a halt. "But I don't think we can take that turnoff."

"Don't argue with me! Keep driving!"

"I'm not arguing," I said. "I'm perfectly happy to keep driving, but I doubt if even your Subaru can get through that. Want me to go ahead and bury us in the snow?"

Werzel studied the snow bank for a while.

"Damn," he said, finally. "This really screws up my plans."

"If I were you, I'd just leave town," I said. "While the police are still busy with Norris Pruitt."

"What do you mean, busy with him? They didn't find him, did they?"

"A few hours ago."

"Lucky for me you mentioned that," he said. "That changes my plans completely."

"Just what are—were your plans?" I asked. "I realize you might not want to tell me, but I'd kick myself if I didn't ask."

After I said it, I worried that my sarcasm would anger

him. But he didn't even answer for a few moments. I could see in the rearview mirror that he was frowning at the box on the seat beside him.

"Well," he said finally. "I was going to make it look as if Norris Pruitt had killed you and your brother while trying to retrieve whatever Doleson was using to blackmail him."

"Which building were you going to torch, the Spare Attic or the Whispering Pines?"

He gave me a startled look, then relaxed.

"You saw the kerosene, right? I hadn't really decided. Maybe both. But if Pruitt's already been arrested . . . of course, I could rig something to look like a delayed fuse. You say he was only arrested a few hours ago?"

I nodded. I didn't like the way this was going.

"Do you know where?"

I was trying to think of a suitable lie—one that wouldn't result in him dragging Rob and me off to some deserted corner of town where he could carry out his revised plan without interference. But bright ideas weren't happening.

"I said where!" he said, waving the gun. I suddenly realized the truth was better than any lie I could think of.

"The stables," I said.

"What stables?"

"The college stables. That's where we're keeping the animals from the parade until the storm's past and we can get them home. Norris was looking after them."

"Probably filled with nice, flammable hay," he said. "That'll do. Let's go."

I tried not to let him see how relieved I was. Short of convincing him to pull up in front of the police station and drop me off, the stables were the best possible destination. Deputy Sammy would be dropping by to see to the animals. Dropping by more frequently than needed, thanks to my hint that Rose Noire might be checking on them. For that matter, Rose Noire might well drop by to soothe the ruffled fur and feathers of the barn's inhabitants. And I was positive Clarence would look in if he was out of jail. And if Dad and Dr. Blake were in town, surely they'd check on the animals' welfare before heading over to the drama department for Michael's show. I could think of any number of people who might drop by and could help, or at least provide a distraction.

"It's close to the edge of town," I said. He'd be suspicious if I didn't put up some kind of argument. "They may not be plowing over there, either. Could be rough going."

"We'll just have to go and see. Move it."

I eased the Subaru into motion and began lumbering slowly toward the stables. Keeping my eye out for passing vehicles, of course. No need for a showdown at the stables if I could pretend to lose control of the car and spin us into the path of a patrol car or one of the Shiffleys' snowplows.

I glanced in the rear view mirror again. Werzel was staring out the window, apparently lost in thought. I didn't want him thinking. I wanted him off balance.

"So did you kill Emerson Drood?" I asked.

"Kill him? No! Absolutely not!"

"Yeah, right," I said. "That's what Doleson had on you, isn't it—that you killed Drood?"

"I didn't kill him," Werzel said. "He was already dead when I got there, so if someone killed him, it wasn't me."

"If he was already dead when you got there—then the big interview was a fake. That's what Doleson was blackmailing you about."

Silence in the back seat for a while.

"Yeah," Werzel said at last. "Far as I know, it was a suicide, but if they've decided it wasn't, they should look at

Doleson. He took pictures of the body—hoping to sell them to the tabloids. And then I came along and gave him a better idea. There's a limit to how much the tabloids would pay for a shot of a small-town politico who'd hanged himself in a cheap motel room, but he knew he could milk me forever."

"He had Polaroids, right?"

"Yeah. Pictures of me going into the room, and running out, and then more pictures of the body after I'd left. And then he just sat on them."

"Until after you wrote your bogus interview."

In the rearview mirror, I could see Werzel shrug.

"The early reports said it was suicide, so I figured, what the hell. I told my editor I'd done this interview, but I wasn't sure it was tasteful, now that the guy was dead. And he fell for it. Everyone did. Got me an award—did you know that?"

"Congratulations."

"Of course, by that time, Doleson had his hooks into me," Werzel said. He was tapping the gun against his hand as if he wanted to smack something with it. "Everybody forgot about the award in a few weeks, but I still had Doleson popping up like clockwork for his payoffs."

"So what made you finally kill him?" I asked. "Did you come down planning to do it, or was that a spur-of-the-moment decision?"

No answer for a few moments, and then he chuckled.

"Bit of both, actually," he said. "I only intended this as a scouting trip. When he found out I'd gone to work for the *Trib*, he started asking for more money. 'You're getting paid more, so I should get paid more,' was how he put it. I couldn't get him to understand that when you factored in the higher cost of living in D.C., I was earning a lot less."

I wondered if he realized how odd it sounded, the idea of discussing the cost of living with your blackmailer. As if the problem were merely the amount he was charging, not the blackmail itself.

"So you just used the parade as an excuse to come down here," I said. "You didn't know Doleson was involved."

"Not until I saw him booting your mutt out of that shed," Werzel said. "I didn't know if he'd spotted me, so I went in to talk to him and as luck would have it, I found someone had left that sharp stick lying just outside the door—well, I realized it was the perfect opportunity."

"Your idea of perfect opportunity must be a lot different from mine," I said. "I'd have thought sometime when there was no one else around to see you would be a lot more perfect. Like late at night out at the Pines."

"That's where you're wrong," he said. "A place like that is never completely deserted, and if you're spotted there, you're done for. But at your parade—that's an opportunity! Hundreds of people milling all around, and knowing Doleson, a few dozen of them were bound to have it in for him. And I'm not local, so no one would have any reason to suspect I had a grudge against the guy, and I had a perfectly legit reason for being there. So I knew as long as I could engineer getting out of the shed without being seen, I'd be home free!"

"Home free, once you got rid of a few bits of evidence," I said. "Whatever possessed you to take his picture just before you killed him?"

"I wasn't really taking his picture," Werzel said. "I knew the flash would blind him just long enough for me to get the drop on him. Of course, I didn't count on misplacing the camera before I got a chance to delete the picture. That was a problem. All fixed now, though."

He smiled and patted the pocket where he'd stashed the camera.

"Now all you need to do is get rid of the original evidence Doleson had on you," I said. "That's what's in all those boxes, right?"

"He didn't have that much on me," Werzel said. "Just this."

He held up a nine-by-twelve-inch manila envelope with "Werzel, Ainsley," written neatly along one edge. Clearly Ralph Doleson had been an organized blackmailer.

"I wasn't his only victim, you know," Werzel was saying. "He had three boxes full of envelopes. I'm keeping a few that might be useful, and the rest are going into the bonfire."

"Useful how?" I asked. "Are you planning on writing exposés, or picking up where Doleson left off?"

"That depends on the *Trib*," he said. "They're setting me up to fire me—I can tell. Sending me on nothing assignments and then complaining when I don't get a scoop. And then when I do get a scoop on Doleson's murder, they take away my byline. Well, they'll see."

I wondered briefly if the *Trib*'s editorial staff were next on his hit list. But before I could ask, we reached the barn. The parking lot outside was empty, except for Michael's truck, now covered with at least six inches of snow.

"Don't pull in very far," Werzel cautioned as I turned into the parking lot. "That's far enough. In fact, turn around so I don't have to do it when I'm ready to leave."

I backed and turned until I had the car facing the exit. I did angle it to maximize the chances that he'd steer into the ditch that flanked the entrance, now visible only as a pair of slight indentations on either side of the rough track leading into the parking lot. Murderers shouldn't expect their intended victims to make it easy for them.

"Inside," Werzel said.

With Werzel keeping the gun aimed at me from a safe distance, there wasn't much I could do, so I opened the back of the Subaru, shouldered Rob again, and staggered toward the barn door. The air was so numbingly cold that even the short walk from the car to the barn set my teeth chattering. I breathed a sigh of relief when I felt the warm, welcoming air inside. Various animals stuck their heads over stall doors and I heard soft moos, baas, and whatever you call the humming noise llamas make.

Werzel looked around and shuddered as if he'd walked into a cage of hungry hyenas.

"Damn, this place reeks," he exclaimed.

Reeks? It smelled of dung and hay and the wet-wool odor of damp sheep. Maybe I was getting more used to the country than I thought. To me, the smell seemed familiar and almost pleasant.

"What a typical urban reaction to the normal, healthy smells of nature," came a voice from one of the stalls. Caroline Willner, echoing my own thoughts.

"Who the hell's there?" Werzel asked. He scuttled so he could put me and Rob between him and the voice.

"Who the hell wants to know?" Dr. Blake. Coming from the same stall.

"Meg?" Dad poked his head out of the stall in question. "Why aren't you over at the drama department? And what's wrong with Rob?"

"Come out with your hands up!" Werzel shouted.

"What the devil?" I could hear Dr. Blake mutter.

The stall door opened, and Dad hurried out. He stopped short and threw his hands up when he saw Werzel waving the gun, and was almost bowled over when Dr. Blake and

Caroline Willner rushed out and collided with him. I waited, hoping someone else would emerge—Clarence, for example, or Sammy, or Seth Early. I'd have settled for almost anyone not already eligible for Social Security. No such luck.

"Back in the cell, all of you!" Werzel snapped.

"Cell?" Dad echoed. "It's a stall."

"Come out, go in—you could make up your mind," Caroline Willner grumbled.

"This is unacceptable," Dr. Blake said.

"Look, can I put Rob down?" I asked.

"Shut up, all of you!" Werzel shouted. "Into the cell—stall—now! No, wait—what's that?"

He pointed to a door at the far end of the barn that was slightly ajar.

"The feed room," Dad said. "That's where—"

"Great," Werzel said. "Better than the stall—it's got walls all the way up to the ceiling and a nice sturdy door. Into the feed room, everyone."

"Why is this man holding us at gunpoint?" Caroline asked.

"Because he's the killer," Rob said, startling all of us.

"Rob! You're all right!" Dr. Blake exclaimed.

"No, I'm not," Rob said. "My head hurts, and Meg's holding me upside down."

"It's the only way I can carry you," I said. "Despite being my brother, you're extremely heavy."

"Ha, ha," he mumbled.

"Into the feed room," Werzel said again. "Now!"

To emphasize the "now" part, he fired the gun into the air. Or, more accurately, toward the rafters. We all flinched, and a flock of chickens who had been roosting on the

overhead beams scattered in all directions. Including
down, which was alarming to witness, since none of them
were particularly skilled at flying. Several of them made in-
terim stops on the walls or doors of the stalls—presumably
the reverse of how they'd gotten up onto the rafters in the
first place. One made a temporary landing on Dad's head
before hopping down to the floor, and Caroline had to
catch another plummeting hen. But apparently Werzel had
missed them all. None seemed hurt, though you'd have a
hard time convincing them of that—they were all running
around the rafters or the barn floor squawking as if the sky
were indeed falling.

"You idiot," Dr. Blake roared. "You could have killed one
of those poor birds."

"He's planning to kill us," I said, as I dodged another
downward fluttering hen. "Why would he worry about a
few chickens?"

"Into the feed room," Werzel said. "I don't need all of
you as hostages. I could make my life a whole lot easier if
I finished off a few of you right now. Don't tempt me."

"Come on, Monty," Caroline said. "Let's not get ourselves
shot by this lunatic."

She marched into the feed room, taking off her cardi-
gan as she went, as if she planned to settle in and make
herself at home. Dr. Blake and Dad followed more slowly,
and I trudged in last and set Rob down on the floor as gently as I could.

"If only I had my medical bag," Dad said, as he knelt
down beside Rob and busied himself with an examination.

Werzel stayed at the doorway, checking the room. Apparently he liked what he saw. Dr. Blake was standing in
the corner with his arms crossed, frowning thunderously

at Werzel. Caroline had hung her sweater up on the wall and was sitting primly on a bale of hay.

"Okay," Werzel said. "You can all stay here. Except for you. I still need you."

He was pointing the gun at me.

Chapter 32

Back out in the main barn, it was still intermittently rain-ing hysterical hens, and the other animals were growing restless.

"Let's fetch those boxes," Werzel said.

The louse could at least have given me a coat.

When I came back in with the first box, I heard raised voices coming from the feed room.

"Don't be an idiot!" Dr. Blake was bellowing.

"But we have to do something!" Dad yelled back.

"Well, that's a stupid plan," Dr. Blake countered.

"Can you think of a better one?" Dad asked.

"Will you two old fools shut up so I can think!" Caro-line boomed.

They continued to haggle loudly the whole time I was carrying boxes in from Werzel's Subaru. If they really did have some kind of plan, I wished they'd keep their voices down while they were discussing it. Were any of them re-ally that hard of hearing? Or perhaps they didn't think they could be heard over the mooing of the cows, the baa-ing of the sheep, and the squawking of the hens, most of whom had made it down to solid ground and were prac-ticing wind sprints up and down the barn floor.

Werzel had me stack the boxes on the middle of the barn floor just outside the feed room door. Yes, if I were going to burn the barn down with my prisoners locked in the feed room, that was where I'd start the blaze.

I was on the last load, with the can of kerosene perched on top of the box, by the time I finally thought of a plan. I was going to pretend to be losing my grip on the box, stop to shift it, and then drop it, whirl around, and brain him with the kerosene can. Not a brilliant plan, but the best I could think of.

I was tensing to strike when I tripped over one of the hens. The box I was carrying overturned, spilling out its contents—several dozen brown nine-by-twelve labeled envelopes.

"Get up! And pick that stuff up!" Werzel snapped.

"Okay," I wheezed, as if I'd had the wind knocked out of me in the fall. I pretended to be struggling to get up on one knee, paused as if getting my breath, and began grabbing envelopes. I noticed a familiar local name on one envelope—one of the Pruitts—and then made a determined effort not to read any others.

"Hurry up!" Werzel said.

"I'm hurrying," I said. I pretended to hurry, chattering my teeth slightly and shaking my hands to make it more plausible that I was fumbling the envelopes so badly.

I fumbled them all out of my hands when I got to the kerosene can, the better to grab it and swing as hard as I could at Werzel.

Unfortunately, I missed.

"Nice try," he said, stepping all too easily out of the way. "But I'm not—yech!"

As he stepped back, Ernest the llama spat at him—not ordinary spit, either, but the nasty-smelling greenish stuff llamas produce when they're really vexed. The horrid gob landed directly on his face. Werzel scrambled as far from Ernest as possible, reaching down as he went for a handful of hay to scrub off the llama-spit. When he stood up again, he backed up against the other side of the central aisle.

"That's it," he said. The traces of green goop still running down his face only made his smug smile even nastier. "You've outlived your usefulness. Time for—owww!"

He'd backed up against Cousin the donkey's stall. Cousin's head suddenly appeared over the stall door, and he sank his enormous yellow teeth into Werzel's upraised gun arm.

Werzel yelped and dropped the gun. I dived for it. Unfortunately, since Cousin wasn't a bulldog, he let go to try for another bite, allowing Werzel to dive for the gun, too.

We cracked skulls so hard that I saw stars. Werzel must have, too, though, and it slowed him down long enough for me to emerge with the gun.

I scrambled to my feet and backed away. After one of his police training sessions, Horace had told me how many feet away you needed to be from a running assailant to ensure that you could shoot him before he reached you. Unfortunately, I couldn't remember the exact distance—ten feet? Twenty feet? Or was that yards? All I could remember was that it was a lot farther than I would have guessed. I kept backing as fast as I could without tripping over the rampaging hens, and Werzel staggered to his feet.

"Give me that," he said, taking a step toward me.

"I don't think so." I stopped backing, put both hands on the gun, and aimed it at him.

He started backing away again. I felt relieved until I realized he was backing toward the feed room door. Did I dare shoot? If I missed, would the bullets go through the wall where they could hit Dad, Dr. Blake, or Caroline?

"Stop or I'll shoot!" I said.

He kept backing.

I pulled the trigger.

Nothing happened.

I tried again. The trigger clicked slightly.

Werzel looked puzzled.

"I could have sworn I had more bullets," he said.

"You jerk," I said. The idea that he'd held me at gunpoint for the last hour with an unloaded gun was the last straw. I switched my grip on the gun so I could use it as a club and took a step toward him.

Maybe not the smartest move. Werzel grabbed a nearby pitchfork and aimed it at me, the nasty smile returning to his green goo-stained face.

Just then the feed room door fell backward off its hinges into the feed room and Caroline Willner stepped out holding a club.

No, on closer inspection, I realized she was carrying a plaster replica of a cow's hind leg. What the—

"Take that, you fiend!" she shouted, as she cracked Werzel over the head with the fake cow leg.

The weapon crumbled, but it did the trick. Werzel staggered and fell over, and Caroline and Dad both raced to sit on him.

"Quick!" Dad shouted. "Take the pitchfork away!"

"Get some rope!" Caroline ordered.

I wrested the pitchfork out of Werzel's hand and was tying him up with a dog leash I found hanging on the wall when the door at the other end of the barn flew open.

"Hands up!"

Chief Burke and Sammy entered in a gust of snowflakes, guns drawn and pointing at us.

"About time," Dr. Blake grumbled. "Thanks, Debbie Anne. The cavalry's here."

Debbie Anne? I realized he was holding the handset of a wall phone. He put the handset back on the phone. Then he hung Caroline's sweater back over the phone and winked at me.

So that's why they'd been talking so loudly—so Werzel wouldn't hear them taking the pinions out of the door hinges and calling the police.

"These people attacked me!" Werzel shouted.

"Nonsense," Caroline said. "Arrest him for animal endangerment."

"And murder," I said. "Let's not forget murder."

"I'm innocent!" Werzel wailed.

"Shut up," Dr. Blake said, "or Caroline will smite you again."

He handed Caroline another plaster cow's leg. She scrambled off Werzel's back and stood over him, holding the leg by the hoof and tapping it gently into her left hand, as if impatient to wield it. Dr. Blake picked up the pitchfork and went to stand on the other side of Werzel, scowling with plausible menace. Werzel glanced back and forth between them, hunched his shoulders, and shut up.

Dad emerged with Rob leaning heavily on his shoulder.

"You take over, Chief," he said. "I've got to get Rob down to the hospital."

"What the hell is going on here?" the chief asked.

Dad and Rob shambled out. The others—even Werzel—looked at me. I took a deep breath.

The door slammed open again and Michael ran in, brandishing the poker from Cousin Horace's fireplace set. He'd probably picked it up in his office when he saw the signs of Rob's scuffle with Werzel. Nice to know we had the same good taste in weapons.

"Where's Meg?" he shouted. "And what happened to Rob? And what's going on?"

"It's a long story," I said.

Chapter 33

The stables made surprisingly comfortable temporary quarters. Of course, the last few hours had been so exhausting I'd have found a concrete pavement comfortable. After we gave our statements to Chief Burke, Michael and I raced back to the drama department for the one-man show. Then we spent several hours fending off questions from family, friends, neighbors, and the press—though fortunately the only reporters still in town and not incarcerated in the county jail were the editor of the *Caerphilly Clarion* and a part-time stringer for the college radio station. It was nearly ten by the time we got back to Michael's office, and people kept dropping by to see us, so in spite of the fact that both of us were tired enough to fall asleep in one of the two-foot snowdrifts the twin storms had left behind, we took advantage of a lull between visitors to pack up our essential gear, sneak out, and hike back to the stables.

"It's the last place anyone would look for us tonight," Michael said with satisfaction, once we'd put the feed room door back on its hinges and spread out our sleeping bags inside the room. We'd thrown a blanket over some of the hay bales just outside the feed room, and were lounging there, finishing our dinner.

We'd had to take a rain check on the planned steak and shiraz but we'd unwrapped a few gifts intended for various relatives—a bottle of merlot, some gourmet cold cuts and cheeses, and four different kinds of Christmas cookies. If we all made it to Mother and Dad's for Christmas tomorrow, the intended recipients would understand why we hadn't brought their presents.

Michael had brought his iPod and a tiny set of speakers, so we had nonstop Christmas carols, courtesy of the college radio station. We lit a couple of battery-powered lanterns that the Ag Department kept around to use during power outages, and we even had our own elaborately decorated little Victorian-themed Christmas tree, stolen from the German department down the block.

"Borrowed," Michael kept insisting. "We'll have it back long before they even notice it's gone. And it adds the perfect touch to our holiday feast."

We'd spread the presents for each other around the base of the tiny tree and hung our stockings on one of the stall doors.

We were lying in a comfortable pile of hay just outside the feed room door drinking the wine out of Michael's office coffee mugs and eating slices of cold cuts and cheese with our fingers, but it seemed like the most sumptuous feast imaginable. Of course, still being alive had just a little to do with my exhilaration.

"You can't imagine how I felt when Spike came running into my dressing room, covered with blood and barking his head off," Michael said again.

"And I did him such an injustice, assuming that the last thing he'd do was go for help."

"He's no Lassie, but he did the job."

I stuffed another bit of cheese through the mesh at the front of Spike's crate, by way of a thank you and Christmas treat, but he was so overstuffed from all the previous treats of cheese, prosciutto, and salami that he barely opened his eyes. It was the first time I'd ever seen Spike ignore food, and I was willing to bet it would be the last. In nearby stalls, Cousin and Ernest were still munching on an extra ration of oats. In fact, every animal in the barn was joining in the feast except for the chickens, who had gone back to roost in the rafters. We decided that for now they'd prefer sleep to food, so they'd be getting their Christmas treat in the morning.

"Just what was that thing Caroline whacked Werzel with, anyway?" Michael asked. "It looked like a plaster model of a cow's leg."

"That's exactly what it was," I said. "Dad was planning to make reindeer tracks in the yards of a few children—Chief Burke's grandson, and Cousin Mildred's kids. So he went over to the zoo a few days ago, made molds from one of the deer, and cast some plaster hooves."

"Cool," Michael said. "Even better than dancing on the roof with sleigh bells, and it's not every year you get snow to do it in."

"Yes, but when the snow forecast changed to feet instead of inches, he realized he needed more than just the hooves. He needed the whole legs. He decided that a cow was the best substitute available on short notice, and the only cows in town were in the college barn. Caroline and Dr. Blake came along to help him. They were making molds of the cow's legs in the stall, and using the feed room to pour the plaster and dry the legs. Lucky for me they were still at it when Werzel and I showed up."

"I'm sure you'd have found a way to foil him anyway," Michael said. "Or at least hold him off until I got here. Just one thing bothers me—was Doleson just a blackmailer, or do you think he also murdered that politician?"

"Drood? No idea. I gather the chief's going to reopen

the case. See if there's any evidence to prove whether it's suicide or murder."

"Time will tell, I suppose," Michael said. "And what happens to all Doleson's blackmail files?"

"Under lock and key in the chief's office," I said. I wriggled into a slightly more comfortable spot in the hay and decided it wasn't worth the effort of reaching for another slice of ham.

"Bet a few people will get a little nervous when that comes out," Michael said, suppressing a yawn.

"I imagine anyone in those files has been more than a little nervous since the news of Doleson's death got out. The chief didn't say much about what he planned, but from what I got out of Horace, I gather that except for anything that would constitute a prosecutable crime, the rest of the files won't ever see the light of day."

"That's good. Speaking of prosecutable crimes—does the chief have enough evidence without those photos Werzel deleted?"

"Werzel may have deleted them, but as any of Rob's techies will tell you, deleted doesn't mean gone for good. The computer techs have probably already got those photos back. And I'm sure they can find some traces of blood on the lens."

"Outstanding," Michael murmured.

We listened to the carols in comfortable silence for a few minutes. "Chestnuts Roasting on an Open Fire" gave way to "O Little Town of Bethlehem." I was about to suggest that we call it a night and retire to the feed room when—

"Meg! Michael! What are you two doing here?"

I started and opened my eyes to see Dad, Dr. Blake, Caroline, Randall Shiffley, Clarence, and Mother standing over us.

"Getting away from the crowds," Michael said. "At least that was the idea," he added, sotto voce.

"What are all of *you* doing here?" I countered.

"Got to replace that reindeer hoof Caroline broke over the killer's head," Dad said.

"Reindeer hoof?"

"He means the plaster cow leg," Caroline explained. "Unless the police messed with the molds, they should still be in here."

They all trooped into the feed room where Michael and I had set up our sleeping bags. Well, most of them trooped in—the feed room was a little small to hold them all. Mother and Caroline stood outside looking on.

"Is this going to take long?" Michael asked, rather plaintively.

"Only an hour or so," Mother said.

"Isn't it going to be a little difficult to make plausible reindeer tracks in this much snow?" I asked. "I remember the last time Dad did this, there were only patches of snow, and it was pretty easy to keep from making human footprints too near the reindeer tracks. But in this much snow—"

"That's the beauty of it," Caroline said. "We're going to use the boom lift!"

"I'll put the arm out level to the ground," Randall said, sticking his head out of the door. "And move it along real slow, so they can make beautiful hoof prints ten or fifteen feet out in the middle of that unspoiled patch of snow in the town square."

"And sleigh tracks!" Clarence exclaimed. "We've got a pair of sleigh runners so we can make the sleigh tracks, too!"

"That sounds like fun," Michael said. He sounded as if

he was almost tempted to help. But then he yawned prodigiously.

"James," Mother said, "why don't you do that out here?"

"Why?" Dad said, from in the feed room.

"Because Meg and Michael have had a very long day," Mother said. "And I think they would like to rest."

From anyone else, it would have sounded like a suggestion, and the plaster hoofcasters might have protested. But Mother was using the "she who must be obeyed" voice, and even Dr. Blake obediently helped pick up their gear and carry it to the far end of the barn.

"And try to be quiet," Mother said. "After all—"

"What's that?"

We all stopped and listened.

"Could that be bells?" Caroline asked.

Yes, it definitely sounded like sleigh bells going by the barn. Actually, more like over the barn.

"Who's running around with sleigh bells at this hour of the night?" Dad asked. What he really meant, of course, was, who else had stolen his idea? He dashed for the door, and the others followed him out into the snow. We could hear them stumbling about outside and shouting to each other.

"They went that way!" we heard Clarence call.

"Impossible!" Dr. Blake shouted.

"I'll have them keep it down when they get tired and come back in," Mother said. "Good night, dears."

She gave us each a kiss on the cheek and a slight but definite shove in the direction of the feed room. I noticed that our previously limp stockings were now bulging with goodies—how had she managed that in so short a time?

The sleigh bells jingled by again—this time they were definitely overhead.

"Good night, Mother," I said. "And say good night to Dad and Grandfather and Caroline and Clarence and—"

"And all the rest of the Waltons, yes," she said. "Merry Christmas to all, and to all a good night."

For once I decided to let Mother have the last word.

Duck the Halls

Acknowledgments

Thanks, as always, to everyone at St. Martins/Minotaur including (but not limited to) Matt Baldacci, Anne Brewer, Hector DeJean, Kymberlee Giacoppe, Lauren Hesse, Andrew Martin, Sarah Melnyk, Matthew Shear, and my editor, Pete Wolverton. And thanks again to the Art Department for yet another fabulous (and very Christmassy) cover.

More thanks to my agent, Ellen Geiger, and the staff at the Frances Goldin Literary Agency for handling the boring (to me) practical stuff so I can focus on writing, and to Dave Barbor at Curtis Brown for taking Meg abroad.

Many thanks to the friends—writers and readers alike—who brainstorm and critique with me, give me good ideas, or help keep me sane while I'm writing: Stuart, Elke, Aidan, and Liam Andrews, Renee Brown, Erin Bush, Carla Coupe, Meriah Crawford, Ellen Crosby, Kathy Deligianis, Laura Durham, Suzanne Frisbee, John Gilstrap, Barb Goffman, Peggy Hansen, C. Ellett Logan, David Niemi, Alan Orloff, Valerie Patterson, Shelley Shearer, Art Taylor, Robin Templeton, Dina Willner, and Sandi Wilson. Thanks for all kinds of moral support and practical help to my blog sisters and brother at the Femmes Fatales: Dana Cameron, Charlaine Harris, Dean James, Toni L.P. Kelner, Catriona McPherson, Kris Neri, Hank Phillippi Ryan, Mary Saums, Marcia Talley, and Elaine Viets. And thanks to all the TeaBuds for years of friendship.

Three characters in the book were named in honor of real people. Charlie Gardner's sister, B. G. Ritts, made a generous donation to benefit literacy at the Bouchercon auction to win the right to have her brother in the book. Robyn Smith, the Episcopalian rector, is named after a longtime reader who could recite plots, characters, and dialogues from the Meg books. About the time I was starting this book, Robyn died after a long illness, and her friend and fellow reader Ginnie Schoepf asked if there was any possibility I could mention Robyn in a future book. As luck would have it, I was just looking around for a name to give Caerphilly's new Episcopalian rector. And my friend Joni Langevoort answered all my questions about things Episcopalian—I still wish I could have seen the look on Father Rick's face when she asked him what he'd do if they found a dead body in the basement of Holy Comforter. In return for all her help, and at Joni's suggestion, I named the retired rector of Trinity Episcopal Dr. Rufus J. Womble in honor of the priest who baptized her. As always, any resemblance between the characters and the real people after whom they were named is purely coincidental.

Chapter 1

The buzzing noise woke me from an already restless sleep. In my dream, it was Christmas morning. We were opening presents and all the boxes I'd wrapped so neatly had suddenly become empty. Or worse, they contained odd, inappropriate objects, like bottles of vodka for my four-year-old twin sons and a subscription to *Guns & Ammo* for my cousin Rose Noire, who couldn't even stand to see anyone use a flyswatter for its intended purpose.

"What interesting choices," Mother was murmuring, holding up the power drill that had been in her box. Where had the drill come from? And why did she keep turning it on and off, on and off, making that irritating noise?

Just then I woke up. I fumbled on my bedside table for my phone. It was a little past 4:00 A.M. December twenty-first, not the twenty-fifth.

"Only a dream," I murmured.

The buzzing wasn't coming from my phone and I could still hear it. Not a power drill. It appeared to be coming from Michael's side of the bed, from under the pillow. Some battery-operated toy, perhaps, that the boys had dropped while Michael had been reading them *How the Grinch Stole Christmas* before bedtime?

Michael stirred.

"Blast." His voice was sleepy and annoyed. Then he sat

bolt upright and began searching frantically under his pillow.

"What is it?" I asked.

"My pager." He found the offending object, pressed something, and the buzzing stopped. A female voice took its place.

"Box fourteen oh four for the structure fire. One thirteen Clay County Road. Engine companies fourteen and two, truck twelve, rescue squad two, ambulance fourteen respond. Oh four fourteen."

I recognized the voice of Debbie Ann, the local police and emergency dispatcher. And the "oh four fourteen" part must be the time. As for the rest—

"We have a call!" Michael sounded excited and leaped out of bed.

My stomach clenched. Ever since Michael, in a burst of civic zeal, had joined the Caerphilly Volunteer Firefighters, I'd been dreading this moment. The pager had been his constant companion since he'd finished his training a week ago. And now here it was: His first fire.

The address sounded familiar, too. I had the feeling if I were a little more awake, I'd remember exactly what was located at 113 Clay County Road.

Michael dove into the walk-in closet.

"Maybe you should wake Rob," he called over his shoulder.

"Doesn't he have a pager, too?"

"You know Rob."

Yes. My brother—also a newly fledged firefighter—was capable of sleeping with a brass band rehearsing at the foot of his bed. I got up and winced when my feet hit the cold floor. It was in the twenties outside, and didn't seem much warmer inside. Not a night for running around barefoot or in pajamas. I threw on my clothes, then raced out into the hall, and headed up the stairs to the third floor of our overlarge Victorian farmhouse, where my brother lived in one of our many spare rooms.

On my way upstairs I passed my cousin Rose Noire who occupied yet another third-floor spare room.

"Rob's awake," she said. "His pager woke me from across the hall, so I woke him. I'll make them some coffee."

I could hear thuds and exclamations from down the hall. Rob was in motion. Had the noise awakened my twin sons? They'd only recently moved to separate bedrooms. Although it had been their own request and they were vastly proud of their new solo lairs, they were both still a little anxious when awakened in the middle of the night and prone to creeping into our room or each other's.

I went back down and peeked into Josh's room first. A few less beloved stuffed animals were scattered across the royal blue sheets and blankets on his bed. Both boys were fast asleep in Jamie's room, curled up together beneath the bright red bedding. I pulled the door closed to make sure they didn't wake when Rob came thundering down the stairs in full gear, including the world's noisiest boots. He'd probably have tried sliding down the banister for greater speed if the polished oak hadn't been completely swathed in evergreen and tinsel. Then when the noise died down, I slipped out again. Rob was standing in the hallway outside Michael's and my bedroom door.

"Where's Michael?" he stage-whispered.

"Here." Michael stepped out of our room, still fastening bits of gear. "I'll drive."

"Right," Rob said. "Meet you out front."

I pitched in to help Michael with his gear. Rob clattered the rest of the way down to the front hall, where Rose

Noire was standing beside the Christmas tree, holding two travel coffee mugs.

"It's only instant," she said as she handed one to Rob. "So I added just a hint of nutmeg."

"But it's caffeinated, right?" he asked as he grabbed the mug and opened the door.

"Of course." Rose Noire looked mildly affronted that he'd doubted her, but given her fondness for trying to reform everyone else's caffeine habits with odd-tasting herbal concoctions, I could understand why he'd asked.

Rob ran out. I finished fastening the last buckle holding bits of gear to Michael's belt.

"Thanks," he said, giving me a kiss. "And yes, I'll be careful."

"Where's the fire?" Rose Noire asked.

"At one thirteen Clay County Road," I said. "Whatever that is."

"The New Life Baptist Church." Michael frowned. "At least I think. It would help if they just came out and said it."

"Sounds right to me," I said. "Somewhere in town—you can have Rob look it up on his cell phone well before you need to make any turns."

"Good idea." Michael took the second travel mug, murmured his thanks, and followed Rob.

Rose Noire and I looked at each other. We knew many of the New Life congregation—particularly Henry Burke, our local police chief, and his wife, Minerva. And I'd been over at the church last night when a friend who had to work the night shift asked me to take her daughter to choir rehearsal.

We heard Michael's car start up and race off.

"It's four twenty—a.m.," Rose Noire added, as if she

thought I might not have noticed the darkness. "I doubt if there would be anyone there now."

If she was trying to make me feel better, it wasn't working.

"Which could mean the fire would have plenty of time to become big and dangerous before anyone reported it," I said. "Watch the boys, will you? I'm heading over there."

I grabbed my coat from the enormous Victorian hat rack and my purse and keys from the hall table and dashed out into the bitter cold night.

Then I dashed in again, and upstairs to add another layer of clothes.

Even though I prided myself on how quickly I could get dressed and ready in the morning, I was at least five minutes behind Michael and Rob when I set out. Maybe ten.

A good thing this hadn't happened two nights ago, when we'd had near-blizzard conditions. Or last night, when the plows still hadn't finished moving the foot of snow off our roads. All we had tonight was the bitter cold, which meant the huge mounds of snow lining the roads weren't going away any time soon.

I was relieved when I drew near the New Life Church and could still see its enormous steeple rising proudly into the air, illuminated by floodlights below—and with no flames or smoke.

By the time I pulled into the parking lot, I was not just relieved but downright puzzled. The church looked unharmed. All three of Caerphilly County's fire vehicles were there, along with four police cruisers. All their lights were flashing. The firefighters and deputies were all standing around in clumps, staring at the church, except for one larger group that seemed to be staring at something at the back of the ambulance.

I scanned the scene. No, the church was fine. Not just the church but the entire sprawling complex, including two wings and a small outbuilding, all filled with classrooms, meeting rooms, and the multiple rehearsal rooms for New Life's nationally renowned gospel choir. The floodlit façade was serene and unmarred by any signs of a conflagration.

I pulled into a parking space toward the side of the lot, about twenty feet from the ambulance, and close to where Michael and the other firefighters had parked. I was aiming to be far enough away that I wouldn't be underfoot, but close enough that I might overhear what was going on. And my chosen spot was partly behind one of the mountains of snow that the snowplows had piled up, so maybe the firefighters wouldn't notice me quite as easily.

As I turned the engine off, I saw a particularly tall fireman detach himself from the group around the ambulance and stride over toward my car. So much for my attempt to stay unnoticed. I braced myself to defend my right to rubberneck, and then relaxed. It was Michael. I opened the door and stepped out.

"The good news is there's no fire," he said.

"What's the bad— Oh, gross!"

The wind had shifted, bringing with it an unmistakable odor, like garlic, rotten eggs, and burned rubber all mixed together.

"Is that what I think it is?" I asked.

"Yes. The church has been skunked."

Chapter 2

"Skunked?" came a voice from nearby. I glanced over to see that I wasn't the only spectator. I'd assumed the other cars in the lot belonged to the firefighters, but in several of them I could see people huddled, with their motors still running, trying to keep warm. Other spectators who were more hardy—or perhaps, like me, had taken the time to dress for the weather before coming out—stood by their cars, talking in twos or threes as they stared at the church. It was one of those groups that had overheard Michael's words.

"It appears so," Michael said. "No fire, and no apparent damage to the church, but the stench is awful."

The group passed his words down to the next group, and soon the entire crowd was buzzing.

Just who were these spectators? Members of the New Life Baptist congregation? Worried relatives of other new firefighters? Surely not just curious bystanders drawn by the sirens—not at four thirty on a cold morning like this.

I could see another car turning into the parking lot, and more headlights farther down the road.

"What's happening over there?" I pointed to the crowd around the ambulance.

"The guy who found the skunks," Michael said. "Apparently one of them sprayed him right in the eyes and—oh, here's your father. Good—the EMTs don't have a lot of experience with skunk attacks."

7

Dad's familiar blue minivan zoomed past us to park near the ambulance. The sleigh bells he'd fastened to the bumpers and the door handles to amuse Josh and Jamie were jingling madly.

"Did they call him?" I asked. "Or do you suppose he's been having insomnia again and whiling away the time by listening to the police and fire department bands on his radio?"

"No idea," Michael said. "But thank goodness he's here."

We both headed toward the ambulance.

By the time we joined the cluster of firefighters and police officers at the back of the ambulance, Dad's familiar black doctor's bag was sitting nearby and he was bent over his patient, an elderly black man wearing a bulky down jacket over striped pajama pants and fleece-lined bedroom slippers. I recognized him as Nelson Dandridge, the church's caretaker.

The two EMTs had stepped back, apparently happy to let Dad take over. They stood nearby, holding wads of white gauze over their noses. Some of the other bystanders were doing likewise, while the rest merely wore pained expressions. I didn't need to ask why—I could smell the reason. Apparently poor Mr. Dandridge had taken a direct hit from the skunk.

"Try not to move your head," Dad was saying. He was holding one of Mr. Dandridge's eyes open and peering in with a small flashlight. Mr. Dandridge moaned and stopped trying to toss his head, but he began twitching his feet slightly as if some kind of motion would ease the pain.

"You'll be fine." Dad was peering into the other eye.

"But I can't see!" Mr. Dandridge whispered. "And it burns."

"Perfectly normal," Dad said. "And you'll probably feel some discomfort for the next few hours."

"Discomfort?" From his tone it was obvious that Mr. Dandridge thought the word wholly inadequate for what he was feeling.

"Let's continue the ocular irrigation for a little bit before we take him down to the hospital." Dad turned to the EMTs who, to their credit, only hesitated for a few moments before returning to their patient's side.

"'Hospital,'" Mr. Dandridge repeated. He sounded unsure whether to feel happy that his condition was being taken seriously or worried that it might be more serious than Dad was telling him. The medics had taken up posts on either side of his head and were squirting saline into his eyes.

"There's always a chance of complications," Dad said. "Skunk spray is very caustic. Occasionally you see corneal ulceration, or uveitis, or conjunctivitis. And occasionally—"

"Dad," I said. "I think you're alarming Mr. Dandridge."

Mr. Dandridge had begun moaning again and moving his head back and forth, impeding the medics' efforts.

"But all those are very unusual," Dad hastened to add. "And the best way to prevent them is for us to do a very thorough irrigation here at the scene. Try not to thrash around quite so much."

With a visible effort, Mr. Dandridge stilled his head, but his feet began twitching again.

"I'll see if I can arrange for an ophthalmologist to meet us at the hospital, just in case." Dad stepped aside and pulled out his iPhone.

"That would be Dr. Garza," I said. "Unless Caerphilly has recently acquired a second ophthalmologist."

"Doc, can we scrub him with the tomato juice now?" one of the medics asked.

"Please do," Dad said.

"Tomato juice?" Chief Burke asked.

"We actually carry it in the ambulance just in case," one of the EMTs said. "Can't say I've ever seen it used before."

"Do we have an ETA on that change of clothes for him?" one of the medics asked.

"I'll go check," Michael said. He ran off—away from the church, I noted with relief.

Two more firefighters stepped forward to help the medics by swabbing Mr. Dandridge's hands and face with rags dripping with thick red liquid. Mr. Dandridge opened one eye slightly and then closed it again tightly. I wasn't sure if he couldn't see or didn't like what he saw.

"Does that tomato juice wash out?" Mr. Dandridge asked.

"A darn sight better than the skunk odor," a medic replied.

"May we ask Mr. Dandridge a few questions while the medics are working?" Chief Burke. Standing at his side was Jim Featherstone, Caerphilly's new volunteer fire chief.

The medics nodded. With visible effort the chief came closer and squatted down at Mr. Dandridge's side.

"Nelson, it's Henry Burke," he said. "I'm sorry to bother you, but we need to know a few things."

Mr. Dandridge nodded slightly and assumed a stoic expression.

"Like why the devil did you call the fire department?" Chief Featherstone demanded.

"Because the county doesn't have a skunk department," Mr. Dandridge said. "Anyway, I didn't ask for the fire department. I just called 911."

"But you said the church was burning."

"I never said the *church* was burning." Mr. Dandridge tried to sit up and was prevented by the EMTs. "I said that I was *in* the church and that I'd been sprayed by skunks, and my *eyes* were burning. But perhaps I wasn't speaking too clearly. Those miserable skunks were still trying to spray me."

"Skunks?" Chief Burke asked. "Plural? How many? And where were they?"

"In the choir loft," Mr. Dandridge said. "And I have no idea how many of them there were. I thought it was cats at first, and I went closer to see why someone had left a whole cage of cats in the church—"

"Cage?" Chief Burke and Chief Featherstone said in unison.

"Yes, cage. And I have no idea how many of them there were in the cage. A whole swarm of them."

"Actually, the traditional term is a 'surfeit of skunks,'" Dad put in. "I was just talking to Debbie Ann—she's arranging for the ophthalmologist—and it's pretty obvious what happened. Mr. Dandridge called her to say that he thought there were intruders in the church—"

"I saw the lights on from my house," Mr. Dandridge put in. "I live just across the road."

"And as Debbie Ann was urging him to leave the building and wait for the arrival of a deputy, he began shouting 'It's burning! It's burning!' Which was a perfectly natural reaction to being sprayed in the eyes by a skunk."

"Skunks," Mr. Dandridge corrected. "Could be dozens of them."

"And of course Debbie Ann made the logical assumption that he was talking about the church," Dad concluded.

The chiefs looked mollified.

"I've sent in two of my men wearing SCBAs to check out

the church thoroughly, to make sure there's definitely no fire and no other hazards," Chief Featherstone said.

"SCBAs?" Chief Burke repeated.

"Self-contained breathing apparatus. I can lend you some if you want your men to investigate."

"Thanks," Chief Burke said. "I'd appreciate the gear—I plan to go in myself. I'm pretty familiar with the layout of the church."

"I told my men to stay away from the choir loft as much as possible," Chief Featherstone said. "At least until Eli Slattery from animal control gets here to remove the skunks."

"Did he say how soon he'd get here?" Chief Burke asked.

"No idea." The fire chief was frowning. "I left a message on his voice mail."

"Eli's a sound sleeper," one of the firefighters put in.

Chief Featherstone's frown deepened.

"Chief," another firefighter said. "We could just call Osgood Shiffley down at the service station. He's open all night, and only a few blocks from Eli's house. He could probably pop over and pound on Eli's door."

Chief Featherstone blinked in surprise. He had retired after twenty years in a big-city fire department and moved to Caerphilly to take over leadership of our volunteer force. He was still getting used to life in Caerphilly, and looked as if he wasn't sure whether to be pleased or horrified by this kind of small-town solution to the problem.

"Let's give Eli a chance to respond," he said finally. "But I'll keep the idea in mind if the delay becomes too inconvenient."

"Maybe someone should just try to take the skunks out," one of the firefighters said. "I always heard that after they spray they can't do it again immediately."

"Not what I've heard," another firefighter said.

"Besides," Chief Featherstone said. "Mr. Dandridge says there are multiple skunks. We have no idea if they all sprayed him or if some of them didn't and are just waiting to go after the next person to stick his nose in the choir loft. Anyone want to take that chance?"

The firefighters fell silent.

"So we wait for animal control," Chief Burke said.

"Do you have any more questions?" Dad asked. "Because I'd like to transport him to the hospital." Dad looked at his watch. "The ophthalmologist will be meeting us there within the half hour."

Both chiefs nodded their approval. Dad packed his bag and hopped into the back of the ambulance. The two medics helped Mr. Dandridge in. Then they conferred briefly, and one stepped into the back of the ambulance with the patient. The other almost skipped on his way to the less odorous driver's seat. Michael and another firefighter came running up.

"Wait a sec," Michael called. "We've got his change of clothes."

The back door of the ambulance opened. Dad leaned out to take the clothes, and looked around until he spotted me.

"Meg," he said. "Your grandfather's in my car. Could you see that he gets home safely?"

"Why in the world did you bring him along?" I asked. While Grandfather was hale and hearty for someone in his nineties, I didn't think either the weather or the hour were suitable for dragging him out of his comfortable bed in my parents' guest room.

"I didn't exactly bring him," Dad said. "He heard the sirens. And when I got out to the car, he was already sitting there, ready to go. No use even trying to talk him out of coming. And once we figured out there was no fire, he decided to stay in the car and sulk."

He sounded uncharacteristically exasperated—with me, or with his headstrong father? No telling. He slammed the door and the ambulance set out, steering a careful course through the growing throng of onlookers.

"Well, that might solve the skunk removal problem," I said to the chiefs.

Chief Featherstone looked puzzled and glanced at Chief Burke as if seeking enlightenment.

"Meg's grandfather is Dr. Montgomery Blake," Chief Burke explained. "A very distinguished zoologist."

"Blake?" Chief Featherstone frowned slightly, no doubt puzzled that Dad and his father had different surnames. Since he was new in town, presumably he hadn't already heard about how Dad had been abandoned at birth, adopted, and only recently reunited with his long-lost father. Then he spoke again.

"The one you always see on Animal Planet?" he asked. "Getting bitten and peed on by exotic animals?"

"That's him," I said. "And I happen to know he's particularly fond of skunks. He likes their attitude."

"I'm glad someone does," Chief Burke said. "Could you ask him if he'll help, please?"

Chapter 3

I took my time approaching Dad's van. I had misgivings about the whole idea of involving Grandfather in the skunk removal. Yes, he was a seasoned zoologist, but he'd also spent years filming nature documentaries. No documentary about skunks would be complete without showing how they sprayed their would-be attackers. And that was precisely what we wanted to avoid. What if Grandfather forgot, even momentarily, that there weren't any cameras rolling?

Dad had left the van running, obviously so the heat would stay on. Grandfather had reclined the front passenger seat as far as it would go and was fast asleep and snoring vigorously.

"Grandfather?" I touched his shoulder gently.

He started upright.

"What the hell is going on?" he asked. "Where's James?"

"Dad went to the hospital with his patient," I said.

"Well, take me home, then," he said. "Nothing to see here. So much for your big exciting fire. Should have stayed in bed and taken care of my cold."

"I can take you right away," I said. "Unless you feel up to helping us with a wildlife problem."

"Ah! What's the problem?" He unfastened his seatbelt and buttoned up his coat.

"Skunks. There are skunks in the church."

"Impossible."

"Impossible?" Couldn't he smell them? Oh—the head cold. I wasn't sure whether to order him back into bed or envy him his apparent immunity to the prevailing stench.

"Or at least highly unlikely," he continued, as he reached over and pulled the seatbelt back across his body. "They'd all be asleep."

"You mean skunks hibernate?"

"No, but they sleep a lot more in the winter. Especially when it's cold. And with this much snow on the ground, they'd probably be snowed in their dens. Sleeping the weather out. Someone probably just saw a black-and-white cat." He closed his eyes and appeared to be settling back to continue his nap.

"Well, then we've got a whole cage of black-and-white cats, and at least one of them did a pretty good imitation of a skunk. Good enough to fool Mr. Dandridge into thinking he'd been sprayed in the eyes."

Grandfather opened one eye.

"Good enough to fool Dad into taking Mr. Dandridge down to the hospital to see an ophthalmologist."

Grandfather made a growling noise.

"Well, that could be, then," he said. "And they wouldn't like it if someone dragged them out of their dens in weather like this. And if you woke them up, they'd be downright peeved."

Apparently they weren't the only ones.

"So do you want to see the peeved skunks or do you want to go back to your den and sleep the weather out?"

He reached over, pulled a tissue from a box on the floor, and blew his nose. Then his eyes lit up.

"Ah, yes!" He sniffed appreciatively a few times, like a

wine connoisseur assessing the bouquet of a rare vintage. "You could be right. Help me out of this wretched seat," he added, as he unfastened the seatbelt again.

I brought the seat back to its upright position and helped him down from the van. Then I turned off the engine, took the keys, locked the van, and scrambled to catch up with Grandfather, who had apparently regained his energy and was striding over to the two chiefs. I hoped he didn't hit an ice patch on the way.

"I hear you have a skunk problem," Grandfather said.

"Indeed," Chief Burke said. "I don't think you've met our new fire chief."

After a round of introductions, Chief Featherstone held up a piece of headgear that looked like a cross between an astronaut's helmet and a praying mantis's head.

"You can put this on to go inside," he said. "Can someone help Dr. Blake with the air tank?"

" 'Air tank'? Nonsense," Grandfather boomed. "What do we need that for? I thought there wasn't a fire."

"There isn't, but the skunk smell's pretty overwhelming," Chief Burke said. "We thought—"

"Nonsense," Grandfather said. "I've smelled a few skunks in my time. Hasn't killed me yet. Come on; let's get inside. It's damned cold out here."

With that he began striding toward the front doors of the church.

"I should go with him," I said to Chief Burke, and took off in Grandfather's wake.

The two chiefs followed more slowly, probably because they stopped to put on their own helmets and strap oxygen tanks on their backs. Another firefighter followed in their wake with an armload of some kind of gear. The half dozen gleaming white steps leading up to the church slowed Grandfather down and we all stepped together into the vestibule. It was a large entryway decorated from floor to ceiling with evergreens, gold tinsel, and red velvet bows. Along the walls were brightly colored felt appliquéd banners that looked to be the work of the Sunday school classes, each illustrating a different beloved Christmas carol. The contrast between the beautiful Christmas decorations and the overpowering skunk odor would have been funny if I wasn't having so much trouble breathing.

Even Grandfather halted with a surprised look on his face. Evidently his head cold wasn't giving him total immunity.

"Where did you say the spraying happened?" he asked.

"In the choir loft." Chief Featherstone's voice was muffled by the breathing apparatus. He and Chief Burke looked rather insectoid, and the mechanical sound of their breathing was curiously unnerving, like sharing space with a pair of Darth Vaders.

Chief Featherstone marched across the vestibule and flung open the broad double doors into the sanctuary. As he was silhouetted in the doorway, I realized that even without the mask he was rather an odd figure, with a stout, barrel-shaped body perched on the thinnest legs I'd ever seen.

We followed him and stood just inside the doorway. I was beginning to regret hastily scampering after Grandfather without demanding that the fire chief lend me my own breathing apparatus.

The New Life sanctuary always overwhelmed me when I first walked in. Not so much because of its beauty, although the soaring expanses of light oak and whitewashed walls looked particularly elegant with all the evergreen, tinsel, and ribbon. No, it was the size that always got me—the place was so incredibly huge. The stained-glass windows wouldn't have been out of place in a medieval cathedral. And at the back of the church the choir loft, looming high over the altar, could probably fit almost as many people as the entire sanctuary of Trinity Episcopal, where Michael, the boys, and I had begun going a lot more regularly now that Mother had been elected to the vestry.

The sanctuary was also lined with the Christmas carol banners whose bright, cheerful colors contrasted strangely with the rank odor that was assaulting our noses. I wondered if the felt was absorbing the odor, and whether it would be possible to fumigate the banners.

"Up there." Chief Featherstone pointed at the choir loft, which was top-heavy with great looping ropes of ribbon-trimmed greenery.

"Pretty powerful odor to be coming from way up there." Grandfather sounded dubious.

"Unfortunately, it's not just coming from up there," Chief Featherstone said. "One of my men reported that in spraying Mr. Dandridge, the skunk or skunks also appear to have scored a direct hit on an intake duct for the air circulation system."

"That's going to be a challenge for the church, isn't it?" Grandfather said. "Well, how do we get up there?"

He struck a familiar pose: shoulders back, chin high, mouth firmly set, visibly determined to push through all obstacles. If we were filming one of his nature specials, this would be the signal that he was about to jump in the tank with the sharks, crawl into the lion's den, step out into the path of the charging elephant, grasp the rattle-snake's head, or whatever other foolhardy and camera-worthy stunt he'd come up with.

It would have looked more dramatic if he hadn't chosen to pose in front of a banner filled with several dozen cotton-ball sheep with broad black pipe-cleaner grins.

"I don't think there are enough handholds to do a free climb up there," I said. "But we could get some ropes and rappel up. Or— Wait! There's no camera crew. Why don't we just take the stairs?"

"Better yet, there's an elevator," Chief Burke said. "We installed it to make sure the less spry members of the choir could save their breath for singing."

"I'm perfectly able to climb a few steps," Grandfather began.

"And so am I," Chief Burke replied. "But since it doesn't look as if we'll be finished here any time soon, I think we should save our energy. Follow me."

He set off at a brisk pace toward the back of the church and to my relief, Grandfather followed.

The elevator was so small it could only fit two people at a time, so the fire chief and I waited below while Chief Burke and Grandfather went up. As soon as the elevator door closed, Chief Featherstone beckoned to the firefighter who had been trailing us. The firefighter handed me something. Another insectoid helmet.

"In case you change your mind when we get up there," Chief Featherstone said.

"I already have." With his help, I donned the helmet. The firefighter strapped on the attached oxygen tank and I sucked greedily at air that was gloriously free of skunk odor.

"Thanks," I said.

"I'm having another brought up," he said. "Maybe we can shove your grandfather into it before he pukes."

The elevator returned and we rode up in anxious silence. My heart was beating a little fast when the door opened to reveal ground zero of the skunk smell.

Chapter 4

Luckily we peered out before exiting. The skunk cage—a huge thing, six feet square and nearly as tall—was perilously close to the elevator door. Easy to see how Mr. Dandridge had stumbled into it. Several of the skunks turned when the elevator door opened and were hissing at us. One of them appeared to be pounding his front feet on the ground. Several others were doing the same thing in the other direction, where Grandfather and Chief Burke were. Apparently they'd managed to make their way to the other side of the choir loft, where there was room to stand a lot farther from the cage.

"How far can those things spray?" I called over to Grandfather.

"Maybe twenty-five or thirty feet," he said. "But they're only accurate to about ten feet."

Since the cage was only about twelve or fifteen feet from the open elevator door, I didn't find that reassuring.

"Come out of the elevator very slowly," Grandfather said. "And hug the wall all the way to the back of the loft. Then you can work your way across to here. And if one of them turns around and lifts his tail really high, run like hell."

Chief Featherstone and I looked at each other.

"Well, let's get this over with," I said.

I went first. The skunks seemed to hiss a lot more, and

two of them hurled themselves against the side of the cage, as if trying to charge me. They became even more agitated when the fire chief followed me, but seemed to calm down in direct proportion to how far we were from the cage. Eventually, we joined the others, who were studying the cage from the safer distance of about thirty feet.

I also found myself studying the choir loft with amusement. The top half—everything that could be seen from the main body of the church below—was pristine and festooned, like the rest of the church, with evergreen, gold tinsel, and red velvet. Red velvet cushions softened the pews at the back and the sturdy wooden folding chairs in the remaining space. But at floor level, where the congregation couldn't see, I could see untidy stacks of music books and loose sheet music, trash cans overflowing with water bottles and candy wrappers, odd misplaced garments— the same sort of homely clutter that I'd seen accumulate backstage at the shows Michael directed or acted in at the college.

And how much of it, decorations and personal clutter, had been ruined by skunk spray and would have to be thrown out. I glanced back at the skunk cage.

"Someone has a sense of humor." I pointed to one corner of the cage, which was decorated with a single, bright-red stick-on bow.

"There's no way that cage came up in the elevator," Chief Featherstone said.

"I suspect it's also too big for the stairs," Chief Burke said. "Which means either the perpetrators brought up the pieces and assembled it here before putting in the skunks or, more likely, they winched it up over the front of the choir loft."

"Probably the only feasible way for us to get it down." Chief Featherstone was leaning out over the edge of the balcony and studying the beams.

"Agreed," Chief Burke said. "But I want my crime scene specialist to examine those beams first, for any trace evidence."

"You have a full-time crime scene specialist?" Chief Featherstone sounded surprised.

"Officially he's a deputy," Chief Burke said. "But he was a full-time crime scene specialist for York County before joining my staff, so when we do need forensic work, he's available."

I felt sorry for the crime scene specialist, who happened to be my cousin Horace Hollingsworth. He wasn't keen on heights, and I was pretty sure he'd be spooked at having to do forensics in close proximity to so many skunks. And if I got the chance, I'd warn him not to pass up the offer of breathing apparatus.

Just then the firefighter who'd trailed us into the church emerged from a doorway behind us. Evidently there was a stairwell on this side of the loft. I wasn't sure whether to feel relieved that I didn't have to go near the skunks on the way out or annoyed that no one had properly explained the geography before we'd come up to the loft. The firefighter began outfitting Grandfather with his own helmet and oxygen tank. Grandfather made surprisingly little protest.

"How many of the blasted things are there?" Chief Burke asked.

"I count twelve." My grandfather had pulled out the pocket binoculars he always carried and was studying the skunks through them. "Nine full grown and three half grown."

"Definitely a surfeit of skunks," Chief Featherstone said, with a chuckle.

"If you ask me, one skunk's a surfeit when it's someplace you don't want it," Chief Burke said.

"More interesting is the fact that at least one of them isn't a common striped skunk." Grandfather pointed toward the cage. "See that one that's gray and white instead of black and white? That would appear to be a domesticated skunk—possibly gone feral."

"Pet skunks aren't legal in Virginia," Chief Burke said.

"Then you'll have one more thing to charge the perpetrators with when we find them," I said.

"Which shouldn't be too hard." Chief Featherstone was becoming almost jovial, perhaps because this call was turning out to be everyone's problem but his. "Look for the guys who reek like polecats."

"Actually, they might have managed to avoid being sprayed," Grandfather said. "If they knew something about safely handling skunks."

"There's a safe way to handle skunks?" Chief Featherstone asked.

"If I wanted to move that cage without getting skunked," Grandfather said. "First thing I'd do is make a cover for it."

"What kind of cover?" Chief Burke asked.

"Opaque," Grandfather said. "Something that covers all four sides and the top. If you look close, you'll see the bottom is solid." He handed the Chief Burke his binoculars.

"So they're less likely to spray if they can't see us?" Chief Burke was peering intently at the cage. "Why is that?"

"They're smart," Grandfather said. "They know they have a finite amount of spray before they run out, and if they use it all up, it could take a day or two to replenish. And if a predator figures out they can't spray, they're dead ducks. So they're much less likely to spray if they don't see a good target. That's why they do all that hissing and foot stomping we saw. Usually they can scare off predators without having to spray."

"So we put a cover on the cage and they won't spray us?" Chief Burke said.

"Probably won't spray us," Grandfather corrected. "I'd still keep my distance. The adolescents might be a little trigger-happy."

Chief Burke nodded.

"I think I'll call Randall Shiffley about this," he said. And then, turning to Chief Featherstone he added, "Mayor Shiffley's family owns both a construction company and a moving company. Between the two of them, they should be able to figure out how to get this confounded cage out of the choir loft."

He turned back to Grandfather.

"So who, apart from zoologists, would know about how to handle a caged skunk safely?" he asked.

"Hmmm." Grandfather looked thoughtful. "Animal control officers. Veterinarians, as long as they've worked at a zoo or wildlife shelter. Maybe hunters. Domestic skunk breeders. Maybe someone who works at a pest control company, one that includes wild animal relocation in its services."

"Great," I said. "We're in a county full of hunters, where wild animals regularly stray into people's yards and houses, near a college with a graduate zoology program, and just down the street from a small but world-famous private zoo. Isn't there anything we can think of to narrow the chief's pool of suspects?"

Everyone fell silent for a few moments. We were all frowning and thinking—except for Grandfather, who had returned to studying the skunks through his binoculars. Then Chief Featherstone spoke up.

"We saw no signs of a break-in," he offered. "So it would have to be someone who knows something about skunks and has access to the church."

Chief Burke frowned, no doubt because that meant the prankster was more than likely a fellow member of the New Life congregation.

"Not necessarily," I said. "There were a lot of people at the choir rehearsal last night."

"Weren't they mostly family of choir members?" Chief Burke asked.

"Not entirely." I shook my head. "I was there. Aida Butler was on patrol last night, so I brought her daughter to the rehearsal."

"One of my deputies," Chief Burke said to Chief Featherstone.

"And I saw Abe and Rivka Sass." I was ticking off the non-Baptists in attendance on my fingers. "They're taking off on a cruise tomorrow and won't get to see tonight's concert so I assume they got permission to come to the dress rehearsal. And they weren't the only ones. There's pretty much an open door for rehearsals."

Chief Burke winced and nodded.

"What's all this about a concert?" Chief Featherstone asked.

"Everyone wants to hear the New Life choir's Christmas performance," I said. "But most people also want to attend Christmas services at their own church, and on top of that on Christmas the New Life Church is full to overflowing with just the congregation. So they always give a concert on the last Saturday before Christmas. This year, it's tonight."

"You may have to reschedule the concert, then," Chief Featherstone said. " 'Cause there's no way this church is going to be fit for human habitation by tonight."

I winced. I didn't look forward to breaking the news to Jamie and Josh if the concert were canceled.

A deputy popped in from the stairwell just behind us.

"Chief," the deputy said. "Reverend Wilson's downstairs. Wants to know what's happening with his church."

From the chief's pained expression, I deduced that he did not relish breaking the bad news to his pastor.

"Want me to go along and help?" Chief Featherstone said.

"I appreciate the offer, but maybe I should be the one," Chief Burke said.

With that we all trooped down the stairs. Even Grandfather, who looked preoccupied.

Chapter 5

When we exited the church we spotted Reverend Wilson's small, stooped frame at the bottom of the building's front steps. He looked every one of his eighty-some years, and the expression on his round dark face was one of profound anxiety—almost pain. Michael was standing just behind him, breathing apparatus pushed back on top of his head. He appeared to be hovering, as if worried about the elderly minister.

"How bad is it, Henry?" Reverend Wilson called out when we appeared in the doorway.

"Pretty bad, Ambrose," Chief Burke said.

Chief Burke pushed back his mask and went down the steps and stood talking to Reverend Wilson in a low tone. Someone had turned on all the outside illumination, including all the strings of holiday lights, which twinkled with incongruous gaiety behind them.

Chief Featherstone strolled back inside the vestibule to confer with some of his men. Grandfather and I stood on the steps of the church. I realized I was feeling a little claustrophobic in the breathing apparatus, so I pushed the mask back and took a few deep breaths. Grandfather followed suit. The air might have smelled pretty bad to anyone who hadn't been inside the church, but I found it refreshing. Grandfather seemed to feel the same, so we stood side by side for a few moments, breathing and surveying the scene below.

The church looked almost festive now, with the holiday lights twinkling and spotlights illuminating the larger-than-life plaster Nativity scene on the front lawn. You could almost imagine that the small groups of people dotting the parking lot had come to carol. Even the flashing red and blue lights of the fire engines and police cruisers seemed to add a curiously festive note.

"So tell me," Grandfather said. "Did I sleep through the part where we found out who did this stupid prank and why?"

"No," I said. "Still a mystery." Although I wondered if it was necessarily a complete mystery to Chief Burke. Quite apart from the knowledge of Caerphilly and its inhabitants he'd picked up in his years as police chief and deputy sheriff, he was a member of the New Life Baptist congregation. If the church had enemies outside or malcontents within, he probably already knew all about it.

And fat chance getting him to say anything before he was ready.

"Well, time's a-wasting," Grandfather said. "We need to get Caroline over here." His old friend and frequent partner in mischief, Caroline Willner, ran a wildlife sanctuary about an hour's drive from Caerphilly. "We could use her help with these skunks."

"I thought you were the skunk expert," I said.

"Yes, but she's had a lot more hands-on experience with skunk removals," he said. "I suppose it's a little too early to call her."

"It's a lot too early to call her." I pulled out my cell phone and checked the time. "It's only a little past five. Let me take you home where it's warm."

"I should wait till six," he said.

"You should wait till nine, at least," I said. "She needs

her sleep, especially if you want her to drive all the way up here to—"

"Ah," he said. "There she is now. She must have heard the sirens, too."

He hurried down the steps to where he had spotted the short, plump figure of Caroline Willner. Beside her was Mother, looking as tall and willowy as ever in spite of the heavy winter coat she was wearing.

"No one tells me anything," I muttered as I fell in step beside Grandfather. "I gather she came up for the holidays?"

"And to see my new marmots," Grandfather said. "We're having a special exhibit to raise funds for the Vancouver Island marmot. Fascinating creatures."

"I should have known a mere human holiday wouldn't be enough to drag her up here," I replied.

"Merry Christmas, Meg!" Caroline enveloped me in a hug as we joined them.

Mother leaned over to give me a kiss on the cheek.

"Such a relief that it's not actually a fire," she murmured. "What are Michael and Rob thinking, volunteering for something so dangerous? You'd think they were still in their twenties."

I shook my head. If she was expecting an explanation, she'd have to get it from Michael and Rob—I agreed with her.

"We need to help the fire and police departments," Grandfather was saying to Caroline. "Someone brought a cage into the church that contains twelve *Mephitis mephitis*."

"Twelve!" Caroline looked startled. "Oh, my. That's a very large family group."

"From what I've observed of their behavior, I don't think

they're all related," Grandfather said. "Are you missing any skunks?"

"No." Caroline shook her head firmly. "It's been an unusually slow season for skunks, ever since about September. Normally this time of year, between nearby county animal control officers and the private companies that specialize in wild animal removals, we'd have gotten a few injured ones to rehabilitate and a couple dozen to rehome, but we've only had three all season."

The two of them immediately drew aside and fell into an intense discussion about whether rabies, distemper, canine hepatitis, leptospirosis, or several other polysyllabic diseases were affecting the local skunk population enough to reduce the number of rescues she was seeing. I focused on whether I should tell the chief about Caroline's skunk shortage, since it seemed to give a potentially useful clue to finding out where the skunks had come from. If there were any animal control officers or pest removal experts nearby with a grudge against the New Life Baptist Church—

"Meg, dear." Mother was looking stern. "How bad is it?"

"The church, you mean?" I asked. "It reeks. They have a hideous cleanup ahead of them, and for all I know, they might have to replace some of the wood and fabric that got sprayed. I'm not sure you can ever get the smell out of something organic."

Mother nodded grimly.

"I'm glad I got to hear the dress rehearsal last night," I added. "Because there's no way they're going to be able to give a concert in there tonight. And the boys will be inconsolable. What a pity."

"We must do something!" Mother was using her Joan of Arc voice.

I felt a sudden wave of tiredness wash over me and yawned, hoping against hope that I wasn't going to be included in her "we."

"They will need a great deal of help for the cleanup," Mother said. "And the concert must go on! I will speak to the rector. And the ladies of St. Clotilda's Guild."

I was relieved. So far I'd managed to resist Mother's attempts to enlist me in the guild, which was Trinity Episcopal's chief women's organization for church and community good works. So while I probably couldn't escape being sucked into the cleanup and whatever Mother had in mind for finding the concert a new venue, at least her organizing talents would be spread across the entire membership of the guild, and not focused solely on me.

"And look!" Mother's voice held a note of warm approval. "There's the dear rector now."

I still did a double take when Mother used "dear rector" to refer to the new pastor of Trinity Episcopal. Most people just called her Robyn. Sometimes Reverend Smith if they didn't know her that well, and in a few cases "that new girl" if they were traditionalists and disapproved of her gender and relative youth. Mother had fallen initially into the "new girl" camp until she figured out that Robyn's theological stance corresponded almost exactly to her own: liberal social views and a very traditional high-church liturgy. And when Mother had discovered that Robyn shared her fascination with interior decorating, she skipped over the "Robyn" and "Reverend Smith" phases entirely.

"This is terrible!" Robyn was exclaiming. "I hear their church will be unusable for days. What a sore trial at any time, but at Christmas! We must do something!"

"Several somethings," Mother agreed. "What did you have in mind?"

"As soon as it's decent, we should start calling people," Robyn went on. "We can get together a work detail to help with the cleanup."

"I doubt if they'll have the skunks removed and the crime scene processed for several hours," I said. "You'll have plenty of time to organize the work detail."

I didn't add that given the enormous size of the New Life congregation, they might not be all that short of helping hands. Why rain on an impulse that was both neighborly and ecumenical?

"I think the bigger problem may be finding a space for their concert," I went on. "It could be a day or two before the church is habitable."

"They're welcome to use our sanctuary," Robyn said. "I'm not sure we could fit in half the people who want to come. But we'll work out something."

"Reverend Wilson!" Mother called.

Reverend Wilson, who was still talking to Chief Burke and Michael, looked up. He returned Mother's wave and the three of them headed over to join us.

"What a trial for you and your congregation!" Robyn said, taking both of Reverend Wilson's hands in hers. "All our prayers are with you, of course. And we're going to bring in some hands to help with cleanup. Have you thought of another space for the concert yet?"

"Sadly, no." Reverend Wilson looked uncharacteristically doleful. "Nor for all our other Christmas worship and fellowship events."

"I'm going to see if the college can offer some space," Michael said. "Normally at this time of year there would be any number of classrooms and auditoriums standing empty. But since the college is hosting those big basketball and debate tournaments this weekend, I'm not optimistic."

"The college has even borrowed some of the larger spaces in the county office buildings," Chief Burke added. "So that option's out."

"And apart from the college and the county, I'm not sure anyone has a space large enough for our concert," Reverend Wilson said.

"Could you have two concerts?" Mother asked. "One tonight and one Sunday night?"

"Trinity Episcopal could host one," Robyn said. "Possibly both—let me check our calendar. And we can contact all the other local churches. I'm sure among us we can find sufficient spaces for everything."

"That would be wonderful," Reverend Wilson said. "Take quite a bit of work to arrange, though."

I'd already figured that out. And since the last few weeks of nonstop holiday preparations had left me feeling stretched a little thin, I began trying to think of a tactful way to leave before a big chunk of that work landed on my plate. Luckily, Grandfather helped me out.

"Meg!" He appeared at my side, looking his usual impatient self. "Caroline's going to stay here to supervise the skunk removal. Can you take me over to the zoo? We've got to get a temporary habitat ready for these skunks."

Chapter 6

Perfect. Even if readying the skunk habitat took hours, I decided that chauffeuring Grandfather offered the best chance of seeing my bed sometime before nightfall.

"I'll be happy to take you out to the zoo," I said. And then, before Mother could protest that she needed me here, I added, "The sooner we have a place to put them, the sooner the cleanup can begin."

Mother nodded her approval and returned her attention to the two ministers. Robyn had already taken out her Day-Timer and was scribbling notes. A woman after my own heart, although my notebook-that-tells-me-when-to-breathe, as I called my giant to-do list, was currently housed not in a Day-Timer but a small well-worn, tooled-leather ring binder made by a fellow craft show artist.

Reverend Wilson was looking less glum. The situation was in hand; I could sneak off with a clear conscience.

Grandfather brooded quietly on the way over to the zoo, only breaking his silence occasionally to favor me with some tidbit of information about skunks. I'm not sure why he felt obliged to tell me that the Great Horned Owl, due to its nearly nonexistent sense of smell, was the skunk's only serious predator. And while I found it interesting that the Native Americans used skunk oil as a mild liniment or healing balm, I hoped he wouldn't repeat this information in front of Rose Noire. Given her fascination with natural remedies, I could easily see her collecting skunk spray and smearing it all over any family member who seemed in need of healing.

The zoo's night-shift head keeper met us at the gate. He looked pale and anxious as he swung open one half of the enormous wreath-laden metal front gate. I pulled my car into the small gravel circle that served as a loading zone when the zoo was open and Grandfather's private parking when it was not. A dozen live potted evergreens edged the circle, each decked with ribbon-trimmed seed balls and chunks of suet. Was this Grandfather's idea or one of Caroline's suggestions?

"Morning, Victor," Grandfather called out as he climbed out of my car. "Have you finished checking on the animals the way I asked?"

"Oh, yes," he said. "Both of our skunks are there. All of the animals are there except . . . except . . ."

"Out with it, man!"

"Cleopatra's missing."

"Missing?" Grandfather exclaimed. "How? Did someone leave her cage unlocked?"

"Who or what is Cleopatra?" I asked.

"The emerald tree boa," Grandfather said. "Unusually large specimen. Nearly seven feet long."

"Wouldn't she be hibernating this time of year?" I suggested. "That's what snakes do in the winter, right? Maybe she's just burrowed under whatever bedding's in her cage."

"It's called brumating in a snake," Grandfather said. "And yes, she'd be doing it now—she might wake up if the weather became unseasonably warm, but with the air this cold, she'd be asleep. We keep the snake house cold enough that they'll sleep, but not so cold as to be dangerous. Victor, I assume you checked the bedding thoroughly."

"Thoroughly!" Victor nodded vigorously. "And every

corner of the snake house, from drains to rafters. She's not there. And there are no cracks or crevices she could have used to escape."

"And no Cleopatra-sized bulges in any of the other large snakes, I assume," I added.

"Of course not," Victor snapped. "I'd have noticed. And we only have one or two snakes anywhere near her size."

"She couldn't get far, surely, on a night like this?" I asked.

"In the unlikely event that she got outside, she'd go dormant almost immediately," Grandfather said. "And likely die if she wasn't found soon enough."

"She wasn't lying dormant anywhere within ten feet of the snake house," Victor said. "We checked even though it was obvious she didn't leave on her own."

"You think she was stolen?" Grandfather frowned.

"It's the only reasonable explanation," Victor said. "I checked her cage last night, the way I always do when I make my rounds. She was there and the padlock was in place. And I closed the snake house door after me and made sure it was secure—I know how dangerous a draft could be. When I went 'round just now, the padlock was gone and the cage door was wide open. Someone must have cut off the padlock and taken her."

Grandfather looked grim.

"I do not like the direction these pranks are taking," he said. "First someone puts a surfeit of skunks in a highly unsuitable environment, where they are in serious danger of being harmed by hysterical people—"

How like Grandfather to side with the skunks.

"—and now someone has quite irresponsibly removed an innocent reptile from its habitat and exposed it to weather that could be injurious to its health. When will people learn—"

"Let's tell the chief." I pulled out my cell phone and dialed 911. "I have no idea if this is in any way related to the skunk thing, but he will want to know. Hello, Debbie Ann? I'd like report a missing snake."

I wouldn't have thought the words "snake" and "skunk" were that easily confused, but it took us a while to sort out the mix-up. Debbie Ann relayed the stolen snake report to the chief, along with a warning to keep an eye open for Cleopatra in the church.

"She wouldn't be the least bit bothered by the skunks' spray," Grandfather said. "And it's been a while since she was fed, so one of those smaller, adolescent skunks might look rather tempting to her. Have the chief put out an APB."

I relayed this suggestion—though coming from Grandfather, it sounded more like an order.

"I'll see what I can do," Debbie Ann said. "After all, it wouldn't be the strangest APB we've put out here in Caerphilly. But is there any particular reason to think it's in the church?"

"No," I said. "Except that it seems a little far-fetched to think that there would be two people—or groups of people—pulling animal-related pranks on the same night. What if whoever put the skunks in the church also turned Cleopatra loose there?"

"Oh, my."

Debbie Ann hung up, presumably to put out a snake alert to those working in the church.

"We must go down there and look for her," Grandfather said.

"What about the skunk habitat?"

Grandfather hesitated.

"It will only take me a little while to show Victor what I have in mind," he said finally. "You wait here."

He and Victor bustled off. I called home to make sure the boys were okay and after Rose Noire assured me all was well, I stretched out on the couch in Grandfather's office and closed my eyes. If my luck held, once they got started, Grandfather would insist on supervising every detail of the skunk habitat, and I could get a nap.

I managed an hour before Grandfather stormed back in, intent on returning to the church.

He entertained me on the way back to town with amusing trivia about emerald tree boas, including the fact that they gave birth to live young in litters of six to fourteen, and that the newborns were not emerald green like their parents but a distinctive brick red or orange color—information I fervently hoped would never be of any practical use to me.

It was past dawn when we arrived back at the New Life Church, although the sky was still gray and overcast with the threat of more snow. Its parking lot was now half full and the crowd had swelled—although I was relieved to see that most of the newcomers appeared to be men and women carrying buckets, mops, and totes full of cleaning supplies. They were all staring at the church doors, which were flung wide open to the cold.

A gasp ran through the crowd when four men emerged from the front door, carrying what appeared to be one end of a telephone pole. They held the pole above their heads as if in triumph, and the crowd cheered in response. Then they began picking their way carefully down the front steps. The rest of the pole was slowly emerging from the church door until suddenly a large black object appeared—the skunk cage, thoroughly swathed with black tarps and supported by a huge net suspended from the pole. The men had to lift the front of the pole very high indeed to drag the cage over the top of the steps and they were moving very slowly, to avoid jarring the skunks any more than they could help. After the cage, the other end of the pole lengthened until finally four more men emerged, holding their end of the pole high over their heads.

When the black-clad cage finally reached the bottom of the steps, the crowd fell back to a respectful distance as the men carried it to a waiting flatbed truck, incongruously decorated with evergreen garlands and red ribbons. No doubt it had recently been used as the platform for one of the floats in the town's annual holiday parade. The men lifted the cage onto the bed of the truck. More cheers from the crowd. Then another half dozen men raced over to assist with sliding the pole out of the loops at the top of the net while others threw tie-down ropes over the cage, darted forward to secure them to the bed of the truck and raced back to a safe distance.

"Take me over there," Grandfather said, pointing to the truck. I pulled up as close as I could without interfering with the crew.

Another cheer went up when the crew finally stepped back, presumably to declare the loading operation complete. The men began slapping each other on the back in celebration—I assumed because this phase of the skunk removal had been accomplished without additional spraying. Caroline Willner's diminutive figure appeared in the midst of the men, patting them on the arm or the back.

"Time to get this show on the road," Grandfather said. He scrambled out of my car and trotted over to the truck. Once there, he had a hasty conference with Caroline and some of the firefighters. I deduced that he was sharing the news about Cleopatra, which seemed to break up the celebration. Several firefighters dashed back into the church with serious expressions. Two of the remaining crew hopped into the cab of the flatbed truck while Grandfather and Caroline and the rest of them boarded a nearby van. The truck set off at a slow pace, probably to keep the skunks from being annoyed or dislodged, and the van followed.

As I watched the truck's stately progression out of the parking lot, Michael came up to stand at my side.

"Almost looks like another parade," he said.

"We could be seeing the formation of another holiday tradition," I said. "The annual procession of the skunks."

"Good grief—I hope not." Michael shuddered at the thought. "Please don't mention that idea to Randall Shiffley—it's just the kind of thing that would strike our mayor as a unique tourist attraction."

"My lips are sealed," I said. "How close are you to going home to get some sleep?"

"Not sure," he said. "But I don't think it can be that much longer. I should head back in. I've been helping Horace with the forensics. Now that the skunks are gone, he's got to finish up the last part of the choir loft."

He gave me a quick kiss, took a few deep breaths, and strode back toward the church.

"Meg, dear." I turned to find Mother and Minerva Burke, the chief's wife standing nearby. Minerva headed up the Ladies' Auxiliary, the New Life Baptist Church's equivalent of the St. Clotilda's Guild that Mother now ran at Trinity Episcopal. From the way they were both beaming at me, I deduced they were about to draft me for some chore. Probably scrubbing down the choir loft when Horace had finished with it. I braced myself.

"The dear rector has already contacted all the local clergy," Mother said. "And everyone is simply delighted to offer what space they can to help out the New Life congregation."

"Fabulous," I said.

"She's a wonder, that Robyn," Minerva said. "But it's starting to get dreadfully complicated—everyone's got their own program of holiday events."

"Except for the temple," Mother put in. "Thank goodness Hanukkah came early this year, so they only have their usual activities."

"And somebody's got to figure out a schedule that works everything in, and then manage it," Minerva said.

"And you're so good at that sort of thing," Mother said.

I cringed. It sounded like a tedious, time-consuming task, one that would probably require every bit of diplomacy and negotiating skill I possessed. The last thing I needed to take on in the busy holiday season. And from what I could see, Robyn was very good at organizing herself.

Of course, this was already Robyn's busiest season, and I'd already begun to worry about her. She was looking tired. Not just tired, but frayed around the edges. And Caerphilly College's winter break had begun, which meant that Michael would be not only free to take care of the boys as much as needed but eager to spend more time with them.

Most important of all, the organizing tasks would probably last at least as long as the cleanup operation and give me a perfect excuse not to go back into the New Life choir loft.

"I'll do it," I said. "Provided Robyn can get everyone to send me their calendars."

"She's already working on that," Mother said. "And she has a room you can use as a small temporary office over at Trinity."

An office? I wasn't sure why I would need an office at the church—surely this was something that could be solved in a few hours with a telephone and a computer, or even just a good supply of paper and ink. But Trinity was several miles from the stench of the choir loft, so although the office was clearly overkill, I didn't mind the idea.

"Can you give us a ride over there?" Minerva asked.

"We're going to start getting things ready for tonight's concert," Mother added.

"Which is the one nonnegotiable item on that schedule of yours," Minerva said. "The first concert will go on at eight o'clock tonight at Trinity Episcopal."

"Your carriage awaits." I opened the front and rear passenger doors of my car and Mother and Minerva climbed in.

Chapter 7

"It's small, but I think it will work," Robyn said as she opened the door to my new temporary office.

The room itself wasn't actually that small—it might have been a little larger than her own comfortable study. But it was filled almost literally to the ceiling with boxes and pieces of furniture, all of them either old, broken, shabby, ugly, or all of the above.

"Unfortunately, we're using it right now as a kind of storage room," Robyn said as she showed me in. "For stuff that doesn't fit into the undercroft."

It took me a moment to remember that what Robyn—and Mother—referred to as the church's undercroft was what plebian souls like me called the basement.

"Most of these old relics used to be in my study," Robyn went on. "I'd have exiled them to the undercroft until this spring's rummage sale, but the undercroft's already packed tight with Mrs. Thornefield's belongings."

"Mrs. Thornefield?" The name sounded familiar. "Oh—the lady who left her entire estate to the church."

"God rest her soul," Robyn said. "Yes, and we got a very good offer a few weeks ago for the house—well above its real value, if you ask me."

Clearly she wasn't yet familiar with Caerphilly's chronic housing shortage.

"But the offer was contingent on the buyer being able to move in by Thanksgiving," she went on. "So we had to empty the house, and rather than spend money on storage, we just brought all the stuff here and stowed it in the undercroft. Where frankly it's driving me bonkers."

I could understand why—Robyn clearly shared my preference for clean, uncluttered surroundings. I still couldn't get over how she'd transformed the previous rector's dark, claustrophobic study into a bright, inviting, airy space.

"But that's a problem for another day," she said, in her brisk, businesslike tone. "Here you go." She pointed to the sturdy, battered desk that turned the space just inside the door into a cramped but usable work space. The top of the desk was empty except for a telephone, a legal pad, and a few pens and pencils stuck into a cracked coffee mug with the red, white, and blue Episcopal shield on it.

"The other churches are either dropping off their schedules or e-mailing them to you," she went on. "Here's the password for our wireless router. Dial nine to get an outside line. And if you need anything, I'll be out in the sanctuary, helping with the setup. And Riddick will be in his office next door. I'm sure he'd be happy to help as well if you need anything."

I nodded, though I doubted I'd want to ask for help from Riddick Hedges, Trinity Episcopal's office manager, bookkeeper, and general factotum. Apart from the sexton he was Trinity's one paid staff member. I had no idea whether he was genuinely overworked or merely bad at multitasking and constantly feeling overwhelmed as a result, but he could generally be seen darting about the church in a state of high anxiety, wringing his hands and getting in the way of anyone who was performing actual useful work.

Robyn hurried out. I sat down at the desk and looked at the papers she had left me. First was a photocopy of the

St. Byblig's schedule for the holy season. They had a lot going on, but I noted some possible empty spaces that the Baptists might use. Next up was a schedule from Temple Beth-El of Caerphilly—obviously printed out from a computer file. Seeing it made me realize that I needed more information from St. Byblig's—the temple schedule didn't just tell me the times and locations of each event, it had a column for each available space, and included the duration, the name of the event's leader or other responsible person, the anticipated number of attendees, and any special needs, like a projector or a coffee setup. I was about to give Rabbi Grossman top marks for thoroughness until I found the Trinity schedule Robyn had prepared. It was a printout similar to the Temple Beth-El's, but Robyn had also given the capacity of each room, attached a list of the people I might need to call about rescheduling their events, and penciled in useful if offbeat suggestions of where some of the Trinity events could be located to free up space for the Baptists.

And she noted that she'd sent me an electronic copy as well. Fabulous. There was no need to reinvent the wheel—I could just take her file and add another column for each room available in the county's unskunked churches and whatever other venues we could find. Sorting the events into the available spaces would be easy.

Okay, not easy. Doable.

But to do that I'd need to run home to get my laptop. And speaking of home—I pulled out my cell phone. Nine o'clock. Not too early to call Rose Noire and check on the boys.

I called home. Michael answered.

"Jamie and Josh's residence." I could hear peals of childish laughter in the background.

"Good," I said. "Chief Featherstone finally sent you home."

"I feel guilty," he said. "Some of the guys are still there helping with the cleanup. But I got a reprieve because I spent so much time helping Horace in the choir loft. The chief assigned someone else to stay with him till the bitter end. And I do mean bitter."

"You're going to get some rest now, right?"

"I'm going to take the boys to town this morning to shop for your Christmas present."

"Hamsters!" piped up a small voice in the background.

"Sshh! Want surprise Mommy," said another small voice.

"Please convince them that I don't need any hamsters," I said. "I know the boys think they're cute and cuddly, but they're just rodents to me. And if you ask me, we have more than enough pets already."

"I've told them," he said. "Hang on a sec." I heard foot-steps, and then a door closing. "Back," he said. "Out in the hall, so they can't hear me. I completely agree with you about the hamster thing. I have no intention of tak-ing them anywhere near the pet store or any other estab-lishment where rodents of any kind can be acquired."

"Just make sure they don't talk Rob into taking them," I said. "Or Dad."

"Or your grandfather, or my mother," Michael said. "Un-derstood. I've spoken to the owner of the pet shop and the manager of the animal shelter. If anyone from either of our families shows up attempting to buy or adopt ham-sters, guinea pigs, gerbils, rats, or mice, they'll be told that all the available rodents are already bought or ad-opted and are waiting for their new families to pick them up. There will be no rodents on the Waterston-Langslow homestead, apart from those the barn cats are supposed to be dealing with."

"Thanks," I said. "I wish you'd just stay home and rest, but if you're coming into town anyway, could you drop my laptop off at Trinity Episcopal? I'm helping out with the effort to find places to relocate all the New Life concerts, services, classes, and social events."

"Can do," he said. "And don't worry. As soon as I talk the boys into some kind of sensible presents for you, I'll bring them home so we can all nap in preparation for tonight's concert."

"Good plan."

We signed off and I returned to my task. I discovered that in addition to her very detailed schedule, Robyn had given me a list of the other clergymen in town, with their e-mails, office, and cell phones.

I had been fond of Father Rufus, our previous rector, a genial soul who habitually walked about so deep in thought that he bumped into walls and had been known to get lost while traveling from his study to the pulpit. Not everyone liked the tidal wave of energy and efficiency Robyn brought to the parish, but if you asked me, they were exactly what it needed.

And it looked as if she'd already done a good half of the job I'd been assigned.

I couldn't do much more until Michael arrived with my laptop, so I decided to see how the concert preparations were going.

Chapter 8

I stepped outside my temporary office and walked up the small hallway, past Robyn's study and toward the archway that opened into the vestibule. I stopped in the archway and stared in amazement at the frantic activity taking place. I recognized several Shiffleys—relatives of the mayor and probably employees of his family's construction company—hauling lumber and tools into the main body of the church, from which sounds of sawing and hammering emerged. Matrons from the Ladies' Auxiliary and St. Clotilda's Guild were scurrying back and forth carrying stacks of prayer books and hymnals; music stands; bundles of red satin and gold lamé choir robes; armloads of holly, ivy, and evergreen; real and battery-operated candles; and the several dozen near life-sized figures from the enormous Nativity scene that for the last few weeks had occupied the space between the communion rail and the first row of pews.

I could see why they were moving the Nativity scene—no doubt they needed the space to fit in all the New Life choir members. And having it there had made navigation difficult. But it had been fun watching several of the more curmudgeonly parishioners who habitually sat in the front row either propping their feet up on the outlying sheep or hanging their canes over the wise men's outstretched arms.

Since I had no pressing reason to go out in the vestibule and didn't want to risk getting trampled by the busy masses of volunteers, I was about to pop back into my temporary office to await Michael's arrival. Then I overheard two women having a conversation that caught my interest.

"It's racial, I tell you," the first one said. "An attack like that on an African-American church?"

"Historically African-American," the second corrected. "These days they're getting pretty diverse. But I think if it was racially motivated they'd do something really nasty."

"You don't think the skunks are really nasty?"

"Only silly nasty. If you ask me, it's those Pruitts."

The other woman pondered that for a while. As did I. At one time, the Pruitts had been the self-proclaimed leading citizens of Caerphilly County, but in the last few years they'd lost most of their money and all their political power. The ones not in jail for various sorts of embezzlement had retreated to neighboring Clay County to lick their wounds and, no doubt, plot their comeback. They certainly had it in for Caerphilly. But why would they choose the New Life church as their target? And besides, however much I disapproved of the skunking, I had to admit that executing it required a degree of organization, ingenuity, and boldness that I had a hard time imagining any Pruitt displaying.

"Too clever for a Pruitt," the first woman said, echoing my thoughts. "And not nearly nasty enough."

I hoped they were wrong about that, and about the possible racial motivation as well. But of course the chief had to keep that in mind in doing his investigation. In fact, that possibility, even more than his own membership in the New Life church, probably accounted for how seriously he was taking the prank. I wasn't sure he'd normally have had Horace do forensics on what would otherwise amount to a misdemeanor.

The two women strolled off, still arguing.

As soon as they were out of earshot, I heard muffled snickers from just outside the doorway.

"Oh, man," a young male voice said.

"Yeah," said another.

"At least they have no idea," the first voice said.

"Have you heard anything about old man Dandridge?"

"He'll be fine." The voice didn't sound that confident. "Let's go look useful."

I realized that they probably had no idea I was there. The hallway was dimly lit while the vestibule blazed with light. So I crept forward a little—just far enough to see who had been speaking.

Two teenagers. I recognized one—he was short and compact, with a café au lait complexion and large, slightly almond eyes. My friend Aida Butler's nephew, Ronnie. I couldn't put a name to the other, who was tall, lanky, pale, and freckled, but if he wasn't a Shiffley, he was one of their first cousins. And I recognized the look on their faces—the eager, smiling, "Who, me?" look of someone who has something to hide and thinks he's getting away with it. If I found one of my sons wearing that look, I'd search the immediate area for broken objects and scraps of forbidden treats.

Was I looking at the perpetrators of the skunking?

But what reason could they have for doing it? I knew of no grudge that any of the Shiffleys had against the New Life Baptist Church, and Ronnie Butler was a member of the congregation.

But still. I kept my eyes on them. One of the older Shiffleys called out "Caleb!" and the Shiffley boy hurried to help him carry some lumber. I didn't recall where Caleb fit into the Shiffley family tree, but it wouldn't be hard to find out. Ronnie was standing at attention in front of Minerva Burke, as if eager to receive an assignment. Both boys' faces looked innocent—ostentatiously innocent.

I made a mental note to tell Chief Burke what I'd overheard as soon as I was someplace where I couldn't easily be overheard.

"This is impossible!"

Jerome Lightfoot, the New Life choir director, was standing in the middle of the vestibule, hands raised to the ceiling in a theatrical gesture. Since he was even taller than Michael—probably about six foot six—he'd have stood out even if the bustling crowd hadn't fallen back respectfully to give him room.

"What are these people thinking?" Lightfoot wailed. He had now grasped his hair with both hands, as if about to tear it out in despair, although I noticed that he wasn't really gripping it hard enough to muss it up, much less yank any out.

I'd seen him carry on like this last night, at the rehearsal, when one of the soloists had made some mistake undetectable to me. He'd berated the poor girl for a good five minutes, and she'd been visibly on the verge of tears. Afterward, when I was dropping off Aida's daughter Kayla I asked her if this was typical.

"Yeah," she'd said. "Especially on the eve of a concert. The worse his nerves get, the more he takes it out on us. I was up for that solo, you know. Really bummed me out when I didn't get it. But maybe losing it wasn't so bad after all. At least I don't get chewed out like that."

And Lightfoot was no better today. Everyone was giving him a wide berth, murmuring polite little apologies as they went past.

"Do I have to do everything myself?" As Lightfoot said

this he glared at the people surrounding him. Clearly, since no one jumped to his side offering assistance, everyone assumed this was a rhetorical question. Lightfoot snorted with impatience and strode toward the archway where I was standing.

Given how dim the hall was compared to the brightly lit vestibule, perhaps it wasn't entirely his fault that he slammed into me, knocking me into the wall with a thud. But he could have been more polite about it.

"Watch it!" he said, as if I were the one who'd done something wrong.

The lack of sleep combined with the shooting pains through my shoulder did me in and I lost my temper.

" 'Watch it'?" I snapped. "You practically knock me down and all you say is 'watch it'? Where the hell did you learn your manners—a stable?"

"Well, why were you standing there blocking the hallway?" he shouted.

"I wasn't blocking the hallway," I snapped. "I was just standing in it. If you weren't so hell-bent on making sure everyone saw your little temper tantrum, maybe you'd have seen me."

His eyes narrowed, and he took a step toward me, fists clenched. Out in the vestibule, I heard several people gasp, and I found myself wondering if he'd ever been physically abusive to any of the choir members. I remembered how some of the younger ones almost flinched when he came near them.

But my temper was up, and I had no intention of letting him see me cower, so in spite of the throbbing waves of pain in my shoulder, I took a step forward, too, lifted my chin, and glared right back at him. I didn't really think he'd try to strike me, but if he tried, in spite of the shoulder and the eight-inch difference in our heights, I was betting I'd come out on top. Working as a blacksmith had made me a lot stronger than most women, and I still hadn't completely forgotten what I'd learned in several years of martial arts training. Lightfoot, on the other hand, had the weedy, hollow-chested, pasty look of someone who never bothered to exercise and was thin only because he didn't really care about food.

And just now he looked a little startled, as if not used to people standing up to him.

"Hmph!" he said. Then he turned and stalked down the hall. I watched him barge into Riddick Hedges's office. Then I turned and saw that everyone in the foyer was staring my way in stunned amazement. Or maybe in accusation—had I just spoiled everyone's holiday mood?

"I can't wait to find out," I said. "Which one of us gets the title role in *How the Grinch Stole Christmas*."

Not much of a joke, but it broke the tension. People laughed far more than it deserved, and a few even applauded.

Minerva Burke appeared at my side.

"You go, girl," she said. "I think he'll get the part, but you deserve a medal. Not many people stand up to old Bigfoot."

"Probably just as well, since that means he doesn't dislocate that many people's shoulders." I was trying to move my arm—fortunately, the left arm—and feeling a little faint from the resulting waves of pain.

"You're serious, aren't you?" Minerva said.

I was fumbling in my pocket for my cell phone.

"I'm calling Dad," I said.

Chapter 9

I pulled out my cell phone, but I didn't want to move my left arm, and trying to hold the cell phone and dial it with my one good hand wasn't working too well.

"Here," Minerva said, taking it out of my fingers. "Let me do that. Let's get you sitting down someplace. Ronnie! Virgil! Come help Ms. Meg!"

I had to admit, it was nice to be half carried into my temporary office and sit back with my eyes closed while Minerva called Dad and ordered him to come over and see to me.

Next door we could hear occasional bellows from Lightfoot, interspersed with the nasal whine of Riddick's voice.

With her phone call made, Minerva pulled over a convenient box for me to put my feet on and another to sit on herself. The two of us, by unspoken agreement, fell silent and tried to figure out what all the fuss next door was about.

"—very sorry," Riddick was saying. "But it's just not practical to remove the altar rail and the first few rows of pews just for the concert—"

"Then how am I to give a concert in this wretched little sty!" Lightfoot bellowed.

"Some of the choir will just have to stand in front of the communion rail," Riddick went on.

"I was told we'd get complete cooperation!" Lightfoot shrieked.

They went back and forth that way for several minutes.

"I confess," Minerva said. "I won't be sorry to see him go."

"Go? Lightfoot? You mean he's leaving?" The news was almost as good as a Percocet.

"Well, he doesn't know it yet," she said. "And I'd appreciate it if you'd keep this to yourself, but yes. We voted not to renew his contract. Unfortunately, it doesn't run out till the end of August, so that means we still have to suffer with him for another eight months. But at least we know there's an end in sight."

"You think maybe he knows?" I asked. "And that's why he's in such a bad mood?"

"I haven't noticed that he's been in a particularly bad mood—for him," she said. "This is pretty much what he's like most of the time."

"Meg, dear." Mother. She swept in, visibly alarmed. "Are you all right?"

"Possible dislocated shoulder," I said. "And I doubt if I have a temperature," I added, as she put a hand to my forehead.

"You never know," she said. "Your father should be here very shortly."

Just then I saw another figure pass the open door, no doubt heading for Riddick's office.

"Who was that?" Mother asked, glancing over her shoulder.

"Barliman Vess," I answered.

Mother uttered a small sigh of exasperation.

"Mr. Vess is a member of our vestry," I added to Minerva. "An elderly retired banker, a lifelong Trinity parishioner, and Mother's particular bête noire."

"He's not my bête noire, dear," Mother murmured. "He has good intentions, even if he is sometimes a little trying."

"This is ridiculous!" Vess's high, cracked voice carried easily through the wall, and probably as far as the vestibule.

"I can handle it," Riddick said.

"We've already gone to considerable expense to accommodate your unreasonable demands," Vess said.

Mother sniffed dismissively.

"Likes to think he's the watchdog over all of Trinity's financial and administrative affairs," she murmured. "As if the rest of us were incapable of grasping it all."

Vess and Lightfoot began bellowing back and forth at each other. I spotted Riddick slipping down the hall, looking back over his shoulder with an angry look on his face. Then he stopped, closed his eyes, took a couple of deep breaths, moved his lips slightly—whether praying or cursing I couldn't tell—and resumed his customary calm if slightly anxious expression.

"That man!" Mother muttered.

I waited to hear whether she was talking about Vess, Riddick, or Lightfoot, any of whom could possibly have provoked her displeasure.

"I hate to speak ill of someone," she went on. "Especially at this time of year—but Ebenezer Scrooge has nothing on him."

That would be Vess.

" 'A tightfisted hand at the grindstone, Scrooge!' " I quoted. Thanks to Michael's annual one-man dramatic readings of *A Christmas Carol,* I could quote Dickens with the best of them. " 'A squeezing, wrenching, grasping, scraping, clutching, covetous, old sinner! Hard and sharp as flint, from which no steel had ever struck out generous fire; secret, and self-contained, and solitary as an oyster.' "

"Precisely," Mother said. "If he posts one more notice

asking who used the church office phones to make an unauthorized ninety-cent long-distance call to California, I may have words with him! And to make it worse, he has the manners of a troll."

"What's he done?" Minerva asked.

"Just last week he tried to have the cleaning service fired for not doing a good enough job," Mother said. "And if you ask me, they were doing a perfectly adequate job."

Coming from Mother that was high praise indeed— her "perfectly adequate" was equivalent to someone else's "fabulous." From Minerva's nod, I could tell she understood this.

"What he really wanted," Mother went on, "was to get rid of the cleaning service altogether, to cut expenses, and have the ladies of St. Clotilda volunteer to do the cleaning. We straightened him out on that notion."

"I should think so," Minerva exclaimed.

"Wasn't it him who tried to get the twelve-step groups banned from using the church building?" I asked.

"Yes," Mother said. "He claimed they weren't leaving enough change to cover the number of coffee packets they used during their meetings. I realize that in these difficult times we all have to keep expenses down, but to begrudge a few pots of coffee to people who are struggling to rebuild their lives!"

"I completely agree," Minerva said. "If he keeps it up, tell him that the Baptist Ladies' Auxiliary would be happy to donate as much coffee as the twelve-step groups could possibly need."

"I think we've already squelched him on that one," Mother said. "But thank you. And perhaps if I could mention your offer, it would shame him into abandoning that particular crusade."

"Please do," Minerva said.

We listened for a few more moments as Vess and Lightfoot bellowed at each other. Vess, predictably, was complaining about the unnecessary expense and trouble the choir was causing, while Lightfoot was bellowing that Vess was a philistine with no appreciation of art. They weren't even arguing with each other, really, just venting.

"If Josh and Jamie were behaving like that, I'd put them both in a time-out," I said.

"One of us should go in and break it up," Minerva said, with a sigh.

"Or both of us," Mother said, with a matching sigh.

"Let's hold off for a few minutes," I said. "At the rate they're going, I think there's a good chance that they'll kill each other off, like the cats of Kilkenny."

Mother and Minerva burst out laughing.

"Besides," I added. "The choir can't begin rehearsing until the Shiffleys have finished whatever it is they're building, so maybe it's a good thing someone's keeping Mr. Lightfoot busy."

"True, dear," Mother said. "And it really isn't funny: You should have seen that wretched Mr. Lightfoot carrying on! He was actually throwing things around in the sanctuary!"

"The Shiffleys' tools and your vases and hymnals," Minerva said. "It's a disgrace!"

Then they looked at each other and burst out giggling again.

"Kilkenny cats!" Minerva spluttered.

"Well, obviously things can't be so bad." Dad appeared in the doorway, holding his trusty medical bag. "What seems to be the trouble?"

Dad agreed with my diagnosis of a possible dislocated shoulder, and he insisted on bustling me down to the Caerphilly Hospital. We nearly came to grief before we even left the parking lot. His van hit a patch of black ice and skidded to a stop against a mound of snow and his medical bag, which unlike us was not strapped in, launched itself out of the backseat into my shoulder, sending more waves of pain through my arm. By the time we reached the hospital, I was mutinous and refused to be taken down for X-rays until they gave me a painkiller of some kind.

Dad and the orthopedic surgeon whiled away the time waiting for the results by trading stories of dislocated joints they had seen in their careers. Since most of the stories involved ghastly complications rather than boringly successful outcomes, after the fourth or fifth story I told them what I thought of their bedside manner and shooed them out of my cubicle.

I was overjoyed when the X-rays finally showed that my shoulder wasn't dislocated. Very badly bruised, but either it hadn't been dislocated in the first place, or it was only partially dislocated and something had popped it back in. My money was on our close encounter with the snow mound in the parking lot.

Dad and the orthopedist were more restrained, cautioning me that there could still be muscle and tendon damage and insisting on an MRI. I found myself wondering, briefly, if they were disappointed that they weren't getting a chance to perform a reduction on me, which I had by now figured out was a euphemism for forcibly shoving my dislocated shoulder back into place. But I had to admit that it was a relief when the MRI showed no serious damage.

Of course, my shoulder still hurt. And I would still need to wear a sling until the abused muscles healed a bit. And even in a small hospital, with Dad urging everyone on, the whole thing took quite a long time. Luckily, while I was waiting my turn in the MRI machine. Michael and the boys dropped by with my laptop. The boys were a little worried until I demonstrated that I had no visible wounds, after which they relaxed and began to explore all the exciting new opportunities for mischief that the ER provided. When they began fighting over who got to ride in the wheelchair and who had to push, Michael and I decided it was time for him to whisk them away to resume their Christmas shopping mission. I whiled away the long wait by finishing up a provisional schedule for relocating all the various church services, classes, pageants, rehearsals, dinners, brunches, and other events. It was a little annoying, having to type one-handed, but still—without my laptop and my cell phone, this would have been an impossible feat.

Of course, in a world without laptops and cell phones, Robyn would have had to find someone else to do the organizing after I'd gone to the hospital. And I could have had whatever pain meds Dad was willing to prescribe, instead of asking him for something that wouldn't muddle my mind.

When I emerged from the MRI, I found that Dad and the orthopedist and several of the nurses had decided to go caroling up and down the halls of the hospital as soon as they finished treating me.

"You're welcome to join us," Dad said.

"I have a few things to do back at Trinity," I said. "And then I think I'll go home and rest."

So Dad took me back to the church, singing "Good King Wenceslas" with great enthusiasm, although he did interrupt himself after nearly every verse to see how I was feeling.

Chapter 10

I arrived back at Trinity with my left arm in a sling, feeling extraordinarily cheerful thanks to the tranquilizer Dad provided, which didn't do much to relieve the pain in my shoulder, but did make me feel curiously detached from it.

I continued to feel cheerful, mellow, and detached for two hours as everyone I talked to picked holes in my draft schedule. In short order I made not one but three complete revisions.

Along the way, I developed a whole new sense of how hard Robyn's job was. Her study saw a steady stream of visitors. Most of them, from the small bits I could overhear, were well-meaning volunteers who wanted her to make some decision that I'd have made myself. Her voice carried better than most of theirs, so I had a chance to appreciate her patient, gentle attempts to empower them to make their own decisions. Me, I'd have been tempted to just shout "I don't care! Figure it out yourself!"

At least every ten minutes either Lightfoot or Vess would appear in her office. Sometimes both at once. I never had any trouble overhearing every word they said. Usually they were complaining about each other, although both occasionally took a few verbal jabs at the Shiffleys doing the construction. Randall Shiffley showed up a couple of times to repeat that if everyone would stop bothering him and his crew they could have the construction finished by

three o'clock when the choir practice was due to start.
And Minerva Burke showed up a few times to calm down
Lightfoot, who kept declaring the concert off. I finally
decided he was serious, and apparently so did Minerva.
A few minutes later, Reverend Wilson arrived and told
Lightfoot off in the tone of voice he usually reserved for his
summer revival hellfire and damnation sermons.

"And if you still feel unable to continue," the reverend
boomed, in tones people could probably hear in the next
county. "I'm sure Sister Burke here would be happy to
take your place. The concert must and will go on!"

After that Lightfoot made himself scarce for a while.

Although after both Reverend Wilson and Robyn left,
he and Vess both showed up again and turned their wrath
on poor Riddick. After his first encounter with them, the
poor man actually ducked into my office to hide from
Lightfoot, only to be so startled at finding me there that he
jumped and hit his head on the corner of a broken-down
five-drawer wooden file cabinet.

I jumped up to make sure he was all right, and closed
my office door partway to conceal him.

"Why do they have to be here?" he whispered. He was
holding the heel of his hand to the brow ridge just above
his right eye, and I remembered Mother saying that he
was a martyr to migraines.

"Well, Robyn did offer Reverend Wilson the use of Trinity for the concert," I said. "And it's a wonderful chance to
show how well the church looks for the holiday. But I
think you have a point. Mr. Lightfoot doesn't seem to appreciate our hospitality, so while I'm rearranging, I'll see
if I can move any other events he's involved in to other
churches. The Catholics have a big sanctuary. Maybe I could
schedule him there."

Riddick gave a weak smile and closed his eyes. I went back to my work, and he stood there, motionless, until the hallway outside grew silent again. Then he slipped out without saying anything.

Would the church become more peaceful when the construction was finished and music took the place of hammering? Probably not. From what I'd seen at the last rehearsal, Lightfoot wouldn't let them sing more than a few bars without cursing at them. Although at least he'd be yelling from farther away, not next door.

And waiting for the chief to call me back was also wearing on my nerves. I'd called him shortly after arriving back at the church to tell him what I'd overheard. Of course I got his voice mail. Not knowing who might be around when he played it back, I'd made my message noncommittal.

"Hi. It's Meg Langslow. I overheard something this afternoon that might be relevant to the question of who pulled off that prank. Would be happy to fill you in at your convenience."

Was the investigation going so badly that he had no time to return my call? Or so well that my small clue was of no importance? Every time the phone rang, I had to remind myself not to sound cranky—it wasn't my callers' fault that they weren't the chief.

But it was their fault that they weren't all being as organized and cooperative as they could be. Randall Shiffley strolled into my temporary office about the time my meds were wearing off, to hear me barking into the phone at the secretary of the Methodist church.

"I said I'll fix the problem!" I said. "But until further notice, the schedule stands!"

I hung up and looked at Randall, fully expecting him

to make some unreasonable request or point out some aspect of my schedule that was less than perfect. He held up both hands as if surrendering.

"I just stopped in to see how you're feeling," he said.

"Cranky," I answered, with a sigh. "And rude. That was rude. I shall probably feel obliged to apologize to Mrs. Dahlgren later."

"What's the old biddy on about now?" Clearly Randall knew Mrs. Dahlgren. He crossed his arms and leaned against the massive Victorian breakfront that formed one boundary of my office space.

"She tells me they can't possibly host the Baptist Ladies' Auxiliary potluck dinner tonight because they don't have enough bathrooms."

"You could tell her that you'll ask all the Baptists to be patient while they wait in line," he said.

"I did," I said. "I also told her if the lines got really bad we could arrange for people to pee next door with the Unitarians."

"I reckon she wasn't too pleased with that idea." He was smothering a chuckle.

And he was holding a large hammer. Evidently he'd been helping out with whatever the Shiffley Construction Company had been doing in the sanctuary. Construction. An idea started forming in my mind—much more slowly than usual, thanks to the meds, but still forming.

"Just what have you guys been building, anyway?" I asked.

"A stage to fill in the area behind the altar rail," he said. "And risers for the choir to stand on. You want to come see?"

"Later," I said. "Do you have any of those construction site portapotties you could take over to the Methodist church?"

"We do," he said. "It's a slow season for construction right now, so they're not much in demand. But if you think Mrs. Dahlgren is upset now—"

"Deliver half a dozen of them," I said. "I'll ask Mother to send over some of the ladies of St. Clotilda's with some wreaths and tinsel to make them look a little more festive. Can you do that?"

"I can," he said. "If you really think—"

"HALLELUJAH! HALLELUJAH!"

We both jumped as the opening of Handel's "Hallelujah Chorus" rang out from down the hall in the sanctuary.

We listened for a few bars, and then the music abruptly stopped. We could hear angry voices instead. We both remained silent, straining to hear what was being said. Eventually Lightfoot's voice came through more clearly.

"I said get out and stay out!"

"Only Lightfoot abusing the choir," I said.

"They should get rid of him before he ruins that choir," Randall said.

"He's not a good choir director?"

"Not that I'm an expert," Randall said. "But I've been talking to some people who are. He's got good credentials from a good school. Decent knowledge of music, they say. But he's a train wreck with people. If you ask me, they were in too much of a hurry to hire when their old choir director died so suddenly. Any day now, New Life Baptist Church is going to start leaking members like nobody's business."

I thought about what Minerva had said. I couldn't repeat what she told me, but . . .

"I wouldn't worry about it," I said.

"You know something I don't know?"

"No," I said. "But do you really think the Baptists haven't noticed? Besides—"

"You need to do something about this!" Barliman Vess erupted into my office. "That man has taken over the sanctuary! He's not scheduled to start his rehearsal until three! It's only half past two."

He shook a copy of the master schedule in my face.

"We were supposed to have it for the riser construction until three," Randall said. "But we finished early, so I told Mr. Lightfoot he could get started if he wanted to."

"But that's not on the schedule!"

"Technically, no." Randall's voice sounded a little less calm than usual. I suspected Vess had already been getting on his nerves during the construction. "But since—"

"Hold on!" I swiveled back to my laptop and with a few keystrokes, changed the schedule so the choir rehearsal began at two thirty. Then I swiveled back.

"As duly appointed schedule coordinator, I hereby issue the latest revised schedule," I said. "Choir practice begins at two thirty. Would you like a clean copy?"

I pointed to the printer. Vess shook his head.

"Anything else?" I asked, in my sweetest voice.

Vess frowned down at the paper in his hand, obviously still angry, but curiously unable to argue now that Lightfoot's trespass had been legitimized. I found myself noticing all the liver spots on his bald head and how the skin on the back of his hands was crinkled like tissue. I suddenly felt very sorry for Vess. He'd been retired for at least twenty years and a widower for almost that long. Maybe fussing over the fine details of Trinity's finances and organization were the only things that kept him going.

"Hmph!" he said. He glared at me, and then at Randall for a few seconds, before stomping out.

"I guess he blames you for messing up the schedule," I said. "Though I doubt if he's too pleased with me, either. Mother will get an earful."

"Oh, Mr. Vess already had it in for me," he said. "Kept coming up and complaining about how long our construction was taking. 'How long can it take to nail down a few boards?' And sneaking up behind us to see if we're damaging any of the original 1870s woodwork. And in case you didn't have time to notice, we're not just nailing down a few boards."

"I can see that," I said.

"We designed and built a removable stage and a set of risers that are custom fitted to the space here at Trinity," Randall said. "With all due respect to Mr. Vess, I can appreciate a fine bit of craftsmanship when I see it, and that's why I wanted a solution that didn't require driving a single nail into your beautiful hundred-and-fifty-year-old oak woodwork. After tonight's concert, it won't take more than half an hour to disassemble it so y'all can have services tomorrow morning as usual, and then after the last church service we'll put it back up again for tomorrow night's concert. If there's a single scratch or nail hole I'll personally make it good as new. And Trinity gets to keep the whole thing, so if you ever need a stage, with or without risers again, you've got one. Your minister's pleased as punch—what's Vess's problem? He's been riding us all day."

I couldn't remember the last time I'd seen Randall this provoked. My sympathy for Vess was fading.

"Robyn's sane," I said. "Vess, not so much. If the congregation took a vote on who they most wished would get fed up with Trinity and join some other church—any other church—I'm betting Vess would win, hands down."

"Just don't sic him on First Presbyterian," Randall said. "Sorry. Didn't mean to rant at you. I think I'll make myself scarce before he comes back."

"And as soon as I send out what I fondly hope is the final schedule, I'm going home to shower and rest," I said. "So maybe I'll be able to enjoy some time with Michael and the boys when they get back from Christmas shopping. Don't forget those portapotties."

"I won't." He stood up, nodded, and strolled out.

I scanned the schedule and made one more change. Not much I could do about today, but tomorrow? Lightfoot had a couple of hours' worth of rehearsals with his soloists scheduled for Sunday afternoon. I swapped them into the Methodist church, so Mrs. Dahlgren could enjoy his company for a while.

I sent out a group e-mail with the new schedule, sent a copy to the printer, saved the file, and packed up my things. I made sure I had the meds Dad had provided, but decided to wait until I got home to take more of them. Detachment was great for coping with recalcitrant people, but my current alert—if cranky—state seemed better for dealing with snowy driving conditions.

Just as I entered the vestibule, the choir started another song.

"There's a star in the east on Christmas morn," sang a soaring soprano soloist.

"Rise up, shepherds, and follow," answered the choir.

I stepped into the sanctuary and perched on a pew to listen, just for few minutes. The soloist and choir both sounded wonderful to me, but from Mr. Lightfoot's gestures and facial expressions, I could tell he wasn't happy.

Just as the soloist was beginning the third verse, my cell phone rang. It wasn't loud, and I had the ring tone set to a single chime, which was not as intrusive as the loud and intricate tunes so many people seemed to favor, but Lightfoot turned and glared at me as if about to shout "Off with her head."

I pressed the answer button before the phone rang a second time and ran out into the vestibule to take the call. In fact, for good measure, I ran all the way outside the church.

"Meg, dear?" Mother. "Is this a bad time?"

Chapter 11

I was tempted to lie and say I was busy, before she had a chance to ask whatever she was calling me to ask. But I felt a little superstitious about uttering falsehoods on the steps of a church.

"Not a bad time for me," I said. "Mr. Lightfoot may yet kill me for interrupting his choir practice."

"Mr. Lightfoot should be very grateful to you that he has a place to practice," Mother said. "Speaking of finding places . . ."

I winced. I could already see my latest carefully arranged schedule collapsing like a house of cards. I leaned against one of the bright red double front doors, brushed a aside a stray frond of spruce from the wreath that was trying to tickle me, closed my eyes, and braced myself.

"We need a place to hold a sewing bee," she said. "The cleaning company says there's nothing they can do about the seat cushions that were sprayed by the skunks. So we're going to make all new ones."

"Do we have to do it now?" I asked. "And who's 'we'?" I hoped she hadn't forgotten how meager my sewing skills were.

"The New Life Ladies' Auxiliary and St. Clotilda's Guild," Mother said. "And yes, we need to do it now because there's a chance we can get the church back in operation for Christmas Day services. If the cleaning service manages to get the smell out of the heating system and Randall's crew can finish replacing the wood that soaked up the scent and we can handle the cushions, the church will be as good as new!"

I was working on a tactful way of suggesting that once the cleaning service got the ducts clean, the Baptists could have their services back with folding chairs instead of new pews and upholstery, and maybe the sewing bee could wait until after Christmas. Suddenly the church's outdoor decoratives came on, outlining every tree, bush, lamppost, and fence post with fairy lights. No similarly sudden illumination flooded my brain—only a mild curiosity about whether someone had just turned them on or whether they were on a timer. Then Mother spoke again.

"We were thinking of using your library, dear. If that's okay with you. It's big enough, and we wouldn't really be in your way."

It sounded like such an easy solution. True, I'd resisted offering the library when I was compiling my schedule, in no small part because Michael and I were still very much enjoying having it to ourselves. We'd lent the space, along with our barn, to the county for several years during the financial crisis, when Caerphilly had lost possession of its library building and needed someplace to house the books. But now that we had it back, I wasn't keen on making it a public space again.

"And of course we'd be happy to watch the boys if you and Michael need to do a little last-minute Christmas shopping."

Mothers of twins can be induced to do many things with an offer of free babysitting.

"Fine," I said. "But just the library—not Michael's office, which is where we've hidden all the Christmas presents.

Except for yours, which are somewhere else entirely and already wrapped," I added.

"Of course, dear." Mother was almost purring. "I wouldn't think of peeking. I'll be over in half an hour or so to make sure everything's ready."

"Surely you weren't planning to start tonight?" I asked. "Won't a lot of people want to be at the concert?"

"We're starting bright and early at eight tomorrow," Mother said. "For those who aren't attending early services, of course; they can come later."

"Why don't I just make sure all our stuff is out of the library when I get home?" I asked. "I'll be there soon."

"That would be perfect, dear," Mother said. "And I'll see to the decorations," she added.

" 'Decorations'? Mother, you already decorated our house weeks ago—remember?"

"Yes, dear," she said. "But that was weeks ago. Things might need a little sprucing up. And back then I was just decorating for you—not for the Ladies' Auxiliary and St. Clotilda's. See you soon."

With that she hung up.

I wasn't sure I wanted to find out what feats of decorating Mother was capable of when she was trying to impress not one but two church women's groups. At least between my bruised shoulder, my job as location tsarina, and most important, Michael and the boys, I'd have plenty of very valid excuses to avoid getting involved if Mother tried to enlist my help.

I ducked back inside. In my haste to remove my offending phone from choir practice, I'd left my purse, my coat, and the tote containing my laptop in the pew where I'd been sitting. I slipped into the sanctuary and collected my gear. Lightfoot was so busy yelling at the baritones for sloppy enunciation that he didn't notice my arrival.

As I was about to leave, I realized I hadn't collected the hard copy of the latest schedule from my printer. I plodded down the dark little hallway to my temporary office. I unlocked my door, went in, and closed it after me, because I suddenly felt a little light-headed and didn't want anyone to see me wilt into my desk chair.

Definitely time to go home and rest. Past time. And maybe a good time to take that next dose of the tranquilizer after all. I set down my tote and began to rummage through it one-handed for the water bottle I usually kept there.

Then I heard a noise from the office next door. From Riddick's office. Which had been closed when I walked down the hall, with no line of light under the doorway.

I was opening my mouth to ask who was there when it occurred to me that maybe someone who was sitting in an office with the lights off might be doing something that wasn't on the up-and-up.

I put down my tote and the water bottle and tried to stand up quietly. I was taking slow, careful steps toward the door—

And tripped over my purse. I twisted to avoid landing on my shoulder, and ended up knocking over the office chair, which landed with a noisy clatter on the linoleum floor. I scrambled up as quickly as I could, but I heard soft, rapid footsteps going down the hall.

By the time I opened the door, the hallway was empty.

And now Riddick's office door was standing open.

I walked in.

At first I thought that Riddick had made a clumsy attempt to decorate his office for Christmas. Then I realized that the decorations piled on his desk, his shelves, and his floor were actually church castoffs—broken angels, half-melted candles, an ancient fly-specked Santa. All the worn-out items Mother and the ladies of St. Clotilda had winnowed out and marked for donation or disposal when they'd decorated the church. Was he keeping the junk out of some sense of thrift or feeling of nostalgia? Or was it merely, like so many other things at Trinity, a case of Riddick just not yet getting around to dealing with the detritus?

Maybe the mounds of paper covering every horizontal surface were similar signs of neglect rather than busyness. It would take someone more familiar with them—perhaps only Riddick himself—to tell if anyone had been messing with them. But I did notice that his computer was on. Would he have gone home and left it on? Many people did, of course. If I were Riddick and knew Barliman Vess might come snooping around at any time, alert to every nanowatt of waste, I wouldn't, but maybe Riddick was used to Vess's nagging.

I stepped inside to see what was on the screen. It appeared to be the alumni directory for a prestigious school of music. Someone had done a search on the name "Lightfoot." I scrolled down to see the results. Only one Lightfoot, and he was Arnold, not Jerome. The picture didn't look right, either—the choir director was a tall, skinny, light-skinned African-American. This Lightfoot was a short, bespectacled white guy with thinning blond hair. About the only similarity was their age—at a guess, they were both in their forties.

Of course, the fact that our Lightfoot hadn't showed up didn't necessarily mean anything. I wondered if the University of Virginia, my alma mater, had an online searchable directory—one accessible to anyone who went to the alumni Web site. If they did, they certainly wouldn't have a recent picture of me. Maybe Lightfoot just hadn't signed up for the directory. It seemed largely calculated to let students and alumni look for jobs and network with people who might be interested in musical collaborations and jamming. Lightfoot had a job, and I didn't see him as the collaborating type.

Up until a few weeks ago I wouldn't have had the slightest idea how to extract any more information from Riddick's computer, but it had occurred to me that given how precocious Josh and Jamie were, all too soon they would start playing with our computers and getting into who knows what sort of trouble. One of the perks of Rob owning a computer game company was access to expert tech support whenever we needed it. Rob had been happy to send over someone from his help desk to set up parental controls on all our computers and to teach me a few basics on how to check up after the boys—knowledge I hoped I wouldn't have to use for a few more years.

As a result, I knew how to find the list of other pages this browser had recently visited. It was a moderately interesting list. Someone had searched for Lightfoot's name, alone and in combination with the music school and with the name of a Baptist church in Detroit.

Someone was suddenly very interested in Mr. Lightfoot.

Of course, this fact would be a lot more useful if I knew who was doing the snooping. It could have been Riddick, before he left. Or any of the dozens of other people who had been coming and going from the church all day, including whoever had fled when I'd knocked over my chair.

I pulled out my phone and took a picture of the history,

and then another of the page showing the wrong Lightfoot. Then I turned off the computer and shut and locked Riddick's door.

I collected my purse and tote and locked up my office, too.

In the vestibule, I opened the door to peek into the sanctuary. Several dozen people were listening to the rehearsal. Including Mr. Vess, who did not appear to be enjoying himself. He was standing in the back, glaring at Lightfoot.

I closed the door and was about to leave when I heard a loud thud followed by some clanking noises to the left side of the vestibule, where another corridor led to the classrooms and the parish hall.

Two Shiffleys were each holding one end of a small stack of long boards and looking down at a small toolbox lying on the floor with some of its contents spilled out. Clearly the metal tools were the source of the clanking noises.

"What's up?" I said.

They both jumped when I spoke, and then relaxed.

"We thought you were him for a minute," one said.

"Let's get the rest of this stuff loaded before he does come out again," the other one said.

"Meg, could you put that toolbox on top of the boards?" the first asked.

"She's injured," the other said. "You can't ask her to—"

"It's okay," I said. "I can do it one-handed." I put down my stuff, dumped the tools back in the box, and set it as securely as possible on top of the boards.

"Thanks," one of them said.

"Come on," the other said, looking around nervously. "Let's go before he comes out here again."

I followed them out. They thanked me again as they

threw the boards and then the kit roughly into the back of a Shiffley Construction Company truck. Then they roared off before I'd finished stowing my stuff in the car.

Had Lightfoot unnerved them so much? Or something else?

I shoved the thought aside, got into the car, and headed for home.

Chapter 12

It was snowing again, so I decided maybe it was a good thing I'd been distracted before I took another pill. The ride home promised to be a little slippery.

But I did enjoy the part of it that led through the town square of Caerphilly. Nearly every building was decorated, some with tasteful wreaths and natural evergreens, others with twinkling lights. The county's annual holiday parade had already taken place, but many of the floats had been installed as decorations in the town square, at the foot of the county's living Christmas tree, a specially planted Colorado blue spruce that, according to Randall, was "just a smidgen shorter than the national Christmas tree."

I was pleased to see that the town square was still covered with snow. If the snow didn't melt by Christmas Eve, Randall would set the plows to clearing out a space at the foot of the Christmas tree so the crowds could gather to watch the living Nativity pageant across the street at the Methodist church and then gather around the county tree for the community carol sing. But for now, the large expanse of snow, unbroken except for occasional footprints from birds or foxes, was magical.

A surprising number of people were trooping up and down the sidewalks and in and out of all the shops around the town square. Maybe Randall's campaign to promote holiday tourism was working. I wasn't sure why "Christmas in Caerphilly" had a Victorian theme—maybe Randall, like me, had seen *A Christmas Carol* too many times at an impressionable age—but I enjoyed it. Nearly every corner had a band of carolers in Victorian costume, entertaining passersby while collecting donations for local charities. The outdoor stalls, also for charity, were doing a brisk business in hot beverages—coffee, tea, chocolate, and cider mulled with spices—and hot snacks, including muffins, cookies, candied apples, and roasted chestnuts. There were long lines for the hay rides, in reproduction farm wagons pulled by teams of sleek draft horses, specially chosen because they weren't spooked by the constant jingling of all the bells on their harnesses. And even longer lines to have pictures taken in borrowed Victorian costumes either in front of the town Christmas tree or in a genuine one-horse sleigh with a beautiful dappled gray horse harnessed to it.

It was more peaceful when I reached the residential areas of town, although I doubt if I spotted a single house without some kind of Christmas or winter decoration. On the outskirts of town I passed by several hills and ravines bristling with sledders and snowboarders. And when I got out into the country, I passed the occasional group of people who in spite of the fact that they were rapidly traversing the frozen fields on cross-country skis still found the energy to wave their poles and me and shout "Merry Christmas!" and "Happy holidays!"

For a moment I tried to imagine trekking that way across the countryside with Michael and the boys. And then I gave it up. My arm had begun bothering me on the way home. I waited until I was safely parked in the driveway, then took the pill with a long pull from the water bottle and walked inside. Michael's car was there, which meant he and the boys were home from their shopping.

James and Josh were very glad to see me, and only the sight of my sling prevented them from hurling themselves upon me. They kept staring at the sling and asking what it was until I finally led them into the kitchen and made each of them a dish-towel sling.

The boys were delighted, and began racing around to find someone to admire their new accessories. Mother, when she arrived, was startled.

"What have they done to themselves now?" she asked.

"Swing, Gamma!" Josh explained.

Jamie just held his sling up so Mother could see.

"They *both* fell off the swing?" Mother asked. "What were they doing outside in this weather?"

"That was 'sling,' " I pointed to my own sling. "They're fine. Monkey see, monkey do."

"Oh, I see," she said. "Very elegant. You both look quite dashing."

"Where's Daddy?" I asked. "Do you want to show him your slings?"

"Show Daddy!" both boys shouted, and ran upstairs.

"And how are you doing, dear?"

"Long day," I said. "But I'm home, and planning to rest now."

Which was intended as a subtle hint that if she was planning to enlist me in the redecorating, it wasn't going to work.

"That's nice, dear. Yes, it needs a little something." She was gazing around the hallway with a small frown on her face, so I deduced that last part was about the decor, not my napping plans.

" 'A little something'?" I followed her gaze. The whole hall was decorated within an inch of its life. Evergreen garlands alternated with gold tinsel garlands, all ornamented with red velvet ribbons. Every horizontal surface contained at least a few branches of holly sporting clusters of red berries. Several dozen poinsettias were massed along the walls—elegant silk ones, of course, rather than real ones that might be poisonous to the dogs. In the front corner was a rather elongated tree, chosen specially to reach as close to the ceiling as possible without occupying so much floor space that we couldn't open the door. It was completely decked with red and gold ornaments. We had two Nativity scenes, one small and traditional on the hall table, the other large and modernistic, on the floor beside the tree. Two handmade baskets held the Christmas cards we'd received. Special red and gold bowls scattered throughout held Rose Noire's special potpourri blends—spruce and pine scent near the tree, cinnamon and apple flanking the arch to the living room, and clove and nutmeg in the hallway leading back into the kitchen.

Arriving guests generally spent the first fifteen minutes of their visit exclaiming over the decorations, which actually wasn't as inconvenient as it might sound, since it usually took me five or ten minutes to hack my way through the decorations to get to the hall closet or the coatrack to hang their wraps. And once I finally pried the guests out of the hall, the marveling usually continued. Mother referred to her efforts in the living room and dining room as more restrained, though of course they were only so in comparison to the hall. It was all fine for social visits, but whenever anyone came on any business I'd taken to leading them to the kitchen, where they wouldn't spend their entire time sightseeing and could be more easily induced to help consume some of the surplus of holiday cake, cookies, candy, and fruit that was piling up.

Mother had even incorporated our two dogs into the decorating scheme. The original plan was to put large red velvet bows on both dogs' collars and to have them sleep on matching red velvet cushions on the hearth. I felt sorry for Horace, who'd been drafted to help with this part of the decorating. Tinkerbell, Rob's enormous Irish Wolfhound, gave him no trouble—in fact, she actually seemed to like the red bow—but Horace had ended up making a trip to the ER after trying to decorate Spike, our nine-pound furball, whose personality resembled a cross between a saber-toothed tiger and a wolverine. By the time Horace got back, Spike had established ownership rights to the wolfhound-sized cushion. The cushion intended for his use was barely large enough to fit Tinkerbell's enormous shaggy head, but she curled up on it anyway. Fortunately Mother found the resulting tableau cute, since any attempts to rearrange it would probably have resulted in more trips to the ER.

Mother had gone particularly overboard in the dining room, where she'd adopted an angel theme. Legions of angels marched up and down the dining room table, holding trumpets or songbooks or candles. More angels lolled on the sideboard and peeked out from behind the plates and pitchers in the built-in china cabinet. Angels rioted along the evergreen garlands that festooned all four walls, climbed and dangled from the chandelier. There wasn't actually a lot of room left for serving food or seating people, which hadn't been much of a problem so far—we'd just taken to eating a lot more often at our oversized kitchen table—but was definitely going to cause some tension when Michael's mother arrived to carry out her plan of using our house to prepare and serve her entry in the two dueling Christmas Day meals we were expected to attend. Mother would be serving her own meal over at the cottage, as she'd taken to calling the rambling farmhouse she and Dad had bought to stay in during their increasingly frequent and lengthy visits to Caerphilly. Was I wrong in suspecting that the decor in her dining room would be equally over the top but far less impractical in which to serve a meal?

Looking around, I tried to imagine what Mother could possibly think was missing.

"Didn't some famous interior designer say when you finished decorating you should take a look and remove at least one thing?" I asked.

"It was Coco Chanel," Mother said. "And she was talking about a woman getting dressed—not interior decorating, and certainly not decorating for Christmas, where a certain feeling of luxurious excess is quite appropriate."

She was shuffling through one of the Christmas card baskets, making sure that the top cards were all elegant ones that matched the red, gold, and green color scheme, and banishing any that did not meet her aesthetic standards to the bottom of the basket.

"I'll leave you in charge of the luxurious excess," I said. "I'm going to take a nap so I'll be fit to go to the concert tonight."

"Splendid," she said absently. She was holding up both hands making the suggestion of a picture frame and squinting through it at the stairway.

I headed upstairs, resigned to the probability that the hallway would be unrecognizable the next time I saw it.

When I was halfway up, Michael and the boys appeared.

"Mommy, go sledding!" Josh called.

Jamie just raced downstairs and began digging through the coat closet for his snow gear.

"They already napped," Michael said. "And I assume you still need to. So since there's fresh snow falling . . ."

"Wonderful idea," I said. "How about feeding them while you're out, and I'll meet up with you all at the concert?"

I helped stuff the boys into their snowsuits and boots and then climbed upstairs again, ignoring the fact that Mother was still busy with her measuring tape and notebook. I put my cell phone where I would hear it if the chief finally returned my call and fell asleep secure in the knowledge that the boys were safe, and happy, and that I could take a nice long nap before I saw them again.

My phone alarm woke me up a few hours later with just enough time to throw my clothes on and drive into town for the concert. In fact, not quite enough time, since I had to park half a dozen blocks from Trinity.

I despaired of getting a seat for the concert, and was resigned to standing in the back. Or maybe sitting on the floor of the vestibule—I wouldn't see much but at least I could hear. But when I peeked into the sanctuary, I spotted Michael and the boys, sitting in one of the front row pews, with Robyn and her husband sitting on one side of them and Mother, Dad, Grandfather, Caroline, Rose Noire, and Rob on the other. Robyn caught sight of me and waved, and I hurried to take the seat they were saving for me.

If I'd been picking the seats, I wouldn't have picked the front pew. Because of limited space, the first two rows of choir members were standing in front of the communion rail, almost stepping on our feet, so we had to crane our heads up to see them and couldn't get a glimpse of the rest of the choir. I was afraid we'd get blasted when they opened their mouths and began to sing, and the fact that Jerome Lightfoot had set up his music stand not six feet away, in the center aisle, didn't exactly make me any happier. But the boys were very excited at being so close to the choir, and it was all we could do to keep them from reaching out and grabbing the red velvet and gold lame of their special Christmas robes.

And we couldn't keep the boys from standing on the pews when a hush fell over the church and Lightfoot nodded to the organist, who had been playing soft background music. The organist struck up the first few chords of "O Come, All Ye Faithful" and the choir all lifted their hymnals purposefully.

Suddenly something shifted in the evergreens over the choir's heads, and a bright green snake's head popped out of the foliage, followed by three or four writhing feet of body.

Chapter 13

Scattered screams erupted from both the choir and the audience, and I was terrified that a stampede would take place. Cleopatra, by contrast, seemed remarkably calm.

Fortunately, Grandfather saved the day by scrambling up onto the seat of our pew, and then beginning to bellow out orders and exclamations.

"Cleopatra! Well done! You've found her! Quiet, everyone! She's easily startled. Get a ladder, someone! Let's get her down before she falls!"

A few people still fled out into the halls, but nearly everyone sat quietly and watched with interest as several sturdy basses and baritones lifted up other, lighter choir members onto their shoulders. Following Grandfather's bellowed instructions, they carefully untangled Cleopatra from the greenery, carried her down, and placed her across Grandfather's shoulders. The choir and congregation burst into applause as Grandfather, still wearing his scaly boa, shook the hands of Cleopatra's rescuers. He and Caroline drafted Horace to help them drive Cleopatra back to the zoo and strode out. Once Cleopatra was gone, everyone—even the people who had briefly fled the sanctuary—seemed in an unusually good humor, and Lightfoot had a little trouble getting them all to settle down so the concert could resume.

In fact, Lightfoot was the only person who seemed at all upset over the incident. He was in a completely foul humor.

And kept glaring over at me. Did he suspect me of having arranged Cleopatra's appearance, to upstage his concert? Or was he just staring at the sling Dad insisted I still wear? People tended to notice it, and a lot of them came over to commiserate with me, shooting him frowning glances as they did, but I wouldn't have taken him for someone who cared what others thought.

Then again, maybe he was afraid I'd sue. That seemed more in character. I made a point of beaming graciously at him the next time I caught him glancing my way, which seemed to disconcert him more than all the whispering and finger-pointing.

The audience finally settled down, and Lightfoot raised his baton and the concert resumed.

"O Come, All Ye Faithful!" was followed by "Hark! The Herald Angels Sing" and then "Ding Dong Merrily on High," "Go Tell It on the Mountain," "Glory, Glory, Glory to the Newborn King," "When Was Jesus Born?" "O, Holy Night," and "Children, Go Where I Send Thee."

Josh was clearly enjoying the concert immensely—he was nodding his head, tapping his feet, and slapping his knees in time to the music, even during the slow songs. I loved watching him, but I had to admit, I was glad he had crawled into Michael's lap, not mine. I was holding Jamie, who was sitting with his mouth and eyes wide open, utterly motionless, as if afraid the whole thing would vanish if he moved a muscle or made a sound.

Satisfied that the boys were having fun, I settled back against Michael's shoulder, closed my eyes, and gave myself over to enjoying the music.

It was well past the boys' bedtime when the concert ended, so rather than wait for the slow procession out the main doors, where both Robyn and Reverend Wilson were shaking the hands of the departing audience, we ducked to one of the side doors—where we found Riddick Hedges standing guard. He frowned at us.

"Good evening, Riddick," Mother said. "Lovely to see you." With that she sailed toward the door, clearly assuming he would open it by the time she reached it. Riddick blinked, and then scrambled to comply.

"Good evening, ma'am," Riddick said. He didn't quite bow, but he was clearly tempted.

We all followed in Mother's wake, wishing Riddick good evening—except for the boys who were fast asleep on Michael's and Rob's shoulders.

"I was supposed to be keeping this door secure," he muttered as I approached, bringing up the rear of our party.

"Against intrusion, I assume," I said. "Or did Robyn tell you to lock it up so no one could escape her handshake?"

"Never had such foolishness before," he muttered. "Skunks! Snakes! What next?"

"Nothing, let's hope," I said. "Or at least, with you on guard, nothing here."

"The chief sent out orders for everyone to lock up tight tonight," he said. "I remember when nobody had to lock his front door here in Caerphilly."

"I'll let you know if I spot anyone suspicious lurking outside," I said.

"Right," he said, with a grudging nod of approval as he held the door for me.

As I followed the rest of the family, I heard him testing the lock behind us.

On the first part of the way home the boys woke up long enough to serenade us with some of the songs the choir had performed. The results might have been more melodic if they were old enough to have any idea of pitch and key and if they could have been persuaded to sing the same song at the same time, but Michael and I enjoyed it anyway. I wasn't quite so sure about Rob. Still, I was relieved when both of their voices began to fade—bedtime would go so much more easily if we could just carry them to bed and tuck them in, still unconscious.

"I see your mother's been busy again," Michael murmured as he walked into the foyer with Jamie over his shoulder.

"It's like living at the North Pole," Rob muttered as he hauled Josh upstairs.

I was relieved to see that Mother hadn't rearranged everything—just added a little more of everything. More greenery. More ribbons. More tinsel. About the only annoying thing she'd done was arrange for someone to fit out the entire downstairs with little wireless speakers to pipe in an endless supply of soft instrumental Christmas music. It took me fifteen minutes to find the central source of the music—an iPod set up in the kitchen pantry—and silence it for the night.

I checked to make sure the library was ready for the sewing bee and Michael's office, with its dangerous cargo of unwrapped presents was locked. Then, after a quick visit to the boys' rooms to plant good night kisses on their sleeping foreheads, I fell into bed. It was still dark the next morning when my cell phone rang.

Chapter 14

It was my phone ringing, not Michael's pager—something to be thankful for, I supposed. I fumbled to answer it.

"Meg?" It was Robyn. "I hope I didn't wake you."

I knew it was customary under such circumstances to protest that no, of course, she hadn't awakened me, I had been up for hours. But it was 6:00 A.M. and I wasn't sure I could manage the obligatory cheerful tone with any grace, so I skipped to the point.

"What's wrong?" I asked.

"Can you come in and work your magic on the schedule again?"

I blinked for a few moments, puzzled.

"Is there something wrong with the schedule everyone agreed to last night?" I asked finally.

"Of course not! It would have been perfect except there's been another incident."

Suddenly I felt a lot more awake. I sat upright and began fumbling for the light.

"What kind of incident?"

"Someone left a flock of ducks overnight in the sanctuary at St. Byblig's."

"Ducks?"

"What's wrong?" Michael muttered.

I pressed my cell phone's speaker button so he could hear what Robyn was saying.

"Father Donnelly came in to get ready for the early mass,"

she reported. "And he found the ducks, several hundred of them, roosting on the pews, and a few of them waddling up and down the aisles. And more down in the Sunday school classrooms. And they'd obviously been there for hours, and the place was a mess—no way they could celebrate mass in there till after a good cleanup. So he canceled the mass, and most of the parishioners who showed up for it are already on their way home to change into work clothes and start cleaning. But the cleanup could take a while, and he doesn't yet know if the building has to be reconsecrated, so he needs to know where he can celebrate mass today—several masses, actually—and you're the only one who knows the master schedule well enough to figure that out. Can you come down to St. Byblig's and help us cope?"

"Be there in half an hour," I said.

"Bless you!" With that, she hung up.

"Ducks," Michael mused. "Well, at least evicting them won't be dangerous. Geese, now, might put up quite a fight, but ducks are pretty mild-mannered."

"Does this mean you're volunteering to help with the duck removal?" I asked. I was slipping on my jeans and a fairly warm sweater, since I'd probably be spending a lot of time either outside or in a church building whose doors and windows had been flung open to bring in the fresh air.

"Someone has to watch the boys," he said.

"True," I said. "And they had a late night last night, so if by some miracle they actually sleep in, let's let them. I have no idea how long this will take, but I'll keep you posted."

"Maybe the boys and I can come over and help when they are up," he said. "But not until the ducks are gone—they'd want to bring some home, and I don't think we want any more additions to the livestock just yet."

"Agreed." I grabbed my laptop, which was still perched on top of the dresser where I'd dumped it before going to bed, and headed out.

It was snowing, but only lightly, and the roads were fine, so I made good time. And while my shoulder wasn't back to normal, it didn't hurt as long as I refrained from raising my hand too high or trying to lift anything heavy.

St. Byblig's was a quaint little gray stone building nestled into the side of a hill on the outskirts of Caerphilly. The roofs were covered with snow, the surrounding grove of evergreens all had a light dusting of snow that outlined every needle, and the whole thing looked like a picture postcard. Well, except for the long line of people well bundled in overcoats and down jackets, trudging into the church with their gloved hands empty and then out again, each carrying a snowy white duck. It was a memorable scene, and a reporter from *The Caerphilly Clarion* was taking pictures to document it.

The line continued down to a small panel truck from the Shiffley Construction Company, parked at the foot of the church steps. Here the process was reversed—people walked in carrying ducks and walked out empty-handed, to join the procession back into the church.

I parked my car as close to the door as I could, and peeked into the panel truck on my way into the church. Someone had done a quick conversion job with chicken wire and a rough door frame, transforming most of the space inside the truck into a giant duck cage.

"Morning, Meg." Inside the truck, Caroline Willner was minding the gate, holding it open just enough for each arriving human to tuck his or her duck inside, and then shutting it so the ducks already in residence couldn't escape.

"Where are they going?" I asked.

"Down to the zoo for now," she said. "Your grandfather's got his men clearing out some space."

"Odds are they won't have to stay there long," I said. "Sooner or later, some farmer is going to wake up and notice his ducks are gone."

"I'm surprised it hasn't happened already," she said. "Of course, when someone does show up, we'll need some proof of ownership. No way we're just going to turn over several hundred valuable Pekin ducks to any old person who shows up claiming to have lost some. We're nearly full here—can you stick your head out and see if the other truck's back?"

I did as ordered.

"No other truck in sight," I reported.

"Blast. Well, send in the next dozen ducks, and have the rest wait back in the church till the truck's here."

I relayed her instructions to the duck-laden conga line. The first twelve queued up outside the truck door while the rest trudged back into the church, calling out "Hold up! Waiting for the next truck!" to those still emerging from the church.

By the time I reached St. Byblig's vestibule, it was filled with people standing around holding ducks in their arms and chatting cheerfully with one another—a little loudly, to be heard over all the quacking.

"There she is!" Robyn and Father Donnelly waved me over.

"Let's talk in my office," Father Donnelly said. Normally his round ruddy face would have worn a broad smile, but this morning he looked harried. "More peaceful away from all the livestock. It's the wrong season for the blessing of the animals."

"Can I see the scene of the crime first?" I asked.

"Help yourself." He shuddered, and gestured to the doors leading to the sanctuary.

I peered in. Dozens of white ducks were still waddling about the floor, resting on the pew seats and kneelers, or perched on the top of the pews. Considering the number of ducks in the truck outside, in a holding pattern in the vestibule, or already on their way to their temporary quarters at the zoo, the original duck infestation must have been impressive.

"Quite a lot of them," I said aloud.

"Hundreds," he said. "For all I know it could be thousands. I expect someone is counting them, if you're curious. I have no doubt they'll want to publish the statistic in the newspaper. At least I can report one blessing—they all seemed to have stayed on this side of the altar railing. So while there's a lot of soiling in the nave and some of the nearby meeting rooms, the chancel area, thanks be to God, seems untouched."

"And we had the Shiffley Construction workmen rig that netting to make sure it stays that way." Robyn pointed to the far end of the church, where several expanses of ten-foot-tall deer netting divided the main part of the church from the raised area with the altar.

"Good idea," I said. "Well, let's get started."

It took two hours and countless phone calls to devise a workable solution, and in the end we only managed it because the Methodist and Lutheran ministers offered to hold an ecumenical service at the Methodist church, freeing up a time slot at the Lutheran church for one of the masses for the refugees from St. Byblig's. Also, in a novel idea, the Caerphilly Bowl-o-Rama, which didn't normally open till one on Sunday, offered the use of its space until that time and we relocated all the St. Byblig's Sunday school classes there. Father Donnelly made a quick call to his arch-diocese, where a sleepy monsignor gave the chancery's approval to our revised plans.

"The Bowl-o-Rama," Father Donnelly said. "I never thought I'd see the day."

" 'Wherever two or more of you are gathered in His name,' " Robyn quoted.

"Yes," Father Donnelly said. "But thank the Lord for the Lutherans and Methodists. I'm not sure how the chancery would have reacted if I'd asked to hold the mass in a bowling alley."

I decided not to point out that it could come to that, if Caerphilly's reigning prankster continued unchecked. From the look on his face, I suspected that thought had already occurred to him.

"Perhaps I should ask now, just in case," he murmured, picking up the telephone again.

"Let's get the e-mails and telephone trees going," Robyn said.

Since it was Sunday morning and most of the clergy were conducting services and not apt to be near their computers any time soon, I printed out two dozen copies of the schedule (version seven) and drove around to the various churches to hand deliver them. At the Methodist church, Mrs. Dahlgren, the secretary, give me a particularly poisonous look. I couldn't pretend not to know why so I just ignored it. And the portapotties didn't look that bad. Randall's crew had set them up right behind the life-sized Nativity scene on the grass in front of the church—which would, with the figures removed, be the venue for the live-action Nativity on Christmas Eve. Someone—probably at Mother's direction—had screened the portapotties as much as possible with a lot of very leafy fake palm trees. They'd even painted the white portapotties with faux doors and windows and rooftop terraces, so they looked remarkably like the little dioramas of Bethlehem I remembered building in my childhood Sunday school classes, even down to a light dusting of snow to soften everything.

Mrs. Dahlgren may have been vexed, but a great many of the congregation—particularly the children—were charmed with the dramatic addition to their Nativity scene. As I left, I could see Reverend Trask beaming as he and Reverend Larsen supervised a joint task force of Methodist and Lutheran children who were dusting the snow off all the human figures in the scene. He waved back at me cheerfully and gave me a double thumbs-up. So there, Mrs. Dahlgren.

As I drove around, I found it was gnawing at me that I still hadn't managed to tell the chief about overhearing Caleb and Ronnie. I wasn't sure whether to be irritated at the chief for not calling me, or with myself, for not persisting. I finally pulled over and called again. And once again I reached only his voice mail.

"This is Meg Langslow," I said. "Just wanted to remind you that I may have some information on who's pulling these pranks."

At the First Presbyterian Church a service was letting out. I ran into Randall Shiffley and learned that progress had been made in solving the mystery of who owned the ducks.

Chapter 15

"We're pretty sure the ducks belong to my cousin Quincy," Randall explained. "He's been in the hospital, recovering from heart surgery. He's a bachelor, so there'd be no one at his farm to notice someone loading up the ducks. We've all been taking turns going over to look after them, but we haven't had anyone sleeping there, so the place was wide open for the duck thief. Looks like they even used his big truck to do the hauling."

I almost asked if his nephew Caleb was one of the ones who'd been helping with the duck care, but thought better of it. I'd let the chief sort that one out.

"I gather he has a lot of ducks?" I asked instead. "So whoever was doing the feeding wouldn't necessarily miss the borrowed ones immediately?"

"Does he ever!" Randall exclaimed. "Man, but I hope he gets well before my next turn to go over there. Do you have any idea how much poop eight or nine hundred ducks can produce?"

"Yes, I saw St. Byblig's," I said.

"Maybe I should go apologize to old Barliman Vess," Randall says. "He keeps filing complaints about Quincy with the health department and the police and any other agency he can think of."

"Complaints about what?"

"The noise and the smell and the fact that occasionally the ducks get into his garden and eat his plants," Randall said. "And I understand how Vess feels—I wouldn't want to live there myself—but fair's fair. Quincy was there first, and that part of the county is zoned for agricultural use. What kind of idiot moves in next to a working duck farm and then starts complaining that his neighbors are quacking and pooping too much? City folks."

I nodded, feeling just a little flattered. Having the locals complain to you about city folks was, I knew, a distinct step up from being city folks yourself.

"I think the biggest problem is that Quincy's operating as a free-range farm," Randall said. "If he was running a conventional duck farm with the birds all cooped up in tiny little cages—which is what Vess kept suggesting—they probably could have gotten along okay. But these days, at least around here, the money's in raising free-range, organic birds for the premium market."

"And Quincy's birds are a little too free-ranging for Mr. Vess's taste?"

"Yup." Randall nodded. "Well, I should be off. Got to move the ducks back to Quincy's farm before your grandfather gets fed up and starts feeding them to his wolves."

I hoped Randall was kidding. Then again, while Grandfather was devoted in theory to the welfare of all animals, he did have a sneaking fondness for carnivores and predators.

I had saved Trinity Episcopal for last, figuring if I had any energy left I could attend the ten o'clock service. But by the time I got there, my energy was nearly gone.

Trinity was hopping. The classrooms were filled with Episcopal and Baptist Sunday school classes. Father Donnelly was galloping through a briskly paced Catholic mass in the sanctuary, no doubt confusing a few Episcopalians who hadn't gotten the word that the usual nine o'clock service had been pushed back to ten. The vestibule was filled with Episcopalians waiting patiently for their service to begin, and not seeming to mind the wait much, because they all had so much news and gossip to catch up on.

I ran into Mother, resplendent in a new red-and-gold hat.

"Meg! Would you like to sit with me and the ladies?"

"Another time," I said. "I've been up since before dawn working on the schedule, and my arm is bothering me." I realized as I said it that this wasn't a white lie. My arm was starting to ache slightly.

"We'll tell you all about it later," one of the ladies said. "When we come out for the sewing bee."

"And Michael and the boys can sit with us," Mother said.

The boys looked very fine in their little suits, including special red and green plaid ties in honor of the season. I shuddered, briefly, imagining how hard it had been for Michael to achieve their sartorial splendor, and made sure both they and Michael knew how impressed I was.

"We're staying afterward for the rehearsal," Michael said.

" 'Rehearsal'? Oh, for the Christmas pageant." Trinity always had what we called a Christmas pageant. It was actually a lot like the live Nativity that the Methodists had on their front lawn on Christmas Eve. But since we held it in the sanctuary, children in costume acted the parts of the animals, along with Mary, Joseph, the wise men, the shepherds, and the angels.

The part of baby Jesus was normally played by a startlingly lifelike doll. The year the boys were born the well-meaning volunteer in charge of the pageant decided it would be adorable to have a real baby play the part. She recruited Josh and Jamie, on the rather unsound theory that they wouldn't both be cranky and crying at showtime. In her defense, it had been at least twenty years since her own children were infants, and she was the first to admit that we should bring back the doll after the first rehearsal, when Jamie projectile vomited on Melchior and a couple of helpless sheep.

This year, Robyn had recruited Michael to read the Christmas story as the children acted it out, while the choir would lead the congregation in a few musical selections, like "While Shepherds Watched Their Flocks By Night" when all the sheep milled on stage and "We Three Kings" when the wise men made their entrance. I was looking forward to the performance, but I hadn't realized Michael had signed the boys up to participate. Though I was glad to hear that in spite of their previous attempt to turn the Christmas story into *The Exorcist* the boys were still welcome back.

"That's good," I said. "What are the boys—sheep?" Most of the smaller children ended up as sheep.

"They're going to wear their Halloween costumes," Michael said.

"But they were dinosaurs for Halloween," I pointed out. "I don't think there were a lot of dinosaurs in Bethlehem in biblical times."

"Picky, picky," Michael said. "Robyn's got a more expansive approach to the pageant. Wait till you see it."

I felt a brief twinge of guilt at weaseling out of the service, but my eyelids were drooping more and more. And if Michael and the boys were attending not only the service but also the rehearsal, I might have time for a proper nap.

With visions of soft pillows and our down comforter dancing through my head, I headed for the exit. Unfortunately I got caught up in the human traffic jam in the vestibule, as several hundred Catholics tried to leave the sanctuary at the same time that a similar number of Episcopalians tried to enter. It wasn't just the sheer numbers but the fact that everyone wanted to clump in little groups to share news and gossip with friends they didn't usually get to see on Sunday morning. And by the time I managed to escape to the parking lot, so had a lot of the departing Catholics, while late-arriving Episcopalians were cruising up and down the lanes, looking for vacant spaces that would have been a lot easier to create if the impatient new arrivals would stop blocking in the departing cars.

By the time I was finally out of the parking lot and on my way, I felt distinctly low on Christmas cheer. The words "Bah! Humbug!" kept trying to escape from my lips. Clearly I needed an attitude adjustment, so I turned on the radio and tuned in the Caerphilly College station.

Normally at this time of year KCAE radio was short-handed because most of the student staff left for the holidays. The few who remained usually filled airtime with long, interrupted sequences of Christmas carols. My spirits rose at the prospect.

Unfortunately today the radio station appeared to have fallen into the hands of a few students who were either more enterprising or perhaps enjoying the opportunity to play around with minimal faculty or editorial supervision. I quickly deduced that they'd been running around interviewing various people in town about the pranks, and then interspersing audio clips from the interviews with clips from the Marx Brothers' *Duck Soup*. I couldn't quite decide whether the juxtaposition made the interviewees sound a lot funnier or a lot less intelligent. Or both.

I finally punched the off button and tried to hum for

the rest of the way home. And for some reason as soon as I spotted the first few sheep belonging to Seth Early, our neighbor across the road, I cheered up immensely and began singing aloud.

"Shepherds shake off your drowsy sleep, rise and leave your silly sheep."

Although I hoped Seth wouldn't hear me referring to his dignified Lincoln sheep as silly. And I had to admit there wasn't anything silly about them, since he'd resisted Mother's suggestion that he decorate them all for the holiday with big red bows.

At least twenty additional cars were parked up and down both sides of the road in front of our house. Several women with piecework totes or brown paper grocery bags were trotting down the path that ran along the left side of the house and led to the backyard where the library had its own entrance.

A real hostess would have gone and greeted the ladies, made sure they had enough light, offered them coffee and tea.

Instead, I scurried up the path and let myself into the house, looking over my shoulder, and managed to shut the door just as another car pulled up.

I took a deep breath. And then another. The house wasn't quiet—soft instrumental carols were playing through the sound system Mother had set up. But it was peaceful. I inhaled the cinnamon, clove, and evergreen smells. I looked around. Mother had upped the ante on the decorations, all right. The foyer didn't look like our foyer. It looked like a set for a movie. A movie set at Christmas, back in Victorian times. Maybe a new remake of *A Christmas Carol*. Any second a director would yell action and a flock of actors would walk in, the women in crinolines and the men in frock coats and—

"Meg?"

Rose Noire was standing in the hallway from the kitchen, holding the large coffee urn we used for parties and looking at me with a worried expression.

"Is something wrong?" she asked. "You were just standing there staring at the chandelier."

"Sorry," I said. "Long day already."

"Yes," she said. "And you need to be very, very careful over there."

"Careful?" I said. "I'm only over at Trinity. It's not exactly hazardous duty."

"Not physically, no." She set the urn down on the floor by the stairs, stood up, and clasped her hands dramatically. "But I sense unseen danger there."

"You can sense it all the way out here?" I tried not to sound too incredulous.

"I went in yesterday to take lunch to your Mother after Michael came back to stay with the boys," she said. "I sensed something at Trinity."

"Something?" I repeated. "Like evil?"

"Danger."

Her voice carried a note of firm conviction that alarmed me. I didn't quite believe Rose Noire had the psychic ability to sense danger. But I didn't ignore her premonitions, which all too often turned out to be accurate. My theory was that she was very good at observing facts and danger signs and even subconsciously adding them up but either unable or utterly unwilling to recognize that she was making deductions rather than having premonitions.

"I don't trust that man," she murmured. And then, before I could ask, she clarified: "Mr. Lightfoot. His aura is very dark and troubled. He's not what he seems. And it's infecting the whole choir. I sense nothing but pain and unhappiness around them."

"Doesn't take a psychic to figure that out," I said. "I could tell as much just from attending a rehearsal."

"Your instincts are good," she said, nodding with approval. "He has something to do with the pranks."

Not unless I was completely wrong about Ronnie and Caleb.

"Lightfoot?" I said aloud. "Seems unlikely. Why would he try to sabotage his own concert?"

"Your mother didn't believe me either," she said. "And I think the man she was talking to only pretended to. A tall, elderly man she was arguing with," she added, seeing my inquiring look. "I think he has something to do with running the church."

"That would be Mr. Vess, Trinity's resident gadfly," I said. "And I'm sure he's quite willing to believe anything negative about Lightfoot."

"I hope he takes it seriously, then," she said. "He could be in danger, too."

Perhaps he had taken her warning. Was it Vess who'd tried to look up Lightfoot's history on the computer? And was he acting on his own suspicions or because of Rose Noire's warning? I had a hard time seeing him as a believer in premonitions, but if Rose Noire hadn't bothered to share the source of her conviction that Lightfoot was not what he seemed . . .

"Well, I'm taking this to the sewing ladies," she said, stooping over to pick up the urn. "Are you going to join them?"

"Maybe later," I said. "I was up before dawn, and I need a break."

"Your arm is hurting you," she said.

"Not that much—" I began.

She frowned slightly.

"Why, yes," I said. "I hadn't noticed it till now, but I think it is hurting me. I'd better go up, take some of those painkillers, and lie down."

She smiled happily.

I glanced into the living room. Spike and Tinkerbell were curled up in front of the hearth, where a much larger than usual fire was blazing merrily—no doubt to impress the sewing circle attendees if they wandered into the living room. If Michael and I had to chop and split our own wood, I'd have protested the extravagance of the huge fire, but since I knew every log was helping put food on the family dinner table for one of Randall's poorer cousins, I just pulled out my notebook and jotted down a reminder to check the level of firewood in the barn and call for a new supply if necessary. Tinkerbell raised her head and thumped her tail on the floor in greeting. Spike opened one eye, sniffed vigorously for a few moments, and then, having detected no trace odors of anything edible, went back to sleep.

"I don't think those two have left the fireplace in days," I said. "What did Mother do, glue them to the cushions?"

"She might as well have," Rose Noire said. "They're heated cushions."

She sailed off toward the library, carrying the huge coffee urn.

Okay, now it made sense. I cast an envious glance at the cushions before trudging upstairs. Maybe it was time to break down and buy an electric blanket. I didn't like the idea of sleeping under a tangle of wires, but if the weather kept on being this cold . . .

I'd worry about it later. I fell onto the bed. In a few minutes I'd gather enough energy to crawl under the covers, I told myself.

Then I realized that I felt grungy. I hadn't had time for a shower before racing off this morning, and I'd been spending a lot of time in close proximity to duck poop.

I had plenty of time to take a shower before my nap. In fact—I felt a twinge of deliciously guilty pleasure at the thought—I had enough time to take a good, hot, soaking bath.

I ran down into the basement, because while I'd done a lot of laundry over the last several days, none of it had yet traveled upstairs from the enormous folding table I'd installed. "Getting dressed in the basement" was my own private shorthand for being woefully behind not just on niceties but on essential household chores. I needed to tackle the folding table soon.

But not right now. I collected clean clothes and a clean bath sheet. I heard voices coming down the hall from the library, and voices coming up the front step. Someone else would have to deal with them. I ran upstairs, laid out the clean clothes on my side of the bed, then dumped my dirty clothes in the hamper, snagged my fuzzy robe, and marched into the bathroom. I was trying to decide between the cinnamon-apple-spice bubble bath Michael's mother had given me last Christmas—nice enough, but not my favorite, although, it would be tactful to finish it off before she arrived, probably bearing this year's bubble bath offering—or Rose Noire's homemade rose and lavender soak, which was my favorite, and tended to vanish almost as soon as a new supply arrived. And after my bath—

I was reaching to turn the faucet when I heard a noise behind me.

"Quack-quack-quack!"

I whirled, throwing my robe around me as I did.

A large white duck waddled out of the shower stall.

Chapter 16

I pulled on my robe and belted it as I peered into every cranny of the bathroom.

No one there. Just the duck. Which looked up at me expectantly.

"Quack-quack-quack!" it said again. It fluttered up to the rim of the tub and marched up and down, looking down at the tub and then up again at me.

I could see that the plug was in the tub. The old, worn-out plug, which leaked slightly—replacing it was another one of those neglected tasks. I suspected that someone had filled the tub with water, put the duck in it, and then left, not realizing that eventually our winged visitor would be left high and dry.

"No," I said. "I am not filling the bathtub for you."

I left the bathroom, closing the door carefully behind me. I put my nice clean clothes on, which seemed a bit of a waste, since I hadn't managed to get myself clean to go with them, but I didn't fancy digging the dirty ones out of the hamper.

I pulled out my cell phone. Should I call 911? No. I put it away again. The duck didn't necessarily mean that our house had been hit by the prankster. There could be some other perfectly logical reason for the duck in our tub. Maybe it was intended as a Christmas present. Not for me or Michael, presumably, or the giver wouldn't have hidden it in our bathroom. And I had a hard time imagining anyone in my family giving the boys a duck. My nephew Eric had had a pet duck for many years, and they all knew how much trouble it had been. And they all knew we'd only just adjusted to the amount of work required by the chickens we'd acquired this fall. I'd spent the last several months making it very clear to anyone I could even imagine giving the boys a present exactly how we'd feel if they inflicted more livestock on us.

Maybe someone in the family had been helping with the duck removal at St. Byblig's and failed to notice one of the trespassers stowing away in his vehicle. And by someone in the family I mainly meant either Rob or Dad. Anyone else would have noticed a stowaway duck long before they got all the way out here or, failing to notice it, would find something a lot more sensible to do with it—either taking it back to town or stowing it in the barn for the time being. I couldn't imagine anyone but Rob or maybe Dad putting the duck in our tub.

I could tell by glancing at the cars outside that neither of my prime suspects was around to be confronted.

And I really needed that nap.

So I collected the duck, took him upstairs to Rob's bathroom, drew him an inch or so of water in the tub, and made sure the door was closed firmly.

I wasn't keen on having that soaking bath until I'd cleaned the bathroom thoroughly to remove the last vestiges of the duck's occupancy, so I settled for a hot shower before my nap.

And I actually did manage to sleep for an hour and a half before my notebook-that-tells-me-when-to-breathe began whispering in my ear that I should be paying attention to it. After that, sleep was impossible, so I went downstairs to see what was up.

I ran into Rose Noire in the hall.

"Do you have any idea why there was a duck in Rob's bathroom?" she asked.

"I put it there," I said.

She blinked.

"Okay," she said finally. "Why did you put the duck in Rob's bathroom?"

"I was afraid it would keep me awake if I left it in Michael's and my bathroom. And before you ask, I have no idea why there was a duck in our bathroom. Maybe it's left over from the church prank."

"I think we should take it outside," Rose Noire said. "I can set up a nice place for it in one of the sheds and—"

"No," I said. "It's not staying. It needs to go back to wherever it came from as soon as possible, before the boys see it and want to keep it."

"Oh, dear." Rose Noire glanced toward the kitchen.

I suddenly realized that I could hear Spike barking in the kitchen.

I had a bad feeling about this. I strode down the hallway and burst into the kitchen.

The duck was in the middle of the kitchen, inside the plastic fencing that we had used as a portable playpen for the boys before they figured out how to climb over it. The boys were inside the pen, petting the duck. Spike and Tinkerbell had deserted their heated cushions to inspect the newcomer. Tinkerbell was just sitting outside the pen, sniffing occasionally, and wagging her tail. Spike was scurrying around the outside of the pen, growling nonstop, except when he erupted into brief fits of barking. Rob was standing just outside the pen with his hands in his pockets, looking worried. Mother was setting the kitchen table. Michael was tending two pans on the stove, and Dad was slicing ham. From the haste all the adults were displaying—well, Michael and Dad, at least—I deduced that the boys had returned from rehearsal hungry and perhaps a little cranky, and they were hurrying to get food ready before the distraction of the duck wore off and they remembered their tummies.

"Rob brought him down," Rose Noire said. "And I left him there while I went out to fix a place for him . . ."

"I get it," I said. "I'm more interested in where the duck came from in the first place."

Rob and Michael both winced. That surprised me; I hadn't suspected Michael of any involvement in the duck's arrival. Mother and Dad looked as if they'd also like to hear the answer.

"Mom sent a grocery list of things she wanted for her Christmas dinner," Michael said. "I was pretty busy yesterday, so Rob offered to get everything."

"And I did," Rob said. "Except for the duck. The market didn't have fresh ducks. And she was very specific—not a frozen duck."

"You should have gotten a frozen one," Michael said. "We could have taken the wrapper off and hid it till it was thawed. She'd never have known."

"Now he tells me," Rob said. "Anyway, I ran into one of the Shiffleys who said he could get me a fresh duck. Said he'd deliver it this morning. It seemed like a good idea at the time."

"Unfortunately, the duck is a little too fresh," Michael said.

We all looked in dismay at the boys, who were happily chasing the duck around the perimeter of the playpen while Spike kept pace with them on the outside. The duck didn't seem to mind. Dad took up a station just outside the pen and began handing the boys little bits of ham or cheese each time they passed.

"The first thing to do is to get the duck out of sight," I said. "Jamie! Josh! It's nearly time for lunch. Go wash your hands."

"Can I feed ducky?" Josh asked.

"The duck has to go outside," I said. "Ducks don't belong in the kitchen."

"Nooo!" Josh wailed.

"Want ducky," Jamie whined.

Think fast, I told myself, if you don't want to start a flock of ducks on top of all the chickens.

"We have to hide the duck," I said. "It's a present for someone else," I said.

Both boys' faces fell, and I could tell that tears, in large quantities, were moments away.

"But don't worry," I said. "You'll be able to see him all the time."

The boys looked hopeful. As I glanced around, seeking inspiration, I could see that every adult in the room was staring at me in dismay. Mother was shaking her head almost imperceptibly.

"Where is everybody? And when's lunch?"

Grandfather strode into the room.

Chapter 17

Although giving animals to Grandfather made about as much sense as trying to give Mother a decorating book she didn't already have, he was probably the only adult in the room who wouldn't hate me if I gave him the duck.

"Darn," I said. "Looks as if we've spoiled the surprise. I guess there's nothing to do but give it to him a little early."

I picked up the duck, strode over, and handed it to Grandfather.

"Merry Christmas," I said, giving him a kiss on the cheek.

Grandfather stared for a few moments at the duck in his hands as if he'd never seen one before.

"Gampy like duck?" Josh said. He sounded anxious.

"Why, yes!" Grandfather said. "What a surprise!"

"Better than a tie," Rob put in.

"Wear it in good health," Michael said, lifting a water glass and then gulping down half its contents.

"And a fine, fat bird," Grandfather said. He poked the duck's ample, downy white breast and nodded appreciatively. "Well, I shall look forward to having this with—"

"With all the other animals in your petting zoo," I said.

"Not sure we need any more—" he began

"Because he's a very fine duck," I said. "I'm sure the children who come to the zoo will enjoy visiting him."

"But what's wrong with a little roast—"

"You know how much little children love ducks," I said. "The boys have already grown fond of him."

As if on cue, they both toddled over to tug at Grandfather's trousers, in a subtle hint that he should hold his present a little lower and let them enjoy it, too. He obliged.

"Ducky!" Jamie cooed happy. He was gently stroking the duck's wing feathers.

"See," I said. "They've already named him."

"That's not a name," Grandfather growled. "It's a generic description."

"Ducky Lucky!" Josh said. He was pounding the duck on the head with the same vigor one would use on a large and rambunctious dog. Ducky Lucky seemed to take it all in stride.

"I rest my case."

"Hmph!" Grandfather said.

"And see?" Michael put in. "He's obviously quite tame enough to be a great addition to the petting zoo."

Grandfather shook his head. But it wasn't a "Hell, no!" headshake. More of a "What now?" He turned his attention to Ducky Lucky and his two human acolytes.

"Feel how oily his feathers are." Grandfather demonstrated for the boys by stroking the duck's feathers gently. "You know why that is?"

Both boys shook their heads and began massaging the duck's feathers with enthusiasm.

"It makes them waterproof and keeps them warm. Come on—Let's take Lucky out to the barn and I'll teach you a few things about ducks."

He strode out, and his tiny pupils tried to follow, though we had to stop them and stuff them into their winter wraps before we let them out. Dad grabbed several newly made ham-and-cheese sandwiches and trailed after them. Everyone else in the room let out a sigh of relief.

"So I guess I should tell Michael's mother I couldn't find a fresh duck?" Rob asked.

"Please," Michael said. "I'm not sure I'll ever want Peking duck again."

"She won't be happy," I said. "Why not call whoever you got it from and demand a replacement that's ready to cook?"

"I can't do that," Rob said. "I mean, he did deliver the duck. Besides, I don't know his name. And I paid cash. I offered to write a check, but he insisted on cash. I got the feeling maybe he wasn't really supposed to be selling the ducks. He was kind of hanging around the poultry section of the market, and came up to me when he overheard that I couldn't get a fresh duck."

"Let me get this straight," Michael said. "The night before several hundred ducks were stolen from Quincy Shiffley's farm, you made arrangements for a random Shiffley to deliver a live duck here."

"A fresh duck," Rob said.

"And sometime this morning you took delivery of what you already suspected might be a stolen duck."

Rob squirmed and nodded. I found myself thinking, not for the first time, that if Michael had gone in for law school instead of drama school, he'd have made a first-class prosecutor. And that the chief might want to check up on the Shiffley who'd delivered our duck.

"It sounds so terrible the way you put it," Rob said.

"How can you be so sure he was a Shiffley?" I asked.

"He looked like a Shiffley," Rob said. "And besides, I saw him helping build the stage at Trinity."

"So maybe he was just working for the Shiffley Construction Company."

"Do all their employees call Randall 'Uncle Randall'?"

I pulled out my cell phone and hit one of my speed dial buttons. Randall Shiffley answered his phone on the first ring.

"What's up?" he said. "Any new schedule changes?"

"Do you have any idea which of your many relatives would have sold my brother a fresh duck last night?"

A pause.

"Was there something wrong with the duck?" he asked finally.

"The duck is just fine," I said. "In perfect health, in fact; he arrived here still alive. And the twins met him, and the newly christened Ducky Lucky will soon be an exhibit at Grandfather's petting zoo rather than the main course of our Christmas dinner."

Randall sighed.

"The only Shiffley I know of who raises ducks is Quincy, and he wasn't hanging around the supermarket flogging them last night, that's for damn sure. I saw him in the hospital this morning and he hadn't been anywhere. But I think I can figure out who did this. You want a replacement duck or shall I just get Rob his money back?"

"Either would be fine," I said. "Do you already have a suspicion who did it, or do you just plan to raise Cain with all the family black sheep until one of them confesses? If it helps, Rob thinks the seller was one of the men doing construction at Trinity."

"I'm going to start with my cousin's boy Duane, who's been known to pull stuff like this before—and yes, he was on the crew over at Trinity. Consider the original duck my gift to the Caerphilly Zoo."

"I'll have Grandfather send you a receipt for your generous donation," I said. "Thanks."

"That works. Someone will drop by with the new ready-to-roast duck tonight."

"After the boys' bedtime?"

"You got it."

"Good!" I said. "And thanks."

We both hung up.

"We're getting a new duck?" Rob asked.

"Make sure there's someone here to receive it tonight," I said. "And can someone figure out what's French for 'Peking duck' and explain to Michael's mother why we all have to call it that when the boys are around."

Dad pulled out his iPhone.

"I'm going to check on the sewing bee," Mother said.

"Lunch in a few minutes," Michael said.

"*Canard laqué de Pékin,*" Dad said, looking up from his iPhone.

"I'll come with you," I told Mother.

We left the men to finish putting lunch on the table and went through the foyer to the long hallway that led back to the library. Some ancestor of the previous owner had added it on as a ballroom, back when that was a fairly normal thing to have around the house, and we'd finally finished converting it to the library of our dreams. The boys already loved curling up in the big sofa for story time, and in due course I was looking forward to sitting with them at one of the long oak tables, supervising their homework and helping them with their science projects.

I opened the big double doors to find the entire room had been decorated to the hilt and was filled with red velveteen in various stages of being made into seat covers and curtains. Mother and whoever she recruited to help must have stayed up half the night working in here. Ropes of evergreen framed every one of the tall windows and built-in bookshelves and looped along next to the double-height ceiling. Red and gold tinsel festooned the circular stairway leading up to the second level of shelves, where the tinsel-wrapped railings seemed barely adequate to hold back a small jungle of pointsettias, live spruces, and Norfolk pines. Trailing wicker baskets of red Christmas cactus hung down from the railings so far that I could see some of the sewing circle members having to duck as they bustled around the room, and the baskets were decorated with ribbons holding little silver bells that set up a constant tinkling with the breeze when anyone passed beneath them. Mother and her minions had even gussied up the books—on every shelf, two or three of the volumes had been wrapped with temporary dust jackets of red, gold, green, or purple foil paper. When you added in the soft instrumental carols playing—no doubt from wireless speakers hidden behind the books—and enough Christmas potpourri to send up an almost visible haze of evergreen, clove, cinnamon, and ginger fumes—well, I'd bet anything that the decor stopped everyone in their tracks for at least the first half hour after they arrived.

But now everyone was hard at work. A dozen portable sewing machines were set up in a line on the right-hand table, with a dozen women sewing away busily on them. The center table was covered with cloth on which other women were fitting white pattern pieces and then cutting out various shapes—mostly the red velveteen, along with a sturdy black cotton for curtain linings and parts of the cushions that didn't need to be seen. One end of the left-hand table was piled high with bolts of red and black cloth, while at the other end Minerva Burke had set up her command center.

Mother was immediately drafted to give an opinion on

some fine point of upholstering—not that she ever sewed much, apart from doing the odd bit of crewelwork, because she thought it an elegant thing to be seen doing. But she was a very expert consumer of upholstery services. I strolled over to talk to Minerva.

"How's it going?" I asked.

"I'm optimistic that we'll have everything done by Christmas Eve," she said. "It won't be a problem if we stay up rather late finishing, will it?"

"You'd have to be pretty loud out here for us to hear you," I said. "Just lock up when you leave. How's the smell removal going?"

"Slowly. If I ever catch the wretches who did that to our lovely church—" She broke off and set her jaw, as if forcibly restraining language no self-respecting Baptist matron would know, much less use in public.

"I tell you one thing," she said. "This duck thing has confounded my theory of the crime."

"I find myself wondering if your theory was also the chief's," I said. "But I know better than to ask. What is your theory?"

"That the pranks have something to do with the choir," she said.

I nodded agreement. Should I tell her about what I'd overheard? No, the chief would probably be annoyed if I tried to involve Minerva, and I wasn't at all sure a proper Baptist matron would approve of Rose Noire's premonitions. Besides, she was already keeping a close eye on Lightfoot.

"But I haven't seen any choir events scheduled in the Catholic church," she went on. "So there goes that theory."

"Maybe not," I said. "What if St. Byblig's wasn't the intended target?"

She raised one eyebrow and cocked her head.

"You're keeping the New Life building locked up pretty tight, right?"

"Tight as a tick," she said.

"And I suspect Trinity wasn't left standing wide open last night."

"No," she said. "I was one of the last to leave—I was helping make sure we'd left everything at least as clean as we found it. And your pastor was there to lock the door behind us, and when I told her she should go home and get some rest, she said she would as soon as she made sure everything was secure."

"That fits," I said. "Imagine you're the prankster, and you drive your truck full of ducks up to your intended target and you can't get in. Are you just going to give up and take them back where you stole them? Or are you going to look around for someplace else to cause trouble?"

"Ye-es," she said slowly. "But why the Catholics?"

"St. Byblig's isn't far from Trinity or New Life," I said.

"The Methodists are closer," she said.

"Yes, but the Methodist church faces the town square," I said. "Not exactly the place I'd pick to unload several hundred contraband ducks. Way too public and visible."

"No," she said, with a note of excitement in her voice. "But a church at the edge of town, whose parking lot is completely hidden from the road by trees . . ."

"Exactly."

"And besides," she said. "St. Byblig's has a loading dock."

"It does?"

"No idea why, but it's quite useful," she said. "That's why they're the central distribution point for the county food bank—it's so easy to load and unload. I've put a loading dock down as a feature we'd like at New Life next time we do a little expansion and remodeling. It would make handling the choir equipment a lot easier."

"So once they got into St. Byblig's, they could just drive up to the loading dock, herd the ducks out, and drive off," I said. "Maybe it was the target after all, because of the loading dock."

"Very interesting." She looked preoccupied.

"I should be heading out," I said. "If I stay much longer, someone will force me to sew, and I'd hate to ruin any of that beautiful fabric. But if you happen to talk to Henry, remind him that I have some information for him. About the case," I added.

"Will do," she said. "Thanks again for the use of the room."

I headed back to the foyer. But before I left the long hallway, I heard the library door open. Minerva stepped out into the hallway, closed the door after her, and raised her cell phone to her ear.

The chief had probably already thought of everything we'd been discussing. And maybe he hadn't called me back because he knew what I had to say—I might not be the only one who had overheard Ronnie and Caleb. But just in case he hadn't, it wouldn't hurt to have Minerva remind him to call me.

Chapter 18

Lunch was pleasant, if a little chaotic. Unfortunately one of the interesting facts Grandfather had told the boys about ducks was that having no teeth, they swallowed bits of grit to help grind up their food. I could tell the boys were eager to experiment with this, but fortunately our gravel driveway was currently covered with snow. Perhaps they'd forget by the time the weather warmed up.

After lunch, Michael curled up to have a nap with the boys. I checked my e-mail and voice mail and found that a few small schedule kinks had to be ironed out. Normally I'd have worked on it in Michael's office, where I could use the printer, but I was wary of getting sucked into the sewing frenzy. So I packed up my laptop and headed to town. After all, I could do some shopping while I was there. We were running low on a lot of things, particularly coffee, tea, juice, and sodas, thanks to the enthusiasm with which Rose Noire was keeping the sewing circle refreshed.

While I was at the market, I spent a little time hanging around the poultry section, frowning at everything, but no lurking Shiffleys offered to sell me illicit poultry. Evidently Randall had reined in Duane.

I dropped by the New Life Baptist Church and St. Byblig's so I could check on the progress both sets of cleaners were making. And then I went over to Trinity and settled down into my little office to sort out the schedule once more.

I'd been there for fifteen minutes or so when Barliman Vess walked in. He started when he saw me, so I deduced I wasn't the object of his visit.

"Can I help you?" I asked.

"No," he said.

I was tempted to ask, "Then why are you standing here, hovering over me?" But I decided it would be more effective to ignore him.

I was wrong. He just stood there. After what seemed like an eternity but was really only five minutes according to the clock on my laptop, I looked up again. He was staring at the junk. Or possibly at the window at the far end of the room, behind all the junk.

"It'll be nice when all that junk's gone, won't it?" I said.

"Junk?" He looked over as if startled that I was still there, and frowned thunderously. "Nonsense. Perfectly good furniture. Plenty of use left in it. Complete waste of money, replacing all of it."

He glared at me. I shrugged, because it was less likely to make him angry than saying what I thought—that he was a pigheaded old skinflint to begrudge Robyn a nice office. It wasn't as if the church was broke.

He eventually stopped scowling at me and ran his eyes across the junk filling the room one last time. Then he turned and left without saying another word.

"And a merry Christmas to you, too, Mr. Scrooge," I muttered.

I had barely turned back to my laptop screen when Riddick scurried into my office.

"What did *he* want?" he asked.

"Vess? I have no idea," I said. "Just shedding a little yuletide warmth in my direction, I suppose."

"Didn't he say anything?"

Riddick was clearly overwrought. I turned reluctantly away from my computer again to face him.

"He just stared at all the junk," I said. "And when I said something innocuous about how nice it would be to see it gone, he nearly bit my head off."

"I'm trying to deal with it," Riddick said. "It's not my fault. Even before all these snakes and skunks there's been so much more work with the new rector here, and it's not really the right time of year for a rummage sale, and I can't just get rid of it like that." He snapped his fingers.

"Of course not," I said, in my most soothing tones. Although I couldn't help thinking that anyone with an ounce of common sense and gumption could get rid of everything here pretty quickly. Mother could do it. I could do it. And if she and I could convince Robyn to turn the two of us loose on it . . .

"He wants my job, you know," Riddick said. "Wants to eliminate it," he clarified. "Thinks what I do should be done by volunteers."

"As far as I can tell, he's the only one in the church who feels that way," I said. "I know Mother disagrees. Don't let it worry you. And if you need help dealing with the junk, I'm sure Mother will be able to help. I could, too. But let's not worry about it till after Christmas."

" 'After Christmas,' " he repeated. He didn't exactly look thrilled at my suggestion. But he did look a little less tense. "Yes. Your mother is always very . . . Yes. After Christmas."

He glanced warily at the clutter as if half afraid it would jump out and attack him. Then, with a visible effort, he straightened his spine and forced his face into an unconvincing but very determined smile.

"Thank you," he said. "And merry Christmas."

And then he scurried out.

A few moments later, when I had buried myself back in my schedule, I heard Mr. Vess's voice.

"I need to speak with you for a moment."

I braced myself and looked up, but he wasn't in my office. The words had come from out in the vestibule. Just then the organ began to play, drowning out anything else Vess had to say. According to my schedule, that would be Trinity's regular organist, sneaking in a short rehearsal between Baptist choir rehearsals. I resigned myself to the possibility that Lightfoot might barge in and complain about this minor interruption in his frenzied rehearsal schedule.

A soft instrumental version of "O Little Town of Bethlehem" filled the air. When no one barged into my office, I relaxed and went back to my work, happily humming along with the carols.

I'd thought it would only take a few minutes, once I was finally free of interruptions, but by the time I finished juggling and e-mailing the resulting schedule, I looked up from my laptop to find that the sky outside was getting dark. And since my temporary office had only one small window at the far end of the room, behind all the boxes and old furniture, it had grown very dark indeed.

I sat up, stretched my shoulder gently, and checked my watch. Nearly time for our organist to turn the sanctuary back to the Baptists for their final preconcert prep. I didn't quite share Rose Noire's suspicions of Jerome Lightfoot, but I had no desire to talk to him. And so, time for me to go home and have some Christmas fun with Michael and the boys.

I organized all my papers, turned off my computer and my desk lamp, and was about to stand up and be on my way when I heard low voices outside my door.

"Man, are you crazy?" Ronnie Butler.

"What do you mean?" Caleb Shiffley.

I crept a little closer to the door, the better to eavesdrop.

"That thing with the ducks."

"Shut up—what if someone hears us?"

"No one here," Ronnie said. "The rev is out running the prayer meeting, and old man Hedges went home to nurse his migraine."

And if Caleb was suspicious and decided to check doors, should I try to hide behind some of the old furniture and keep eavesdropping? Or just look startled and pretend I hadn't overheard them?

Luckily I didn't have to make a decision.

"Look," Ronnie went on. "I know you're still mad at Bigfoot about the whole April thing, but enough's enough. The chief's got Horace Hollingsworth doing fingerprints and stuff. They could still catch us for the skunk thing, or the snake. We should lay off with the pranks, not do stupid stuff that might leave more evidence and doesn't have anything to do with old Bigfoot anyway."

"Wait," Caleb said. "You think I put the ducks in St. Byblig's?"

"You mean you didn't?"

There was a brief silence. Presumably Caleb had answered by shaking his head and they were staring at each other in dismay.

"This is creepy," Caleb said at last. "If you didn't, and I didn't—man, they're gonna blame this on us, too."

"If they catch us."

"When they catch us."

"And why would anyone want to cause problems for St. Byblig's?" Ronnie asked. "Everyone likes Father Donnelly."

Another pause.

"Maybe we should go to the chief," Ronnie said. "Or Reverend Wilson."

"You think they'd believe us?"

Silence.

"You know," Caleb said. "I bet it's going to be a lot easier for them to catch whoever did the ducks."

"What do you mean?"

"Think about it," Caleb said. "We were in and out of the New Life Church pretty quick, and the snake didn't even take ten minutes. But somebody had to load all those hundreds of ducks and bring them over there in a truck or something and carry them all into St. Byblig's. That took a lot more time. Which means a lot bigger chance of being seen or leaving evidence."

"Are you suggesting that if they catch whoever did the ducks, we should let them take the blame for the rest?"

A sigh.

"I guess not," Caleb said. "That would be pretty slimy. Though if you ask me, it was slimy of them to do the ducks. Everyone was kind of calming down and then the whole thing with the ducks stirred them up again."

"What makes you think they were calming down?"

A pause. A long pause.

"Well, I think they would have if the pranks had stopped," Caleb said finally.

"Yeah, right." Ronnie sounded unconvinced. "Look, no matter what Bigfoot gets up to, we just sit tight. Agreed?"

"Agreed."

Soft departing footsteps signaled that my eavesdropping was over. I decided to wait for a little bit before emerging. And as soon as the coast was clear, I should call the chief and report what I'd heard. Everything I'd heard—he still hadn't returned my call from yesterday.

And was Rose Noire right about Lightfoot having something to do with the pranks—at least the latest one? And should I relay her suspicions to the chief? I knew he shared my skepticism about premonitions, but did he also share my trust in Rose Noire's subconscious?

As I was crouching there, trying to decide how soon to take out my cell phone, it rang. Michael. I hurried to answer it before it alarmed the departing pranksters.

"Josh has been begging to come to tonight's concert," he said. "I told him I'd ask Mommy if it was okay."

"I have no idea how crowded it will be," I said. "But if nothing else, we can listen from here in my temporary office. You said Josh has been begging—does Jamie have an opinion?"

"He has no objection. He wants to see the snake again. He's asked about it several times."

"Let's hope he's disappointed. Want to meet for dinner someplace before the concert?"

"How about Luigi's?"

"My very thought. I'll head out in five minutes."

Before leaving my now completely dark little office, I called Chief Burke's cell phone. Which went to voice mail. Not knowing who might be around when he played it back, I made my message noncommittal.

"Hi," I said. "It's Meg Langslow. I really need to talk to

you. I've overheard several things that I'm pretty sure are
relevant to the question of who's pulling off these pranks.
Would be happy to fill you in at your convenience."

With that I tucked my phone in my pocket, threw on
my coat, hat and gloves, and headed for my dinner with
the family.

Chapter 19

Dinner was splendid. Luigi's had been one of Michael's and my favorite spots since we'd begun dating, and it was nice the boys were finally old enough that we could take them out for a restaurant meal. At least we could at Luigi's. It was noisy enough to drown out any racket the kids produced. Most of the waitresses were matronly Italian ladies, Luigi's sisters and cousins, who all had a soft spot for handsome bambini. And since the decor was designed to survive the nightly onslaught of dozens of starving college students, whatever damage the kids did would disappear when they swabbed the place down after closing.

The place seemed much more crowded than usual, partly because several tables had been sacrificed to allow space for Christmas decorations and the rest moved even closer together. In the back left corner, Luigi's Christmas tree was, as usual, decorated entirely in green, white, and red, the Italian national colors. In fact, the angel gracing the top was waving a tiny Italian flag. The back right corner contained an eight-foot-tall *ceppo*—a traditional Italian Christmas decoration consisting of a pyramid-shaped set of shelves trimmed with candles and evergreen, with presents, candies, and a small Nativity scene gracing the shelves.

I was a little alarmed to see a pair of white ducks in an evergreen-trimmed cage by the kitchen door. Was this part of some new expansion of the menu—an advertisement for duck marinara, perhaps? I pulled out my phone and figured out that the Italian word for duck was "*anitra,*" so I could scour the menu for it.

But Paolo, our waiter, reassured me.

"Oh, no, they are just pets," he said. "Luigi's grandson, little Tonino, was heartbroken when they took all the ducks out of the church, so we asked Randall if he thought his cousin would sell us a pair. These are going home with Luigi tonight."

"A pair," Michael asked. "Are you planning on raising ducks?"

"No!" Paolo muttered something in Italian while shaking his head. "They are both supposed to be boy ducks, God willing."

We managed to pry the boys away from Tonino's ducks only by promising them a visit soon to Ducky Lucky.

In honor of the season, Luigi's cousin Guiseppe, the failed opera singer, was occupying the small stage in the main room, singing Christmas carols in Italian, accompanied by Zia Filomena on the badly tuned upright piano. Jamie enjoyed the performance enormously, but Josh found it strangely disturbing to hear familiar carols with strange words, even after I explained that it was just another language.

"He's not singing the right words, Mommy!" he said loudly during one of the quieter moments of "*Astro del Ciel*"—better known to Josh as "Silent Night."

I'm not sure he bought my explanation. And I had to admit, when Guiseppe launched into the Italian version of "White Christmas," in a passable imitation of Bing Crosby's mellow baritone, even I found it a little strange.

But listening to Guiseppe was a good appetizer for the New Life choir's second concert, which was just as splendid as the Saturday night version had been, even though we did get stuck sitting in the front row again. Josh insisted on singing with the choir, which would have passed unnoticed if, at the end of "Angels We Have Heard on High" he hadn't gotten carried away and added a few more "Glo-o-o-o-o-rias!" to the song, to the great amusement of both choir and audience. Jamie spent most of the concert craning his neck to look up at the overhead decorations, trying to spot a snake, but at least it kept him occupied.

Even Barliman Vess seemed in a good mood, although I doubted he was enjoying the music. More likely he was comforted by the thought that every verse brought us closer to the moment when Lightfoot and the choir would be leaving Trinity. By the end of the concert he was actually smiling.

As Michael, Rob, and I were filing out with the boys we ran into Robyn. When she spotted us, she looked relieved.

"Is there any chance one of you could do a quick check around the church before you leave?" she asked. "Make sure everything's locked up with no stragglers? I could do it of course, but for now, I have to stay here to make sure everyone really leaves—we think the pranksters got into New Life by staying after the choir rehearsal. And that's going to take a while, and—"

"And if someone checks all the doors and windows and closets while you're guarding the exit, you'll get home all the sooner." I turned to Michael. "I need to drive my car home anyway. Why don't you take the boys home and start the bedtime process? I should be there before you get them tucked in."

"Can do," Michael said. He and Rob exited.

Robyn handed me a key ring and I started my inspection

on the small hallway on the right side of the vestibule that held the offices and several storage rooms. No intruders in Robyn's office, and her windows were all properly locked. Ditto for my small office, although I couldn't actually get anywhere near the window. As far as I could tell from across the room, it was latched; and if it wasn't, any burglar foolish enough to attempt entry would probably impale himself on the upturned legs of the half dozen battered chairs stored just under the window. Riddick's lair looked like a filing clerk's bad dream, untidy stacks of paper covering every horizontal surface, but it was secure and intruder-free. A couple of locked storage rooms finished off the short hallway. I unlocked the doors and peered in, seeing nothing amiss.

I returned to the vestibule, gave Robyn a thumbs-up, and crossed to the other side, where a longer hallway led to several classrooms and eventually the parish hall. I checked them all, methodically—even the bathrooms— and then headed down to the basement. Or should I work on calling it the undercroft, to please Mother and Robyn? A couple more classrooms on the downhill side, which had natural light, and on the side that nestled into the hillside was the furnace room, which also doubled as a huge storeroom.

The classrooms were a little cramped, thanks to the rows and rows of Shiffley Moving Company boxes stacked in the corners.

I had a brief anxious moment when I peered into the furnace room and thought I saw a human figure crouched against the wall at the far end. But when I turned on the light I saw that it was a coat tree covered against the dust with an old sheet that fluttered slightly in the draft from one of the air vents. There were a lot of hulking shapes in the furnace room, with and without dust covers. Like the greater part of my temporary office, it was filled with boxes, interspersed with heavy vintage furniture. Mrs. Thornefield's legacy, no doubt.

"She had some very nice things," I remembered Mother saying, when news came out that Mrs. Thornefield had left her entire estate to Trinity. "I shall look forward to the estate sale."

Presumably the nice things were in the boxes. Unless Mother's taste had changed dramatically, I couldn't imagine her coveting any of the furniture I was seeing. No antiques, nothing light or graceful or elegant. Just a lot of big, heavy, dark, battered furniture with faded, threadbare upholstery and cheap, corroded metal fittings.

And scattered in and around the boxes and furniture I could see the detritus of decades of parish life. Hideous paintings in dusty, ornate frames. Every piece of broken equipment that had ever been banished from the offices above, including an IBM Selectric typewriter, an Apple IIe computer, and what appeared to be a 1950s mimeograph machine. Hulking unidentifiable papier-mâché objects left over from bygone children's pageants. Why did we have a mini trampoline leaning in one corner?

Still, the undercroft was looking better than it had the last time I'd seen it. Shortly after Robyn's arrival, Mother and the ladies of St. Clotilda had renewed their long-standing offer to reorganize all the church storage spaces, from attic to undercroft, and unlike Father Rufus, Robyn had given her approval. The crowded shelves of food that formed the food bank were gone, reorganized into a former junk closet upstairs. The dozens—perhaps hundreds—of cardboard boxes of old files had been sorted, weeded down to the essentials, and stored in neatly labeled waterproof plastic bins in the attic. The basement really was the last bastion of disorder—well, the basement and my office—and once the Christmas season was over and the guild had time to organize the rummage sale, even those would be gone. The very thought made me cheerful.

I ended my inspection at the back door, which opened into a concrete well where a set of steep stairs led up to the churchyard. The stairwell was screened by a thick privet hedge, which made the back stairs precisely the sort of discreet entrance I would use if I were a prankster looking to smuggle ducks, snakes, skunks, or other unwanted livestock into the church. I double- and triple-checked the locks on that door.

And then, having found no stowaways and no security breaches, I took the stairs back up to the ground level and reported to Robyn.

"All secure," I said as I handed over the key ring.

"Thanks," she said. "But keep the key ring. Until the prankster is caught, we'll be locking the church a lot more. Which shouldn't inconvenience anyone with a legitimate reason to be here—we must have a million spare keys out there in various parishioners' hands—no reason you shouldn't have one set, in case you need to get into your office."

"Not that I'm complaining, but shouldn't Riddick be helping with all this checking out and locking up?" I asked.

"He's home with his migraine," she said.

"Again? He had one yesterday, didn't he?"

"He seems to be having a lot of them lately." She shook her head. "Frankly, I doubt if we'll see much of him as long as we have so many people from other congregations coming and going. Intruders, as he calls them."

"He's very protective of the church," I said.

"I'd call it possessive," Robyn said. "And frankly, it's been driving me crazy. Hard enough coming in as the new kid, dealing with people who want an older priest."

"Not to mention a male priest," I put in.

"Yes," she said. "But I seem to have gotten off on a particularly wrong foot with Riddick, and nothing I've done seems to have made any difference. Well, at least the end is in sight."

" 'End'?" I didn't like the sound of this. "What do you mean, 'end'?"

"He's retiring," she said. "Theoretically. It was supposed to be end of the year, but now he's pushed it back to the end of January. And it's his decision, not mine. Retiring and moving to someplace warmer. He asked me not to announce it until he could tell people himself—though I think with only a month to go it's about time we said something to the congregation. I mean, people will want to throw him a good-bye party, won't they?"

We both thought about that for a few moments.

"We'll all feel bad if we don't," I said. "It's the right thing to do."

Robyn shook her head sadly.

"So much for my New Year's resolution to find a way for us to get along better," she said. "I've been talking to Reverend Trask over at the Methodist Church. He has some wonderful wisdom on how to get along with difficult people."

With Mrs. Dahlgren to deal with, no doubt he did. Reverend Trask must be a saint.

"I confess," Robyn went on. "I resented Riddick at first—he had it within his power to make my arrival at Trinity so much easier, and instead he seemed to be putting up obstacles at every turn. But then I took a step away and looked at the situation. He's served the parish for twenty years—all of them under Father Rufus. I'm sure my arrival can't have been easy for him."

No, I suspected it hadn't—particularly since Dr. Rufus J. Womble had been a mild-mannered, easygoing sort, perfectly content to leave all the practical matters to Riddick's marginally more capable hands. The three of them—Riddick, Father Rufus, and Trinity—had quietly moldered away until Father Rufus, while walking around the rectory, as usual, with his nose in a book, had fallen down a flight of stairs and broken both legs, prompting the bishop to decide that he was overdue for retirement. And along came Robyn, with her huge supply of enthusiasm and energy. Even those of us who adored her sometimes felt a little tired. How must it have been for Riddick?

"There's so much I could have learned from him," Robyn said.

"Yes," I said. "Sometimes he's the only one who can get that window in the kitchen to open when it gets stuck. And every year, the decorating committee nearly has a nervous breakdown until he figures out where the boxes of decorations have gotten to."

"I was thinking more of the wisdom he must have learned from working with Father Rufus for so long," Robyn said. "And his deep knowledge of the congregation. But yes, those things are useful. Although Randall Shiffley's promised to find me a carpenter who can fix the window, and once we have that yard sale and clear out thirty years' accumulation of pure junk, finding things around here won't be nearly so difficult."

I could understand why Riddick was leaving, even though I was very much in favor of Robyn's plans.

And it occurred to me that although very few people

knew it yet, two of the most annoying people in my life right now—Riddick and Mr. Lightfoot—were probably leaving town soon. Could life get any better? Well, possibly if Barliman Vess decided to convert to one of the other denominations in town. Unlikely, and I didn't really want to wish him on any of them.

And if Michael's mother would go back to her long-standing tradition of taking a cruise to some warm climate for Christmas and showing up with armloads of presents for Epiphany, thus avoiding the dueling holiday dinner crisis we were having this year. But that was a problem for another day.

"Speaking of clearing out," I said aloud. "Time we both did that."

"Not quite." She closed her eyes briefly, and I could see how tired she was. "I'm not leaving until the night watch gets here."

"Night watch?"

"A small group of parishioners have agreed to stay here in the church overnight," she said. "To guard against any more pranks."

"Smart idea," I said.

"All the churches are doing it," she said. "Just until Chief Burke catches who's pulling these pranks. And did you know the temple has a guard who stays there every night? Times being what they are I'm sure that's wise, but isn't it sad for a house of worship to have to do any of this?"

"Very sad," I said. "How soon are our volunteer guards coming?"

"They were supposed to be here at ten."

We both glanced at our watches. The volunteers were fifteen minutes late. And no doubt at this time of year Robyn had a busy day tomorrow.

"Don't worry," she said, as if reading my mind. "They should be here any minute."

"I could wait for them," I began.

"But you have Michael and those sweet little boys waiting for you," she said. "And when I go home it's to a cold house—my husband had to dash down to North Carolina to see about his great-aunt again."

"Oh, no," I said. "But he'll be back for Christmas, I hope."

"Of course," she said. "And I rather think Matt will be bringing Great-Aunt Brynhild back this time—and not just for Christmas. But tonight I'm footloose and fancy free, so I might just stay here with the watch for a while. For the company."

I wished her a good night and headed home, feeling reassured that Trinity was locked up tight and would soon be watched over by a vigilant group of parishioners.

Chapter 20

I got home in time to hear the last few pages of *How the Grinch Stole Christmas* and participate in the usual bedtime ritual—made somewhat more prolonged by the fact that the boys, who had only the vaguest idea of time, had to be told several times that no, Santa was not coming tonight. Soon, but not tonight. And perhaps they weren't sleepy enough, given all the napping they'd done during the day to allow them to stay up for the concert. But once we were sure the boys were asleep, we assigned Rose Noire to keep an eye on them, and Michael and I retreated to the library to wrap presents.

It was going a lot slower than usual, thanks to my still wonky shoulder—in fact, half the time it was Michael doing the wrapping with me providing sage advice and an occasional finger to hold a ribbon in place.

As we wrapped, I told Michael about what I'd overheard after the concert.

"So we know who the pranksters are," he said.

"One set of pranksters," I said. "They didn't do the duck prank."

"Maybe," he said. "Or maybe they just didn't *both* do it."

"Michael, they both denied it. Strenuously. And they had no idea anyone was listening."

"Except each other. What if one of them did it, thinking the other would approve, only to find out the other was furious. Would he admit to pulling the prank? Or would he pretend to be baffled?"

I closed my eyes and tried to remember their voices.

"They sounded so sincere," I said.

"So would I have at their age," he said. "At least we have a better idea why they did it. Some kind of retribution against Lightfoot—I assume that's who they meant by 'Bigfoot.'"

"'Mad at Bigfoot about the April thing,'" I repeated, as I collected a stack of presents Michael had already wrapped and moved them out of his way. A small stack, that I could carry one-handed. "I'm sure that's what they said. What happened in April?"

"Easter? The New Life choir gave that big sunrise concert down at the lake. Did Lightfoot dislocate anyone else's shoulder for the occasion?"

"Easter was in March," I said.

"Would they remember that? Most people think of Easter as being in April."

"Maybe," I said. "But if Lightfoot did something to upset them back then, why not call it the Easter thing? And why wait nine months?"

Michael shrugged and shook his head.

"Well, I'll tell the chief," I said. "Assuming he ever calls me back. He's in the New Life congregation—maybe he'll have some idea just what happened in April."

"Or maybe he'll convince the boys to spill all," Michael said. "Anyway—you know, we could do this tomorrow."

He'd caught me yawning prodigiously.

"Tomorrow is cutting it awfully close, isn't it?" I asked. "Especially since we've got your *Christmas Carol* performance tomorrow night. And I want to get everything possible wrapped beforehand, so we can save Christmas Eve for assembling things."

"Do we have any more gift tags?" Michael said, holding up a present. "I need to tag this one before I forget who it's for."

"Hand it to me—I'll make some more tags." I grabbed the scissors and a scrap of foil paper and began carefully cutting little rectangles that I could fold into tags.

"And don't forget," I went on. "We'll be helping both mothers with their dinners."

"Right," he said. "So we persevere. It would help if our respective mothers-in-law could work together and throw one big Christmas dinner instead of two."

"It was a major feat of diplomacy to get them to schedule their meals at different times," I said.

"Understood," he said. "And believe me, your diplomatic skills are much appreciated. So is it lunch with your parents and then supper back here with whatever Mom comes up with? Or vice versa?"

"Please!" I said. "They would both be mortally insulted at hearing their banquets described as lunch or supper. Early dinner and late dinner, noon sharp and six p.m."

"And Pepto-Bismol at midnight," he said. "Please tell me they're going for something easy to digest."

"Mother's doing turkey," I said.

"Fabulous! I like a traditional holiday meal."

"Which she is cooking in some odd way she read about on one of those food blogs," I said. "Stuffed with crab, oysters, and lobster."

"Sounds delicious!" And then his face fell. "For those who can eat it. Is she having a seafood-free option, or has she forgotten your allergies again?"

"Mother doesn't approve of my being allergic to anything as elegant and expensive as crab, oysters, and lobster," I said.

"Well, there should be plenty of side dishes."

"And with any luck she won't gussy up all of them with seafood."

"Or if she does, you'll have all the more room for Mom's feast," he said.

"Yes." I tried to sound enthusiastic, but Michael knew me too well.

"So, what's Mom serving?" he asked.

"She's going pan-Asian," I said. "Cantonese-style lobster is the main course."

"Oh, dear."

"Accompanied by Peking duck, squid pancakes, spicy pig's blood soup, thousand-year-old eggs, and charcoal-grilled eel."

"She's clearly trying to impress everyone," Michael said. "She always goes to Asian dishes with . . . unusual ingredients when she wants to impress."

"She said she knew people would be tired of ordinary holiday fare by the time they came to her dinner," I said.

We wrapped in silence for a few minutes.

"You know," I said finally. "I just don't get it."

"Get what?"

"The whole idea of getting tired of the usual holiday fare," I said. "I like holiday fare. Turkey. Gravy. Mashed potatoes. Pumpkin pie. I like them."

"I assume everyone does. Or almost everyone."

"And I never understand all the fuss about how to use up leftover turkey. What's wrong with just eating it the way it comes, at least while the gravy lasts? I'm always a little sad when the turkey runs out."

"I agree," he said.

"But unfortunately neither of our mothers does," I said. "And please don't repeat this to them—"

"Of course not."

"Because I feel horribly ungrateful complaining about this. They're going to a world of trouble, and fixing us fabulous, gourmet fare."

"That you can't eat."

"Some of which I can't eat, but that's beside the point. Even if they fixed something I could eat—something I liked, like steak—I'd still kind of miss the traditional fare. Turkey, cooked in a normal way, not stuffed with crustaceans. And with good old artery-clogging southern gravy. Mashed potatoes. Cranberry sauce. Pumpkin pie. Tomato aspic. Don't make a face—Mother's tomato aspic is more like Bloody Mary–flavored Jell-O."

"Still—aspic?" Michael still sounded dubious. "Did you like it that much?"

"I didn't hate it," I said. "And it was traditional. What I'm trying to say is that I miss all the things I used to have at Thanksgiving and Christmas when I was growing up. Back when Mother drafted Mrs. Fenniman to do her cooking. Mrs. Fenniman was an excellent plain cook. Forget losing weight on her cooking, and if you valued your life, you didn't make a suggestion about how to do something differently, but if you liked good, plain southern cooking, Mrs. Fenniman was the queen."

"I remember," Michael said. "Who's helping your mother this holiday?"

"Some poor cousin from Matthews County whose husband is spending Christmas on the *USS Harry S Truman*," I said. "She's wonderful cook, and willing to put up with Mother's strangest suggestions, and I'm sure it will all be delicious. But it's—it's not the tradition I grew up with. And I feel terrible complaining to you, because I know having strange and unusual food is your Christmas tradition."

"Some tradition," he said. "Every year something different, from some other part of the world. The first time I had a holiday dinner with your family, I thought I'd died and gone to heaven."

"Really?" I put down the scissors and stared. "You never told me. Or if you did, I assumed you were just being polite."

"Your family had the kind of holiday dinners I always longed for," he said. "The kind every other kid on base—or later, in the neighborhood—got to eat. Real old-fashioned meals, like the Pilgrims ate. I wish we could go back to that."

"Yeah," I said.

We fell silent again. I wasn't sure what Michael was thinking, but I was pondering the fact that I already felt better about our mothers' strange and over-the-top holiday menus, knowing Michael didn't like them any more than I did.

"I have a plan," he said finally. "To satisfy the longing we both have for an old-fashioned Christmas dinner."

"We run away and eat with Mrs. Fenniman?"

"Better," he said. "We cook our own."

"And have three Christmas dinners?" I shuddered slightly. "I'm not sure that's much of an improvement."

"We could do ours on Christmas Eve," he said. "Remember that little basement apartment we lived in before we found the house?"

I nodded.

"It's vacant at the moment. And the owner of the house is a friend. He's trying to decide whether to rent it out again or remodel it as part of his house. I'm sure I could arrange for us to borrow the apartment."

"And do what?"

"Cook our own Christmas dinner," he said. "Just you and

me and the boys. Not a big dinner—the kitchen's pretty tiny. But I can drop by the turkey farm and get a small bird."

"It takes a while to cook even a small turkey," I pointed out.

"And you'll probably be swamped with more church-swapping chores," he said. "So I'll pick up the ingredients, and the boys can help me get it started, and then you can join us in the basement apartment for our own little Christmas dinner. The four of us. And then when the tryptophan in the turkey starts working on the boys, we bring them home, put them to bed, and assemble the train tracks and whatever else in a fabulous mood."

"It's a crazy idea," I said. "Let's do it."

We took time off from our wrapping to run to the kitchen for a few cookbooks and make a list of utensils and ingredients we'd need. And by the time we'd finished that, it was well past bedtime, but we lay awake for quite a while, inventing ever more fantastic tales to tell our families about our absence on Christmas Eve, and giggling until I was afraid we'd wake the boys. It was nearly one by the time we fell asleep.

And half past three when Michael's pager went off again.

Chapter 21

"Where is that, I wonder?" Michael asked, after Debbie Anne had rattled off the address. "Someone really should explain to Chief Featherstone that a lot of people in town barely know their own street addresses, and at least half of his firefighters don't own a GPS."

"Temple Beth-El," I said. "I have now memorized the addresses of every church and synagogue in town, and I've practically memorized the phone numbers of all the priests, ministers, and rabbis."

"The prankster again?" He looked grim.

I went up to make sure Rob was stirring. I found Rose Noire knocking on his door, which popped open just as I reached her side.

"All right, all right," he muttered. "Why didn't someone tell me so many of these fires would be in the middle of the night?"

He popped back into his room and from the thumping and scuffling noises, he appeared to be hauling out and donning his gear.

"I'll fix coffee again," Rose Noire said.

"And after that, could you watch the boys again while I trail after the firefighters?" I asked. "I have at least a dozen events scheduled in one or another of the temple's meeting rooms today, and if I'm going to have to rework the schedule again, I'd like to know sooner rather than later."

"Oh, dear," she said. "So it's the prankster again? Of course."

She flitted downstairs and into the kitchen. I went to throw on my clothes. Warm clothes, in case we were in for another long stretch of standing about in the cold.

Temple Beth-El was also on the Clay County Road, a little farther out of town than the New Life Baptist Church. It was fairly new, and very modern, with a lot of floor-to-ceiling glass windows looking out over the surrounding woods. In any other season, the view from those windows was magical, since members of the congregation had subtly improved the natural beauty of the woods by planting dogwoods and redbuds at its edge for spring blossoms and Japanese maples for fall color.

But as I pulled into the temple parking lot and picked my way through the mounds of snow to find a good stopping place, I glanced up at the glass windows and shuddered. Even if they'd gone in for the kind of thick, energy-efficient glass that would make the inside toasty warm in this weather, just having a view of the snow and ice outside would chill me on a night like this. And knowing that every time I walked in front of one of those windows some lurking prankster might be watching me—

"Stop spooking yourself," I muttered as I parked the car.

And my stomach tightened when I realized that this time the fire engines weren't standing idly by. Michael and Rob and their colleagues were unrolling hoses and hauling equipment out of various compartments and then dashing off into the woods to the right of the temple.

Most of the deputies who had arrived on the scene were following them, although I could see a pair of deputies slowly working their way around the left side of the building, checking behind every twig. And my friend Aida Butler was talking to an excitable man in a fur-trimmed down jacket. I strolled over to eavesdrop.

"—and Chief Burke told us all to be on the lookout for the prankster," the man was saying. "So when I saw the flames out in the woods, I called."

"Did you go out to investigate?" Aida asked.

"I didn't dare leave the temple," he said.

Flames in the woods. I watched until the last fireman had disappeared into the woods, then followed the path of the hoses, keeping a good ten feet away from the nearest one. A half-moon shone down from the cloudless sky and reflected on the snow, making it easy to see where I was going.

Pretty soon I spotted the firefighters in a clearing. No flames, but a lot of steam rising from what had probably been a campfire before the hoses had gotten to it. Three hoses were still pouring water into the clearing—Rob was wielding the nozzle on one of them—and a couple of other firefighters were hacking at logs and turning over piles of leaves, presumably to uncover any lingering sparks.

Chief Burke and Chief Featherstone, the fire chief, were standing at the edge of the clearing, watching the excitement.

"You think maybe you could call them off now?" Chief Burke said. "I hate to dampen their enthusiasm, seeing as how for most of them it's their first real fire—"

"But the fire's long gone, and all they're doing now is washing away any evidence that you might like to find," Chief Featherstone said. "I hear you."

He lifted a bullhorn to his mouth and barked out an order. "Stand down! Turn off your hoses and stand by to assist the deputies if needed."

It took a few seconds, but the hoses cut off, and all the firefighters gathered around the clearing, except for a few who were running through the woods shouting "All clear here!" at intervals, and were probably too far away to hear their chief.

Two of the deputies sprang into action, searching the sodden leaves and ashes in the clearing.

"Found something," one called. "Beer bottles. And the contents are still a little fizzy."

He held up a bottle of Gwent Pale, a local microbrew.

"Never heard of that brand," Chief Featherstone said.

"It's not really sold anywhere but Caerphilly," Michael told him. "Two retired agriculture professors from the college started a microbrewery as a hobby. The quality varies wildly, but since they're not trying to make a profit, they keep the cost dirt cheap—making it the beer of choice for a lot of the college students who are old enough to drink."

"And a lot who aren't," the chief added. "But most of the college students have gone home. This looks like teenagers."

I had to agree. I tried to think of a reason why someone old enough to drink legally would take to the woods with a six-pack of Gwent Pale on a night like this, and failed miserably. I saw several other firefighters or deputies nodding as if having the same thought.

"Let's finish up here before all that water freezes over again," the chief said. "And—"

A harsh buzzing broke out, as if a tribe of giant, angry, mutant bees had suddenly descended on the clearing. All the firefighters began digging in their pockets. Chief Featherstone pulled his pager out first and pressed a button.

"Box fourteen oh four for the structure fire. Seventy-two Church Street. Engine companies fourteen and two, truck twelve, rescue squad two, ambulance fourteen respond. Oh three twenty-three."

"Church Street," the Chief Featherstone said. "Let's go."

"Which one is it?" one fireman asked.

"Trinity Episcopal Church," I called over my shoulder. I was already making tracks for the parking lot.

Chapter 22

Since I wasn't hauling heavy equipment, I beat all the fire-fighters and most of the deputies back to the parking lot. But since I was only a civilian, I made sure not to get in the way of any of the emergency vehicles as they roared and squealed out of the parking lot. So I was, of course, the last to arrive at Trinity.

When I pulled into the parking lot, not that far behind the last of the fire engines, I saw five people standing around, stamping their feet and blowing out plumes of vapor as they breathed. None of them was wearing coats, so I suspected they were the night watch, and had evacuated the church in a hurry. And yes, I could see smoke coming out of the church. Out of the basement stairwell, in fact. Not a whole lot, but still. A real fire.

I pulled up to the group of onlookers—I recognized several of them as frequent church volunteers—and rolled down my window.

"Anyone need to warm up?"

They all took me up on it. Four of them, three men and one woman, climbed into the back. It was a tight squeeze, even after we stowed the boys' car seats in the trunk. The fifth, a plump elderly woman, joined me in the front seat.

"What happened?" I asked, as I rolled my window up again.

"We were playing Parcheesi in the social hall," one of the men said. "To help keep awake."

"And we took a break every hour and patrolled," the plump woman said. "Inside, of course—what a beastly night!"

"And just a little while ago, we smelled smoke coming from the undercroft," the man went on. "Hank and I went down to check things out, and there was a fire in the furnace room!"

"We emptied the fire extinguishers on it without doing much good," said another man—Hank, I supposed. "So we called 911."

"And evacuated," the plump woman said. "And would to goodness we'd taken the time to grab our coats."

"Good thing we didn't," the first man said.

"Wouldn't have hurt," the woman said. "Church hasn't burned down yet."

"You didn't see that fire," Hank countered. "Meg, can you pull a little closer to the church so we can see what's going on?"

I started the car again, and carefully crept through the parking lot until I found a spot with a better view of what was going on. Some of the firefighters—including Michael; I recognized him by his height—were dashing in through the front door, dragging hoses behind them while others had gone down into the basement stairwell. But they appeared to have halted there. I could see several of them standing at ground level, holding the hose or their axes, peering down. Then I heard a smashing noise, and the firefighters set up a cheer, and they all disappeared into the basement.

We watched in silence for a few moments.

"Looks a bit more serious than ducks and skunks," one man finally said.

More smoke billowed out of the basement door, and a little out of the front door of the church. Was that a bad thing? A sign that the fire was spreading? More likely it meant the firefighters were pouring water on the blaze.

I noticed two of Chief Burke's deputies working their way around the left side of the church, giving the clouds of smoke a wide berth. The chief himself was standing in the parking lot, well out of the firefighters' way, but visibly impatient for them to finish their job so he could start his.

After a while he spotted my car and strolled over. I rolled down my window.

"Evening, Chief," I said.

"Morning, I think," he said. "One of these days you're going to have to let Michael and Rob go to a fire all by themselves. Are these the folks who called in the alarm?"

My passengers poured out their story, interrupting each other in their haste. The chief heard them out, then took their names and numbers.

"I hate to ask it, but would you good people mind staying here until the fire's out and I can get into the church?" he asked. "I'd like to take your detailed individual statements as soon as possible."

"No problem," Hank said.

"We're the night owls," the plump woman said with a small laugh. "We were planning to stay up all night to watch over the church."

"Looks as if we failed," another man said.

"I wouldn't say that," Chief Burke said. "Looks as if you called 911 in time to save the church."

He pointed to the front doors, where firefighters had begun trickling out. I felt a sudden wave of relief when I saw Michael's tall form among them.

"Is it the same prankster, Chief?" one of the men asked.

"Too early to tell," he said. "Were the five of you the only people in the church?"

"Yes," said the plump woman.

"As far as we know," muttered one of the men.

"The doors and windows all locked?" the chief asked.

"And checked every hour," the plump woman said, nodding vigorously.

"And you didn't let anyone else in at any time?"

The members of the watch all shook their heads, some of them frowning uneasily.

"Good." The chief nodded absently. He appeared to be lost in thought. I hoped the watch members were reassured by the fact that he was staring into space, not at any of them. I know I would have been relieved.

Chief Featherstone came over.

"We're still finishing up in the basement," he said. "But the fire's out, and you're welcome to come in and start your investigation. And I expect these folks would like to get in out of the cold. Okay with me as long as they stay out of the basement."

"And with me as well," Chief Burke said. He turned and strode toward the church. My passengers all murmured thanks to me and scrambled out of the car to follow. I decided to tag along.

Since the night watch had all been in the social hall when the fire broke out, the chief sent them there, with orders not to talk to each other until he'd interviewed them—and a deputy to watch over them and make sure they followed orders. I went along and busied myself making a pot of coffee so I'd look useful enough that they wouldn't kick me out. In fact, I decided, I'd fill the big pot we used for receptions. The firefighters might want some before they went home, and there were bound to be more deputies showing up soon, not to mention curious parishioners.

When the coffee was ready, I grabbed a cup with my good hand and went out to hand it to one of the firefighters or deputies, so I'd have a good excuse for taking a look around. I spotted the two chiefs in the vestibule, talking intently about something. I headed their way.

Then I saw my dad appear in the vestibule, medical bag in hand. He said a few words to the two chiefs, then trotted briskly in my direction.

"Morning, Meg," he said when he spotted me. "Terrible business."

He disappeared down the basement steps.

I went to the head of the stairs and peered down. A deputy was standing at the foot of the stairs. He turned, and I recognized him as Vern Shiffley, one of Randall's many cousins.

"No one's allowed down here," he said.

"Not sure I even want to go down there," I said. "Coffee?"

"Thanks." He trudged up the stairs, looking glum, and took the cup from me.

"What's wrong?" I asked. "Is it bad down there? Was anyone hurt?"

"We have a body," he said. "Looks like the prankster went too far this time."

Chapter 23

"A body?" I flinched at the thought. "Who?"

He looked for a moment as if he were about to tell me to mind my own business, then his face fell.

"It'll get out soon enough. That old gentleman who used to run the First Farmers Bank of Caerphilly before it got bought up by that out-of-state bank."

"Barliman Vess?"

"That's him." Over Vern's shoulder I could see the chief had spotted us talking and was heading our way. I braced myself to be kicked out.

"I gather Mr. Vess works here or something?" Vern asked.

"He's a vestryman."

I could tell from Vern's face that he didn't know the word.

"The vestry is very similar to what you Presbyterians would call the session," I said. "Group of people elected from the congregation to help govern the church."

"So he's what we'd call an elder?" Vern asked.

"Yes," I said. "Hello, Chief," I added.

"Any idea what Mr. Vess was doing in the furnace room at three in the morning?" Chief Burke asked.

"None whatsoever," I said. "We had a night watch staying here in the church—those people who were warming up in my car. They were keeping a lookout in case the prankster came back. But they were all in the social hall, as they told you, playing Parcheesi between patrols. You can ask them if Mr. Vess was with them—though I think they'd have mentioned it if one of their number never made it out of the church."

The chief nodded.

"The only thing I can think of—" I began. And then I stopped myself, because what I had been about to say suddenly seemed foolish.

"Go on," the chief said after a moment.

"Mr. Vess was kind of a gadfly," I explained. "Particularly on church financial issues."

"Useful to have a retired banker for that," the chief said.

"Except he drove everyone crazy," I said. "He was always going on about overspending, and trying to catch people being wasteful—or worse, dishonest. Mother said last year he was putting marked bills in the collection plate to see if the people adding up the offering were honest."

"What could he have been trying to find out in the basement?"

"No idea," I said. "Robyn—Reverend Smith—might know. Or my mother. She's on the vestry with Mr. Vess."

The chief turned to Vern.

"It would help if we knew whether Mr. Vess was killed in the furnace room or whether his body was moved there later," he said.

"I'll ask Dr. Langslow." Vern headed down the stairs.

"So you think he hid in the church after the concert and then came out to do—whatever he came to do," the chief said.

"No, he couldn't possibly have been hiding in the church after the concert," I said. "I locked up for Robyn while she was seeing people out, and I'd have found him."

"He could have been hiding in a closet," the chief said. "Or the men's room."

"The bathrooms are one-person and unisex," I said. "And I checked them all. And all the closets. I remember one time Mr. Vess hid in the broom closet for hours so he could find out who was constantly leaving the lights on after choir practice. So I checked everywhere."

"You were checking for Mr. Vess?" The chief looked confused and a little suspicious.

"No, I was looking for potential pranksters, but I remembered how easily he'd hidden in the closets, so I figured if he could hide in closets, so could they."

"I suppose you checked all the doors," the chief said. "Including that little door at the far end of the basement."

"The door that would be just perfect for sneaking in with a small cage of skunks?" I said. "Absolutely."

"Actually, this time it was rabbits," he said. "And they're fine," he added hastily, seeing the look on my face. "A little frightened, but they were at the far end of the furnace room. The fire didn't get that far."

I nodded, and found I had to blink back tears. For the rescued rabbits, or Barliman Vess? I wasn't sure.

"Only two of them," the chief went on. "Not much of a prank compared to the others."

"Maybe Mr. Vess interrupted the perpetrators while they were unloading the rabbits and they fled with most of them," I said. "You could put out an APB. See if you can find anyone in possession of a suspicious number of rabbits. Just kidding," I added, seeing that the chief didn't seem to like my suggestion.

"Indeed," he said. "Actually, since the rabbits turned out to be stolen from the fifth grade classroom at Caerphilly Elementary, which only had two to begin with, I don't think we'll be uncovering any hoards of contraband leporids."

I decided to wait until he looked less stressed before making my other, more serious suggestion—that perhaps whoever had killed Vess had left the rabbits to make it seem as if Vess's murder was connected to the other pranks. Although the odds were, the chief had already thought of it.

"By the way," I said aloud. "I know no one was hiding in the church when I left, but I'm not sure it's all that significant. I don't think the locks have been rekeyed in twenty years, and both Robyn and Father Rufus have been pretty quick to give a key to anyone with a legitimate purpose. Including some of the people from other churches who were here at Trinity over the last few days. Like Lightfoot and Randall's construction people."

The chief sighed and nodded.

"It's the same at New Life," he said. "The reverend is always more interested in bringing people in than keeping them out. We won't be solving this one based on who has access to my crime scenes. But thanks."

"Chief, there's something else," I said. "Did you get my call last night?" I decided that was more tactful than "Why the heck haven't you returned my last three phone calls?"

He nodded. I looked around to make sure no one else was nearby.

I noticed he did, too.

"You have some relevant information?" he asked, in a low voice.

"Do you know Caleb Shiffley and Ronnie Butler?" I asked.

"Yes." He nodded slightly. "Both fine young men. I believe they're seniors this year. Both on the basketball team, in fact. Ronnie is a member of the New Life congregation, and I believe Caleb, like most of the Shiffleys, attends First Presbyterian. What about them?"

"They were the ones who put the skunks in the choir loft. I overheard them talking about it. And the snake here."

The chief looked at me for few moments, expressionless.

"Yes," he said finally.

"You already know?"

"I didn't quite know," he said. "But I suspected. In fact, I was suspicious of Caleb almost from the start."

"You were?" I exclaimed. "Why?"

"Caleb helps his father out at the Shiffley Exterminating Service. His father usually assigns him to go deep into the woods to release the animals that are being returned to the wild. The most plausible explanation I could come up with for the sudden appearance of so many skunks was that some of the rescued skunks had not been released as planned over the last few months. And Caleb and Ronnie are inseparable. Have been since grade school. I figured if one was in on it, it was almost certain the other was."

"So you were just gathering evidence?" I asked. "Before confronting them or arresting them or whatever?"

He sighed.

"Gathering evidence, yes, but frankly, I was hoping when they realized how much trouble they'd caused, they'd both come forward and offer to make amends. But after the duck incident, I had no choice. I was already planning to bring them and their parents into the station this morning. If only I hadn't waited."

"So you didn't return any of my calls because you already knew about them," I said. "Makes sense."

"I'm sorry." He seemed to be wincing slightly. "There was also the fact that I've gotten at least a hundred calls over the last day and a half, all from people who were sure they knew who had committed the pranks."

"Now I feel guilty, adding to the avalanche," I said. "I probably should have just relayed the information I had to Debbie Anne. Or one of your deputies."

"Actually," the chief said. "I suspected, with all the time you'd been spending around the New Life choir, that your suspicions might be a lot more accurate than most, but I wanted to see if I could induce the boys to come clean first."

"Before I gave you concrete information that forced you to take more drastic action."

"I was . . . well, yes. Precisely. I wanted to handle it privately, with apologies to Reverend Wilson and Father Donnelly, complete financial restitution, and a stiff unofficial course of community service to the two churches."

I nodded. I hoped Josh and Jamie never did anything as stupid as the pranks, but if they did, I hoped the chief was still around to help us deal with it.

"I was wrong," the chief went on. "I let myself be swayed by my good opinion of the young men. My desire to avoid ruining their futures. If I'd only brought them in after the duck prank, perhaps they'd have stopped, and whatever tragic sequence of events happened here last night would never have taken place."

"But they didn't do the duck prank," I said. "And I doubt if they did this. They did the skunks and the snakes—I overheard them talking about it on Saturday. But they had nothing to do with the ducks. That's what I was calling last night to tell you."

Chapter 24

"Didn't do the duck prank?" The chief looked surprised, and a little skeptical. "Are you sure? And how do you know?"

I relayed what I'd heard in the hallway at Trinity on Saturday, what I'd seen on Riddick's computer, and then what I'd overheard Sunday afternoon.

"So you see why I don't think Caleb and Ronnie did anything after the snake incident." I didn't realize until I was finishing up my account how much the information had been weighing on me.

"You believed them, then?"

"Yes," I said. "They had no idea anyone was listening, and they sounded utterly truthful. They were both reproaching the other for committing the duck prank—doing something so stupid, something that was likely to get them caught, after they'd agreed to lie low."

He pondered for a few moments. I glanced down the hallway and saw that a couple of the deputies were looking at us, obviously impatient, but not about to interrupt the chief when he was so intent on a conversation.

"Anything else?" he asked.

Should I tell him about Rose Noire's premonition of danger in the church and her suspicions of Lightfoot? He'd probably only find it annoying. And what good were premonitions about something that had now already happened? I shook my head.

"Keep this to yourself for now," he said finally.

I nodded.

"It's possible that whoever did this is hoping the blame will fall on the boys," he went on.

"And you want the real culprit to think that he's succeeded so you can catch him off his guard. Or her."

"Or them," he added. "Precisely. So tell no one."

"Not even Michael?"

He frowned for a moment.

"I think we may rely on Michael's discretion as well," he said finally. "But no one else."

"Especially not my dad," I said. "Who would probably manage to tell the whole county within a few hours—swearing them all to secrecy, of course."

That got a slight smile out of him.

"Speaking of your father, I need to talk to him. Stick around, if possible. I may need your help to sort out what went on here."

With that he started down the stairway toward the basement. I headed back for the parish hall, to wait with the others there. Just as I was about to enter it, Horace dashed through the front door. The deputies in the vestibule pointed him toward the stairway.

He waved to me before disappearing into the basement.

In the parish hall, four of the watch members were once again playing Parcheesi at one of the long tables we used for meals, while the older woman was seated a little farther down the table, reading an Agatha Christie paperback.

They all looked up when I came in.

"The investigation continues." I slumped in a chair at the same table, but at the far end from the Parcheesi game, and closed my eyes as if too exhausted to speak. I wasn't sure they knew about Vess's death, and if they didn't, I was sure the chief would want to break the news himself and watch their reactions.

A few minutes later the chief came in, accompanied by Robyn. Several deputies came in after him and stood along the wall.

"Are all of you okay?" Robyn exclaimed. The chief stood by watching while she went around to give each of the watchers a few words and a quick hug. She ended up with me.

"So sorry," she said. "I have a feeling we're going to be rearranging again."

I nodded.

"Ladies and gentlemen," the chief said. "I want to have a brief word with each of you. But first, I have to tell you that tonight's incident is more than just a prank. There's been a murder."

The watch and Robyn all reacted with gasps and exclamations of "Oh, no!" or "Who?"

I just watched, trying to detect any false notes in their reactions—probably just what the chief and the deputies were doing. Maybe the chief spotted something suspicious but I didn't.

"We've identified the deceased as Mr. Barliman Vess," the chief added.

I don't think I was imagining the looks of relief that crossed all of their faces—quickly replaced with looks that clearly said, "Of course, it's still a terrible thing."

"May I remind all of you not to discuss what you heard and saw tonight until after I've interviewed you?" the chief said.

The watchers and Robyn all murmured their agreement.

"You, too, Ms. Langslow," the chief added. "Michael

asked me to tell you that he's heading home and will see to the boys till you get back."

I nodded. So much for going home and catching up on my sleep.

The chief left with one of the watchers—the Christie reader—while the Parcheesi players seemed to have lost interest in their game.

"What on earth was he doing here?" one of them asked. "Sorry, forget I said that," he added, glancing up at the deputy.

"We could talk about what's going to happen with our Christmas services," the remaining woman watcher said. "That's not against the chief's orders, is it?"

The deputy shook his head.

"That will depend on how long the church is unavailable to us," Robyn said. "If it continues to be a crime scene after today, we must trust Meg to find us a solution."

"But having a death so close to Christmas," another watcher said. "Surely that will cast a pall over all our celebrations."

"Not if we remember the true meaning of those celebrations," Robyn said. "The reason Christ was born among us."

" 'Born that we no more may die,' " one of the men sang softly. I recognized the tune and some of the words from the little-sung third verse of "Hark! The Herald Angels."

" 'Born to raise us from the earth,' " the singer went on. Two of the others joined in on the next line, " 'Born to give us second birth.' "

Another deputy stuck his head in, looking a bit surprised, but apparently warbling Christmas carols wasn't against the chief's orders, so both deputies joined in the last two familiar lines: " 'Hark! The herald angels sing, Glory to the newborn king!' "

"Very good," Robyn said. I wasn't sure whether she meant the singing or the sentiments, but everyone seemed more cheerful. "Charles Wesley did have a way with a hymn, didn't he?"

"On a practical note," the remaining woman said. "If we get the church back in time, will we need to reconsecrate it after this?"

The others all glanced over at the deputy, as if checking to see if this line of conversation was allowed.

"I think not," Robyn said. "I'll have to check with the bishop, of course, but I think the appropriate action is a prayer service for the Restoring of Things Profaned."

"I don't recall seeing that in the Book of Common Prayer," one of the men said.

"Book of Occasional Services," Robyn said. "I've actually used it once at my previous parish—one of the parishioners had a psychotic episode and willfully injured himself."

The watchers all nodded. One of them walked over to a bookshelf, picked out a volume, and walked back to the table with it.

"Here it is," he said. "Book of Occasional Services." Two of the others crowded around to look over his shoulder.

"Does Mr. Vess have family?" I asked Robyn.

"A son on the West Coast." She pulled out her Day-Timer and scribbled a few items in it, and then glanced at her watch. "I'll check with the chief to see if I should do the notification or wait until after he makes the call. I do hope he doesn't declare the whole church a crime scene, although I suppose we should be prepared for that."

"I think the best thing I can do to prepare is rework the

schedule again," I said. "After which I hope no one will think me rude if I try to nap."

"Would you like my laptop?" Robyn reached into her oversized purse and pulled it out. "I've got your latest schedule on it, and you should be able to access the network from here. Or if you really need to sleep, do!"

She gestured toward the far end of the room where there was a nest of cast-off armchairs and couches.

"Thanks," I said. "That would be great. And while I'm thinking of it, do you think perhaps it might make sense to rekey the church? Since by now we have no idea where most of those million spare keys have gone."

"I hate the idea," Robyn said. "But it's probably necessary. Long overdue, in fact." She pulled out her Day-Timer.

I curled up on one of the couches and pulled up the latest schedule. A quick call to Father Donnelly confirmed that St. Byblig's was back in play, and I was now so thoroughly familiar with all the available spaces in the local churches that it took me only a few minutes to move all the events scheduled today in Trinity to the equivalent spaces in St. Byblig's. Of course it helped that since today was Monday, and only the twenty-third, it was a relatively quiet lull between the weekend and the holiday itself.

And then, after e-mailing my ever-growing list of people who needed to be informed of every single change in the schedule, and recruiting one of them—the office manager at the Unitarian church—to print out and drop off some signs that would tell anyone who showed up at Trinity where to go, I curled up on the most comfortable-looking couch. Napping was probably not going to happen, but at least I could rest my eyes. Yes, lovely to rest my eyes, and . . .

"Meg?" I woke with a start to find a uniformed deputy looming over me.

Chapter 25

Evidently I had napped. For two hours, unless my watch was wrong. The room was empty except for me and the deputy. It was Sammy Wendell, one of Rose Noire's many beaus.

"Meg?"

"Sorry," I said. "I was fast asleep. I gather the chief wants to see me."

"No, the chief just took off," Sammy said. "We're locking down the building. I'm afraid you need to leave."

"Locking down the building? For how long?"

Sammy shrugged apologetically.

I followed him out. Our steps echoed in the empty building. It was so quiet that I started when I heard the sound of hammering coming from downstairs.

"One of the Shiffleys is boarding up the basement door," Sammy said. "The one the firefighters had to break to get in."

Out in the parking lot I could see groups of people. Some were standing and staring at the silent, empty church, as if unwilling to accept that the drama was over. Others were turning to leave and climbing into their cars. I saw Riddick standing on the sidewalk, wringing his hands and leaning forward slightly as if poised to run back into the church if the chief changed his mind and took away the crime scene tape.

Robyn, Mother, and several ladies I recognized as members of St. Clotilda's Guild were standing in a cluster. Robyn was holding open what appeared to be a prayer book.

"If you've been reduced to holding services in the parking lot, maybe it's time I woke up and got back to my job," I said.

"The new schedule's fine," Robyn said. "We're just making plans for the Restoring of Things Profaned. Though I think we've done all we can do until we learn when we're getting the church back."

"Poor Horace is still in there working," Mother said.

"And covering every inch of the inside with that horrible fingerprint powder," one of the ladies exclaimed.

"Which we all think should be cleaned up before we have the ceremony," Robyn said. "Of course, that's not liturgically necessary."

"But it just won't really feel restored if we don't," one of the ladies said.

"And it's going to be difficult, first getting out the news about the cleanup, and then the ceremony," Robyn said.

"Why not schedule your cleaning and ceremony for some specific time?" I said. "Like seven a.m. tomorrow morning for the cleaning, followed by nine for the ceremony. If we have to postpone, we can, but at least people can get it on their schedules. And I'll talk to the chief and see what his timetable is. Would it work to have the upstairs back if he still wants to keep the basement—sorry, undercroft—off-limits for a while?"

"It would be fine if we just had the upstairs, " Robyn said. "That's a brilliant idea."

"Yes, dear." Mother looked pleased, and all the ladies were murmuring agreement. It didn't seem like a particularly brilliant plan to me, but by now I suppose they were all accustomed to having me schedule things for them.

"And we've decided to hold Barliman's funeral on Friday the twenty-seventh," Robyn said to me. "Apparently his son is the only family he has left, and we're to make all the arrangements as we think his father would have wanted them. He'll be flying in Thursday afternoon."

I scribbled a note in my notebook to add that to the master calendar when I got back to my laptop. I was hoping the master calendar wouldn't be necessary by Boxing Day, but that wouldn't happen until all the churches were back in working order and the pranksters caught.

"If anyone needs me, call my cell phone," Robyn said. "I'm going to drop by the hospital and then visit my shut-ins. Meg, if you need a room to work in here in town, Father Donnelly has one for you."

"I think I'll try working from home for a while," I said.

Robyn hurried off.

"Poor Mr. Vess," Mother said.

Quite a change from "that wretched miser" or "that horrible man."

"To have no more family than that," she went on.

I had to admit, I sometimes thought I had a little too much family, at least on Mother's side. But I wouldn't have traded with Vess.

"We shall have to do him proud at the funeral," one of the other ladies said.

"And we should plan a really nice buffet for afterwards."

"Let's go out to Meg's house," Mother said. "We can join the sewing bee and plan the buffet at the same time."

This proved a popular idea, and they all hurried over to their cars.

"I'm surprised we're waiting till Friday," one of the ladies said, pausing with car keys in hand.

"Tomorrow's Christmas Eve," Mother said. "We can't very well have it then or on Christmas Day. I suppose we could have it on Boxing Day, but I gather his poor son can't get here any sooner."

I decided not to mention the possibility that if the chief hadn't solved the murder by Friday, he might not release the body. They could always have a memorial service without it.

"The chief will be disappointed at the delay, won't he?" the lady asked. "Don't the killers usually show up at the funerals of their victims to gloat?"

"I'm not sure they do outside of the television shows and mystery books," I said. "But even if they do, I expect the whole town will show up to gawk at Mr. Vess's funeral, so the killer would be lost in the crowd."

"Yes," Mother shook her head sadly. "Everyone who feels guilty about having uncharitable thoughts toward him will show up at the funeral. We might need to borrow the Baptist church to hold everyone."

"He did have a gift for inspiring uncharitable thoughts, didn't he?" I said.

"The vestry meetings will certainly be much less stressful," the lady said. "I can't believe the amount of time and energy we spent on trivial expenditures."

"All that fuss over how fast the toilet paper disappeared." Mother shook her head.

"And that ninety-cent phone call he wouldn't stop harping about."

"And his ongoing crusade to get rid of poor Riddick."

We all glanced over at Riddick, who appeared to be working off his anxiety by picking up bits of litter in the parking lot.

"Remember what a fuss poor Mr. Vess used to make if he found so much as a gum wrapper on the grounds?" the lady said. "So much fuss over such trifles."

A thoughtful look crossed Mother's face.

"Of course, every once in a while, poor Mr. Vess did uncover something genuine," she said. "Petty, but genuine."

"But can you imagine him uncovering anything worth killing over?" I asked.

"No," she said. "But still. He had been acting very smug and cheerful lately. I've never seen him that way unless he was about to expose someone's sins. You don't suppose he had uncovered something that led to his death. If—"

"No," I said. "I'm sure it was just an accident. He was probably down in the undercroft counting dust bunnies or something when the prankster came in."

"I'm sure you're right, dear," Mother said. "I'm sure it's nothing to worry about."

"But if you think it's a possibility," I added. "Tell the chief."

"Of course, dear. I'm sure it's nothing."

I could tell she was lying.

Just then Rob ambled up.

"Hey, Meg, can you give me a ride?" he asked. "I came in with Michael."

"You can come with us, dear." Mother pulled out her car keys and headed for her own car.

"I'm not going home," Rob said. "I need to get over to Judge Jane Shiffley's farm ASAP. I have a client out there."

"A client?" Although Rob had graduated from the competitive and not inexpensive University of Virginia School of Law and subsequently passed the bar exam with a bare minimum of study, he hadn't ever actually practiced law. "No offense intended, Rob, but—"

"Yeah, I know," he said. "My legal prowess isn't exactly legendary. But the chief has arrested a couple of teenagers for pulling the pranks—"

"Ronnie Butler and Caleb Shiffley?" I asked.

"Wow, word really gets around fast," he said. "Yeah, and Caleb is Randall's second cousin once removed, and Randall's having trouble getting hold of any of the local defense attorneys, so he's hired me to go down and hold the kid's hand till the big guns get there."

"Rob, I don't want to cast aspersions—" I began.

"I know I'm not qualified to represent the kid in something that could turn into a murder rap," he said. "But I can make sure he keeps his trap shut until a real defense attorney arrives. I know my limitations. And so does Randall. He's still making calls."

"If the Butlers are having the same problem finding a lawyer, keep an eye out for Ronnie, too," I said.

"I will if I can get there," he said. "I wish someone would tell me why half the time Judge Shiffley insists on holding court in her barn when there are several perfectly good courtrooms over there in the town hall."

"Because she can," I said. "And she likes barns better than courtrooms."

"Whatever," he said. "Can you take me?"

"Let me check with Michael," I said, pulling out my phone.

"He and the boys went to pick up his mother at the airport," Rob said. "They're going to keep her out of your hair until this evening."

"Did he actually say that?"

"No," Rob said. "But that's what he meant."

I called Michael anyway.

"We're just waiting for Mom's luggage," he said. "And

once we get her settled at the house, she wants to take the boys down to the pond, so we can start teaching them to ice-skate. Want to join us?"

"I do, but my shoulder doesn't," I said. "I'll see you back at home later."

I hung up and turned to Rob, who was glancing at his watch and dancing from foot to foot.

"I assume if you're out there representing Caleb and Ronnie that the chief is out there, too."

"Far as I know," he said.

"Good," I said. "I need to talk to him, so I'll take you out there. Assuming the roads are clear that far."

"Awesome," he said. "Let's go."

Chapter 26

Maybe Rob thought I was kidding about the roads. I wasn't. Judge Jane Shiffley's farm was about as far as you could get from the center of town and still be in Caerphilly County. To go there, you drove along the Clay County Road to within a mile of the county line, then turned off onto a smaller, gravel-paved road for several grueling miles, and then onto an even smaller dirt road for the final stretch. I was fully expecting the plowed roadway to end long before we reached the county line.

But I was surprised. The main road continued clear until we got to the point where we turned off on the gravel road to Judge Jane's farm. After that, I could see that we'd have needed a sleigh to continue on the main road, but fortunately the gravel road was as neatly and thoroughly plowed as the main road had been up to the turnoff.

"Well, why not?" Rob said when I pointed this out. "After all, why would anybody want to go to Clay County at the best of times?"

"Someone could want to go through Clay County," I suggested. "To Tappahannock, maybe?"

"Then they'd be out of luck when they hit the county line," Rob said. "I don't think Clay County has working snowplows anymore. They figure anyone who can't be bothered to buy a truck with four-wheel drive can just wait till it thaws."

He had a point. But here in Caerphilly, even the final stretch of dirt road was pretty clear—obviously the Shiffley clan, who had the plowing contract, took good care of their aunt Jane. Or maybe they'd gotten into the habit of plowing her road this way a few years ago when the county had temporarily lost possession of its town hall and Jane's barn was the only courthouse available—just as she was the only judge not either in jail or under indictment.

I could recall summer days when court was in session in her barn and the entire dirt road would be lined with cars. You could see lawyers and their clients pacing up and down in the pastures, since that was the only way to have a private conversation, given the absence of conference rooms. People waiting for their cases to be called would often picnic by the side of the road, and a couple of deputies would patrol the area, making sure defendants and the witnesses against them weren't thrown too close together. Some of the local churches and civic organizations set up stands to sell lemonade and sodas, while the children took turns riding the several gentle old horses Judge Jane kept around for her own grandchildren.

Even though the town had reclaimed its courthouse, the judge still often preferred to hear cases in her barn, and most of the time, nobody much minded.

Things were slow today, no doubt in part because of the weather. Only a few cars and trucks were parked in her farmyard, mostly patrol cars and the chief's blue sedan.

I saw two figures, both heavily bundled, pacing up and down in the snow nearby. One I recognized as a local attorney who specialized in representing drunk drivers. He appeared to be lecturing the other figure, and I noticed a deputy standing just outside the barn door, watching them.

This time of year, the lack of conference rooms made for some pretty brisk attorney-client meetings.

Rob nodded to the deputy and hurried inside. I stopped to say hello—it was Vern Shiffley.

"She in a good mood?" I asked, nodding toward the barn.

"With one of her own family arrested for something like this?" Vern shook his head. "Man, will I be glad to get out of here."

I braced myself and stepped inside.

The interior of the barn was warm, and humid from the breath of all the two- and four-legged creatures within. I inhaled the rich farm odor, a composite of hay, feed grain, and manure.

This end of the barn was a wide corridor flanked by stalls and boxes. Several of Judge Jane's Morgan horses or prize Guernsey cows peered over the stall doors as if interested in the proceedings going on at the far end. I started slightly when I heard a duck quack almost underfoot, but it turned out to be a large buff-colored duck—presumably one of the Saxony ducks I'd heard Judge Jane raised, rather than yet another refugee from St. Byblig's.

Judge Jane was sitting in state on the judge's bench, which was formed by putting an antique captain's chair on the bed of an old farm wagon. The chair was pulled up close to the raised driver's seat, so the judge would have a place to stow any documents she needed close at hand—and more importantly, so she'd have a good solid surface on which to pound her gavel, which she tended to do a lot when presiding.

A dozen or so of the judge's black-and-brown hound dogs lay sleeping in piles of hay, either in the bed of the wagon or on the barn floor, as close as they could get to the judge's feet. The dogs weren't fond of loud voices, overlarge gestures, or anything they suspected was a threat toward their mistress. Their menacing stares and occasional low growls usually kept most defendants and attorneys from getting anywhere near a contempt of court citation. Judge Jane called the dogs her assistant bailiffs.

Rob was already sprawled on one of the hay bales that served as seating, talking quietly to Caleb Shiffley and Ronnie Butler, and absently petting a couple of the hounds. Nearby, I recognized Ronnie's and Caleb's parents, huddled on several other hay bales, looking anxious. I tried to imagine what I'd feel if I were in their place—if Josh or Jamie had committed what he thought was a harmless prank only to have everything go so completely wrong.

Judge Jane was reading a document with a fierce scowl on her face, Chief Burke and several of his deputies were waiting nearby.

Chief Burke looked up and saw me. He pursed his lips and shook his head with a sad expression on his face.

Did that mean that he was sorry, but he didn't believe the conversation I'd repeated to him, the one that seemed to clear Caleb and Ronnie of everything but the first two pranks? Or that he did believe it and was telling me to shut up because this was all part of a plan—perhaps a plan to scare the boys straight, or smoke out the person who'd really committed the last few pranks, or maybe both?

I strolled over and sat on the other end of the chief's hay bale.

"Do you have any idea how much longer you'll be keeping Trinity closed off as a crime scene?" I asked. "Not that we're trying to hurry you or Horace or anybody, because we completely understand that you need to process all the evidence to catch whoever killed Mr. Vess, and we can work around whatever timeframe you give us—"

"But you have a whole bunch of Christmas events coming up and it would be nice to know if you can hold any of them in your church," he said. "I understand."

"It's the sanctuary we need the most," I said. "We could live without the undercroft if need be."

"The what?"

"Sorry," I said. "The basement. Mother and the rector and a lot of the gung ho parishioners seem to prefer the medieval term 'undercroft.'"

"Ah." He nodded. "Getting back to opening up the church—I discussed that very issue with Horace not half an hour ago. He's working to finish up in the main floor within a couple of hours. We'll probably keep the basement—er, undercroft—a little longer, till tomorrow, at least."

"That helps. Thanks."

He seemed to be preoccupied, so I retreated to a bale farther back and tapped out a quick text message to Robyn. I had just finished sending it when Judge Jane rapped her gavel nine or ten times on the wagon seat. All the dogs woke up—a few of the younger ones scrambled to their feet—and they stared out at the rest of the courtroom as if daring us to get up to something.

"All stand," the bailiff bellowed, and we all bolted to our feet—even the remaining dogs—and stayed there while he continued with his rapid fire chant. "Oyez, oyez, oyez! This honorable court is now open and sitting for the dispatch of its business. God save the state of Virginia and this honorable court. Judge Jane Shiffley presiding. You may be seated."

The dogs kept a keen eye on the rest of us until we'd all seated ourselves on the hay bales. Then they began the traditional canine ritual of turning around three times and settling down again in the hay. The judge waited until the prolonged rustling had stopped before continuing.

"Let's pick up where we left off," she said. "Are the defendants now represented by counsel?"

"They are, your honor," Rob said. "Robert James Langslow, attorney-at-law, appearing for Caleb Shiffley and Ronald Butler."

Rob was wearing what we called his Lancelot expression—the male equivalent of Mother's Joan of Arc look. Judge Jane regarded him dyspeptically.

"You represented many clients on potential death-penalty cases?" she said at last.

One of the defendants uttered a small squeak. I couldn't tell which one.

The county prosecutor stepped forward. She was dressed in jeans and a red-and-white Rudolf the Red-nosed Reindeer sweater rather than her usual elegant pinstriped suit, but somehow it didn't make her less imposing.

"The district attorney's office is not asking for the death penalty, your honor. In fact, at present, we're not filing any changes related to the death of Mr. Barliman Vess."

"But you could be eventually," the judge said. "What if in the course of his investigation the chief finds out these two little hooligans had it in for poor Mr. Vess? And you two decide the whole thing was not the unfortunate accidental consequence of a stupid prank but a deliberate, premeditated murder?"

More squeaking from at least one of the defendants.

"Your honor," Rob said. "I'm only representing the defendants for the purposes of arraignment and, dare I hope, bail. They will be represented by experienced defense attorneys as soon as possible. Seems as if every other lawyer in the county is off spending the holiday in a warmer climate."

"And every other judge," Judge Jane growled. "Or I wouldn't be hearing this." She glared at Rob for a while. He stood, wearing the sort of innocent, trustworthy look he used to put on as a teenager when he was trying, against all odds, to talk Dad into letting him drive the car. His two clients looked anxiously from him to the judge and back again.

"Let's get this over with, then," Judge Jane said, with a few whacks from the gavel to underline her point.

In a matter of minutes, Ronnie and Caleb were arraigned on charges of trespassing, vandalism, statutory burglary, assault and battery, grand and petty larceny, arson, cruelty to animals, and illegal possession of a wild animal. And denied bail.

"But your honor!" Rob protested.

"I'm going to have to recuse myself from this case, so in the morning you—or your replacement—can ask my replacement to reconsider bail. It'll probably be Judge Brodie, and he'll probably give it to them, but I'm not going to have it said that those young rapscallions had it easy because one of them was my kin. So—bail denied."

"Has your honor considered the effect on the community?" Rob went on. I had to admit, I was pleasantly surprised that he had the nerve to stand up to her.

Judge Jane looked surprised, too, though not necessarily pleasantly.

"To have these two boys torn from the arms of their loving and very large families this close to Christmas!" Rob went on. "A holiday that's all about family, not to mention peace on earth and good will to all people. A holiday—"

"Chief," Judge Jane snapped. "You got any of those electronic bracelets you can put on these two? The kind that will raise holy hell if either of them sticks his nose outside his parents' door?"

"We do, your honor," Chief Burke said. "The ones we have are actually anklets. We can program them to notify us the second they leave their houses."

"Make it so," the judge said. "Caleb Shiffley!"

"Ma'am?" Caleb jumped up, as if someone had run an electric charge through his hay bale, and stood bolt upright before the judge.

"Ronald Butler?"

"Your honor?" Ronnie yelped, following Caleb's example.

"I'm releasing you two into your parents' custody," the judge said.

I heard sighs of relief from the hay bales where the parents were sitting.

"You're under house arrest," the judge went on. "I don't want either one of you to set foot outside your parents' houses without Chief Burke's permission. And I want you both to do some long, hard thinking tonight. Do I make myself clear?"

The two murmured assent.

"Chief, fit them out with the anklets and then release them to their parents' custody. Anything else?" Judge Jane looked around as if daring anyone to speak up.

"There's that DUI," the bailiff began.

"Tell that son of a gun he's getting a continuance until after Christmas, and he should be glad of it," she said. "Way I feel now . . . Anything else?"

No one else spoke up.

"Court adjourned," she said, with a single powerful thud of the gavel.

"Oyez, oyez, oyez," the bailiff began chanting.

"Meg Langslow!" Judge Jane snapped.

Chapter 27

When Judge Jane barked out my name, I didn't react quite as badly as Caleb and Ronnie, but I couldn't help looking startled.

"Your honor?"

The judge was climbing down off the bench, with the help of a nearby deputy. The dogs all rose, and the ones who had been reclining in the wagon bed poured over the side to join the others in a happily milling pack around her feet.

"I need a drink. And I don't believe in drinking alone. Your brother can ride back to town with his clients. Come have an eggnog."

With that she strode toward the exit.

Not the most gracious invitation I'd ever received, but I fell in at the tail end of the pack. Once we got outside the barn she waited for me and we walked side by side up to the farmhouse.

The front door opened into the great room, as she called it; a huge combination kitchen, dining room, and family room with a roaring fire in the oversized hearth. I sat down on a chair near the fire—a battered-looking armchair that probably only looked tweed because of the dog hair, but proved to be utterly comfortable.

The judge hadn't gone overboard on decorating. A wreath on the door, and a big spruce Christmas tree in the corner covered with multicolored ornaments, most of them old-fashioned and a little chipped or tarnished. Mother would have described them as vintage and enthused over their patina. I just found it homey and comfortable.

But where she beat all Mother's efforts was in the smell department. The whole house teemed with authentic Christmassy scents—the sharp evergreen odors of the tree and the wreath and the mouthwatering scents of gingerbread and cinnamon-spiced cider.

"What the hell is going on here, anyway?" Judge Jane asked. "Let me hang your coat up, and then I'll get the eggnog. Did those two boys actually kill that poor old man?"

"I don't think so." I leaned back and put my feet up on a well-worn footstool. "But why ask me?"

"Because I can't ask any of them." She was standing at the stove, and gestured over her shoulder in the general direction of the barn. The smell of warming eggnog joined the other holiday scents. "It would be completely irregular. Ex parte communication. Hell, I couldn't ask you if I hadn't just recused myself. But I'm off the case now, and you're a civilian. Does Henry Burke really think they did it?"

"He knows they did the first two pranks," I said. "The skunks and the snake. He has a witness who overheard them discussing it."

"A reliable witness?"

"I don't know," I said. "Do you consider me reliable?"

She sighed. Then she handed me a glass of eggnog and sat down on another dog-tweed armchair with her own glass in hand.

"Tell me what you heard. Please," she added, as if remembering that she wasn't wearing her judge's robes at the moment.

I gave her the gist of what I'd overheard last night, in between sips of her delicious and highly potent eggnog.

"Interesting," she said when I'd finished. "Of course, it doesn't rule out the possibility that one of them was lying to his friend."

"Agreed," I said. "But I don't think either of them is that good a liar. That phrase Ronnie used—'I know you're still mad about the April thing'—do you have any idea what happened in April to upset them?"

She frowned and shook her head.

"No idea," she said. "Must have been something pretty bad if they're still upset about it eight months later."

"Or maybe it's something that they're trying to prevent happening this coming April," I suggested.

She continued to frown and shake her head. Then her face cleared.

"Of course," she said, with a chuckle.

"You know what the April thing is?" I asked.

"It's not a what," she said. "It's a who. April Hardaway. Her father owns the John Deere dealership in town. Caleb has been sweet on her for a year or two. Cute little redhead. No idea what she has to do with the pranks, though."

"I think I might know," I said. "Does she sing in the New Life Baptist choir?"

"She does," the judge said. "I confess, I was surprised and a little disappointed that the choir director didn't pick her for a solo."

"He didn't pick Kayla Butler either," I said. "Ronnie's cousin."

"You think those two rascals pulled the whole skunk stunt because Lightfoot didn't pick Ronnie's cousin or Caleb's little sweetheart?"

I nodded.

"Then why the ducks?"

"You're asking why a duck?" I said, in my best Chico Marx accent. "Why not a chicken?"

Judge Jane frowned. Evidently she wasn't a Marx Brothers fan.

"There is no 'why the ducks,'" I said, in my normal voice. "Not with Ronnie and Caleb. Because they didn't do the ducks. Someone else did. And if we knew why, maybe we'd know who."

"*Cui bono*," she said. "Which is Latin for 'follow the money.'"

"Technically, Latin for 'who benefits?'" I said. "And I'm not sure anyone benefits financially from the pranks."

"Same thing." The judge sipped her eggnog slowly. "Mark my words, somewhere down the line, someone will."

A thought came to me and I turned it over in my mind, sipping my eggnog, until I decided that it was something I could safely bring up with the judge.

"It's not just the fact that Caleb is your nephew, is it?" I asked. "There's been bad blood before between Barliman Vess and some of the Shiffleys, right?"

"There has," she said. "Quincy Shiffley is damned lucky he was in the Caerphilly Hospital hooked up to a bunch of machines last night. Otherwise he'd be Henry Burke's prime suspect. He's a known hothead, and he and Vess had exchanged high words more than once."

"And you're worried someone in your family might have been mad enough to do this to Vess?"

"Yes." She shook her head in dismay. "Quincy and Vess have been sniping at each other for years. And a lot of the family blame Vess for Quincy's coronary. Never mind the fact that Quincy has spent the past forty years eating, drinking, and smoking too much and ignoring all his doctors' advice. Just because Quincy keeled over after their latest argument doesn't mean it was Vess's fault. And in case you were wondering, yes, Chief Burke knows about the bad blood. I made sure of that, when I told him I was going to recuse myself."

I wondered how the chief had felt about finding out an as-yet-unidentified Shiffley might be one of his prime suspects. The Shiffleys were a large and very close-knit family. Most of the ones I'd met were honest and law-abiding, and I couldn't imagine them trying to protect a murderer, even if he was family.

But I didn't know all the Shiffleys. Every family had its black sheep. And while I wasn't exactly city folk—an insult that fell somewhere between carpetbaggers and horse thieves in the minds of the locals—I wasn't originally from around here, either. Maybe I wasn't in the best position to judge what one Shiffley would do for another.

"Chief's got to get to the bottom of this one," the judge said softly. "If he can't figure out who killed Mr. Vess, those boys are going to have suspicion hanging over them the rest of their natural lives."

I nodded and sipped the last of my eggnog. Then after a diplomatic pause I got to my feet.

"I'd love to stay—" I began.

"But you have a million things to do and I've already taken too much of your time," she said.

"On the contrary, you've given me a very relaxing break," I said. "And since you're constrained by your office from asking too many people what's going on, if I find out anything interesting, maybe I'll drop by for a little more eggnog."

"It's a deal," she said. "And bring the boys next time. The dogs love playing with kids."

Halfway back to town my cell phone rang: Michael. I pulled over and answered it.

"And where are you and the boys and Granny Waterston?" I asked. "Still skating?"

"No, Mom stole all our wrapping paper and locked herself in her room to wrap things," he said. "The boys are home, being looked after by all the sewing ladies. I asked your mother if I could leave them there while I went out looking for a Christmas present for you."

"I thoroughly approve."

"Yes, except I lied," he said. "I'm not looking for a present for you—I'm out at the free-range organic turkey farm."

"It wasn't a lie, then," I said. "If you're picking up that small turkey for tomorrow night, you're definitely getting what could end up being my very favorite present."

"It's not going to be that small a turkey," he said. "Apparently they don't come all that small these days. This bird would be plenty to feed a family of twelve."

"Even better," I said. "Then it can feed our family a couple of times. As long as it's fresh."

"Very fresh," Michael said. "I just barely avoided being introduced to it. And they're still off . . . um . . . preparing it. Which means unless I want to come all the way back into town and back out again later, I'll be stuck out here a while. Could you do something for me?"

"Sure."

"My friend Charlie—the one who owns the basement apartment—is waiting for me in his office," he said. "As soon as he hands over his spare keys, he's free to split, so if there's any chance you could swing by the college—"

"I'll be going right by it soon," I said. "Where's his office?"

"Peake Hall, room two twelve," Michael said. "Thanks."

I started the car again, and as I drove the rest of the way back to town, I figured out the quickest route to Peake Hall. Wasn't it an administration building rather than an academic one? Odd—Michael's friends tended to come from the faculty rather than the administrators. Then again, since the current chair of the drama department was grooming Michael to be his successor, maybe I should be overjoyed if my husband was making friends in the bureaucracy.

Although as I climbed the stairs to the second floor, I wondered if I should call back and ask Charlie's last name.

Chapter 28

One mystery was solved when I reached room 212, which was a rather imposing office with a sign on the door that read CHARLES GARDNER. REGISTRAR. Aha. Michael's friend Charlie was a moderately important bureaucrat.

The secretary who would normally have been guarding his door against all comers had apparently already started her holidays. I knocked, peered inside, and instantly recognized the occupant as one of the actors in a production Michael had directed last spring.

"Polonius!" I cried.

The distinguished-looking fifty-something man with touches of gray at his temples and in his neatly trimmed goatee looked up with the unmistakable pleasure of the amateur actor whose role has been remembered.

"Only Charlie, now that the play's run is over." He stood and held out his hand, glancing briefly at my sling. "How are you, Ms. Langslow? Not a broken arm, I hope."

"Meg," I said, taking the outstretched hand. "And the sling's only to help my semidislocated shoulder heal faster. Michael sent me to release you from your vigil."

"Ah! Thank you," he said. "They're predicting more bad weather. My plan is to put a few hundred miles between me and the closest snowflake by nightfall."

He fished into his pocket and handed over a key ring with an elegant bow that would have been fully in character for the courtier he'd played in *Hamlet*.

"*Mi casa, su casa,*" he said. "At least the subterranean part of it. And I told Michael to feel free to use the refrigerator upstairs or the dishes if you need to. Hope the private getaway is a success. Is there anything else I can do for you?"

"No, I think— Wait. Yes," I said. "Could I ask you a couple of questions? Quick ones," I added. "I know you have a storm to miss."

He looked surprised, but gestured to the chair in front of his desk and sat down again himself.

"Ask away," he said.

"You're the registrar," I said. "Is your office where someone would check to make sure a job applicant really had a degree from Caerphilly?"

"Not anymore, thank goodness," he said. "All the paperwork involved in sending transcripts used to be the bane of our existence, but these days we outsource it. There's a central national clearinghouse for degree verification. We send them the data on all the degrees we award—and then every year when our hundreds of graduates send out thousands of resumes in their initial job searches, the clearinghouse answers all the queries from interested employers—for a modest fee."

"So if I suspect someone has lied about his degree, I should start by finding out if his employer bothered to check with this clearinghouse."

"Correct," he said. "Most large employers do. Smaller ones . . ." He shook his head. "The most common mistake is to take everything a job applicant provides at face value. We had an applicant show up here once with a stellar résumé, complete with what looked like copies of completely authentic reports from the clearinghouse on both his undergraduate and graduate degrees. Fortunately, we ran a check anyway. And did not offer employment. Here"—he picked up a pen, jotted something on a notepad, then handed it to me—"if you really think someone is committing degree fraud, you could start by checking him out here."

"Or advising his employer to." I took the paper, which contained a Web site's URL. "Thanks."

I stood, and Charlie followed suit.

"I hope your suspicions are unfounded," he said, offering his hand.

"Caerphilly would be a better place if they are," I said as we shook hands.

"Ah! Then I hope you get the sneaky degree forger dead to rights," he said with a laugh. "I'll ask Michael all about it when I'm back. Have a merry Christmas and a happy New Year!"

He bent down and picked up something from behind his desk. A small cage containing a rather large white duck.

"A present for my nieces," he said, seeing my startled look. "I'm told they make wonderful pets."

I tried to figure out a tactful way to ask him if he was sure it wasn't a stolen duck, but inspiration failed me, so I just wished him a merry Christmas and watched him hurrying down to his car with his cage in hand.

I hiked back to my own car in a thoughtful mood. Should I say something to someone at the New Life Baptist Church? I gathered from what Minerva had said that Lightfoot's departure was already a settled thing. Would it make any difference whether or not he'd lied on his application?

No, but he didn't know he was already on an exit path. So if he had lied and then found someone checking up on him, it could be very material to the chief's murder investigation.

Of course, how could I tactfully ask anyone at the New Life Baptist Church if they'd failed to do an adequate job checking out their new choir director?

I decided to talk to Minerva Burke.

Who, as I recalled, was at my house now, supervising the sewing circle and helping keep an eye on Josh and Jamie.

I got into my car and headed home. I made the mistake of taking a route that led me past some of the dorms where many of the high school and college students attending the debate and basketball tournaments were now packing up to go home. Buses, vans, and cars clogged the roads, and the departing students darted everywhere— laughing, shouting good-byes and holiday greetings, taking pictures of each other, holding impromptu snow battles. Obviously they hadn't all won their games or competitions, but I didn't see any discouraged faces. Only happy kids, excited at the prospect of going home for the holidays.

Their enthusiasm lifted my mood, even while I was dodging them. And that was even before it occurred to me that the end of their events meant that any number of rooms at the college might now be available if any more pranks put any more churches out of commission. I should keep that in mind while working on my schedule.

Back at the house I was relieved to find that except for the sewing circle, no one was around. Before going down to the library, I seized the opportunity to fill a few bags with things Michael and I would need for our Christmas Eve dinner, and managed to get the bags into my trunk without being seen.

And then I made myself a cup of tea—the old-fashioned way, by boiling the water in a kettle and steeping loose tea in the pot instead of nuking a mug of water with a tea bag in it—and sat down in the living room with one of the baskets of Christmas cards.

For a minute or so, I had to fight the urge to be doing something useful with them. Entering any new addresses or e-mails in my address book. Or checking the cards against my list of Christmas cards we'd sent so I could fire off belated greetings to anyone we'd forgotten.

"Breathe," I told myself. It took a minute or two, but I managed to relax and see the cards not as looming chores but as what they were supposed to be—expressions of love and friendship from people we might not be able to see this holiday season.

I found myself just looking at the pictures. The Blankes—a retired colleague of Michael's and his wife—posing at sunset on a beach in Bali. Eileen and Steven, whose wedding had been partially responsible for Michael's and my meeting in the first place, on the porch of their North Carolina farm with their five kids, all in matching Christmas sweaters. Dr. Smoot, Caerphilly's former medical examiner, standing in front of Bran Castle in Transylvania, smiling so broadly that you could easily see his fake fangs. A lovely action shot of the Mountain Morris Mallet Men, a troupe of friends who were croquet-loving Morris dancers. A picture of my friend Karen and her son Timmy—could he really be seven now?—in front of Neuschwanstein Castle. Pictures of other friends with children who seemed to shoot up faster than was possible from year to year.

I decided to stick to looking at the pictures and read the printed Christmas letters and handwritten notes later.

Plenty of time to figure out if Eileen and Steven and their tribe were planning to arrive the same week as the Morris men, who'd established a tradition of camping on Mother and Dad's farm for a week or two every summer and challenging all comers to freewheeling games of Xtreme croquet. And to learn if this was the year single-mother Karen got transferred back to the States and announced her intention of once again leaving Timmy with us for an unspecified number of months until she got settled. To read the note from cousin Wesley, which would probably once again ask us to come and testify at his bail hearing. Or the Christmas letter from cousin Dolores, who made Job seem fortunate and Eeyore cheerful. For now, I decided, it was a time just to enjoy looking at the familiar faces and thinking of all those who were dear to us.

"'A good time,'" I found myself murmuring—by now I knew *A Christmas Carol* as well as Michael. Even the boys could quote bits of it. "'A kind, forgiving, charitable, pleasant time; the only time I know of, in the long calendar of the year, when men and women seem by one consent to open their shut-up hearts freely, and to think of people below them as if they really were fellow travelers to the grave, and not another race of creatures bound on other journeys.'"

I finished up my tea, reluctantly replaced the card basket in the front hall, and headed down the long hallway to talk to Minerva and check on the boys.

When I peeked into the library, the boys were nowhere to be seen. And Minerva seemed delighted to see me. She hurried over to the door, and I braced myself to remind her of my nearly nonexistent sewing skills.

"There you are!"

"Where are the boys?"

"They're fine," she said. "They were getting a bit restless, so your father and grandfather took them out to the zoo."

I decided not to ask exactly what she meant by "restless." Minerva would have used stronger words if either blood or broken valuable objects were involved. She shooed me back into the hall, followed me out, and closed the door behind her.

"Good Lord, but your mother's been on quite a tear," she said.

"She has? About what?"

"Barliman Vess. If you'd asked me yesterday what your mother thought of him, I'd have said she couldn't stand the man."

"And you'd have been right," I said. "What makes you think she's changed her mind now that he's dead?"

"She hasn't really. But now she's convinced he was onto something."

" 'Onto something'?" I echoed. "Like what?"

"She doesn't know," Minerva said. "As she keeps saying to anyone who will listen, he was cut off in his prime because he knew something dangerous or was asking the wrong questions or some such thing."

"And she could be right," I said. "Not about the cutting off in his prime—the man was eighty if he was a day. But he could very well have been killed because of something he knew."

"Seems that way to me, too," Minerva said. "I'm not arguing with her on that. I just question how wise it is to go around saying so to every blessed person in creation. *And* promising she's going to pick up Mr. Vess's mantle and carry on his crusade, whatever the dickens it was."

"Oh, good grief." I lowered my voice and took a step closer. "You do realize what she's trying to do, don't you?"

"Of course." Minerva followed suit, and looked around to see if anyone were eavesdropping. "Trying to flush out the killer by making herself a target. And a damn fool thing to do, if you ask me."

"I agree." I suddenly felt enormously tired. "I'll try to talk some sense into her. Where is she, anyway?"

Minerva pursed her lips as if almost too exasperated to speak.

"After carrying on like that here for near an hour, she suddenly announced to the whole world that poor Mr. Vess's cat must be starving, and she was going to go to the rescue. I called Henry the minute she left, but it's not as if the department doesn't have a few other things to do. And he can't very well put out an APB on a law-abiding citizen. For what? Intent to commit feline nutrition?"

"I'll go after her," I said.

Chapter 29

From the look on Minerva's face, I could see she approved.

"I doubt if your mother went straight to Mr. Vess's house," she said. "Because obviously there's no guarantee that the killer's here at the sewing bee."

"I'd be pretty surprised if the killer was here," I said. "Of course, maybe she knows something we don't."

"More than likely she's carrying on the same way all over town. Back at your church, if they've opened it up again. Over at the Caerphilly Market. And the post office. And the garden store. And—"

"Understood," I said. "Which gives me time to get over to Mr. Vess's house and intercept her. Where does he live, anyway?"

Minerva handed me a sheet of paper on which, in her neat handwriting, she'd written not only Mr. Vess's address but also detailed instructions, including the landmarks that would tell me I'd overshot my target.

"Before I go," I said. "May I ask you something?"

"Of course, dearie," she said. "Ask away."

"How carefully did the church vet Mr. Lightfoot's credentials before hiring him?" I asked.

She blinked and frowned slightly before answering.

"Not carefully enough, by a long shot," she said finally. "Although if you ask me the problem's with the man, not the credentials. We should have paid a lot less attention to the fancy school he went to and a lot more to what a miserable human being he is. Why—do you know something we don't?"

"No," I said. "But someone was suspicious enough of Lightfoot to start checking him out." I explained what I'd seen on Riddick's computer, and what I'd heard from Michael's friend the college registrar.

"Now that's interesting," she said. "And I purely don't know if the search committee did the kind of check you're talking about. In fact, knowing who was on the committee, I'd be surprised if they did. They spent a lot of time interviewing him, and a lot more time praying for guidance."

"Both very good things to do," I said.

"But we fell down on the practical part," she said. "Although I do know they called all his references, and they all gave him a glowing report."

"Which is why he picked them," I said.

"And of course we only have his word for it that they're really people from his old church," she said. "I will certainly have a thing or two to say when we start forming the committee to find Mr. Lightfoot's replacement. Right now we're arguing over how soon to tell him. Some people think we should wait till August, when his contract's up, but I think we need to start a lot sooner than that. And yes, we should check out his credentials—properly, this time. Won't do us any good now, of course, but if we were bamboozled, I'd like to know the whole of it."

"Better yet, if he got the job with false credentials, you might be able to get rid of him a lot sooner than August," I said. "Most contracts have escape clauses in case one party's committing fraud."

She blinked for a few moments, and then a smile slowly crept across her face.

"So how do we go about vetting his files?" she asked.

I was about to fish in my pocket for the slip of paper Charles Gardner had given me. Then a thought hit me.

"You know," I said. "I bet the chief could find out today. Seeing as how this could be related to a homicide."

Her face fell.

"It's an interesting theory," she said. "But I'm not sure I see Lightfoot as a killer. He's a blowhard."

"He didn't dislocate your arm," I said, glancing down at my sling.

She flinched slightly, and nodded.

"Look, I agree," I said. "I can't see Lightfoot carefully plotting something and flawlessly executing it. But losing his temper?"

She nodded.

"And lashing out at Vess?" I went on. "Striking him down in the heat of anger and then, when he realized what he'd done, starting that fire in the furnace room as a clumsy attempt to make the whole thing look like a prank?"

"You're right," she said. "It's a possibility. I'll call Henry." She pulled out her phone but remained pensive, looking at it.

"But?" I asked.

"Obviously you think Barliman Vess is the one who was looking up Lightfoot on the computer."

"You don't think so?" I asked. "Why not? Was he not very computer savvy?"

"Oh, he was savvy enough," she said. "Surprisingly so for such an old . . . old-fashioned person."

I suspect she'd been about to say "old codger," or possibly "old coot."

"According to Henry, he was always sending things he'd printed out from the Internet to justify all his suggestions and complaints," she said. "But I can't imagine why he would care that much about Lightfoot."

"I suppose it could have been Riddick, since it was his computer, but I think he'd gone home by then," I said.

"Or it could have been one of those Shiffleys," she said. "The two who were hanging around after the construction finished. Cleaning up, they said. Seemed to take them a right long time for a simple cleanup job."

"Perhaps they had to move slowly to keep the noise level down when the choir was singing," I suggested. "Mr. Lightfoot doesn't like noise during his rehearsals."

"I caught one of them coming out of that hallway where your office was," she said. "Duane Shiffley, I think it was. Maybe it wasn't my place to say anything, but he looked a little furtive, so I asked him what he was looking for, and he said the bathroom. I pointed it out to him and kept an eye on him till he went in."

"You think Duane was up to something?"

"Maybe," she said. "What if he did come back Sunday night to snoop around some more, and Mr. Vess accosted him the way I did?"

"We should tell the chief," I said. "Not our job to sort all this out."

"Thank the Lord!" With that she began dialing.

I hurried out to my car and set out.

Barliman Vess lived along the Richmond Road—so called not because it led all that directly to the state capital, but because before the interstate came through north of town, it was the first road you took on your long, roundabout journey there. Thanks to the interstate, Richmond Road had remained a pleasant country road, winding around hills through mile after mile of rolling green farmland.

Vess's house was small and unpretentious but well maintained. It had obviously once been a farmhouse, and had just as obviously been sold off separate from the farm itself—not unlike the much larger farmhouse Michael and I now lived in. A neatly whitewashed picket fence separated a modest yard from the pasture that surrounded it on three sides. A detached garage sat to the right of the house, and to the left about a third of the yard was set off from the rest by its own stretch of picket fencing—no doubt the garden, in summertime. The bushes around the house looked tidy and well pruned under their caps of snow. The driveway and front walk had been neatly shoveled before last night's light dusting of snow had fallen on them.

I walked carefully up to the door in case there was any ice hidden under the dusting, because I had a good idea how much it would hurt if I fell on my shoulder and undid whatever healing it had done. No lights in the house. I knocked on the door, hoping Mother was inside. No answer.

Maybe Mother hadn't gotten here yet. Or had come and gone.

No, there were no footsteps on the walk or the front stoop other than my own. And none marking the expanse of virgin snow around the house.

I pulled out my cell phone and called. Mother's voice mail answered.

"I'm at Barliman Vess's house," I said. "I need to talk to you before you get here. Call me."

Should I go back to town or wait here for Mother?

Or should I see if I could get into the house myself?

I looked under the doormat to see if he had left a key. No luck. But then when I dropped the coconut-fiber mat back down it hit the brick stoop with a dull but metallic ping. I flipped it up again and looked at the underside. A key was neatly affixed to the bottom of the mat with a small strip of duct tape. A slight improvement over just tucking the thing under the mat, I supposed.

What I was contemplating was, of course, trespassing. But I could always say that I'd misinterpreted some message from Mother and believed she had asked me to feed Mr. Vess's cat. Minerva would back me up.

I pulled the key off the mat and unlocked the front door.

I'd half expected the cat to greet me at the door, but the front hall was empty and unnervingly still. The loud ticking of a huge antique grandfather clock to my left only emphasized how quiet everything else was. Was there really a cat, or was Mother just making one up as an excuse to come out here?

I closed the door behind me and locked it. I reached for the light switch, then stopped. Why advertise my presence? I began fumbling in my purse for the flashlight I always carried.

Of course, with my car parked in the driveway, I was already advertising. I gave up the flashlight search and flipped on the lights.

My first thought was that Mr. Vess clearly had taste and money, but his life must be a little lonely. Well-worn but expensive-looking oriental rugs covered small patches of the polished hardwood floors. The furniture all looked either antique—mostly Colonial—or of good quality, if very understated. But while I couldn't put my finger on the reason, I had the strong sense that not a lot of people ever came here.

To the right of the door was the living room, which looked chilly, underused, and a little brittle, as if everything might crumble if I turned even one of my boys loose in it for a few minutes. To the left, a small dining room that looked a little less as if everything was glued in place. Over the sideboard hung a modern oil painting of an attractive woman in her fifties. The late Mrs. Vess, no doubt. She was smiling slightly and her eyes looked warm and kind. If the artist had accurately captured her personality . . .

"Poor man," I said aloud. She was clearly someone who had been missed.

The kitchen was also small, with no breakfast area, so Mr. Vess probably had to eat in the dining room. It was neat and functional, but not very personal. Maybe it was sexist of me, but I couldn't help thinking that a woman would have had more decorations in her kitchen. More individual touches.

Upstairs were two bedrooms and a small bath. One bedroom was clearly Mr. Vess's. The bed was covered with an old-fashioned white chenille spread. The bedside table to the left held a lamp, a vintage fifties electric alarm clock, a small water carafe with a top that doubled as a glass, three library books, and a pair of reading glasses. The right bedside table held only a lamp identical to the left one.

The other bedroom was fitted up as a study. A comfortable-looking reading chair stood by the front window, and the table beside it and the floor around it contained more books. At the other side of the room was a small mahogany secretary with a sleek modern laptop perched incongruously on its writing surface. A wooden file cabinet sat nearby.

I couldn't resist scanning the books first. They were a mix of well-worn literature, apparently from Vess's own library, and brand-new spy thrillers in plastic library covers. Then I made a beeline for the desk.

Not surprisingly, most of the papers had to do either with Mr. Vess's investments—which were not unimpressive—or his work with the Trinity vestry. Fat files of paperwork from the search for the new rector. Notebooks full of financial reports going back fifteen years. More fat files of memos Vess had sent to the vestry about various issues, like the cost savings to be gained from installing lower wattage lightbulbs in the hallways and the shockingly extravagant use of toilet paper in the ladies' toilets.

I wondered if Vess had built his comfortable home through lightbulb and toilet-paper economies. I hadn't noticed any dimness in his lights, and I checked his bathroom and found that he had used fairly cushy double-ply toilet paper.

His desk file drawer contained what I assumed were his active projects—a series of files, each in its own neatly labeled hanging folder. LIGHTING USAGE SURVEY—that must be his project of hiding in the closet to see who was leaving lights on. COSTS/DAMAGES FROM CHRISTMAS INCURSIONS—good grief; he had already started a file with his complaints about our church-swapping activities. RECTOR PERSONNEL EVALUATION NOTES—I glanced through that to see that it was a laundry list of petty or imaginary transgressions by Robyn. He also had files on all the vestry members—including Mother. I had to leaf through that one. The gist of it was that he found Mother extravagant and much too insistent on having her own way, so he wasn't completely incompetent at judging character.

I hoped his executor consigned these files to the shredder. I had trouble reconciling their pettiness with this house, with its mix of elegant functionality and quiet, understated beauty.

Maybe the house was Mrs. Vess's creation. I remembered Mother talking about how Vess had fought the rest of the vestry tooth and nail over the very minor expenditures involved in sprucing up Robyn's study—mainly a few gallons of paint, to be applied by volunteer labor.

"The man doesn't seem to understand," Mother had said. "Even if the styles haven't changed, things just wear out."

Maybe he'd kept the decor here untouched after his wife's death. I hadn't seen anything that couldn't have been here for ten years, or even twenty. I could see him living here, blind to the house's beauty but well aware of its comfort. Keeping everything unchanged not out of sentimentality but because that was the cheapest and easiest option.

Odd that one hanging folder was completely empty—the one marked THORNEFIELD INVESTIGATION.

I searched the rest of the file cabinet and the desktop. No THORNEFIELD INVESTIGATION misfiled under OFFICE SUPPLY INVENTORY or HOUSEKEEPING SAVINGS PROPOSAL or any of the other projects.

I was deeply immersed in the files when I heard a loud bang outside and started.

Chapter 30

I slipped over to the window on the side of the house where the sound had come from and peered out, careful to stay back far enough to minimize the chances that I'd be seen.

The back windows of Mr. Vess's offices had a sweeping view of rolling pastures leading down to a large pond and a series of long, low, whitewashed sheds. One of the barns had a faded sign on the side reading PLEASANT VALLEY DUCK FARM.

A tall, lean figure in jeans and a faded corduroy coat came out of one of the sheds and I heard the loud noise again—it was the shed door being slammed closed.

I was willing to bet that I was looking at Quincy Shiffley's farm, with one of his cousins dropping by to tend the ducks. A cousin who was slamming doors in a bit of a temper because he really didn't want to be out in the cold feeding a bunch of ducks.

I was a little alarmed when the cousin began striding across the snow-covered pasture in my direction. But I soon realized he wasn't aiming for the house. Two large white ducks were perched on the fence between Vess's yard and the duck farm. In summer, no doubt they'd have fluttered down into the garden and begun foraging, but now they merely stared down at the snow as if disappointed. I watched from behind the curtain as the visiting Shiffley captured them—they looked cold and not really all that eager to escape—and strode back up the hill to the barns with one under each arm.

I peered out the front windows to make sure there was nothing there, and then went back to hunting.

Vess hadn't been prone to clutter, so it didn't take long at all to search the small house and confirm that the missing file wasn't anywhere else. Not in the office. Not in the dresser or the bedside table. Not in any of the closets. Not in the attic, which was actually empty. Not in the garage, which contained only a bare minimum of lawn and garden tools.

Of course, that didn't necessarily mean the file was missing—only that it wasn't here. Perhaps Vess had left it in his car. Or had lent it to another member of the vestry, seeking their support.

I drifted back up to his office and wondered it I should turn on his computer. Not that I would expect to find much there—I'd already noticed that apart from the occasional letter or memo, most of the contents of his complaining files were handwritten.

And I was no computer forensics analyst, so why muddy the waters if the chief eventually did send someone to check the laptop. I left the laptop alone. It was time to go.

Though not before I fed the cat. If there even was a cat.

I went back to the kitchen. There, on the floor of the utility room, was a beige plastic mat with two bowls on it, both empty. You couldn't even tell which was the food bowl and which was the water—both had been licked clean and dry.

There was dry cat food in a cabinet overhead. I rinsed out both bowls, shook a decent amount of food into one, and filled the other with water.

Just then the doorbell rang. I hurried to peer out a

window and spotted Mother's car. I opened the door to let her in.

"Hello, dear," she said, giving me a peck on the cheek as she came in. "Did you also come to look after poor Barliman's cat?"

"I came to look after you," I said. "Given the fact that we don't have any idea who killed Mr. Vess, don't you think it was a little foolhardy to make such a fuss about continuing his quest, once you found out what it was, and then letting the whole world know you were coming out here by yourself to feed his cat?"

"I knew you'd come after me as soon as you heard," she said. "And didn't it give you a lovely excuse to come out here and poke around? Did you find anything interesting?"

"Maybe," I said. "I'll show you."

I led her up to the office and pulled out the drawer containing Mr. Vess's files.

"Good heavens," she said. "I wish I could say I was surprised, but I'm not. Someone should destroy these files—the way J. Edgar Hoover's blackmail files were destroyed after his death."

"I was thinking more about Sherlock Holmes burning Charles Augustus Milverton's files," I said. "And I'd be in complete agreement except for the small fact that there might be some clue in these files to help the chief find Vess's killer."

"Then why are you taking this file?" she asked, tapping one manicured nail on the hanging folder labeled THORNE-FIELD INVESTIGATION.

"I'm not," I said. "It was already missing when I came. Do you have any idea what it could be about?"

"He usually kept his little investigations close to the vest," she said. "I have no idea. But if he thought there was anything the least bit suspicious about Mrs. Thornefield, he's very much mistaken. She was a gracious and generous lady with impeccable taste."

"If you say so," I said, thinking of that heavy furniture in the church basement. "Maybe Vess was inspired by her generosity and was investigating how she went about arranging her legacy to the church. Maybe he was thinking of following suit."

"Maybe." She glanced around with an appreciative air. "It would be nice, of course, but I'm not holding my breath. Maybe he has—had—some bee in his bonnet about the legacy causing us a tax problem. Or an insurance problem, from storing all that stuff in the undercroft. Though that would be his own fault—he was the one who vetoed short-term storage, even though the Shiffley Moving Company would have given us a bargain rate."

"Keep your eyes open, then," I said. "And let's get out of here before someone catches us trespassing."

"Did you feed the cat, dear?"

"Yes," I said. I walked down the hall to the kitchen and poked my head in. I could see, in the utility room beyond, the hindquarters and tail of a small gray cat, and by the sound of it she was bolting down her food. I backed away as quietly as I could.

"Mission accomplished," I told Mom. "By the way, what will happen to the cat?"

"Robyn has half a dozen volunteers to take her if the son doesn't want her," Mother said. "She'll be fine."

She looked around and shook her head.

"Such a lonely man," Mother said.

"At least he had a cat for company," I said.

"He was always complaining that she was an incompetent mouser," Mother said.

"But did he get rid of her because of that?"

Mother held her hands up as if conceding my point.

"I can think of one thing that his missing file could be about," she said. "It was just after Mrs. Thornefield died that our former rector broke his legs, poor dear. And with him laid up, and not the most practical soul at the best of times, he put Riddick in charge of disposing of Mrs. Thornefield's belongings. And since Riddick had no idea whatsoever what any of it was worth, he was just going to call in a junk dealer to give him a bid on the lot. Imagine how much we would have lost if he had and the junk dealer he'd called had been a sharp or dishonest operator!"

"And Mr. Vess found out about it and sounded the alarm?" I asked.

"He most certainly did not," she said. "He was as clueless as Riddick. But I'd been to see Mrs. Thornefield often enough, and I knew she had some very nice things, so I put a stop to the junk dealer plan."

She was back to her Joan of Arc pose.

"So we're having a rummage sale instead?"

"A very elegant auction and estate sale," Mother said. "Poor Riddick took it hard. He was so mortified at the mistake he'd been about to make that he handed in his resignation. Dr. Womble talked him out of it, of course—made him promise that he'd at least see the new rector in. Maybe the missing file is about that whole unfortunate episode. But of course even Barliman could see that it wasn't Riddick's fault. He blamed Dr. Womble for not supervising him properly."

"Do you think that's what led to the rector's retirement?"

"Oh, no," she said. "The bishop had been ignoring Barliman's complaints about dear Dr. Womble for years. It was the broken legs that made him realize the poor man just wasn't up to it any more. And now that Robyn's here, perhaps Barliman archived the missing file and just didn't yet remove the hanging folder. "

"It wasn't in any of the file drawers," I said. "Maybe he just moved the contents to the file he's keeping on Riddick."

"He's keeping a file on Riddick, too?" Mother exclaimed.

"He keeps files on everyone," I said. "He's even got one on you."

Mother insisted on going back up to the office to see her file. She seemed to find its contents alternately amusing and exasperating. I was feeling a little down because my one potentially exciting and significant find seemed to be dwindling to just another of Vess's petty, misguided crusades. Riddick's file did contain a lot of notes about how he'd almost mishandled the Thornefield estate, although from reading the file you'd have gotten the idea that it was Mr. Vess, not Mother, who'd saved the day. So Mother might have explained away the one interesting thing I'd found.

When Mother had finished laughing over her own file and the general petty nature of Vess's files, we left the house, and I locked up and taped the key back under the mat. And then I scuffed the snow around enough to disguise the fact that the mat had been moved.

"Doesn't make much of an effort for the holiday, does he?" Mother said.

She was right. No wreaths, no candles, no tree—not even any Christmas cards lying about. Maybe that was what had made the place seem so curiously forlorn.

"How does he get away with it, I wonder," I said. "Doesn't Caerphilly have some kind of ordinance requiring every household to make at least a minimum holiday decorating effort?"

"I wish it did," Mother said. I had been joking. She was probably serious.

"Speaking of making an effort for the holiday," I said. "I'm heading back to town. I have things to do."

"I'm going to get the groceries for my Christmas dinner," Mother said. "Your brother was going to help me carry everything—I don't suppose you could—"

"I'll help you hunt him down, no problem," I said, hoping to head off a request that I take her shopping. "Just don't ask him for any fresh ducks."

"What are you doing now, dear?" she asked.

If that was an attempt to enlist me in the shopping, I was prepared.

"I'm going to drop by and talk to the chief," I said. "And figure out some way to get him to look for that missing file without getting both of us thrown in jail for trespassing and interfering with an investigation."

"The file we noticed was missing while we were looking for Mr. Vess's poor starving cat?" Mother said.

"Yeah, that will work," I said. "And then I'm going to go home, take another pain pill, and rest my arm until it's time to get the boys ready for Michael's show."

"Feel better, dear," she said. "And I'll see you at the theater."

Chapter 31

I did feel better on the way back to town. Partly because my arm, although only giving me occasional twinges of pain, was proving to be such a useful tool for weaseling out of things I didn't want to do. And partly because the college radio station was back to its usual policy of non-stop Christmas music, and was playing a wonderful program of medieval carols. I was singing along with "The Holly and the Ivy" when I pulled into the police station parking lot. I was lingering in the car to hear the ending when my phone rang. I was in such a good mood that I answered it without thinking.

"Hello?"

"I don't have any animals!"

I pulled the phone away from my ear, turned down the radio, and looked at the caller ID. It was the Methodist church. Almost certainly Mrs. Dahlgren.

"I beg your pardon," I said into the phone. "I didn't quite get that."

"I don't have any animals! I'm supposed to be getting some animals! Where are they?"

Were the Methodists—or at least Mrs. Dahlgren—feeling slighted because the prankster hadn't hit them, too?

"Most of the churches that have received animals have been rather glad to get rid of them," I said. "I'm not sure I understand why you're complaining."

"For the live Nativity!" she shrieked. "We need cows,

sheep, pigs, goats, donkeys, and some ducks or chickens. The rehearsal's in two hours."

"I'm afraid I'm still confused," I said. "Where do you usually get the animals?"

"Usually we get them from farmers who belong to the congregation," she said. "But they're upset because of the pranks, and none of them want to risk their animals. I assumed you'd be getting me some animals."

"Me?"

"Aren't you in charge of taking care of all the problems caused by these ridiculous pranks?" she demanded. "Didn't you get my message?"

"No, I didn't get any kind of message from you," I said. "And I'm only in charge of scheduling, to make sure everyone's holiday events can go on in spite of the pranks."

"Well, we're an event! And we won't go on if you can't schedule us some barnyard animals."

With that she hung up.

I took a deep breath and muttered several very uncharitable things about Mrs. Dahlgren.

And then I reminded myself that the live Nativity pageant wasn't just a Methodist event. They hosted it, because they were the only church that faced the town square, but like the New Life Baptist concert, the Nativity was more a community event. And in a farming community, a live Nativity pageant with no animals wasn't much of a show.

And clearly Mrs. Dahlgren was in no state of mind to make any practical arrangements. So if I wanted the town's holiday celebrations to continue successfully . . .

It occurred to me that sheep were one of the mainstays of biblical agriculture. And Michael and I did live across the road from a sheep farm. I called home and found Rose Noire.

"Do you think you could talk Seth Early into bringing a few sheep to town for the live Nativity pageant rehearsal," I asked her.

"Of course!" she said. "How many?"

"I don't know." I tried to remember last year's pageant. "Half a dozen, maybe? The more the merrier, actually. The Methodist farmers are nervous about bringing their animals in, so the sheep might be the main friendly beasts there. And make sure Seth's okay with it."

"You know how he loves to show off his sheep," Rose Noire said.

Yes, and I also knew that he was one of the legion of men who were smitten by Rose Noire—that was the main reason I delegated the sheep roundup to her.

"And bring a few of our chickens in," I said. "Whichever ones you think are likely to behave during the pageant."

"Of course!"

Okay, so there would be sheep and chickens for the rehearsal. Maybe I should rest on my laurels. Though it would be nice to find someone to bring a few cows, goats, and maybe even a donkey. And surely with all the ducks that seemed to be popping up all over town, I could find one or two to grace the stables.

It occurred to me that Grandfather had all of those in his petting zoo. I called him.

"The boys are fine," he said, before I even asked. "James is making sure they don't go near any of the carnivores."

"That's good," I said. "I was calling to ask if the Methodists could borrow some animals for the live Nativity scene."

"Hmmm," he said. "I've only got the two camels right now, but I suppose it's better than none."

Camels! Mrs. Dahlgren certainly wouldn't be expecting

the camels. I began to feel almost smug, imagining the look on her face.

"That would be excellent," I said. "And is there any chance you could bring a few docile barnyard animals from the petting zoo? A donkey, a cow or two, and perhaps a few goats."

"Yes, yes," he said. "But why stop there? Let's make this thing impressive!"

I liked his enthusiasm, but I wasn't sure what he had in mind.

"I could bring the wolves," he said. "They make quite an impression, especially the Arctic Wolf."

"I'm not sure wolves are quite what people are expecting at the Nativity," I said. "It's not really biblical."

"The wolf also shall dwell with the lamb, and the leopard shall lie down with the kid," Grandfather quoted.

"Yes, but not at the Nativity," I said. "I know you find wild animals a lot more interesting, but people will be expecting domestic animals. It's tradition."

"I've even got a fairly tame leopard," he said.

"'Fairly tame'?" I repeated.

"You're missing a wonderful opportunity to put a whole new multicultural spin on this thing." I could almost see him pouting.

"Cows. Goats. Donkeys."

"Oh, all right. When and where do you need them?"

I gave him the time and place of the pageant rehearsal, thanked him, and hung up. Then I took a couple of deep, calming breaths.

"You okay?"

I looked up to see Randall Shiffley peering into my window. I nodded, grabbed my purse, and opened the door.

"I'm fine," I said. "Just settling my temper before going

inside, because I figure on general principles you should never be thinking murderous thoughts when walking into a police station."

"I'm going in to see the chief myself," Randall said, and we fell into step together. "So who's your intended victim, and when do you need an alibi?"

"Mrs. Dahlgren, and I don't know yet."

He winced.

"Okay, so I guess you already heard about how she needs some animals for the live Nativity."

"I have now."

"I'm sorry." He pulled out a small notebook—his equivalent of my notebook-that-tells-me-when-to-breathe—and frowned at it, as if the missed signal was the notebook's fault instead of user error. "I was supposed to tell you about the animals, and I was going to just as soon as—"

"Life happens." I stopped about ten feet from the entrance. "You want to make it up to me? Answer me something."

"Sure thing."

"What's Duane Shiffley's story?"

Randall stiffened, then closed his eyes and shook his head.

"What's he done now?" he asked.

"You tell me."

"Nothing, lately," Randall said. "That I know of. Apart from appropriating a few ducks from Quincy's flock and selling them, but you already knew that. He seemed to think Quincy owed him something for pitching in to help at the farm. We straightened him out on that score, and he's paying Quincy back."

"You were awfully quick to suspect him when I called to ask who might have sold Rob a duck," I said.

"Was I?"

I just waited.

"Black sheep," he said finally. "Every family has a few. Duane had a drug problem. Did some prison time, and some time in a residential treatment facility. He's clean now. Far as I know. If you know different, tell me, so we can deal with it."

"He's been seen lurking around Trinity," I said.

"He works for Shiffley Construction," Randall said. "Hard for someone with his record to get hired anywhere else. He was one of the workmen who got the place ready for the choir concert."

"I figured," I said. "Couple of people thought he was behaving a little furtively."

"If these were people who know about his problems—"

"Not all of them," I said. "Because one of them would be me, and I didn't know. I didn't even know his name at the time."

"Yeah," Randall said. "Duane's other problem—well, one of his minor problems—has always been that he looks guilty, even when he's behaving himself. I'll look into it."

"Does he go to twelve-step meetings?" I asked.

"All the time," Randall said. "It was a condition of his parole and still is a condition of his employment."

"That could partly explain it," I said. "Trinity hosts a lot of them."

"Yes." Randall sounded angry all of a sudden. "So if you're suggesting maybe Duane wandered out of a twelve-step meeting, ran into Mr. Vess and killed him—"

"Not what I was suggesting." I held up my hands in a gesture of surrender. "I was just thinking that if someone spotted Duane when he was on his way to a twelve-step meeting, he might have looked a little . . . uncomfortable."

"Try anxious and guilt-ridden and yes, more than a little furtive," Randall said. "I like that theory better. He hates going, but he knows he has to. Look—I don't think Duane was up to anything. But I can't swear to it. All I can say is that if he was, we're not going to protect him. And in case you're curious, yes, the chief knows what he's been up to with the stolen ducks. And I aim to find out if he's been up to anything else."

He looked upset.

"As you say, every family has its black sheep," I said. "Remind me to tell you about some of ours some time."

He smiled slightly.

"When things are quieter, I just might take you up on that."

He nodded and strode off.

Chapter 32

I wasn't sure if I felt reassured or more anxious about Duane Shiffley. I felt sure Randall would find out everything his cousin had been up to. And a good thing, too, since nothing Randall had said explained why Duane would have wandered down the hallway that housed only a few offices and locked storage closets.

Though maybe I could come up with an explanation of my own. Yes, Trinity hosted a lot of twelve-step meetings, but every church in town hosted a few, along with a variety of outreach and support groups. They'd all been pieces on my schedule—smaller pieces, pieces I'd tried to move as little as possible, because I sensed the attendees might be a lot less comfortable about relocating than catechism students or participants in the quilting circle. Maybe Duane was trying to find someone he could ask where to find a meeting he'd been planning to attend. Or looking for a posted schedule.

I realized I hadn't even asked Randall about the incredible coincidence of Duane's selling Rob—and presumably a few other people—stolen ducks on the same night someone had stolen all those hundreds of ducks from Quincy's farm.

And I wondered what Randall had been coming to see the chief about. Not, I hoped, something important, since he was now driving away. Going to deal with Duane, perhaps?

I strolled inside the police station. On the counter inside was a little two-foot Christmas tree that looked pretty normal until you got close enough to realize that instead of ordinary ornaments it was festooned with gold-colored toy police badges and tiny silver guns. The silver garland wound around it was made of dozens of miniature silver handcuffs linked together, and the angel on top was actually a blond police officer Barbie doll with glitter-flecked gossamer wings attached to the back of her blue uniform.

"Hey, girl!" It was my friend Aida Butler, one of the chief's deputies, who was sitting behind the front desk. "What did you think of Kayla at the concert?"

I enthused for a while over the concert. I wanted to ask about her nephew Ronnie, but I couldn't figure out a good way to bring it up. I settled for praising her daughter.

"I don't understand why Kayla didn't do the solo," I said. "The girl who did it was okay, but Kayla's better."

"Yeah," Aida said. "Of course, the soloist's father is the church treasurer—maybe Lightfoot's angling for a raise. Or it could just be that Kayla's mouthy. And before you say it, yeah, she takes after her mother that way. She made the mistake of talking back to Lightfoot and now fat chance of her getting a solo while he's in charge. And she's not the only one. The man is ruining our choir."

"Maybe they won't renew his contract." I was dying to tell her what Minerva had said, but I didn't dare.

"Let's hope so. Lord forgive me, when I heard about the murder, I couldn't help wondering for a moment if Lightfoot was the victim. Not hoping, mind you, but wondering. And I wasn't a bit relieved when I found out it was that harmless old man instead."

"He wasn't that harmless," I said.

"A lot of people wished him ill, then?" Aida perked up as if she found this interesting news.

"The chief already knows that he was not well liked at Trinity," I said. "I couldn't stand him myself. But I didn't wish him ill—just elsewhere."

"Same with me and Lightfoot," she said.

"Speaking of the chief, is he very busy?" I asked.

"I don't actually know," she said. "He's over at your church—checking out whether Horace is finished and we can release it."

"Great!" I said. "That's actually what I wanted to ask him about." Well, one of the things. "I'll head over there now."

"Don't push him about it," she said. "He knows you need the church back but he's cranky as all get-out. See you later?"

"Thanks for the warning," I said.

There were two police cruisers and several other cars in the Trinity parking lot. Vern Shiffley was on duty at the door.

"I dropped by to see if you had any word on when we get the church back," I called out when Vern opened the door.

Before Vern could answer, the chief appeared in the vestibule.

"Meg," he said. "Can I talk to you for a minute?"

Vern held the door open, and I stepped inside. The chief led the way down the hall and into my temporary office.

"Hope you don't mind," he said. "Horace and I have been using your office while we've been working here."

"My temporary office," I said. "And you're welcome to it."

The chief was sitting at my temporary desk, and he had added a folding chair for his interview subjects.

"I won't keep you long," he said. "I just have a few questions."

"And I have something to tell you," I said.

"Yes?" He picked up his notebook and pen.

"I have no idea if this has anything to do with his murder, and you probably know this already, but it could be significant that Barliman Vess kept files on stuff."

From the look on the chief's face, I could tell he found this revelation underwhelming.

"I'm not sure I see the relevance," he said. "I myself keep a modest filing system—financial records, family information, professional development materials. I should think everyone does."

"Barliman kept files on problems," I said. "And the people he thought were causing them."

A pause.

"Are you suggesting these were blackmail files?"

I hadn't been but it was an interesting thought.

"More like harassment files, I hope," I said aloud. "He was a would-be whistleblower cursed with a shortage of major smoking guns. If he didn't like how something worked around the church, he'd start keeping a dossier on the situation. And sending memos to the vestry."

"Yes," the chief said. "I believe your mother refers to them as 'Barligrams.' And it wasn't just the church. He maintained an active correspondence with the mayor, the health department, animal control—pretty much every agency in town. I have a folder full of them myself. Everyone in the town and county government got their share of Barligrams."

"So you don't think the files are significant?"

"I didn't say that." He leaned back, rubbed his forehead as if noticing the start of a headache, and looked at me for a few moments. "I understand you went out to Mr. Vess's house. Did you notice anything interesting in his files?"

"I didn't go out there to read his files!" I protested. "I fed his cat." It wasn't technically a lie.

"And completely resisted the temptation to snoop around?"

I gave up.

"No," I said. "But it's not as if I read all the files. The only thing unusual I noticed was that one of his files was missing." I explained about the empty hanging folder marked THORNEFIELD INVESTIGATION.

"I might know what happened to that folder," the chief said. "Apparently a few days ago Mr. Vess reported the basement of Trinity Episcopal as a hazard to our new fire chief—who, as you probably know, doubles as the new county fire marshal."

"Because of all the stuff from Mrs. Thornefield's estate?"

The chief nodded.

"The jerk. It was Vess's idea to put it all there."

"That would seem consistent with Mr. Vess's modus operandi," the chief said. "I'll check with Chief Featherstone to see if the missing file happens to be in his office."

"So what's happening with the church basement?" I said. "Please tell me Chief Featherstone isn't going to close the church down." If he did, Robyn would expect me to come up with yet another iteration of the schedule, and I wasn't sure there were enough rooms left in the county.

Chief Burke sighed.

"Chief Featherstone was dragging his heels on doing the inspection," he said. "Because he knew this was the worst possible time for Trinity to have to deal with a major basement cleanup. But after the fire, he couldn't very well look the other way."

"Blast," I said. "How soon is he doing his inspection?"

"He and Reverend Smith are down there as we speak," the chief said. "I gather he's giving Trinity a week to resolve the problem before he has to close you down."

"A week!"

"I know it's not very long—"

"On the contrary, it's more than enough time." I suspected Mother and Robyn would try to enlist me to deal with the problem, and I already had some ideas. My fingers were itching to pull out my notebook and start a page for the project.

"But wait," I said. "How can Chief Featherstone expect us to deal with the basement when the whole building's still a crime scene?"

"It won't be in a few minutes," the chief said.

"That's good," I said.

"Nice to see someone happy." He was frowning and staring into space.

"If I wasn't afraid you'd think I was prying, I'd ask how your investigation was going," I said.

"Very oddly," he said. "I have to confess, it's not often I get to interview someone just before he becomes a murder victim."

"You were investigating Mr. Vess?"

"I said interviewing, but yes," he said. "I know you assumed I was ignoring the information you gave me—"

"That Ronnie and Caleb didn't pull the duck prank—"

"But I did listen. And I wasn't focusing only on the boys. Mr. Vess also seemed a credible suspect for the duck theft."

I nodded. He seemed to be talking to himself as much as to me.

"It's a little hard to figure out the motive for such a peculiar prank," he said. "But he certainly had means and opportunity. And it's difficult to imagine anyone else getting away with it without Mr. Vess noticing."

"Yes," I said. "From his back windows, he'd have had a grandstand view."

"And last night was a cloudless night with a half-moon," the chief said.

"And it must have taken quite a while to load all those ducks," I said. "And caused considerable commotion."

"Yes." The chief nodded. "Mr. Vess's unfortunate demise does nothing to prove or disprove the possibility that he committed the duck prank. But there's also the possibility that he witnessed the theft of the ducks and was killed because he was trying to confront—or even blackmail—the persons responsible."

"Persons," I said. "Are we back to suspecting Caleb and Ronnie?"

"Not necessarily," he said. "But they're not out of the woods. Their fingerprints were on the half-empty beer bottles near the campfire at Temple Beth-El. And we found two more bottles near Trinity. No fingerprints, but same brand."

"And they're the only underage drinkers in town who favor Gwent Pale?" I asked.

The chief nodded as if conceding the point.

"They are, however, the only underage drinkers already known to be responsible for some of this week's unfortunate events," the chief said.

"So you think Mr. Vess was blackmailing them?" I asked.

"Or perhaps he caught them in the act of staging another prank," the chief said.

"Or someone is trying to frame them," I said. "But why?"

"I have no idea," the chief said. "Not yet, anyway." He was staring at his notebook.

"Is that it?" I asked, after a minute or so.

"Is what it?"

"You said you wanted to talk to me," I reminded him. "Was that what you wanted to talk to me about?"

"No." He sat up straighter in his chair, turned a few pages in his notebook, then looked back up at me. "Is Trinity thinking of hiring Jerome Lightfoot away from the New Life Baptist Church?" he asked.

Chapter 33

I blinked for a moment in surprise.

"Not even on the list of questions I thought you'd be asking," I said. "Not that I know of. And if anyone at Trinity had been thinking of it, I should think watching Lightfoot in action over the last several days would have made them think better of the notion. No, don't start thinking the New Life Baptist Church can get rid of him by pawning him off on us. It's not that easy."

The chief smiled slightly. Then his face turned somber.

"Then do you have any idea why Barliman Vess would have called the church where Lightfoot worked before he came here to check him out?"

"Did he?" I asked. "And why not ask them?"

"I did," he said. "I know what he told them. I also know what several members of your vestry think. I was asking you."

"That he was probably trying to cause trouble for Lightfoot," I said. "It's the only reason I can think of. Our Trinity choir director's a volunteer, and as far as I know everyone is completely happy with her. Hiring someone would be overkill—the most we do is have the choir rehearse and sing one hymn each week. But Vess really clashed with Lightfoot once the choir rehearsals moved over here. I can well imagine him trying to dig up some dirt. That's the way his mind works."

The chief nodded. He pointed to an object that was

standing on the desk beside him, a two-foot-tall Arts and Crafts–style candlestick made of silver and oak.

"Recognize that?" he asked.

"It looks like one of the candlesticks that stand at either end of the altar. Here at Trinity," I added, since over the last few days we'd been talking about more than one church.

"Where is it stored?"

"Stored? I don't think it is. I think they leave the candlesticks on the altar. They're heavier than they look— why would anyone haul them around if they didn't have to?"

"Someone wouldn't take it away to be polished or something?"

"The Altar Guild fusses over the church every Saturday afternoon—I expect they give the candlesticks a dab of silver polish most weeks, so they never really need major cleaning. Although come to think of it, I suppose someone had to move the candlesticks before the concerts Saturday and Sunday nights. The New Life choir took over the whole area behind the altar rail."

"And if you were someone helping move things, where would you put the candlesticks?"

"In the sacristy," I said. "Which is that small room off to the right behind the altar. They store the chalices and all the other altar equipment there."

"No one would have a reason to haul it into the basement?"

"Why would they?" I asked. "And even if they did, the Shiffley Construction Company team took the stage and the risers down last night. I assume someone from Trinity would have been there to put everything back to get ready for any services today."

The chief nodded. From his reaction—or lack thereof—I deduced that I wasn't telling him anything he hadn't heard before. He leaned back and studied something in his notebook.

"You can ask Robyn if it was there at the altar last night," I said. "She was staying till everyone left but the night watch. I expect she'd have noticed if anything was amiss in the sanctuary."

I suddenly realized there was something attached to the candlestick.

"Is that an evidence tag?" I asked.

He nodded. I stared at the candlestick for a few moments.

"It's the murder weapon, isn't it?" I asked.

"We don't know yet." He tightened his mouth. "Probably."

"I hope not," I said. "Mother will have a conniption fit."

"We'll know soon enough," he said. "I'm expecting—Ah, Dr. Langslow. Welcome."

Dad bustled in.

"So, you think you've found the murder weapon?" Dad sounded very excited at the thought.

The chief pointed to the candlestick. Dad's face fell.

"Oh, dear." He glanced at me. "Your mother will be very distressed."

"Meg already suggested as much." The chief was holding out a pair of gloves. "Here. Take a look and see if you think it matches the wound."

"Is that fingerprint powder on it?" I asked.

"Yes," the chief said. He was holding the candlestick while Dad tugged on the gloves. "Horace has already processed it for fingerprints and other trace evidence."

Dad took the candlestick and examined it from top to

bottom, both through and over his glasses. Then he raised it up in the air and brought it down in a slow arc.

"Yes," he said. "It's the right size and shape. If you like I can borrow the matching candlestick and Horace and I can run a few tests. But if this isn't the murder weapon, you'd be looking for something very like it."

Vern and Horace appeared in the doorway.

"We're in luck, Chief," Horace said. "We've got a match on the fingerprints."

Horace paused. Was he merely being dramatic, or was he giving the chief a chance to kick me and Dad out?

"Well," the chief prompted.

"Jerome Lightfoot."

Chapter 34

The chief didn't seem thrilled to hear this.

"I can see the headlines already," he said. "'Baptist Choir Director Bludgeons Elderly Man in Church Basement.'"

"'Elderly Blackmailer,'" I suggested.

"Not much better," the chief said. "We need to pick him up. Vern, Horace—hang on; I'll get his exact address from Debbie Ann."

"And she can put out a BOLO, in case he's not home," Vern said.

The chief nodded. He was already punching buttons on his cell phone.

"Debbie Ann," he said. "I need an address on Jerome Lightfoot . . . One fourteen West Street. Right. He's a suspect in the murder. . . . Right."

I pulled my latest schedule copy out of my purse and scanned it.

"He's supposed to be over at the Lutheran church right now," I said. "He had me schedule another rehearsal with some of his soloists. Of course, there's no guarantee he'll be there, especially if he suspects you're on to him."

"You heard the lady," the chief said. "Horace, you go to West Street. Vern, hit the church."

Vern and Horace nodded and disappeared.

"Who's going to direct the choir at services tomorrow and on Christmas Day if you arrest Lightfoot?" I asked.

"That's for the choir to decide," the chief said. "Though

I do know Minerva has been saying for weeks that she could do a better job than Lightfoot even if she was blindfolded with one hand tied behind her back. Well, the place is all yours." The chief stood up and rubbed his back as if it ached. "I'm going to break the news to Minerva and Reverend Wilson."

I pulled out my cell phone. I should probably call a few people and tell them that Trinity was available. Or have a small celebration that I didn't have to do yet another draft of the schedule to move all of Trinity's many Christmas Eve events to someplace else. Or notify Randall and Aida that at least their nephews were off the hook for the murder.

No time to do any of it. I glanced at my watch and realized it was high time I headed home. Michael was performing his one-man show of *A Christmas Carol* in a few hours, and between now and then I had to get myself and the boys fed and dressed.

Probably best just to let today's schedule run its course. And luckily I'd left tomorrow's schedule alone, hoping that the chief would finish with Trinity today, so I didn't have to rearrange that at all.

I turned out the light, left my office, and trudged down to the parish hall where the coffee machine was kept. I decided a little caffeine would help my trip home.

As I waited for the water to trickle down into my cup, I dug into my purse and dropped some change into the jar kept for that purpose. As dark and quiet as the church was, I could well imagine the ghost of Barliman Vess appearing to chide me if I didn't.

I sipped my coffee as I headed back to the vestibule.

And just as I was about to go out the front door, I noticed that the lights were back on in my little office.

I walked down to it as quietly as I could, more than half expecting to find it filled with sheep or wombats.

Instead I found Robyn and Chief Featherstone.

"Oh, dear." Robyn was shaking her head while looking around at all the furniture and boxes that filled all but the tiny space around my desk.

"What's wrong?" I asked.

"Hi, Meg. I'm afraid the fire chief isn't happy with your office."

"It's a fire hazard," Chief Featherstone said.

"It's not Meg's fault," Robyn hurried to say. "She's only been using it a few days."

"I had a report last week that there were parts of the church that constituted a fire hazard," Chief Featherstone said to me. "I told the reverend here that I'd try to put off inspecting it until after the holidays. But now, with what's happened . . ." He shook his head.

"I assume the basement is also in your sights," I said.

He nodded.

"I completely understand," Robyn said. "I know we should have done something about it weeks and weeks ago."

"By 'we' don't you mean Riddick?" I asked. "Wasn't he the one who was supposed to arrange the estate sale?"

"Yes, but he was clearly in over his head," Robyn said. "I've been trying for weeks to figure out a way to reassign the project without hurting his feelings."

"Do you have someone willing to take it on?" I asked. Clearing out the basement was one thing, but arranging an auction and an estate sale? I had a premonition that the church-swapping schedule was suddenly going to need more work—at least it would if she was planning to enlist me.

"Your mother seems quite willing to take it on," she said. "She's already started planning—she thinks we'll raise more money if we have an auction for the more valuable stuff. It all sounds fabulous to me. I've just been trying to bring Riddick around. But we can't wait any longer, so even though he's out sick—"

"Again?" I asked.

"Or still," she said. "I never can tell. At any rate, since Chief Featherstone has only given us till New Year's Day to get this done, we can't afford to wait any longer."

I had the feeling that far from being unwelcome, the chief's ultimatum had given her the solution to one of her knottiest problems.

"I'll leave you to it," Chief Featherstone said. "Merry Christmas to both of you, and apologies again for delivering such unseasonably bad news."

With that he left.

"So if Mother's going to take on the project, have you told her about the deadline?" I asked.

"A few minutes ago," she said. "She seemed to have a plan for where to put the stuff."

"And did she say what her plan was?" I was willing to bet I already knew.

"She thought it would be nice to have the estate sale in a barn," Robyn said. "Or possibly two barns—I gather the one on your parents' farm is on the small side for all the stuff we've got, so we'd need either a second barn somewhere else, or possibly some tents for the yard—though that would mean waiting till it's warmer, and I gather she's as eager to hold the sale as I am to see all this stuff leave. She's going to look around and see if she can find a barn large enough to hold it all."

Just then my cell phone rang. I glanced at the caller ID. Mother. I answered the phone and put her on speaker so Robyn could hear.

"Yes, Mother," I said, before she could say anything. "You can use our barn for the estate sale."

"Thank you, dear," she said. "Now all I have to do is figure out some way to get everything out there."

"I have some ideas about that," I said. "December twenty-sixth is Boxing Day, right? Let's ask everyone who's got a truck or a large trunk to come and move a few boxes. And you and the ladies of St. Clotilda can supervise."

"Everyone in the congregation?" Robyn said. "What a great idea!"

"And anyone in any other congregation who wants to help out," I said. "With any luck we've built some bridges over the last few days."

"Lovely, dear," Mother said. "And I can probably recruit a few cousins to help."

The last time Mother had recruited a few cousins for a project, we'd ended up fixing sandwiches and finding beds for fifty people. But the project did get done, and in record time.

"I think we have a plan," I said. "Talk to you later."

"Good night, dear," she said, and hung up.

"I hope that's not too inconvenient for you," Robyn said. "Having all that stuff in your barn."

"It won't be for long," I said. "Mother's been champing at the bit, waiting to get her chance to bid on some of Mrs. Thornefield's stuff."

"Then I will eagerly await Boxing Day and the opening of all those boxes," Robyn said. "Goodness! This has certainly been the most unusual Christmas season. Do you suppose I should warn the bishop I'm a murder suspect?"

"Are you?" I asked.

"I quarreled with the victim," she said.

"You'll have to stand in line behind half the congregation on that one," I said. "Most of us have been quarreling with him a lot longer than you have."

"And I knew he was plotting to get me kicked out of Trinity," she said. "He told me as much. My first parish as rector, after all those years as an assistant, and a mere six weeks after I arrive, one of the vestry is already plotting my downfall. That's motive, isn't it?"

"Yes, but nothing like the motive Mother has," I said. "He called her proposed design for redecorating the parish hall 'fussy and old-fashioned.'"

"Mercy!" Robyn said with a smile. "I wouldn't blame her for killing him after that. I'd have helped! So you think I should wait a while before telling the bishop?"

"Probably. Then again, Mr. Vess was always complaining to the bishop about things, and for all I know he could have complained about our bishop to the presiding bishop. Maybe you should tell the bishop to make sure he has an alibi."

Robyn giggled and shook her head. And then her face grew sad.

"Seriously—what a terrible thing, to leave behind such a legacy. I don't think I've met a single person who is genuinely saddened by his death. I'm already fretting over what to say in his eulogy. I can honestly say that he worked hard for the vestry, and took seriously his responsibility of stewardship, but beyond that, I confess, I am stumped."

"Have you seen his house?" I asked.

"I've dropped him off there a time or two, but no, I've never been inside."

"I suspect it's unchanged since his wife's death," I said.

"Perhaps some of the oldtimers can tell you more about her—from her portrait, I suspect she was a kind person. And he bought expensive cat food for his cat, in spite of being disappointed in her mousing abilities."

"Thank you," she said. "I can use all that."

"Go out and look yourself," I said. "You'll get a better sense of the man. The key's taped to the underside of the mat."

"I will," she said. "Thank you. I'm tempted to go over there right now."

"Why not?" I said.

"Because first I've got to find Riddick and tell him I'm taking the rummage sale out of his hands."

"Mother can't possibly schedule anything till January," I said. "Why not wait till after Christmas to tell him?"

I could tell from her face that she was tempted.

"No," she said finally. "I think I'd rather not have it hanging over me. And your mother needs to be able to start planning and organizing without any secrecy. Besides—"

We both started slightly on hearing a door slam in the distance.

"Front door, I think," Robyn said. "I suppose the crime scene tape is down. People will start coming for events."

"We don't have any scheduled here for tonight," I said.

Just then Riddick came into view. He glanced into the doorway and nodded to us.

"I see you heard the news," Robyn called out.

Riddick stopped and turned.

"I heard we finally got our church back to ourselves," Riddick said. From the way he was glowering at us, I wondered if he was blaming me and Robyn for all the unfortunate events that had disturbed his normal routine. And then he put his hand up and massaged his temples, wincing, and I realized that maybe he was just still feeling his migraine.

"All the congregations have their churches back, and everyone's Christmas Eve and Christmas Day services can go on as planned," Robyn said. "Isn't that wonderful?"

Riddick nodded glumly and turned to leave.

Robyn took a deep breath, gave me a brisk nod, and stepped out into the hallway.

"If you have a moment, there's something I'd like to talk to you about," I heard her say.

She and Riddick disappeared into her study. I silently wished her luck and turned to leave.

Chapter 35

I felt surprisingly cheerful on the way home. Or maybe it wasn't so surprising. The chief had solved the murder, and Lightfoot was probably already in custody. Caleb and Ronnie had undoubtedly learned their lessons, which meant the pranks would almost certainly come to an end. I would probably see Randall at Michael's performance tonight, and could apologize to him for casting any aspersions on his cousin Duane's character.

My spirits fell a little when I arrived home and found Horace dashing out of our front door, chewing on a sandwich.

"I thought you'd be down at the station with Jerome Lightfoot," I said.

"So did I," Horace said. "He's flown the coop. Probably sometime last night from what his neighbor said. We're all doing double shifts until he's caught. I just dropped by to grab a bite on my way out to search Caerphilly Creek."

He dashed back to his cruiser.

Rose Noire was standing in the doorway, waving to him as he hurriedly took off.

"Poor thing," she said, as I came in. "He's going to miss Michael's show."

He was also going to be scouring the county for a dangerous killer in twenty-something weather at a time of year when most people would rather be indoors with their families preparing for the upcoming holiday. But I was glad to see she had her priorities straight.

"How is everybody?" I asked.

"Michael is in his office doing his vocal exercises," she said. "The Baptist ladies have finished and taken all the new curtains and seat cushions over to the church. They'll be back tomorrow to clean up and take away the sewing machines. Rob and the boys are in the playroom, watching cartoons. Michael's mother is in the kitchen."

"I should go and say hello," I said. "To Michael's mother, that is."

Rose Noire winced, but I wasn't bothered. These days I actually liked my mother-in-law. Before Michael and I were married, her habit of referring to me as "her" and my family as "the outlaws" had rubbed me the wrong way. She seemed to grow a lot fonder of me once Michael and I had gotten married—though I found myself wondering if she was just resigning herself to the inevitable. But eventually, after a conversation with Rose Noire, I made a resolution to consider everything Mrs. Waterston said to me in a positive light—even if it sounded like criticism.

So if she commented, "You've gained a few pounds, haven't you?" I would say, "Why yes! Thank you!" as if pudging out was something I had been working frantically to achieve. If she mentioned that the boys were a grubby mess, I would beam and say "Yes, isn't it nice that they're so active!" If she mentioned how loud they were I would enthuse, "Yes, is there anything more delightful than hearing the happy voices of children at play?" If she commented on any shortcomings in the housekeeping, I would pretend to think she was complimenting me on achieving a comfortable, unstuffy, lived-in house.

I'd gotten to the point where playing the lemonade game, as I called it, was actually quite enjoyable, and these days, for whatever reason, she gave me far fewer opportunities to do so. I wasn't sure if she was making fewer snide or critical remarks or if I was just less apt to misinterpret random remarks as intended slights, but either way, we got along better.

I strolled into the kitchen. Michael's mother was standing on the stepping stool, rummaging through one of the cabinets. Was she looking for something in particular or just planning to rearrange them again?

"Hi, Mom," I said.

"Hello, dear." She stepped down off the stool and we exchanged kisses on the cheek. Then she held me at arm's length, studied my face for a few moments, and nodded as if I'd passed some test.

"You're looking well," she said.

The old me would have wondered why she had to sound surprised. The new me just noted with pleasure that she sounded sincere.

"Thanks," I said aloud.

"Where's your colander?"

"We have several that live in that cabinet." I pointed to the proper one. "But Rose Noire's been doing rather a lot of soap and potpourri making lately. She may have borrowed them."

And one had gone out to my car in the bag of things we needed to cook our contraband Christmas dinner, but I wasn't about to tell her that.

"I don't need it right now," she said. "Just making sure you have everything I need for my dinner. I'll put it on my list. When I'm finished, you and Rose Noire can take a look. There may be things you have that I'm not finding, and anything else we can buy."

"Good plan." This was the side of Michael's mother I liked. She always checked to see that she had everything she needed before leaving the house. She never started a project without making sure she had all the tools and supplies she required. Most people thought I was a good organizer, but I had to admit, Dahlia Waterston had me beat.

Of course, she'd only had Michael to raise. Perhaps if she'd had to cope with twins—

"What did you do to your arm?" she asked.

"A rude person barged into me and dislocated my shoulder on Saturday," I said. "It's still a little bruised."

"Ah," she said. "You might want to get a new sling for the performance. This one has red stains on it."

She turned her attention back to her list and then darted over to the spice cabinet.

She was right. The sling had red stains. Red wine or marinara sauce? In either case, not suitable for wearing on Michael's big night.

I went out to the library and hunted around until I found a scrap of the black lining fabric that was the right size for a replacement sling. Might as well look a little elegant for tonight's performance, and I was sure the sewing circle wouldn't mind. Then I took a deep breath and went upstairs to face the task of getting the boys ready for *A Christmas Carol*.

At least I didn't have to stuff them into little suits and ties again.

We'd left the boys home last year, and probably should have this year, but hearing Michael practice had stirred them up, and the prospect of being left behind provoked tempests of misery.

So we'd agreed to bring them. After the last two late nights, we'd come up with a new plan. Tonight they would wear pajamas under their snowsuits. And we'd cautioned them that if they got tired of listening to Daddy, they should tell me quietly so I could take them home to bed. Rose Noire and I were driving separately, so if the boys faded at different times we could each ferry one home.

To my delight, the idea of dressing up in pajamas and then going outside in them had just enough flavor of forbidden fruit to delight the boys, so they cooperated unusually well. Then I left them and Rob to continue watching *It's a SpongeBob Christmas* and went upstairs to get cleaned up and dressed myself.

I was wearing a long black dress, and the black sling was almost invisible against the fabric. Was that a bad thing? Should I perhaps go back and borrow a scrap of red velvet, so people could see the sling and perhaps avoid jostling me? No, I decided on elegance. If I got jostled a bit—well, we all have to suffer for beauty.

We all had a quick supper—ham-and-cheese sandwiches and Rose Noire's potato-leek soup. Well, all of us but Michael, who preferred not to eat too close to a performance. But Rob, Grandfather, Caroline, and the boys more than made up for any self-restraint on Michael's part.

"So you do this *Christmas Carol* thing every year?" Caroline asked.

"Every year for five years now," Michael said.

He'd started doing it because he wanted to help to raise money for the local food bank whose supplies usually ran particularly low at the holiday season, and had come up with the idea of doing a dramatic reading of Dickens's *A Christmas Carol*. Not the whole book of course, but luckily Dickens himself had created a condensed version that he could perform on his frequent tours of America.

The first year, a brave fifty or sixty of us filled the first few rows in one of the college's smaller auditoriums. Last year it had been standing-room only in the drama department's main theater. I hoped they didn't have to turn too many people away tonight. Next year we might need to schedule two performances, unless the new drama department building, now under construction on the north side of the campus, was finished slightly ahead of time. The J. Montgomery Blake Center for the Dramatic Arts— Grandfather had donated a good chunk of its cost and browbeat a number of friends and foundations for the rest—would have several performance spaces, including an enormous state-of-the-art theater that could hold twice as many people as the hall we were in tonight. But since it wasn't scheduled to open for another year . . .

We could worry about having two performances— complete with two sets of preperformance jitters—next Christmas.

"And this is the first year the boys are old enough to go!" Michael added, beaming at his sons.

Actually, I wasn't all that optimistic about their chances of staying the course, but they were so eager that I thought we'd at least give them a chance. And if I had to leave early with one or both of them—well, it wasn't as if I hadn't seen the performance before. Thanks to all that rehearsing, I could have recited it along with him.

"And it's time we all took off," I said. "Daddy needs to get there early," I added to the boys.

I drove, since in his preperformance state Michael tended to forget about boring, practical things like turn signals and stoplights. The boys chattered happily about SpongeBob and Frosty the Snowman, which I hoped was enough of a distraction to keep his nerves from starting to fray.

We dropped him off at the stage door of what people were already calling the Old Drama Building. It was built in the overly ornate Gothic-revival style that made the Caerphilly campus so popular for film crews looking for locations for music videos and low-budget vampire films. Fortunately the snow and the addition of wreaths on the doors and candles in the windows created more of a festive Victorian Christmas atmosphere.

"Bweak a leg, Daddy," Jamie said. I'd been coaching him on the fact that it was bad luck to wish an actor good luck.

"Two yegs," Josh said, competitive as usual.

I parked in one of the faculty spaces and then led the boys around to the front door. We probably could have slipped in with Michael, but I wanted the boys to see all the people lining up and paying money to see Daddy. To keep down expenses we didn't print tickets for the show—just took contributions at the door, and attendees could donate any amount they felt comfortable with. Last year we'd taken in a lot more fifty and hundred dollar bills than fives or ones.

Of course we were early, so there weren't too many people lining up. Still, we formally handed over our contributions to the ushers, who were clad in Dickensian costumes. I recognized the one in front of us as one of Michael's graduate drama students.

"Thank you, my good man," the usher said as Josh handed over his dollar. "At this festive season of the year, it is more than usually desirable—"

"That we should make some provision for the poor and destitute," Jamie rattled off.

"Bravo!" Our usher and several others nearby applauded.

"Bah, humbug!" said Josh, not only competitive but contrarian tonight.

The drama students all found this delightful and applauded some more.

"I take it this means that Professor Waterston has learned his lines," our usher said.

"If he forgets any it's not from want of rehearsal," I said, handing over my contribution.

"Thank you, madam," he said, with a bow. "Enjoy the performance. And I look forward to seeing you the day after tomorrow."

"On Christmas Day?"

"Your mother has very kindly invited those of us who cannot go home for the holiday to share in your Christmas dinner. Christmas orphans, she calls us."

"Lovely," I said. And since I wasn't hosting the dinner and had every intention of dodging all attempts to suck me into cooking, I meant it.

The lobby was decorated with whole forests of greenery festooned with red ribbons and flickering faux candles, and with all the ushers and ticket takers dressed in Victorian costumes, the effect was quite splendid. In a far corner, a costumed string quartet was playing a lively version of "Good King Wenceslas."

"Meg, dear!" Mother was standing just inside the door, also dressed in period costume, though her red velvet gown was much more elaborate than those worn by the women ushers. "Come have tea. And some hot cider for the boys."

"Gamma in play, too?" Jamie asked

Josh just trotted past her to the stand where volunteers—mostly women from St. Clotilda's Guild and the New Life Ladies' Auxiliary, resplendent in hoopskirted Victorian dresses in jewel tones—were selling hot tea, coffee, and cider to benefit the cleanup and renovation of the churches of Caerphilly, according to the signs posted nearby. I had a feeling this would be only the first of many benefits.

"Nice to see you," said a familiar voice.

Chapter 36

I had to do a double take before recognizing Robyn, also in a Victorian gown, although I recognized hers as one borrowed from the drama department's wardrobe collection.

Riddick Hedges was also there in costume, which was unfortunate, because unlike Michael and the other men from the drama department, he had no idea how to carry it off well. He was squirming as if the whole outfit was profoundly uncomfortable, and if I'd been casting David Copperfield he'd have been a shoo-in for Uriah Heep. It was perhaps a measure of his discomfort that he was not only willing but eager to fetch pitchers of water to refill the urns, haul away bags of trash, or perform any other chore that allowed him to disappear from view. In between errands he appeared to be attempting to fade into the wallpaper along one side of the lobby. No doubt he was unaware that he was standing directly beneath one of the dozen ornate Victorian mistletoe balls that dotted the room. I suspected he'd be mortified if anyone pointed this out.

I shelled out for tea for me and cider for the boys. Josh bolted his and had to be told to drink his second helping more slowly. Jamie was already sipping so slowly that I suspected he thought he'd be taken home to bed when his cup was empty.

"Take your time," Mother told me. "Rose Noire and your father are saving seats for all of us."

"Unfortunately, no one from Henry's department will be here tonight," Minerva said.

"Are they still trying to locate Jerome Lightfoot?"

"And not having much luck," Minerva said. "It's beginning to look as if after killing poor Mr. Vess he went straight home, packed his suitcases and took off. They've got a bulletin out on his car."

"I hope they catch him soon," I said. "Actually, I hope some other county catches him soon."

"I confess, I agree." Minerva shook her head. "I'd purely love to hear that he's been spotted a good long ways from here and locked up in someone else's jail. I had words with that man, more than once—if I'd known what kind of man he is! A cold-blooded killer!"

"Actually, I'm not sure cold-blooded could ever describe Mr. Lightfoot," one of the other Baptist ladies said. "I've never seen him when he wasn't in a temper over something."

"A hot-tempered killer, then," Minerva said. "And running around loose, and him knowing full well that I'm one of the people who's been trying to get him fired. Makes me feel all funny."

"Sit down, Minerva, dear," Mother said. "And have some tea."

"I can't blame you one bit," the Baptist lady said.

"I don't see how any of us will sleep tonight," exclaimed an Episcopalian.

Most of the church ladies chimed in either with the rumors they'd heard or to say how anxious they were. But by some unspoken agreement they all deferred to Minerva's superior cause for alarm—after all, she was not only a known enemy of the fleeing killer but her husband was even now risking life and limb to bring the fugitive to justice. Several of them vied to see who could refresh her tea.

"I'm sure we'll all be praying for a speedy end to this terrible situation," Robyn said. She clasped Minerva's hands. "And for the safety of our brave law enforcement officers, and for the soul of poor Mr. Vess."

"And for Mr. Lightfoot, too," put in Reverend Wilson, craning around from behind the table, where he was filling cups of cider. "For 'I say to you, that likewise joy shall be in heaven over one sinner that repents, more than over ninety and nine just persons, which need no repentance.' There is still hope for Mr. Lightfoot."

There were murmurs of "amen," from the assembled tea ladies and Minerva lifted her chin and looked comforted.

"Although I hope no one will object if I hope Mr. Lightfoot starts his repenting very soon, and from the inside of a jail cell," I added.

"Lord, yes," Minerva said.

"I look forward to the day when he is safely locked up," Reverend Wilson said. "And I can begin to help him wrestle with the heavy burden of sin he must be carrying."

"I just hope Henry finds him before Christmas Day." Minerva looked anxious. "I remember one terrible year back in Baltimore, not too long after we were married, when he was working twenty hours a day trying to catch a serial arsonist and didn't have time to open our presents until three days after Christmas. And he's not a young man anymore."

"Oh, that reminds me, dear," Mother said. "Before I forget."

She glided over to the tea table, reached underneath, and pulled out a gaily wrapped package.

"This is for you, Meg dear."

I suppressed the urge to ask her why she felt it necessary to give me the present now, when I would either have to run out to the car to stow it or lug it with me during the entire play.

"Thanks," I said instead. I couldn't help noticing that she was displaying none of the delight she normally took in presents, even when they were intended for other people. In fact, she had looked relieved the second it left her hands. "Who's it from?"

"Cousin Sylvia." From her grave tone of voice, she obviously knew how I felt about getting a parcel from Sylvia. For that matter, how everyone felt. We both stared at the parcel for a few moments in silence.

"What's wrong?" Robyn asked.

"Cousin Sylvia is an avid knitter," I said.

"I love hand-knitted presents," Robyn said. "Lucky you!"

"Sylvia's taste is . . . unusual," Mother murmured.

"She has no taste," I said. "And her color choices are so peculiar that I really think someone should find a way to test her for color blindness."

"She tries so hard," Mother said.

"Mostly she does bulky Christmas sweaters," I said. "With Santas or reindeer or Christmas trees or bells. Only she does her own designs, so everything just looks like multi-colored amoebas. Or psychedelic Rorschach tests."

"Still—one could make allowances," Mother said. "If only she'd use natural fibers. Wool. Cotton."

"I don't think it's possible to dye natural fibers in colors garish enough to please Sylvia," I said.

"Now you've roused my curiosity," Robyn said. "You must come and show me this sweater after Christmas."

"I'll show it to you now." I began picking at the tape at one end of the soft, bulky parcel.

"You can't open that now," Mother said.

"Why not?" I asked. "She won't be here to see me open it on Christmas Day. Even if she were, I can tape it up again."

"Well, it would be nice to see what we're all in for this year," Mother said. "Once she comes up with a pattern she likes, she usually does it up in different color combinations for everyone," she added to Robyn.

"I'm just surprised she gave me a present at all," I said. "I thought she wasn't speaking to me. She found out I'd given away some of the sweaters she's made for me and Michael over the years."

"You should never have donated them to the church rummage sale," Mother said.

"She knitted those sweaters you donated to the rummage sale?" Robyn exclaimed. "Oh, my." She regarded the parcel with alarm.

"I knew better than to donate them anywhere else," I said. "I know she haunts every thrift shop for miles around. I just didn't think she'd come to the Trinity rummage sale."

"Next time just mail them to Cousin Alicia in California," Mother said. "That's what I do. She has found someplace that's happy to have them. Possibly some organization that helps the visually impaired. And then— Oh, my!"

I had finally succeeded in removing the paper from the sweater and held it up. Mother and I stared at it, speechless.

"Actually, this one is rather nice," Robyn said.

It wasn't Sylvia's usual bulky horror. It was a soft, boat-neck sweater, all black except for the neckline, hemline, and the ends of the sleeves, which shaded into black flecked with a slight hint of metallic gold. I held it against my body and measured. I'd have to try it on to be sure, but it looked as if it would fit me perfectly. And look good on me. Perhaps Mother had brought the wrong parcel. I checked the tag: TO MEG FROM SYLVIA.

"It's beautiful," I said.

"Of course, given Sylvia's color sense, she probably thinks it's hideous," Mother said.

"Exactly," I said. "She really must hate me. Unless she's suddenly had a complete change of taste since last year. And I think it's wool."

"Wool-cotton blend, if I'm not mistaken." Mother was fingering the sweater with appreciation. "Very nice. And no, your brother opened his early, too. I'd say his is worse than usual. I believe it's meant to be Santa petting Rudolph and the rest of the reindeer—although if so, you'd think she'd have used red and brown instead of orange and purple. Rob thinks it's supposed to be a fruit basket being savaged by mutant hyenas. If that turns out to be a little small for you, let me try it on."

"Hands off!" I pretended to swat her fingers. "I'm the one who insulted Sylvia. I should bear the burden of her displeasure."

"I still have the last sweater or two she sent me and your father," Mother said. "I haven't mailed them to Alicia yet. I could donate them nearby."

"Good idea," I said. "Offend her as soon as possible, before she starts on your gift for next year. Why not donate them to the rummage sale we'll be having with Mrs. Thornefield's things?"

"Estate sale," Mother corrected. "And yes, that's a lovely idea. We need to schedule it soon. Though not until after I've had Sotheby's and Christie's in to look at a few of her things that might bring more at auction."

"Not the furniture, I assume," I said.

"Of course the furniture," Mother said. "Mrs. Thornefield had excellent taste. Sheraton, Chippendale, Hepplewhite."

"Then where did all those old horrors in the basement come from?" I asked. "I can't see anything but big, heavy stuff that I wouldn't give houseroom to."

"Big, heavy stuff?" Mother suddenly looked anxious. "That doesn't sound like Mrs. Thornefield's things."

"They probably put the best stuff at the far end of the basement," Robyn said. "Away from the furnace, not to mention prying eyes. The big stuff's probably church castoffs."

"And there are tons of boxes," I said. "I suppose they might have boxed up anything really fragile."

"We could go over there now," Mother said. "Just to check it out."

"The play's starting in fifteen minutes," I said, glancing at my watch. "And I should put in appearance at the cast party. Let's just get there early on Boxing Day. We told everyone to come at noon, right? We can get there a few hours early."

"Why not tomorrow?" Mother asked.

"Tomorrow's Christmas Eve," I protested. "We all have wrapping and cooking to do."

"It won't take long."

"You haven't seen the basement lately. Even if my shoulder were back to normal, there's no way the two of us could manage all the boxes."

"I can round up several of your more athletic cousins to help us do any shifting around we need."

"As long as we're finished in time for the live Nativity pageant and the carol sing-along," I said.

"Thank you, dear."

"Probably time we all took our seats," Robyn suggested. As we'd been discussing the sweater the incoming crowds had swelled, and now the lights in the foyer blinked to signal that it was time for us to enter the auditorium.

Riddick, who had been hovering nearby for the last several minutes, cleared his throat and stepped forward.

"Is it okay if— I mean, I'm happy to stay on if I'm needed but . . ." He let his words trail off and touched one side of his head gently, as if to remind us of his migraines.

"Go home, then," Robyn said. And then, as if startled by how brusque her words had sounded, she stepped forward and patted his shoulder. "You really don't need to hang around if you don't feel up to it. Or if there's something else you'd rather be doing. Go home and take care of yourself."

He smiled wanly. Then he turned and began walking slowly toward one of the side exits. I noticed that the farther he got from us, the faster his pace became. Clearly there was nothing wrong with his legs.

"Did I sound too impatient?" Robyn asked Mother and me in an undertone. "I confess, I feel impatient. He's been complaining all day. What is one supposed to do with people who insist on hanging around and whining when you've told them multiple times it's perfectly fine for them to leave?"

"Just what you did now," I said. "Tell them it's okay to go."

"Subtlety is lost on Riddick," Mother added.

I discarded Sylvia's wrapping paper in a nearby trash can and carefully stowed my beautiful new sweater in the tote I always carried whenever I went anywhere with the boys. I'd trained myself to call it a tote rather than a diaper bag because I'd long ago realized that even when the boys no longer needed diapers they'd still need the million and one other things I carried in the bag.

"Don't forget to thank Sylvia," Mother said.

"Are you sure I should?" I asked. "What if I thank her and get the mutant purple reindeer next year?"

"So true." Mother frowned.

"I know," I said. "I'll tell her that I like the sweater so much because there are only so many times you can wear a Christmas-themed sweater—or for that matter any brightly colored sweater—but a nice neutral black sweater works fabulously any time."

"Let's hope she takes the hint," Mother said. "Why don't you tell her I said that?"

"Happy to," I said. "Josh? Jamie? Finish off your cider so we can go watch Daddy's play."

Chapter 37

Rose Noire, Dad, and Michael's mother were saving places for us in the front row, so even though Mother, the boys, and I slipped in only a few minutes from curtain time we had good seats. The boys were awed at the number of people who'd come to see their daddy, and we gave in and let them stand on their seats for a few minutes, gazing in wonder at the several hundred audience members. More than a few of the audience had come in costume—some in Victorian garb and others in whatever they'd worn for Halloween. The hall was filled with robots, pirates, vampires, ballerinas, werewolves, mafiosos, cowboys, cartoon superheroes, six-foot cats and rabbits, and innumerable Goths and fairies. The audience sparkled almost as much as the hall, which was decorated not only with the usual evergreen and tinsel but also with tiny multicolored LED lights that pulsed in patterns to the Celtic holiday music that was being piped through the hall's speakers. Clearly the tech crews were having fun tonight.

About the time we got the boys settled down and facing forward again, the lights dimmed and Michael strode out onto the stage, wearing his Victorian costume—a top hat, a black frock coat, a red cravat, and a bright red plaid waistcoat. The audience burst into applause, and the boys jumped up on their chairs again and shouted "Daddy! Daddy!" while applauding wildly. Michael spotted them, and strode to the front of the stage to bow to them. Then he pointed at each one in turn with his forefinger and fixed them with a stern look until they both sat down and assumed expectant expressions. The audience laughed and applauded, and I could hear a few people saying things like "Aren't they adorable!" Well yes—most of the time.

Michael set down his top hat on a nearby prop chair, stepped to the podium, and began.

"Stave One," he announced. "Marley's Ghost. Marley was dead, to begin with."

Josh settled down immediately and stared at Michael as if intent on every word. Jamie spent the first five minutes wiggling and craning his neck around, so he could catch a glimpse of all the people staring at his daddy. Then, after another few minutes of scanning the rafters intently— no doubt in hopes of a cameo appearance by another snake—he settled down with his head against my side and went quietly to sleep. Josh remained rapt, with his mouth hanging open. In fact, occasionally I saw his lips moving, and I realized he was mouthing the words along with Michael.

I was absorbed myself, at least at first. No matter how many times I saw him rehearsing, I was still surprised at how much better it seemed when he took the stage. Was it the lights and the theater setting? Or did he take the energy most people would fret away in stage fright and channel it into his performance? I marveled at how different he made his voice for each character, at how I almost could see what he was describing come alive.

And then he came to the part of the story where Scrooge goes home to his gloomy lodgings and, after the shock of briefly seeing Marley's face where the door knocker should have been, gives way to an uncharacteristic fit of nerves and searches his rooms.

"Nobody under the bed; nobody in the closet; nobody in his dressing gown, which was hanging up in a suspicious attitude against the wall."

There were chuckles at that, and I remembered my own brief moment of fright when I'd been searching the Trinity church basement and had been startled by the coat tree, with its own suspicious attitude.

Thinking of the coat tree reminded me of the whole mass of clutter currently infesting Trinity—in the furnace room, the classrooms, the storage closets, and the office that would soon cease to be mine. Strangely, the clutter no longer oppressed me, perhaps because I knew it would be leaving soon. As Michael acted out the confrontation between Scrooge and Marley's ghost, part of my mind was following him, and the other half was happily making lists. Things we'd need for the church clean-out. Things Michael and I could donate to swell the estate sale. Places where we should publicize the sale.

I felt wonderfully content. I had my family all around me. The boys seemed happy. And I was simultaneously doing two of my favorite things: watching Michael perform and making mental plans for organizing a project.

I glanced over at Mother, who was sitting proudly upright in her Victorian finery and following the performance with the keen appreciation she bestowed on anything belonging to a more genteel bygone era. But she didn't look as content as I felt. Clearly she was still concerned about Mrs. Thornefield's estate. I hoped it turned out that some of the larger boxes held the furniture Mother remembered so fondly.

And if they didn't—well, I remembered hearing that Mrs. Thornefield's house had been rather run-down by the time it had come into Trinity's hands. What if she hadn't been quite as well off as she'd led everyone to believe? What she'd had a cash-flow problem and had solved it by selling a few of her nicest pieces?

Mother would be so disappointed. Maybe I should try to postpone our box-opening visit until after Christmas?

No. It would only prey on her mind. If the Sheraton and Hepplewhite furniture had been sold, best find out as soon as possible.

Jamie woke up after half an hour's nap, and from that point both boys remained wide awake to the end, following Michael's every word, and laughing when the audience did, though I suspected they were laughing not because they understood the funny lines but out of delight, because so many people were laughing at Daddy's jokes.

Michael took ten curtain calls. Afterward we took the boys backstage to see everyone congratulating Daddy in his dressing room. They were incredibly impressed.

And also starting to show signs of impending crash and burn, in spite of the preemptive extra napping earlier in the day.

"Rose Noire and I are going to take them home," I told Michael. "Before they ruin everyone's impression of them as little angels."

Michael's face fell.

"You mean you're not coming to the cast party?" Dad asked. "Your mother and I will be there."

"Your father will," Mother said. "I am worn out and planning to go home to bed."

"Besides," I said. "With a cast of one, how big can it be?"

"Okay, it's also the unofficial departmental Christmas party," Michael said. "And all of my family are invited! And it doesn't start till midnight, after we finish cleaning up the theater, so you could run the boys home and come back for it—if that's okay with Rose Noire."

She had no objection, so after making our good-byes to everyone, we led the boys out to the parking lot. We had to carry them the second half of the way.

"Let's just put them in my car," Rose Noire said. "I'm giving Rob a ride home—he can help me carry them in and you can head to the cast party a little sooner."

By the time we strapped them into their car seats, both boys were fast asleep. So I applied my best good night kisses to their unconscious foreheads and waved as Rose Noire and Rob drove off.

"Does this mean you're coming to the cast party after all?" I turned to see Robyn picking her way across one of the parking lot's many patches of ice. "It sounds like fun."

"I'll be a bit late," I said. "I have to pick up a few things at the grocery store. Don't mention that to Mother if she changes her mind and decides to come," I added.

"Because she would think planning for the rummage sale should trump mere groceries?" Robyn said, with a laugh.

"Something like that," I said. "You have no idea."

"Actually, I do." She looked serious for a moment. "Your mother is a force of nature. I'm just glad she's usually on my side. Call me when you and your mother are coming over tomorrow to inspect the boxes. Matt's back from North Carolina. He and I can help."

My errand at the grocery store didn't take long. I was picking up supplies for tomorrow night's secret Christmas dinner. Cans of refrigerator rolls. Cranberries. Cran-apple juice for the boys to drink—we always served it on festive occasions so they would feel included when we lifted glasses of red wine for toasts. I pondered getting some ice cream, a popular favorite with the boys and Michael. But I wasn't sure there would be room in the tiny freezer compartment of the basement apartment's ancient toy-sized refrigerator for both the ice cream and an ice cube tray.

The store was surprisingly crowded for such a late hour. Some of the people were piling their baskets high with the makings of their own Christmas dinners—turkeys, geese, ham, ribs, pork roasts, potatoes and sweet potatoes, green beans, cranberries, pies, premade pie shells, cans of pumpkin, bags of flour and sugar—looking at other people's carts was giving me an appetite. And just walking down the spice aisles and seeing people filling their carts with cinnamon, cloves, allspice, nutmeg, and other spices made me happy.

In the housewares aisle, I convinced a young, recently married Shiffley that no, a fancy electric mixer would *not* be the perfect present for his wife and suggested he contact Rose Noire, who could put together a deluxe basket of luxurious foods and wonderfully scented sachets, lotions, and potpourris. And then I ended up giving her card to several other present-seeking husbands and boyfriends who had been eavesdropping on our conversation. Tomorrow, I knew, would be one of her busiest days of the year, as the growing number of men who waited till the last minute to start looking for presents for their wives and girlfriends descended on her en masse, all begging for special gift baskets. A good thing she started making up the special baskets before Thanksgiving, though this year business had been going so well that several times in the last month she'd enlisted the rest of the household, even the boys, for several intense evenings of cutting up and wrapping soap, mixing and bagging potpourri, using rubber stamps to create labels, and doing all the other small tasks needed to get her supplies back to a good level.

All in all, I was in a good mood when I left the market. When I got to my car, I put the few things that were going home in the trunk, and the two bags of items going to the basement apartment on the front passenger seat. Probably a good idea to deliver them before I went home, lest one of the mothers come across the cranberries and ask what they were for.

My route to the apartment led near Trinity, and on sudden impulse, I passed the turn that would have been my most direct route to the basement apartment and took a slight detour. I realized that Mother had been on my mind. And I found myself suddenly thinking that perhaps it had been a little too easy to convince Mother to postpone her inspection of the estate sale hoard until tomorrow. And that her decision to go home and rest rather than attend the cast party was slightly suspect. And Mother was on the vestry—wasn't it possible, even probable, that Mother was in possession of one of those million spare keys Robyn had mentioned? And that in spite of Trinity being a deserted recent crime scene, she might decide to drop in to check on Mrs. Thornefield's legacy?

Chapter 38

Sure enough, Mother's gray sedan was in the parking lot. Toward the left side, as close as you could get to the basement door. I didn't see any lights on in the church, but I caught a few flickers of light through the basement windows, as if someone was walking around with a flashlight.

I parked my car next to hers. I put the groceries destined for the apartment on the floor and threw a couple of things on top of them, in case she came out and peeked inside before I found her. Then I headed for the stairwell that led to the basement door. The parking lot was empty except for our two cars, which would have been unheard of, except that there was nothing scheduled here tonight— I'd relocated everything that was supposed to happen here today to other venues, and hadn't rearranged anything after the chief finally released the crime scene. The parking lot would be full enough tomorrow. All the parking lots. But tonight . . .

The basement door was new—no doubt Randall had arranged to replace the one the firefighters had broken down to get to the fire. But to my relief my key still worked. I unlocked the door, holding my key ring tightly so nothing clinked, and turning the lock as quietly as possible.

The hall was dark, but there was enough moonlight streaming in the windows for me to see in the hall. Should I go back and get my flashlight? No, once I'd surprised Mother, we could turn on the lights. I had no idea why she was creeping around with a flashlight. Surely as a member of the vestry she had more right than most to be here.

I found her standing in the furnace room with her hands on her hips—well, the hand that wasn't holding the flashlight—glaring at some of the hulking furniture stored there.

"You see?" I said. "Seriously ugly furniture."

She started slightly.

"Hello, dear," she said. "I am perturbed. These are not Mrs. Thornefield's things."

"Must be some of the stuff from the church attic, then."

"No." She shook her head with quick impatience. "I helped clean out the attic. Remember—just after the dear rector arrived."

"I remember," I said. "I was just thinking the other night how much better the basement looked, even with all Mrs. Thornefield's stuff."

"The guild inspected everything in the attic, the closets, and the basement," Mother went on. "We put all the things the church really needed in neatly labeled plastic bins, and we hauled out bags and bags of trash and recycling, and we boxed up everything that might possibly sell at the rummage sale and had it hauled down here, to the basement. None of this hideous old furniture was here then."

"How can you be sure it's not Mrs. Thornefield's? Even if it wasn't in her living room, maybe she had it in her attic?"

"Mrs. Thornefield enlisted my help," Mother said. She was opening up a box, using a small jeweled metal nail file to slice open the packing tape. "In fact, the guild's help. She didn't entirely trust our old rector. Not his character, of course; the dear man was above reproach. But even those of us who were fondest of him realized that dear Dr. Womble wasn't a very practical person. Mrs. Thornefield was afraid he'd just give her things to the poor, not realizing how valuable they were. So one day she invited the officers of the guild to tea, and she gave us a full tour. Including her basement and attic. There wasn't any ugly old furniture in her attic—only a few seasonal items and a number of banker's boxes containing all her financial records. She wanted us to know where those were. And she showed us her basement so we'd be aware of what a nice wine collection she had. Everything in her house was perfectly organized, spotlessly clean, and in impeccable taste. Nothing like this!"

"How long was that before she died?" I asked. "Maybe she downsized a bit. Sold some of the nicer furniture. To make sure the church got its full value." Or to live on, if I was right about her having financial reverses.

"Only a few months. Look at this . . . this . . . rubbish!" She pulled a few items out of the box she'd been opening up and shook them at me, sending the flashlight beam darting wildly. In her left hand, along with the flashlight, she held a small bronze-colored statue of a scantily clad nymph. In her right she held a superlatively ugly china lamp.

"Maybe someone else donated a few boxes of junk that Robyn—or more likely the old rector—forgot to mention?"

Mother focused the flashlight beam on a label on one side of the box, which read THORNEFIELD ESTATE. BOX 14.

"I've opened up six boxes whose labels claim they are from the Thornefield estate," she said. "And so far I haven't found a single thing Mrs. Thornefield would have allowed in her trash can!"

She strode over to another box and began slicing at the packing tape with her nail file. Surely she wasn't planning to inspect every box in the basement?

"Let's work on that tomorrow," I said. "Preferably once we've already moved the boxes—we're only going to have to tape those up again to move them."

"I can't rest till we get to the bottom of this," she said. But she did stop hacking at the box she was trying to open. "I think someone has stolen Mrs. Thornefield's legacy."

"We can't possibly get to the bottom of it tonight," I said. "And if someone did steal anything, you're making it harder for the chief to figure out what happened. We need to leave those boxes sealed, so the guys from the Shiffley Moving Company can tell us if those boxes are packed and sealed the way they would have done it. That one you were working on—it looks to me as if it could have been opened up and then resealed."

Mother frowned as she looked down at the box.

"How can you tell, dear?"

"The tape that's closed up the top doesn't quite match the tape on the bottom," I said. "It's a little more opaque. And there's a little area right by the tape where it looks as if someone peeled off some tape, and the top layer of the cardboard with it."

Mother bent down to inspect the label more closely.

"You're right, dear. I wonder why I didn't spot that."

"You have to hold the flashlight at just the right angle," I said. "You'd probably have noticed it immediately if you'd turned on the lights to do this." I walked over to the wall and flipped the light switches.

Nothing happened.

I walked out into the hall and flipped a switch out there. Still nothing.

"The lights aren't working, dear," Mother said. "I assume it's something to do with the fire. Or with it being a crime scene."

I thought for a moment, then shook my head.

"The lights were working fine right after the fire," I said. "And I'm pretty sure they were on when I was here this afternoon, talking to the chief and Robyn and the fire chief."

"Then perhaps there was some damage that didn't come to light until now," Mother said.

"If there is, that could be dangerous," I was pulling out my cell phone. "It could be a fire hazard—we should call the fire department. And dammit, I need to cancel all the events we have scheduled here until we're sure the building is safe and—"

"Drop the cell phone."

Mother and I both whirled to find Riddick Hedges standing in the doorway to the furnace room. In his left hand he held a flashlight so large it dwarfed Mother's little pocket light. In his right hand he held a gun.

Chapter 39

"Riddick!" Mother exclaimed. "Just the person we need. There appears to be something wrong with the power. Do you think you can do anything?"

Riddick looked at her for a few moments in disbelief. Actually, I did, too.

"Yes, the power is out because I cut the wires," Riddick said finally. "Now you"—he focused his flashlight beam on me—"I said drop that phone."

I leaned over, put the phone on one of the boxes, and then leaned back and tried to look as if the phone were unreachably far from me instead of a good lunge away.

"Not good enough," he said. "Put it on the ground and kick it over to me."

Reluctantly, I followed his orders. To my chagrin, he managed to bend over and pick it up while still keeping the gun, the flashlight, and his eyes aimed at us. I wouldn't have thought him that agile. I noted that he put my phone in his right pants pocket.

"Riddick, dear," Mother said. "There's really no need for this."

"Don't 'dear' me, you bossy old cow," Riddick said. "You and the witches of St. Clotilda's have had a lot of fun laughing at me all these years, haven't you? 'Poor Riddick—he tries so hard, but he just doesn't understand anything.'"

I had to admit, his imitation of Mother was spot-on.

"I have always tried to be respectful and supportive of you," Mother said. "In fact—"

"Shut up," he said. "There's some duct tape over on top of those boxes. Get it, and start taping up your ankles."

Mother and I looked at each other. She raised one eyebrow—the one on the side away from Riddick.

I realized she was asking me what to do. And looking—nervous. Maybe even scared. I wasn't sure I could remember seeing Mother scared. Or having her ask me for help.

"Sometime this century, ladies," Riddick barked.

Probably not the time for an existential crisis.

"Let's look for the duct tape," I said. And for anything that we could use as a weapon.

If only Mother wasn't here, I thought, as I scanned the nearby floor and the tops of the boxes. I couldn't help thinking that if I were alone, I'd have a much better chance of getting the drop on Riddick. Or if I tried and failed, at least I'd only be failing myself. Mother's slender figure looked alarmingly frail at the moment. And why on earth would anyone over sixty wear boots with dainty little high heels at any time, much less with a foot of snow on the ground? Any escape plan that called for running fast was obviously not going to work.

Mother was playing her tiny flashlight over the top of the boxes. At one point the beam spilled over and illuminated the area around Riddick's feet, just for a second. There was something by his right leg. It looked a lot like the bright red plastic gas can we kept in the garage. Evidently Riddick had come back to have another go at burning up the junk in the basement. The stuff that almost certainly had never belonged to Mrs. Thornefield. I'd bet Riddick had hauled all her valuable things away, and maybe even sold most of them already.

Mother was eyeing her little nail file, but since it was only about five inches long and already warped from hacking through box tape, I didn't think it would do us much good. I was a lot more interested in the tacky bronze nymph, which had a lot of nice sharp edges. But I'd have to get much closer to Riddick to be able to use it.

"What's taking so long?" Riddick asked.

"There is no duct tape here," Mother said.

"There has to be," Riddick snapped.

"What, did you leave it down here when you killed Mr. Vess?" I asked.

"Keep looking," Riddick said.

Fine with me. The longer we could stall Riddick, the better. Surely sooner or later Michael would start worrying that I hadn't shown up at the cast party. Or Dad would wonder what was taking Mother so long. Or one of the deputies would swing by the parking lot, spot our cars, and come to check things out. I wasn't sure why Riddick was so intent on binding us—if I were a cold-blooded killer, I'd have just shot my prisoners and have done with it. Maybe he was a little squeamish about actually shooting us. Or maybe he didn't want to risk the noise. For whatever reason, he obviously preferred to tie us up and let the fire do his dirty work. Well, that was good for us. We needed time. Time, and a distraction.

"Did Vess actually figure out what you were up to?" I asked aloud. "Or were you just afraid he might if he kept poking?"

"Vess was a meddling busybody," Riddick said. "Don't try to pretend you're sad about his death."

"Any man's death diminishes me," Mother quoted. "Oh, look! I found the roll of tape."

She sounded so pleased that I couldn't help shooting her an exasperated look. Did she really not get what was going to happen once Riddick had the tape?

"But I don't think it's going to be very useful," Mother went on. She held up the roll and pulled at the end of the tape. About four inches of tape came away, followed by the brown paper strip that marked the end of the roll.

"That can't be my roll." Riddick sounded cross. "Keep looking."

He followed his own advice, dropping the flashlight beam to scan the floor, starting at his own feet and gradually moving outward.

And I realized that if he was pointing the flashlight at the floor, he couldn't see what we were doing. I reached out, very slowly, and grabbed the ugly china lamp. I wasn't close enough to him to whack him, and it was such an odd shape that I didn't like my odds of throwing it at him accurately but maybe—

I tossed the lamp as far to my right as I could. It landed with a crash near the furnace.

"Who's there?"

As I hoped, Riddick whirled and pointed gun and flashlight in the direction of the crash. I launched myself toward him, taking a few steps and then bringing him down with a flying tackle. I realized too late that I should have taken my arm out of the sling before attacking. We landed hard on the concrete floor, and unfortunately most of my weight landed on my bad arm. I managed not to scream—I kept it down to a loud yelp. I heard something metal skitter across the floor. I hoped it was the gun. Yes, it must be the gun, because I could see the flashlight beam darting about wildly as Riddick started whacking me with it. I raised my good right arm to keep him from hitting my head, and was trying to get my left arm into play so I could hit him back when—

Thunk! Riddick suddenly went limp, and I heard a small metallic tinkling noise on the floor near me.

"Take that, you rude man!" Mother exclaimed.

I grabbed the flashlight from Riddick's now limp hand, scooted out of reach, and turned the beam on him. Mother had hit him with the bronze nymph. The tinkling noise had been one of the statue's slender, graceful arms breaking off on contact with Riddick's skull.

His eyes were closed and I saw a small trickle of blood making its way down his forehead.

I scrambled over to the gun, shifted the flashlight into my left hand, and took firm hold of the weapon.

My left arm wasn't liking this at all, so I walked back and handed the flashlight to Mother.

"Thank you, dear," she said. "If you want to tie him up, I have a full roll of packing tape in my purse."

She kept the flashlight trained on Riddick and the gun at the ready—pointed at the ceiling, thank goodness, not at Riddick and me. I fetched the tape and tied him up. It took rather longer than usual, working with only one good arm. I was relieved that he didn't wake up while I was doing it, but equally relieved to hear him groan slightly as I was finishing off his ankles. I checked his pulse. It was steady, and I saw his eyelids flutter.

I put as much distance as possible between me and him and sat down heavily on a box.

"Here, dear." Mother handed me the gun and the flashlight. "You just rest. I'll go out in the hall where the cell phone reception's better and call Chief Burke."

I sat, watching Riddick regain consciousness and begin

to struggle against the tape. I put the flashlight on the box beside me and the gun in my jacket pocket. My left shoulder was killing me, and I wouldn't have the strength to lift the gun if Riddick wriggled out of the tape.

I wasn't sure if I was relieved or annoyed at hearing the dainty but firm tap-tap-tap of Mother's boot heels as she walked out into the hall.

"Hello, Debbie Ann? Meg and I have caught the *real* killer."

Chapter 40

"I can't believe it! Every church in Caerphilly is back to normal! We can all have our Christmas Eve services as planned! And it's all thanks to you and your mother!"

Robyn was standing in the doorway of Trinity, welcoming the congregation to the ten o'clock service. Maybe the churches were back to normal, but I still hadn't recovered from the previous night's excitement.

Robyn looked as if only the vivid presence of my bright red velvet sling was keeping her from hugging me. I'd chosen the color for that very reason. She settled for patting my undamaged right arm repeatedly.

"Mostly back to normal," I said. "Rumor has it that the Baptist church isn't quite as fresh smelling as they'd like."

"They'll be fine," Robyn said. "Father Donnelly and I gave them some incense yesterday, and just in case they can't quite bring themselves to use it, Randall Shiffley dropped off a couple of cans of pine- and spruce-scented air freshener this morning. Go have a seat down front—you want to get a good view of your boys."

I followed her orders. Mother and Michael's mother were already there in Mother's usual third-row pew, saving me a seat by piling their coats and cameras between them.

I'd gotten about six hours of sleep, thanks in part to the chief's suggestion that I go home after having my shoulder looked at in the ER, and give him my full statement today, after church. Still, never had I so appreciated Robyn's penchant for brief and pithy sermons. Even the parents who hadn't been up late probably felt the same, since we were all keenly aware of the occasional giggles, sneezes, whispers, and sounds of minor combat emanating from the doorways on either side of the church where the children were waiting for their entrances.

Finally the moment came. The organist began softly playing the opening bars of "O Little Town of Bethlehem" and Michael stepped to the podium to begin reading from the book of Luke.

"'In those days Caesar Augustus issued a decree that a census should be taken of the entire Roman world.'"

A sixth-grader in a toga stepped out and held up a scroll made from two empty paper towel rolls, a long sheet of paper, and about a ton of gold glitter. He'd have looked more authentic if his mother hadn't made him wear a turtleneck under the toga but the mother in me approved of her caution.

"'So Joseph also went up from the town of Nazareth in Galilee to Judea, to Bethlehem the town of David . . .'"

As Michael continued to narrate and the organist played softly, Mary and Joseph, seventh-graders chosen for good behavior, entered from the right and headed for the manger. Mary was leading, rather than riding, a donkey whose sneaker-clad rear feet had an alarming tendency to step on the heels of the snow boots his front feet were wearing. Mary abandoned the donkey once she reached the manger, which was right in front of the altar. As soon as the donkey came to a halt, its stomach began to writhe alarmingly, until Joseph kicked both sets of feet several times and stage-whispered "Cut it out, you idiots!"

While her husband was disciplining the donkey, Mary

reached under the manger and matter-of-factly pulled out the doll that represented the infant Jesus and plunked him down in the straw. But then she remembered her character and assumed a beatific expression as she gazed down at the doll.

On this cue, all the animals filed in. In addition to the boys in their dinosaur costumes, the denizens of the stables included a brightly colored parrot, an elephant, a Wookiee, and Winnie-the-Pooh. They all took turns peering down at baby Jesus while the choir led us through all six verses of "Friendly Beasts," after which the Wookiee chivvied the rest of the creatures to the right side of the stage, where they all took their seats on hay bales placed there for their comfort.

"'And there were shepherds living out in the fields nearby, keeping watch over their flocks at night.'"

Several comparatively tall boys and girls dressed as shepherds appeared at the far right, herding twenty smaller children dressed as sheep. The sheep milled about restlessly, being shushed occasionally by their keepers or whacked with crooks, while the choir and the congregation sang "While Shepherds Watched Their Flocks by Night"—thank goodness only the first verse this time. Then the shepherds herded their charges past the manger and got them settled down on the left side of the stage on more hay bales, except for a couple of small boy sheep who insisted on sitting with my two little dinosaurs.

Michael switched over to the book of Matthew.

"'Now after Jesus was born in Bethlehem of Judea in the days of Herod the king, behold, wise men from the east came to Jerusalem.'"

The three children chosen to be wise men—or, in this

case, two wise men and one wise woman—filed out from the left, carefully holding boxes wrapped in gold paper, presumably containing the gold, frankincense, and myrrh, while we all sang the first verse of "We Three Kings." I was relieved to see that there weren't any children in camel suits—especially since the donkey still erupted from time to time with stomach-writhing and alarming sounds of internal conflict and had to be suppressed by Joseph.

" 'Then, opening their treasures, they offered him gifts, gold and frankincense and myrrh.' " The wise persons all popped the tops of their boxes and showed the contents to Mary, who nodded with approval. " 'And being warned in a dream not to return to Herod, they departed to their own country by another way.' " At this, the wise men looked anxiously back the way they'd come, and then set down their boxes at the foot of the manger and tiptoed off in the other direction.

Then the choir started us off with "Joy to the World" and at the end of the song, the wise men came back. All the participants took a bow while we applauded, and then all the parents and grandparents put away their cell phones and cameras and the children scampered out to join their families in the pews for the rest of the service.

A good thing we weren't as tightly scheduled as we had been over the last few days, because after the service was over, everyone milled around for at least half an hour, praising all the pageant participants and sharing the latest gossip and generally reveling in the fact that Trinity was ours, not just for the moment, for the whole rest of the day and all day tomorrow. Doubtless all the other churches were feeling a similar sense of relief.

When everyone finally began drifting away, Michael took

his mother and our two dinosaurs for lunch at Mother and Dad's while I headed over to the police station for my interview with the chief.

I took the long way around, in part so I could drive by as many churches as possible. In fact, I cruised through the parking lots of several. The choir was in full and glorious voice at New Life Baptist Church. The parking lot at St. Byblig's was full, and there were cars parked up and down the road so far in both directions that a couple of parishioners were using their vans to haul latecomers to the door. An early service had just ended at the Presbyterian church and even though it was still below freezing, many of the congregation were lingering in small groups in the parking lot. From the clouds of breath steam rising from most of the groups they were all talking a mile a minute. I exchanged waves with Randall and at least a dozen other Shiffleys. On the lawn of the Methodist church, several people were laughing happily as they hauled away the last few inanimate Nativity figures and shoveled the area, in preparation for this afternoon's live Nativity.

By the time I reached the police station, I was elated from the sight of so many of my friends and neighbors enjoying their Christmas rituals untroubled by pranks. I was looking forward to my interview—I also had a lot of questions, and provided the chief was in a good mood and I was tactful about how I asked, I stood a good chance of getting answers to most of them.

I got a few of my answers before I even went in. As I parked in the visitors' section of the station lot, I saw a Goochland County Sheriff's Department car pull up by the front door. Horace and Vern Shiffley appeared to be watching this new arrival with interest so I went over to wish them good morning and see what I could see.

"Good news," Vern said. "Our friends up in Goochland County have apprehended Jerome Lightfoot."

"But is he still a wanted man?" I asked. "Now that we're pretty sure he isn't the killer, I mean."

"Maybe he's not the killer," Vern said. "But he probably isn't Jerome Lightfoot, either. He had several complete sets of identity papers with him, and they're probably all false. But we sent in his fingerprints, so we should find out who he really is pretty soon. I'm betting the New Life Baptist Church won't be the only place charging him with fraud."

"Speaking of fingerprints," I added. "If he's not the killer, how did his prints get on the murder weapon?"

"He threw it at someone," Horace said. "During one of his tantrums when the choir was rehearsing at Trinity. According to some of the ladies from the Altar Guild, at one point he started heaving anything he could find at people— not just the candlesticks but hymnals and flower vases and seat cushions. The ladies packed up everything that wasn't nailed down and shoved it all in the sacristy for safekeeping. And according to them, Riddick was making himself helpful for a change."

"So when he surprised Vess in the basement—" Vern began.

"Or arranged to meet him in the basement—" Horace put in.

"He brought along the candlestick," Vern finished. "Knowing he could use it to frame Lightfoot. One of the ladies mentioned that she couldn't find it Sunday morning to polish it, but she figured it had just been put away in the wrong place. Riddick had probably hidden it some-place to use when he did away with Vess."

"Which is going to make it a lot easier to prove premed-itation," Horace added.

"You here to see the chief?" Vern asked.

I nodded.

"Wait here until they take Lightfoot through the lobby," Horace said.

"Or whatever his name is," Vern grumbled.

Given what the so-called Lightfoot had done to my shoulder, I thought this was good advice. I spotted several other familiar figures also watching Lightfoot's entrance.

"What's Caleb doing down here?" I asked.

"Just got his anklet taken off," Vern said. "County attor-ney's offering him and Ronnie probation, provided they make financial restitution and do about a zillion hours of community service."

"Good," I said. "Is that Duane Shiffley with him?"

"It is," Vern said. "Seems Duane is dead set against see-ing any more young Shiffleys following in his unfortunate footsteps. Going to stick to Caleb like a burr to a hound dog until he's sure the kid has done all his community service and seen the error of his ways. If Caleb wants to go to the devil he'll have to do it over Duane's dead body. Probably safe to go in now."

I took Vern's advice, wishing Caleb and Duane a merry Christmas as I passed. The chief was standing in the lobby, gazing down the hallway that led to the jail, with a satisfied expression on his face.

"Good morning, Meg," he said. "And merry Christmas. I won't take too much of your time—I know you have a lot on your plate."

And it didn't take much time, probably because he'd

already taken a very detailed statement from Mother last night. I went through my story, and he took a few notes, but that was it. And he was obviously in such a genial mood that I didn't hesitate to ask a few questions of my own.

"So was Mother right?" I asked. "Had Riddick stolen all of Mrs. Thornefield's nice things?"

"Stolen just about everything," the chief said. "And started selling everything off. Fortunately he was keeping good records, so we shouldn't have too much trouble recovering either the items from the buyers or the purchase price from Riddick's bank account, whichever Trinity prefers. And the items he hadn't yet sold were all packed up—apparently he was planning to take it all with him."

"Even the furniture?"

"He had it all loaded in a stolen truck," the chief said. "Quincy Shiffley's truck, in fact. Once we've inventoried it, the Shiffley Moving Company can bring it out to your barn to get ready for that auction."

"What about the stuff in the church basement?" I asked. "Did he steal that, too?"

"No, he bought it all at various junk shops, estate sales and yard sales over the past six months, since Mrs. Thornefield passed away," the chief said. "He knew everyone would get suspicious if there wasn't a house full of furniture and boxes down in the basement. I suppose it never occurred to him that anyone would be that familiar with the contents of Mrs. Thornefield's house."

"He should have known Mother better by now," I said.

"And it's a good thing you knew your mother well enough to suspect she couldn't rest without inspecting the basement," the chief said.

"And did Mr. Vess suspect what was going on?" I asked. "Or was he just unlucky enough to be snooping in the church when Riddick was making his final haul? Or will we ever know?"

"We have a pretty good idea," the chief said. "We've recovered two files Riddick apparently stole from Mr. Vess. The one on the Thornefield estate and one on Riddick himself. Apparently, Vess had been suspicious of Riddick for years."

"But he was suspicious of everybody," I said. "How was anyone supposed to know he was right about Riddick?"

"Precisely! The boy who cried wolf!" The chief leaned back in his chair and clasped his hands behind his head. I recognized the welcome signs that he was in a good mood and felt like sharing the details of his case. "And unfortunately Mr. Vess was rather fixated on the notion that Riddick was stealing money. All Riddick had to do was keep the cash and bank accounts clean and he could steal the church blind without Vess being any the wiser."

"But if Vess had suspected Riddick for years—do you mean this was going on even before Mrs. Thornefield's estate?"

"It's been going on nearly twenty years," the chief said. "Though on a much, much smaller scale," he added, seeing my shocked expression. "Apparently early in their working relationship, Dr. Womble, the previous rector, recognized that Riddick might be finding it difficult to manage on the relatively modest salary the church was paying him. So the good doctor encouraged Riddick to take any little items he might find useful from the rummage sale donations."

" 'Little items'?" I said. "Like that silver Tiffany tea service Mother was burbling about before church this morning?"

"It began with little items," the chief said. "But it wasn't long before Riddick realized the true value of the items donated by more affluent parishioners. That's when he began his practice of replacing valuable objects with cheap counterparts purchased in thrift shops. He also started pretending to sell some of the donated items to antique stores and thrift shops—supposedly for larger sums than they'd bring at the rummage sale. But of course he was selling his thrift shop purchases, not the donations."

"He's lucky no one ever recognized any of his thrift shop junk."

"It's not luck," the chief said. "He stuck to thrift shops at least three hours' drive away."

I shook my head in amazement.

"Riddick, of all people," I said. "And for twenty years?"

"He was only doing it on the large scale for the last six or seven years," the chief said. "Until your mother came along. She's the reason he was leaving Trinity."

"Mother? I thought it was Robyn."

"Robyn annoyed him," the chief said. "All that emphasis on efficiency and decluttering was going to make it harder to run his racket. But his problems really began when your mother was elected to the vestry. Riddick could tell everyone else on the vestry that a thrift shop had offered a few hundred dollars for some old threadbare rugs and they'd say 'Great!' Your mother would want to see the rugs first. She'd almost shut him down even before Robyn arrived."

"Good for Mother!" I exclaimed. "But I guess he couldn't resist going for one more big score with Mrs. Thornefield's estate."

"Yes," the chief said. "He was hoping to use the disruption arising from the change in rectors to cover his tracks. At first, the pranks alarmed him. Having dozens of inquisitive

Baptists swarming all over the church must have made him nervous. But he soon realized that if he kept the pranks going, he could exploit them to help him pull off his final theft. And to get rid of Mr. Vess, whose suspicions were finally becoming inconvenient."

"Don't tell me—after hearing Mother go on about the valuable furniture for the last three or four months, Vess finally took a look at the junk in the basement and figured out what was up?"

"No." The chief was wearing what could only be called a Cheshire Cat grin. "Riddick was planning to move to the greater Los Angeles area, and he was looking for someplace to stash his loot. In late October, he made the mistake of using his office phone to call a storage locker company in Van Nuys. Apparently Vess reads every line of the church phone bill, and when he saw a ninety-cent long-distance charge that didn't seem legit, he couldn't rest till he got an explanation. He'd been bugging everyone about it. What if he called the storage place and they gave him Riddick's name? So Vess had to go."

"Good grief," I said. "I remember all that fuss about the ninety-cent phone call. Our budget's tight, but not that tight."

"Won't be tight at all when we recover what Riddick embezzled," the chief said. "It'll be at least a million."

"A million *dollars*?" My jaw fell.

"At least."

"Well, that answers another question," I said, when I finally got my voice back. "I was still having a hard time believing anyone would commit a murder over a bunch of old furniture, but a million dollars?"

"Definitely ample motive," the chief said. "And if Riddick has any money left after Trinity has taken back what he stole, Quincy Shiffley will probably sue him for mental anguish. He's still convinced some of his ducks are missing."

"So Riddick definitely stole the ducks?"

"Using Quincy Shiffley's truck," the chief said, nodding. "Horace found ample forensic evidence to prove that. We may never know if Riddick committed the duck prank just to cause mischief—because he could see how much the first two pranks and the resulting church-swapping upset Mr. Vess—or if he already had murder in mind. I'm pretty sure he used the ducks in the hope of casting suspicion on Mr. Vess."

"Since Mr. Vess had better access to the ducks than anyone else in the county," I said, nodding.

"And Riddick lit the campfire near Temple Beth-El to make sure all eyes were there and not on Trinity Episcopal," the chief went on. "And he seems to be a belt-and-suspenders kind of crook, so I expect we'll find he planted those beer bottles with the boys' fingerprints on them just in case we didn't believe that Mr. Vess had somehow incinerated himself while trying to fill the Trinity basement with stolen rabbits. So Ronnie and Caleb will have to deal with whatever punishment their parents impose for underage drinking, but I'm convinced they're innocent of the duck and rabbit thefts."

"Good," I said. "I thought they sounded sincere. On another topic—not that I want to pry into New Life Baptist's business, but what's the story on Jerome Lightfoot? Is it just me, or was it a little weird for someone to go to all that trouble just to get a job as a church choir director? Even for such a distinguished choir as yours," I added hastily.

"Indeed," the chief said. "Apparently, to judge from the last three churches at which he worked—two of them under different pseudonyms—his modus operandi is to use his position as choir director to worm his way into the confidence of key church financial officials and then arrange to have the blame fall on them when he absconds with as much church money as he can manage. His previous flights have all taken place either at Christmas or Easter, when he could add substantial cash sums from the collection plate to what he was pillaging from the church bank accounts. I rather doubt he could have pulled it off here in Caerphilly—our treasurer was gratified to have his daughter chosen as a soloist over two arguably more worthy vocalists, but he's not that gullible. Still, you never know."

"And even if he was planning to try this Christmas, I bet all the church-swapping threw a monkey wrench in his plans," I said. "That could account for what a nasty temper he was in every time I saw him over in Trinity."

"His temper was rather nasty at the best of times," the chief said. "But yes, I recall Minerva mentioning that he was behaving badly, even for him. She put it down to tension over the important concert, but perhaps he was merely vexed that he'd have to put up with us till Easter to get another big cash haul. And since poor Mr. Vess was killed after starting an inquiry into Lightfoot's background and Lightfoot took flight so soon after the murder—well, it's a lucky thing you and your mother managed to apprehend the real killer."

We fell silent. I didn't know what the chief was thinking, but I was musing over the fact that however annoying Barliman Vess had been, he had probably helped save Trinity from a good many real financial problems. He'd caught on to Riddick's plot in the end. He'd probably been the first to suspect Lightfoot. He'd still be around to vex us all if he'd trusted Robyn or his fellow vestry members enough to confide in them. We'd be choosing his replacement on the vestry soon, and we'd better find someone else with his unique combination of financial savvy and suspicious nature. I pulled out my notebook and wrote a reminder to think of some good candidates before Mother tried to draft me.

"Well, I won't keep you any longer," the chief said, standing up to signal that our interview was over. "Thanks to you, we're having our full schedule of Christmas Eve activities over at the New Life Baptist Church. Minerva said if you don't have a chance to get home for lunch, you're welcome to drop by for the potluck at noon."

"I'll keep it in mind if anything interrupts me on my way out of town."

Chapter 41

But nothing interrupted me on the way out of town. Mother had saved me a plate, and I arrived in time to help Michael's mother and the boys make Christmas cookies. Michael disappeared—ostensibly to do some last-minute Christmas shopping, though I knew he was actually going over to start cooking our private dinner, especially the turkey, which was larger than expected and would take forever.

"But what happens when you need to leave for the live Nativity and the carol singing?" I asked. "You can't just leave the turkey cooking in an empty house."

"I've hired a sitter," he said.

"For the turkey?"

"One of my students who isn't going home for the holidays will be sitting in the apartment, studying and basting the turkey at half-hour intervals while I'm gone. And no, we don't have to invite him to share the bird he's basting. He'll be at your mother's tomorrow with the rest of the hordes."

When Michael came back from cooking we informed the boys that we were doing something special for dinner after the carol sing. We swore them to secrecy, of course, though I was relying less on their discretion than on the fact that they wouldn't be out of our sight until we took off for the apartment. And if they did babble about the "something special," I planned to say that we were going to take them driving around to see Christmas lights until they dozed off in their car seats.

Around three we all bundled up to go back into town for the live Nativity.

Randall had arranged for a crew to deliver dozens of hay bales to the newly shoveled town square and arrange them in loose rows facing the Methodist church, which was slightly elevated above the square, giving us a good view of the empty stable. Once everyone was seated and just as we were all getting restless and a little cold and wondering when the show would start, we heard baas and bleats and short, sharp barks. We craned our necks to see a flock of sheep coming around the corner into the blocked-off street in front of us. It was Seth Early in a rough homespun shepherd's robe leading at least fifty of his enormous Lincoln sheep, accompanied by half a dozen Methodists, similarly dressed, and Lad, Seth's Border Collie, who did such a good job keeping the flock together and in motion that the humans with their crooks were clearly just for decoration.

Following in the wake of the sheep were the other animals. A dozen cows, complete with old-fashioned bells, marched sedately behind two milkmaids in biblical costume. The half dozen lively goats each had its own keeper and still caused more trouble than all the cows and sheep put together.

I waved to my friend Betsy, who was leading several American Mammoth Jackstock donkeys, including one named Jim-Bob who had helped save my life during the summer. The final donkey pulled a rough wooden cart driven by Rose Noire and piled high with wooden cages containing ducks, geese, and chickens.

Next came the llamas, led by a tall shepherd I recognized

as my brother Rob. Another donkey pulled yet another wooden cart, this one driven by Dad and bearing my grandfather, who was holding the leashes of his three wolves. He was right—the Arctic Wolf was particularly striking.

Caroline Willner followed, riding a small elephant that lived at her wildlife sanctuary. She was followed by more costumed men driving a pair of large pigs, a woman leading a very temperamental zebra, and a small flock of ostriches and emus.

It all made for a very unusual manger scene by the time they finally got all the animals gathered around the stable—except for the wolves, which Grandfather kept a little way down the slope toward the street, since the way they were straining at their leashes indicated that they were far too interested in the other animals.

After all that, the appearance of the holy family and the assorted angels, shepherds, and wise men was almost an anticlimax—well, except for the fact that the three wise men arrived leading two camels with magnificent bejeweled trappings. In spite of the many anachronisms, the pageant was a smashing success.

When it was over and the animals were being led off, we all turned around to face the enormous Christmas tree in the center of the square—which meant that anyone who had a back-row seat for the living Nativity now had a front row seat for the caroling—and after Randall ceremoniously plugged in the tree lights, Minerva Burke led us all in a half hour of Christmas carols before wishing us a merry Christmas and telling us to go home and start celebrating with our families.

Michael ducked out a little early with the boys. I stayed behind to make our excuses—no, we weren't coming over to Mother and Dad's for the evening—the boys were a little tired, and we had presents to assemble before we fell into bed ourselves.

"But we'll see you bright and early on Christmas Day!" I said. Probably too early; all the grandparents were determined to be there when the boys woke up and saw their presents. I'd already made sure Mother and Dad could find their keys to the house so I wouldn't have to let them in.

I took a circuitous route when I left the town square and kept my eye on my rearview mirror. Not that I really expected anyone to be following me for sinister reasons, but I couldn't help worrying about being spotted by some well-meaning friend or relative who might try to catch up with me to congratulate me on my lucky escape or want to hear the details.

I finally turned into the familiar quiet, tree-lined street and then through the familiar gateway in front of the house that Michael's friend Charlie now owned. An eight-foot fence that in summer would be covered with climbing roses and honeysuckle vines instead of snow and ice concealed a surprisingly large parking lot, a legacy from when the house had been chopped into eight or ten cramped apartments. By the time Michael had come to Caerphilly, a prosperous faculty member had turned the building back into a single-family dwelling, except for the basement apartment.

The twinmobile, our van, was already there. I hurried down the narrow brick steps along one side of the house to knock on the low door, whose bright red surface was half hidden by an enormous green wreath festooned not only with a red bow but also a half-price sticker from the Caerphilly Market. I could hear carols playing inside—a very nice choral version of "Adeste Fidelis." Josh opened the door on my first knock—clearly he'd been keeping watch.

"Mommy!" he exclaimed. "Come see playhouse!"

It did seem almost toylike compared with our current house. The ceilings were only seven feet tall so that Michael, at six four, had to duck when he went under an overhead light fixture. It was basically one not-very-large room with alcoves for the kitchen and bath and closet. In our time the kitchen had consisted of a microwave, a toaster oven, and a hotplate on top of a mini refrigerator, and we'd done dishes in the bathroom sink. Now it was fitted out with the smallest stove and kitchen sink I'd ever seen, and a slightly larger and newer mini fridge. Of course, the expanded kitchen took up a few more square feet of what was already a pretty minuscule living space, but it was definitely an improvement.

Charlie had replaced the hideous sofa bed I remembered with a nice new futon sofa. But the bathroom was still separated from the rest of the apartment by the same curtain made of a vintage sixties Indian-print cotton bedspread.

Still, it was cozy. And filled with the most delicious smells—turkey and gingerbread and pumpkin pie. And decorated just as extravagantly as our house was, though clearly by different hands. The bathroom curtain had been drawn aside to reveal a skinny six-foot spruce tree occupying the shower stall—one of the few spaces large enough to hold it. The tree, the rest of the bathroom, and the whole apartment were decorated with red and gold paper chains, lopsided stars cut out of gold paper, and garlands of evergreen held together with Scotch tape, from which I deduced that Michael and the boys had picked the vegetation themselves. A papier-mâché Santa and nine papier-mâché reindeer hung from the ceiling. The power cord to Rudolph's flashing red nose was wrapped in tinsel and taped across the ceiling and down one wall until it could reach a vacant outlet And taped to all the walls were Christmas posters painted by the boys. Wise men riding on beasts that looked a lot more like llamas than camels. Mary and Joseph bending tenderly over a baby Jesus who seemed to be occupying a car seat rather than a manger. Santa Claus, Mrs. Claus, and the elves surrounded by a three-foot-high avalanche of presents—including what I suspected was a giant hamster cage. A giant Christmas tree almost hidden by the wrapped presents piled around it. A mantel from which hung a line of stockings large enough for giants.

"Did you guys do all this?" I asked. "It's beautiful!"

Josh beamed. Jamie, overcome with praise, buried his head in the sofa cushions with his rump sticking up, ostrichlike.

Just then I spotted a completely unexpected sight.

"Did Charlie actually add a fireplace?" I exclaimed.

"Couple years ago," Michael said. "He added one onto the side of his living room, which is right upstairs from here, and decided it wouldn't take too much more to add one down here."

"We can make s'mores now," Jamie suggested.

"After dinner," Michael said.

"Can we hang stockings here, too?" Josh asked.

"No, we've already got stockings at home."

"But Santa could come here, too," Josh protested.

"Mommy, listen," Jamie said. "It's our Baptists." He scrambled over to the end table where the soft strains of a choir singing "O Little Town of Bethlehem" were coming from a portable speaker hooked to Michael's iPod.

Suddenly "Adeste Fidelis" blasted forth at such incredible volume that we all flinched and Michael hurried to turn the volume down.

"Sorry, Daddy," Jamie said.

"It's okay," he said. "He's learned how to operate the iPod," he added to me.

"I'm impressed," I said. "And that does sound like the New Life Baptist choir."

"It is," Michael said. "I got a couple of sound techs from the drama department to record the Saturday night concert. They've cleaned up the files, and now you can buy a copy of the concert on the church Web site for a small donation to their cleanup fund."

"Fabulous," I said.

Since the kitchen really was too small for more than one person, the boys and I sang along with the Baptists while Michael finished the dinner preparations. Finally a timer went off, and he ran upstairs with potholders, then returned carrying an enormous roasting pan.

"Turkey's ready," he said as he lifted the lid, filling the entire apartment with the mouthwatering scent of the turkey. "I actually had to borrow Charlie's oven upstairs to cook it in—I'd forgotten how tiny this kitchen is. But for the rolls of refrigerator biscuits—this oven should work fine."

"Mommy, want gwandbewwy sauce," Jamie said.

"Grandberry?" I echoed. "Oh, cranberry sauce. Right. Do you want me to start on the biscuits or—"

Someone knocked on the door.

"Don't answer it," Michael and I said in unison. But Josh, vastly proud of his doorman's job, was already opening the door.

"Gampa!" he exclaimed. "Come eat turkey?"

"If I'm invited." Dad looked plaintive.

Michael and I exchanged looks. He raised an eyebrow. Well, it wasn't as if we'd been trying to avoid Dad. I nodded.

"You're allowed to stay on one condition," Michael said. "Tell us how you figured out we were here."

"I deduced it." Dad sounded very proud of himself. "This morning at church I was talking to Clyde Flugleman from the turkey farm, and found out Michael had bought a bird, so I knew you were planning something. And then after services, I stopped for gas at Osgood Shiffley's station and overheard him giving directions to a young man who was having trouble finding this address. And when he said he was turkey sitting for his professor—well, I figured it out immediately. But don't worry—your secret's safe with me."

"So much for keeping secrets in a small town," I murmured.

"Have a seat," Michael said.

"I brought some rolls." Dad held up a bag from the Caerphilly Bakery that was large enough to contain a year's supply of bread. "Margie at the bakery made them fresh this morning." He held the bag open slightly and we all sniffed eagerly at the warm, yeasty smell.

"Much better than refrigerator biscuits," I said. "Michael, do we have any wine?"

"Oops," Michael said. "I meant to get some."

"I can go." Dad stood up. "It won't take—"

"No, sit," Michael said. "I can borrow some from Charlie and replace it later."

"Is there anything you want me to do, then?" Dad asked.

"Story," Jamie demanded. He handed Dad the pile of Christmas children's books Michael had brought along to entertain the boys.

Another knock at the door. This time Josh opened it to let in Rob.

"Hey," Rob said. "Any chance of a bite of turkey? I brought a contribution."

He held up a container of ice cream in one hand, and in the other another large bag from the Caerphilly Bakery. From the odor of fresh-baked chocolate that had followed him into the room I suspected the parcel contained either brownies or chocolate chip cookies.

"How did you find us?" I asked. "Not that you're not welcome."

"I knew from the way Dad was acting that he was up to something," Rob said. "So I followed him to the bakery. And then when he left, I went in and Margie told me all about it."

"Oh, dear," Dad said. "It never occurred to me that Margie would spill the beans."

Rob shrugged.

"I'll take those." I relieved him of his parcels. Yes, I was right—brownies *and* chocolate chip cookies. Rob made a beeline for the fire.

"Before you get too comfortable, go upstairs and get a couple more chairs," Michael said, handing Rob a key ring.

"Can do." He bounded out, forgetting to close the door behind him.

" 'Twas the night before Christmas,' " Dad began. " 'When all through the house.' "

"I'm not sure I can fit the ice cream in the freezer," I said.

"Stick it outside the door," Michael said. "It won't melt out there. And while you're at it, shut the door, will you?"

" 'Not a creature was stirring—' "

I stashed the ice cream outside and was turning to come back in when—

"Hello?"

I looked up to see Rose Noire carefully coming down the narrow stairway with a huge covered bowl in her hands.

"Now I know you didn't come for the turkey," I said. Roast turkey was only one of many reasons I couldn't imagine becoming a vegetarian, but Rose Noire never even seemed tempted.

"Heavens, no!" Rose Noire shuddered slightly. "But I am fond of mashed potatoes and cranberry sauce and pumpkin pie. I brought a big salad."

"How in the world did you find us?" I asked.

"That nice Mr. Gardner who lives upstairs bought half a dozen special gift baskets to take to his mother and aunt and sisters," she said. "And when I delivered them yesterday morning, he was down here tidying up a bit, and he told me how sweet it was that his friend was borrowing his old bachelor apartment to have a quiet little Christmas dinner with his wife and twin sons. I knew it had to be you. He probably didn't know we were related. And I wasn't going to barge in until I realized from the hints he was dropping that your father knew and was planning to come."

"He was dropping hints?" I winced. "We'll have the whole family here before long."

"I doubt if any of the others know about Mr. Gardner," she said.

"Well, come in," I said. "We'll have to send Rob back upstairs for more chairs."

We'd gotten everyone seated, Dad's reading was keeping the boys entertained, the rolls were warming in the oven, and Michael was beginning to carve the turkey before the next knock came. This time I answered.

"Horace," I said. "Welcome. Did you follow Dad or Rob or Rose Noire?"

"Actually, I figured from some hints your dad dropped that you guys were up to something," Horace said. "So I put the word out over the department radio and one of the other deputies spotted all your cars here."

"I was not dropping hints!" Dad protested.

"Did you bring anything?" Jamie asked.

"Jamie!" I said. "That's no way to greet a guest."

"Actually, I brought your grandfather and Caroline and Mrs. Waterston, if that's okay," Horace said. "Seems they all have a hankering for an old-fashioned Christmas dinner."

The apartment seemed to get even smaller as they all trooped in.

"Lovely idea," Michael's mother said, handing me a bottle of red wine. "A nice quiet little immediate family event before tomorrow's madhouse."

"Merry Christmas!" Grandfather stepped into the room, holding a second bottle. "Are we in time for dinner?"

"Monty, you old goat!" As she entered, Caroline pretended to swat him with one of the bottles of white wine she was carrying. "You haven't even been asked to stay yet."

"Well, we will be, won't we?" He frowned at me. "You are serving normal food, aren't you? None of this fancy slop."

"Shush!" Caroline hissed.

"Someone go bring the dogs in before they get cold," Michael's mother said. "And the ducks."

"Ducks?" Michael and I spoke in unison, and not without alarm.

Dad and Rob went out and returned. Dad was leading Spike and Tinkerbell, while Rob was carrying a cage containing two ducks.

"Ducks are social animals," Michael's mother said. "Your grandfather thought Ducky Lucky could use a friend."

"Don't worry," Grandfather said. "They're both going back to the zoo with us tonight."

"Now we just need hamsters," Jamie said.

"Guinea pigs," Josh contradicted.

"Okay," Jamie said. "Hamsters *and* guinea pigs."

"I suppose we should be glad they didn't bring the llamas," I muttered.

"Not yet, anyway," Michael said.

"Have a seat, everyone, if you can find one," I said aloud. "Rob, more chairs."

"I'll keep slicing," Michael said.

"Put these on ice," Caroline said, handing me her wine bottles. "Monty, Dahlia, give her the red wine. We should open one to let it breathe a little before dinner."

We kept Rob busy ferrying chairs, dishes, glasses, and silverware down from Charlie's kitchen. He even found a card table upstairs, and a tablecloth large enough to cover both it and the small parson's table that had served Michael and me as both dining table and desk. At last we were all seated, a little tightly packed, but most of us had at least enough space to set down our glasses, if not our plates. The ducks were perched on the coffee table, where they could see the meal—I hoped they either didn't notice we were eating turkey or weren't sentimental about their distant cousins. We'd put food and water down for the dogs, but both preferred to curl up under the table, hoping for handouts. They probably wouldn't be disappointed.

Michael had brought a lot of candles—the LED faux candles we'd taken to using since the boys began walking and grabbing things—and when we finished scattering them all around the room their flickering and the dancing flames of the fire made our makeshift dining table look pretty nice after all.

"Who wants to say grace?" Michael asked.

"God bless us, every one!" Jamie shouted.

"I think that covers the situation," Grandfather said. "I'll take some turkey."

"Gwandbewwy sauce," Jamie said, holding out his plate.

Everyone was so busy passing dishes and waving plates that I was the only one who noticed that someone else had knocked on the door. Rather softly. I was closest, so I went over and opened the door.

Mother. Carrying a small dish.

"Hello, dear," she said.

"Mother," I said. "What a surprise."

Behind me all conversation came to a stop.

"Gamma!" Jamie exclaimed.

"Gamma want turkey?" Josh asked.

"Such a nice idea," Mother said. "Tomorrow's dinners will be so big and formal. A nice little intimate gathering tonight is just the thing."

"A lot less intimate than they were planning," Grandfather said. "With all of us barging in."

"Monty!" Caroline said, swatting him for real.

"I assume Meg and Michael were keeping their plans close to the vest to avoid having too big a crowd," Mother said. "And no doubt would have invited all of us had the unfortunate events of the last day or two not distracted them from getting everything ready as they planned."

Did she really believe that, or was she just giving us a graceful out?

"We should have realized that if we'd reached out, all of you would have been happy to pitch in," I said loud. "As you have without even being asked. Just one question, Mother: How did *you* find out where and when we were having this?"

"I have my methods, dear." She smiled very sweetly, and I knew it was no use. She'd never tell.

"Rob, fetch another chair," I said.

"Roger," he said, and raced out.

"I was planning to surprise you with a small, plain turkey at my dinner," she said. "Will you still want to eat turkey tomorrow?"

"I can always eat turkey," I said.

"I could eat a whole turkey, Gamma," Josh said.

"Me, too," Jamie added.

"I brought tomato aspic," Mother said handing me the bowl. "I know it's always been one of your favorites."

As I nudged dishes aside to find a place for the aspic, Mother stood for a few moments, surveying the apartment. Back when Michael and I had been living there, she had disapproved of it so strongly that she'd showered us with paint and fabric samples and so many decorating books that we'd taken to using stacks of them for our end table and coffee table. I never had managed to convince her that no amount of decorating would make the place any bigger. She reached out toward one of the boys' posters—one that was particularly crooked—and I had to bite my tongue to keep from telling her to leave it alone; I liked it that way.

But she only smoothed down the tape to make sure it was securely fastened and nodded with approval before sitting down at what had been Rob's place. Rob raced back in with another folding chair and found a place to put it where he could set his plate atop the duck cage.

"My, this is nice." Mother surveyed the table with an equally approving eye. "Perhaps I should go retro next year. A very traditional holiday dinner."

I saw Michael's mother frown slightly, and her face took on a familiar competitive look. Dare I hope that next year would see a duel over who could serve not only the most elaborate but the most traditional dinner?

"Merry Christmas, everyone!" Mother said.

She lifted her wineglass—well, it had been Rob's wineglass, but it was hers now. We all followed suit, even the boys, who were drinking cranberry juice in their stemmed glasses.

"Merry Christmas to all," Josh exclaimed.

"And to all a good night," Jamie finished.

Read on for an exclusive story from Donna Andrews,
taking place a few weeks before the start of
Duck the Halls

A Christmas Rescue

"*May the joy of the season fill your heart,*" I read aloud from the glitter-pocked Christmas card I'd just opened.

"Cordelia Lee Mason, if you say 'bah, humbug!' one more time I will let you fetch your own chicken soup," Annabel said. "I don't understand why you're so grumpy."

I plucked a tissue from the box at my side and blew my nose a little ostentatiously. My cousin's stern expression softened.

"I know it's a pain," she said. "Having a cold for Christmas, and the power being out on top of that."

"I do not have a cold for Christmas," I said. "It's only December tenth. I should be fine by the actual holiday. And who needs power when we've got the generator?"

"That's the spirit," Annabel said. "And isn't the snow beautiful?"

"Beautiful." I tried to pump a little enthusiasm into it. I must have succeeded. She smiled, bent her head so the little LED headlamp she wore shone back on the pages of her book, and returned to her reading.

I turned my matching headlamp off, closed my eyes, and leaned back in my chair as if resting.

Annabel was right. I was grumpy. And it wasn't the snow, or the power outage, or the cold, or even our friends' sometimes questionable taste in holiday cards.

I was missing my family. The family who didn't even know I existed. I didn't regret giving up my son all those years ago when I found myself an abandoned unwed teen-aged mother. I arranged for James to be adopted by the Langslows, a wonderful couple who had longed for children for years. They'd raised him right. I was proud of him.

But he'd never known who I was, and after his adoptive parents died we'd lost touch. I'd found ways to keep an eye on him, and rejoiced in his medical career and in the birth of his three wonderful children. I kept an eye on them, too. Not so easy with Pam, the oldest, who'd married an Australian architect and hopped back and forth between the two continents, depending on where his latest commission took them. Reasonably easy with Rob, the youngest, who'd become a famous game developer.

And then there was Meg, the one who looked so like me that it was like staring into a mirror. Well, a mirror and a time machine. I knew you weren't supposed to have favorites, but Meg, so smart and self-assured and in control of her life—so like the me that could have been, if I'd made better choices. I think what I minded the most was not knowing her.

"Nonsense," I muttered to myself. And then I opened my eyes to make sure Annabel hadn't heard.

And the real reason I was so particularly grumpy right now was that the twins—Meg and Michael's two sons, my youngest great-grandchildren—were singing in a children's concert at their church today, and I wasn't going to get to see it. I sometimes went down to Caerphilly for public events that might let me get a glimpse of my family—Easter services at Trinity Episcopal, the town's annual Fourth of July fireworks show, the Christmas parade, Meg's husband's one-man dramatic reading of *A Christmas Carol*. But I kept my distance, and I tried to do it without Annabel finding out. She disapproved of what she called my "stalking."

I'd been planning to recruit Thor Larsen, the local teen who served as our chauffeur and general handyman, to drive me down to Caerphilly for the concert. Annabel didn't need to know where we were going. But between my cold and the snow . . .

Bah, humbug.

I picked up the card that had set me off and studied it. A little on the cutesy side—baby koalas wearing halos. But then it was from friends in Sydney, Australia. Fellow bird lovers. And I was touched by the note, thanking Annabel and me for hosting them when they'd made their trip to Virginia in the spring and urging us to come and stay with them next year.

"Peter and Sarah still want us to come and go kookaburra watching," I said. "Maybe we should."

"It's so far," Annabel said. "And—"

The phone rang, and she jumped up to get it. Normally that was my job—Annabel was painfully shy and hated talking on the phone. She must really be worried about me.

"It's the Reverend Robyn," she said. "Do you feel up to talking?"

"Of course." I held out my hand for the phone. Robyn Smith, Trinity Episcopal's energetic young rector, was someone I'd have liked for her own sake, even without her connection to Meg. Just the thought of talking to her made me feel better.

"We have a problem," Robyn said, after we'd exchanged greetings. "We need a safe place for one of our ladies. Her husband has tracked her down twice now, once at her new job and once at a friend's house. The second time she ended up in the ER. We're arranging relocation to another state, but in the meantime, we're afraid he'll follow her to the shelter. We want to sneak her out of town until the arrangements for her new life are complete."

"You want us to put her up?"

She was silent for a few moments.

"It could be dangerous," she said finally. "If he manages to follow her—"

"I can let our sheriff know we're sheltering someone who may have a stalker," I said. "But it won't be a problem if we can sneak her out without him knowing it."

"Actually, it's sneak *them* out," Robyn said. "She has a five-year-old boy."

Five years old. The same age as Josh and Jamie. Maybe even one of their friends.

"It's a lot to ask," Robyn said.

"Nonsense," I said. "We've got plenty of room. But we need a really foolproof way of sneaking them out of town. Is there anything going on at the church that I could pretend to be coming to see?"

"The children's concert!" Robyn exclaimed. "Everyone in town will be there—it's standing room only."

We quickly hatched our plot. I would arrange for Thor to drive me down to Caerphilly. Robyn would be standing at the door, greeting the audience as they entered. I would palm the spare key to our car and slip it to her when I shook her hand. While the concert was on—and with any luck, while one of Robyn's other volunteers could vouch for the abusive husband's whereabouts—Robyn would sneak the mother and son into my car near the end of the concert. Then Thor and I would whisk them back here to Riverton and keep them safe until Robyn could relocate them.

"Are you sure you're up to this?" Annabel asked, when I'd hung up. "Going out in this weather, and in your condition?"

"Someone has to do it," I said. "Are you game?"

Annabel flinched slightly and shook her head. It wasn't the weather—she was agoraphobic. These days she went out for church and the occasional medical appointment, but apart from that she never left our house.

"Can you take a look at the generator before you leave?" she asked. "I would hate for it to stop while you're gone. Yes, I know that most of the time it just needs to have that switch reset, but you know I hate going near the thing."

So I tended the generator and brought in an armload of firewood while waiting for Thor to pick me up. I had no problem convincing him to drive me—I suspect by doing so he was escaping a lot of unpaid snow shoveling.

By noon we were on our way. The roads were wretched, and I decided after the first couple of miles that I needed to tell Thor the real reason we were going, to keep him from suggesting, every five minutes, that maybe today wasn't the greatest day to be driving fifty miles to see a children's concert. Thor had a soft heart, and after I filled him in on our rescue mission, he buckled down to his driving with new resolve.

"But remember," I said. "It is kind of crazy to drive all this way for a children's concert. So be sure and tell people how you didn't expect it to be this bad. And how you'd have turned back but I had such a bad case of cabin fever that I insisted."

"Right," he said.

Trinity Episcopal was beautiful in the falling snow, with its gray stone and bright red door. More to the point, its parking lot was well and recently plowed, its sidewalks were ice-free—always a concern to those of us over eighty—and the parking spot I wanted was free, a handicapped spot tucked away by the back door that would make it easy for me to get into the church and easy for my passengers to get to the car without being spotted from the street. Thor went to find us seats while I went to the vestibule to hang our coats and go past Robyn's informal receiving line.

The key handoff went without a hitch. I joined Thor in the audience, and we settled in to enjoy the show. At least I was enjoying the show. Thor seemed more interested in catching the eye of a pretty girl about his own age who was helping wrangle the five- and six-year-old performers.

Halfway through the program, I heard some scuffling noises out in the vestibule. And then some muffled shouting. I saw Robyn leave the sanctuary. After a few minutes, when she didn't return, I decided to go snooping. I waited till the end of "Rise Up, Shepherd, and Follow" before standing up.

"Ladies room," I said to Thor, loudly enough that the people immediately around us could hear. Then I pushed past the standees and through the double doors into the vestibule.

I found Robyn talking to a balding middle-aged black man in a heavy overcoat. They both turned slightly, and I saw that the man wore a police uniform.

"Just a moment, chief," Robin said.

Aha. This must be Henry Burke, the local police chief.

"Is anything wrong?" she asked me.

"Nothing wrong," I said. "But it's stuffy in there. I'm feeling a bit faint. Is there any place where I can sit down and cool off for a minute? Maybe have a glass of water?"

"Of course." Robyn took my arm and set off down the hall. "There's a nice easy chair in my office. Chief, Mandy's in there with Meg Langslow. She's seeing if we need to call her father to patch her up. Come with me. It would help if you could reassure Mandy that her husband's under arrest."

If the chief thought it was odd, Robyn bringing a fainting old lady to her office in the middle of what I gathered was another incident with the violent husband of my future guest, he didn't say anything. I did feel a little faint—I'd always managed to avoid coming into too close contact with my granddaughter.

Fortunately, the overhead lights were off in Robin's office—there was only a small table lamp at the far end, by the couch where Meg sat beside a slender, anxious-looking young woman with a nasty bruise on her left cheekbone. Mandy, I assumed. I stayed in the doorway, so the light from the hallway behind me would make it hard to see me well. And Meg was wholly focused on Mandy.

"Are you sure?" she was saying. "Because Dad's right there in the sanctuary. He can come and take a look."

"Frank's done worse than this, more than once," Mandy said. "I'll be fine. I just want to get out of here."

"Mandy, this is Mrs. Mason." Robyn gestured at me. "She lives—well, not in Caerphilly. A good ways away from here. She has volunteered to hide you until we can get you safely to your new home."

The chief glanced at me and nodded approvingly. Meg looked up and gave me a quick smile—not that she could see me that well—and turned back to Mandy.

"You sure you want to take us on?" Mandy's face wore a wry, tremulous smile.

"Absolutely," I said. "And maybe we should get going sooner rather than later."

Then I sat in one of the two overstuffed arm chairs at

the far end of Robyn's office and concentrated on blending into the woodwork.

"I'll go get Joey," Meg said. She patted Mandy on the shoulder and stood up.

"Give me ten minutes or so to interview Mandy before you bring the boy in," the chief said.

Meg nodded and strode out. I breathed what I hoped was an inaudible sigh of relief. I didn't want her to get too used to my face. That could interfere with my ability to keep an eye on her and her family.

Chief Burke gently questioned Mandy. Apparently they'd tried to lay a false trail that would suggest they had gone by bus down to Richmond. Robyn added that her volunteer was sure they hadn't been followed. Neither had any idea how Mandy's husband had tracked them down to Trinity Episcopal.

"I mean, it's not as if Joey'd be in the children's concert here," Mandy said, shaking her head. "We're First Presbyterian."

Just then Meg came back in with Joey. She had to stoop slightly to hold his hand—he was small for five, and skinny. And there were bruises on his face. From his father?

"We're going to sneak you out to Mrs. Mason's car," Robyn said to Mandy. "And then she and the young man who drove her here are going to take you back to her house to stay for a while."

"Until Frank finds us," Mandy said.

"He'll be in jail at least for a few hours," the chief said. "We can slow down the processing that much. Unfortunately, I can't promise he won't get out on bail. Depends on what the judge says."

"And that depends on which judge he gets," Meg said. "If it's Judge Jane, she'll refuse bail, I bet you."

"Unfortunately, it will be Judge Proctor in the morning," the chief said.

I gathered this was bad news.

"Hmm . . ." Meg had a thoughtful look. "Here, Joey. Have a seat."

She picked him up and set him on the other armchair. Robyn handed him a chocolate milk carton.

Meg hurried out.

"Maybe we should take off now," I said. "You could send someone to get Thor. Tell him I'm feeling faint and want to go home. Loudly enough that the people around him will hear."

"Good idea," Robyn said. She bustled out.

"We'll do what we can," the chief said to Mandy.

Mandy started crying softly. The chief took both her hands in his and just let her weep.

I glanced over at Joey. He was sipping his milk and holding something. An iPad. I had one like it—well, almost like it. This was smaller—presumably an iPad mini. He was playing a game. I watched for a few minutes as he steered a small cartoon cat through a series of obstacles. The cat finally smashed into something and screen filled with the words "YOU LOSE!" Joey sighed. He looked up to see me watching him and his eyes grew wary.

"Pretty cool," I said.

"Yeah," he said. "My daddy gave it to me." His face fell. "Back when he was nice. Then he did that." He pointed to the iPad's screen, which was bisected with a spidery crack.

Robyn and Meg came back in with Thor, who hurried to my side.

"You okay, Ms. Delia?" he asked.

"I'm fine," I said. "But we need to get our passengers out of here before the concert ends."

"Okay," he said.

Joey was looking down at his iPad, putting the cat through its paces again.

An idea came to me.

"Thor," I said. "You know that thing you did to my iPad to help me find it when my silly cousin tidies it out of sight and then forgets where she put it?"

"I set up the 'Find My iPad' app," Thor said.

"How's that thing work?" I asked.

"I told you," he said, in that patient voice kids his age use when explaining technology to those of us with gray hair. "The iPad has a built-in GPS. Once you enable the 'Find My iPad' app, you can pick up on its signal from anywhere, as long as it still has power."

We all sat and stared at the iPad for a few moments.

"Glory be," the chief said.

"He's finding us because of Joey's iPad?" Mandy asked.

"Joey." Meg strode over and knelt down next to the boy. "Reverend Robyn told you about going to the new place, right?"

He nodded.

"You know what I think you need?" she said. "I think you need to leave this old iPad behind."

His fingers clutched the iPad and he shook his head.

"And get a new iPad," I said. "With no cracks in the screen. You want another iPad mini, or a full-sized one."

Joey considered that a moment.

"Full-sized," he said.

"I'll get my brother to have his game experts set it up for you," Meg said. "With all the best games. He'll have to take this for a day or two to set it up properly.'

Joey studied her intently for a few moments. Then he nodded and held out the iPad to her.

"Let's call Rob and see if his experts can get rid of the GPS signal," Meg said. "Robyn, I gather you'll know where to send the new one?"

"I have a better idea," I said. "Let me take the old one."

I held out my hand for the iPad.

"But—"

"Joey and his mom can stay here—maybe with people they know?" I said. "And I'll take the iPad with me, and when I get home I'll turn it on. Frank will think they've left town."

"But what if he comes after you?" Thor said.

"Good point," I said. "Let's take it to the police station for safekeeping. And then maybe in a day or so I'll over-night it to some friends on the other side of the country. And I'll tell them to turn it on for a while and then mail to someone else far, far away. If he wants to chase the iPad, I think we can keep him busy for as long as Joey and his mom need to slip away to their new life."

Robyn, Meg, and the chief looked at each other.

"Do it," the chief said.

Meg handed me the iPad and turned back to the chief.

"They can come with me for tonight," Meg said. "I'm sure Mother can find a cousin who can put them up after that."

"After tonight they'll be on their way," Robyn said. "Just as long as we can keep Frank away for tonight—"

"I have good news on that front," Meg said. "Judge Jane called Judge Proctor and offered to switch weekends with him—since she's here in town and he'd have to come all the way in from his farm, in the snow. So if the chief can arrange for Frank to have is bail hearing today or tomor-row, it will be with her, and odds are she'll keep him in-side long enough for Mandy to get a head start."

"And this time, without that iPad to give them away, the head start will do some good!" Robyn said. "Let's roll, folks!"

"I'm going down to the station to get the arraignment moving," the chief said.

"Joey, you and your mom are going to come home to stay with me tonight," Meg said, picking him up. "I have two sons about your age."

"I should get back to the concert," Robyn said.

"Let's head out before the snow gets any worse," I said.

I tucked the iPad into my purse and Thor and I hurried off.

I paused inside the door while Thor went out to clean off the snow and start the car. I heard voices from down the hall.

"So who was that lady who figured out the iPad thing?" Meg asked. I liked that she didn't say "old lady."

"One of my underground battered women's railway volunteers," Robyn said.

"Then I won't pry," Meg said. "Because I know you need to keep that on a need-to-know basis."

On the way back home, while Thor battled the increasingly icy roads, I made a complete study of the contents of Joey's iPad—Thor's idea. He planned to to e-mail Robyn a list of Joey's games as soon as he got power back.

Annabel fussed over us when we finally got home, and insisted on fixing us hot chocolate. Thor stayed long enough for me to pack the iPad and address it to a friend in El Paso, Texas, with instructions on what to do with it.

"I'll take it to the post office in the morning," he said.

"And Thor," I said. "You can't tell anyone about this. Not even your parents."

He nodded and left.

A long day. But a satisfying one. I was a little worried about having spent so much time in close proximity to Meg. But looking back, I thought it was entirely possible that she wouldn't easily recognize me again. The lights had been so dim in Robyn's office that I wouldn't have recognized her if I hadn't already memorized every feature of her face.

"You're in a better mood," Annabel said.

Thor and I had given her the short version of the day's events. I hadn't mentioned Meg's name, and Thor probably didn't know it. No need to upset Annabel.

"Yes, I'm in a much better mood," I said. "It did me good to get out. I think I'm finally getting my holiday spirit."

In fact, it didn't even spoil my mood when the generator suddenly stopped, a little before midnight and just after I'd climbed into bed with a fresh box of tissues at my side. Normally I'd mutter a few curses, vow that it was time to replace the darned thing, and wonder why, just once, Annabel couldn't take care of it, since all the running around hadn't been good for my cold.

But tonight I just shrugged as I climbed out of bed and felt around with my toes for the bedroom slippers. And I found myself thinking very differently about all those sappy Christmas cards. *May the joy of the season fill your heart.* Not so silly after all.

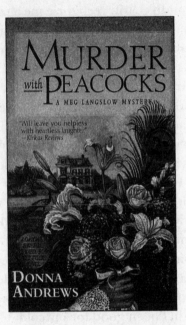